A Song and a Seashell

ISBN: 978-1-60920-073-2
Printed in the United States of America
©2013 Susan Flach

Library of Congress Cataloging-in-Publication Data

API
Ajoyin Publishing, Inc.
P.O. 342
Three Rivers, MI 49093
www.ajoyin.com

Please direct your inquiries to admin@ajoyin.com

For Haley & Chase

A Song and a Seashell

SUSAN K. FLACH

Prologue
Summer 2001

The sun glistens brightly on the blue ocean water as it bounces lightly onto a sandy shoreline. A slight breeze catches a salty sea fragrance mixed with tropical suntan lotion, and it permeates the air. A cloudless day along with eighty-five-degree temperatures has drawn many people in for a leisurely day spent oceanside. Brightly colored umbrellas are scattered like giant thumbtacks on a bulletin board made of sand. Frisbees and footballs are tossed. Sand pails are filled, and Boogie Boards skim across the steady stream of waves that push onto the shore. Families gather to make memories. Teenagers play loud music, relentlessly flirting with one another. A type of energy fills the atmosphere that can only come from a day at the beach.

But all of this is lost to a young boy and girl who are deeply entranced in a world of play farther up the shoreline. To an onlooker the children would appear to be twins. Both with wispy, blond hair and sun-kissed skin. Both possessing a type of natural beauty that draws instant notice. An observer might see their fine-boned facial features and pouty lips, and picture them as models for Gap Kids or Children's Place. The difference between the children—besides the obvious, of one being a boy and the other a girl—lies in their eyes. The girl's are a pale, crystal blue that glistens like the sky on the brightest sunny day. And the boy's are an intense green, resembling the color of a sea turtle or the ocean itself during certain tides. Oblivious to the world around them, the children busy themselves making castles in the sand. Time after time they take turns traipsing their little selves down to the edge of the vast body of water before them. Carefully they scoop up buckets full of salty liquid, only to spill half of it on the trip back to their miniature chateau formations.

As they kneel side by side with the wet skin of their knees digging into the sand, the young boy glances up at the girl, studying her with an intense gaze. When the young girl notices, a blush spreads across her already pink cheekbones, and she quickly looks away. Suddenly the boy playfully flicks her with a spray of water from a nearby bucket in an effort to ease the tension.

"Hey. What was that for?" Her eyes widen in surprise.

The boy's eyes crinkle at the edges as a mischievous smile spreads across his face. He flicks more water. The girl hides her face, trying to block the spray, and quickly grabs the bucket, dumping it over his head. His face briefly registers shock before he turns to grab her. "Hey, you . . ."

But she is already gone, her small, tanned body running across the sand. Laughingly, her blue eyes dare him to chase her.

"Just wait 'til I catch you," he shouts over the sound of the surf.

"You *can't* catch me." She glances over her shoulder and runs for the ocean. He easily closes the gap, and she shrieks, knowing she'll soon be caught. In an effort to avoid him, the girl dives into the water just as a wave rushes over her head. Her sunstreaked, blond hair disappears instantly. The boy's eyes show a flicker of panic as they scan the surrounding whitecaps. Shortly she resurfaces, gasping for air. Quickly and efficiently he swims to where she is and wraps one arm around her, pulling her safely onto the shore. She chokes and gasps for a minute and soon resumes normal breathing.

"You better learn how to swim." The boy pushes a wet strand of hair out of his eyes. His tone is reproachful. "You're lucky I was here to save you."

The whole incident has left the girl subdued, and she nods her head, her eyes round. "Maybe you can teach me." She glances up at him shyly. "You're a good swimmer, aren't you?"

He shrugs indifferently. "Yeah, I'm okay . . . ," he pauses. "Yeah, I *guess* I could teach you."

And so for the next few days that's how it goes. The young, blond boy and the young, blond girl meet up at the same place on the beach, and they work diligently making castles in the sand. And they spend time together frolicking in the ocean, the one trying earnestly to teach the other how to swim.

One day they work mostly in silence, patting and smoothing the wet sand. They are putting the finishing touches on the turrets and bridges that are an intricate part of their castle.

"Who is going to live here?" The boy's voice breaks through the quiet.

"A princess, of course," the girl states, as if the answer is obvious. "And her prince," she adds slowly.

"Oh." They continue shaping and carving and polishing.

"The princess and the prince will eat candy every day . . . and have birthday parties whenever they want. And they can go to the beach all the time . . . 'cuz it's right in their front yard." On and on the young girl describes the life of leisure the royal occupants of their almost-completed beach villas will get to partake in.

The boy listens intently, looking thoughtful. "What if the prince is really a king who lives in the sea?"

The girl looks up and starts to giggle. "A prince doesn't live in the water with fish, silly." She steps back to eye their work. The boy blinks, and for just a moment his face falls. Soon they run down to the water for a swim—castles, prince, and princesses forgotten. Now they are just two carefree children splashing in the ocean, enjoying the moment and each other's company. Afterward, they sit side by side on the shore, not quite touching, toes dug into the sand. Beads of salty water drip from their skin. Presently the little, blond girl stands up and wipes taupe-colored granules off her legs with the palms of her hands.

"My mom and daddy told me we are going home tomorrow. This is my last day at the beach," she announces.

A shocked expression crosses over the boy's fine features, and his eyes widen in surprise. "You . . . are leaving?" His voice seems a little breathless.

"Yep," she answers matter-of-factly, but she refuses to meet his eyes.

"Oh." Silence closes around them.

"Well . . . good-bye," she declares, hand on her hips.

"You're leaving . . . right now?" he asks, the sound of panic rising in his throat.

"We have to pack up all our stuff," she answers, her voice soft. They meet each other's gaze uncomfortably. "Bye." She folds her small hands together, not knowing what else to do.

His green eyes narrow. "Good-bye," he murmurs, looking defeated. And she turns to walk away, toes sifting through the soft, pale sand. "Don't forget to practice swimming," he shouts after her. She looks over her shoulder and nods as bits of her blond hair catch rays of light from the sun. And then, slowly, she turns back around and continues walking, leaving him to watch her form grow smaller as it disappears into the distance.

Chapter One
Summer 2012

I think we were all *soooo* tired of the fighting! That's why we were going away that summer. Well, Mom and Dad didn't exactly tell us that was the reason. They just came to us late one evening in May, soon after my high school graduation, and announced that they had decided it would be a good idea for our family to *get away for a while*—we all needed to *reconnect*. They both looked exhausted as they told us the news. They had found a charming place for us to rent for the summer, up the coast in Rhode Island. In spite of their defeated expressions, I experienced a flicker of hope as they revealed the plans.

We would be staying on the ocean in a summer vacation community called Watch Hill. Maybe this would be the summer of change. Change was definitely needed. Something had crept into our house and was chipping away at the squarely rooted foundation of our family, turning it into a misshapen spear. We had become a runaway ball rolling down a hill. At first the decline was gradual. There were small, intermittent outbreaks of verbal exchanges. Next came the door slamming and the occasional peeling of tires. Now the slope had steepened, and the ball was racing at breakneck speed toward a rocky cliff. It seemed Mom and Dad never got along at all anymore. Dad is a lawyer at a big firm in our hometown of Philadelphia. Over and over again, I'd hear my mom mention how much she hated him being gone so much for his job. But ironically, the more the subject was brought up, the more he seemed to stay away. Lately the heated discussions had progressed into physical exchanges.

"Oh, just leave without answering me . . . that's sooo grown up, Kevin." My mom's voice echoed across the kitchen as my dad gathered papers to stuff into his briefcase. He was ignoring her and heading for the door. "Will you stop? You are infuriating me, you son-of-a—" Her voice escalated, and I watched in horror as she picked up a heavy, glass plate and hurled it at him. It whizzed by his head and bounced off the foyer wall, smashing into pieces as it landed on the floor. Dad froze and turned slowly to face her. Something glinted in his eyes resembling—what? Disgust? Hate?

"Who is acting grown-up, Lisa?" His voice was like ice. He paused for a second, like there was something else he wanted to say, and then turned and walked out the front door instead. Mom cried for the rest of the afternoon. My nine-year-old twin brothers, Josh and Jake, reacted the way they always did as of late. They exited to their bedroom, closing themselves off from the rest of the family, playing only with each other. More and more it was like the two of them, together, equaled one person.

Another time, when a heated discussion arose over who would be picking the twins up from soccer the next day, the word "selfish" was flung across the room. I winced as I witnessed the first actual physical altercation take place between my parents. In a rage, my mom reached up and slapped my dad across the face. I held my breath in anticipation of his retaliation. He was clearly much stronger—what damage would result now? Instantly, he grabbed her by the arms and shoved her against the wall, fire burning in his eyes. He stared at her momentarily and then released her, fists clenched at his side. I could tell he was trying so hard not to return the favor.

"Why did I ever marry you?" He spoke the words slowly, each syllable laced with venom. Then, as always, he walked away. The fight ended, but there was no clear resolution. I breathed a sigh of relief. No one had actually gotten hurt, but somehow, a sting still lingered. I wasn't sure which was more painful: hearing the sound of the slap, or the bite of the words resounding of a life regretted. It wasn't clear to me why I cared so much about whether or not our family stayed together. I would be leaving for Penn State in the fall anyway. I wouldn't be around to witness all the upheaval. But somehow, I just did—I just cared anyway. I cared for me and for the twins, who seemed to disappear into each other more and more with every new fight. And I cared for the Mom and Dad that I used to know, who were a big part of our loving family. So many nights were spent in my quilt-covered double bed, tears running down my cheeks, crying to God—*Please . . . help us!*

Now with every article of clothing that I pack into my red Samsonite suitcase, I feel a small glimmer of hope for the possibilities that might unfold for our family this summer. We scurry around our two-story, brick-sided home, grabbing last-minute items and stuffing them into the nooks and crannies of our white Chevy Tahoe and black Buick LaCrosse. With a parting glance at our now locked-up family dwelling, we load ourselves into the two cars and head onto I-95 North for the ride up to the Ocean State—Rhode Island. We follow Dad on the highway, and I watch as the twins' sandy blond heads dart around in the backseat of his vehicle. I can tell they are excited for the trip. It's been so long since we've done any type of real vacationing together as a family—and now—*wow!*—the whole summer! I'm riding shotgun with Mom in the LaCrosse. Playing with my blond ponytail, I glance over at her. At forty-two, she is an older version of me, with long, blond hair and blue eyes. She still looks pretty youthful for her age, thanks to staying active at her dance studio where she instructs part-time, and periodic shots of Botox that she doesn't like to admit to. But, in spite of all the exercise and pampering, this year has taken a toll on her, and some worry lines have begun to surface. I put my hands on my lap and eye my pale legs. *The Ocean State—beaches.* I am eager to start a much-needed tan, hoping to add a little life to my otherwise too plain features.

Suddenly, I remember I promised to text my best friend Lucy. She is what I'll miss the most about going away for the summer. I smile as I picture her blond, wavy hair and chocolate brown eyes. She's been such a loyal companion to me through all of my growing-up years. I love her like a sister. Even though we'll be apart this summer, there is consolation in knowing we'll be reunited again at Penn State this fall.

We're on our way . . . *(send)*

I put my headphones on and listen to my iPod as I stare out the passenger window. Rihanna is singing to me as I watch the trees and road signs whiz by. My phone starts to vibrate.

(unlock) Take it easy on the Rhode Island boys. Try not to break too many hearts.

I laugh out loud. I've hardly even dated, and I'm hardly a heart-breaker.

Ha! I'll try to take it easy on them . . . maybe! *(send)*

Mom looks over at me and gives me a little smile. "Lucy?"

"Yeah."

"This is going to be a good thing." She feels the need to reassure me. I nod my head, giving a little smile back as I keep listening to the music.

"Are you excited for this summer, Bethany?" She is still trying to have a conversation, so I take out my earbuds and glance in her direction. Somehow she appears a little nervous. My forehead begins to furrow as I contemplate the possible reasons why. Does a whole summer away from home seem like too long? Is she worried about Dad—and her? Will this sabbatical really help our family? Is this going to be it—the one last shot at saving our family? What will happen to the Kuiper family if it doesn't work? I feel a knot forming in my stomach, realizing that I'm becoming nervous too. *Oh no, it's contagious!* Suddenly I feel the need to escape from the car and go running.

The Ocean State. I can't wait to go running on the sandy beaches. I've been a long-distance runner since junior high, and I'm pretty good at it. I don't know why, but it just comes easy to me. They tell me I'm *light on my feet*, so I guess maybe that's it. I just know that while others are panting and turning sweaty and bright red, I seem to just glide on by. I have lots of ribbons hanging from the bulletin board in my bedroom to prove it.

"I think it will be great!" I hope I sound convincing.

"Your dad picked out a nice place for us, right on the ocean." *Dad picked out the place? Maybe he really is on board with the "save the Kuiper family" plan.* I feel slightly reassured again.

"I can't wait to get there."

Traffic slows as we bypass New York City. Stop and go. Stop and go. I look over and see our Chevy Tahoe in the lane next to us. Dad appears solemn as he sits, hands resting on the steering wheel, staring straight ahead. A flurry of movement fills my peripheral vision. I turn toward all the commotion and notice Josh and Jake waving at us for all they're worth. Smiling at them, I wave and give them the peace sign. They nudge each other and break into laughter. Instantly, I get a warm feeling in my chest—it's good to see them this way. Josh and Jake are not identical twins. They both have sandy blond hair, but Josh's is a little more sunbleached, and he looks like Mom. Jake, on the other hand, strongly resembles Dad, except with lighter hair. At forty-four, Dad's full head of normally dark brown hair has begun to reveal tiny flecks of gray, brought on, I'm sure, by the stress of his marital problems. He looks every bit the part of the profession he's in: big city lawyer, all serious in his dark suits and ties. Handsome too—for his age.

After what seems like forever, we exit off I-95 and are driving along Watch Hill Road. I stare out the window, taking in my surroundings intently. This is going to be my home for the next three months. The road winds and dips as it carries us to the small, summertime community. Trees and foliage are everywhere. Beautiful homes are nestled into and onto a hilly terrain. White fences and colorful flower beds decorate the front yards. Some houses look like well-preserved cottages, probably passed down from generation to generation; still others boast of the latest and newest construction.

Wow! This place obviously has a lot of money! The thought is both intimidating and exciting at the same time. We drive past Watch Hill Garage, a charming service station from yesteryear, and turn right onto Foster Cove Road. The farther the car winds down toward the water, the more excited I become. Eventually, we pull into a little gravel drive and park in front of a quaint cottage, sided in dusty blue cedar shakes. This is it. For a second we all pause and take in our surroundings. Then the sound of car doors opening and shutting fills the air, and we emerge on our new summer residence. After the side entrance is unlocked, we enter and check out the rooms. We are first greeted with a little mudroom lined in sea green beadboard and white, tiled flooring. This entry space houses a washer and drier and several hooks on which to hang beach towels, umbrellas, or sweatshirts

The next doorway leads to a great room which consists of a kitchen, dining area, and a giant living space with overstuffed blue and yellow plaid couches. The room is cheery and bright. Large windows allow plenty of sunlight to filter in, giving a springy feel to the area. *Just what the doctor ordered.*

The twins and I had been previously informed of the sleeping arrangements in effort to ward off *I call this room* type of arguments. The main floor houses three bedrooms. On the north side, the rear-facing room will belong to the boys. Opposite of theirs, facing front, is mine. A tingle of excitement spreads briefly across my chest as I discover my room faces the water. On the south side of the great room, a guest bedroom is available for any out-of-town visitors. Probably also available for Mom or Dad pending any fights between them, I imagine begrudgingly. The upstairs consists of a one-room suite with mammoth windows offering a spectacular view. This is where Mom and Dad carry their suitcases.

Making trip after trip to the vehicles, our family resembles a team of professional movers.

"Hey. Bethany." I hear my dad's voice coming from behind me. "There is one more box in the Lacrosse, and it has your name on it."

I roll my eyes, knowing better than to take him literally. "Sure, I'll get it."

"I thought you might." There is a soft edge to his voice. "This place is okay." His eyes encompass the great room. "I guess we can stay."

Is that a grin I see forming on his lips? *Huh!* My steps are a little lighter as I exit the side door next to our parked cars. When I return, the boys come bounding into the kitchen, almost conjoined in appearance.

"When are we getting food?" Jake demands.

"Yeah, we're hungry," Josh confirms.

"Grocery store *after* we get settled." Mom points to a brown bag on the granite countertop. "There are some snacks in there." Greedily, four little hands start sifting through the assortment of items. Soon pieces of whole wheat crackers and green grapes begin filling their mouths.

Continuing to explore our new place, I visit every nook and cranny and soon decide that the best part of the cottage lies just outside the great room's front double doors and wraps itself halfway around the south side of the house—a large, screened-in porch. Standing in the sheltered enclosure, I take in a deep breath of fresh air. Already I can feel the change beginning. The front screen door pushes open easily, and I exit off the porch in search of what I've been so eagerly anticipating—the Atlantic Ocean. Stepping onto our nicely landscaped front lawn, I view the majestic spread of water before me. Instantly I am greeted with several hues of blue, topped with regal whitecaps. I feel breathless, immediately overwhelmed by its beauty. Somewhere deep inside me I feel a sensation—like a pull. Walking down to the sparkling water's edge, I slip off my sandals and stick my toes in. The cool, salty water soothes the skin on my feet as it splashes over them. I stand there for a while inhaling the sea air. Feeling the need to share this experience with Lucy, I pull my smartphone out of the back pocket of my tan shorts.

We're here! *(send)*

A buzzing sensation vibrates my hand almost immediately.

(unlock) So how do you like it?

It's great! The ocean is everywhere! *(send)*

Soon, I start wandering along the water's edge. The sand feels soft beneath my feet, encouraging me to amble farther down the shoreline. A seagull soars overhead, periodically flapping its wings in the air. Our cottage is located in a cove, but I discover that if I walk far enough to the north, I can see the vast ocean stretching out before me. An occasional sailboat litters the horizon. A soft, warm breeze gently presses against the skin on my arms and legs. It all seems so peaceful. Incidentally, I wonder how this summer will unfold. I am enjoying this newfound serenity for the time being, but realistically, I just got here, and how much more peacefulness do I need? Suddenly, a new thought occurs to me.

I hope I won't be bored.

Almost instantly, I feel a pang of regret for leaving Philadelphia. I miss Lucy. I miss her vivacious personality and the way she makes me laugh, even when I don't want to. *Oh no!* I've only been gone a day! Just as I feel a sort of uneasiness set in, I notice a splash in the water several yards offshore. *What was that?* Immediately, my eyes fine-tune to the spot, but minutes go by and nothing more happens. I smile to myself. I'm going to have to adjust to this new life by the sea. Who knows what marine life I might discover leaping from its blue surface? A whale? A swordfish? A shark? I shudder involuntarily at the last thought, and make a mental note to research what types of life inhabit these parts of the Atlantic. I meander a little farther down the coast before heading back toward our cottage. I've already been gone for some time and I don't want Mom and Dad thinking I've been kidnapped our first day on vacation. I am retracing my steps when all at once, there it is again—the splash. Quickly, I scan the water to my left, but all that is visible is the aftermath of ripples spreading across the surface. For some reason, I feel slightly disappointed. *Dang, that rascal is quick!*

My first night of sleep in Rhode Island is restful. I open my bedroom windows and am soothed to sleep by the sound of the ocean surf. When I wake early the next morning, I am greeted by rays of sun. Padding into the kitchen, I grab a peach and a bagel for breakfast and then decide it's time to settle in and organize my room. A charming, white, antique double bed covered in a purple and green duvet is situated in one corner, and a matching dresser sits across the room. Opposite of that is an old, wooden rocker, perfect for throwing things on when I don't feel like putting them away. I begin unloading my myriads of tops, shorts, sweatshirts, and sandals into dresser drawers and a small closet. By late morning I feel like I am ready to leave the house. Setting out to explore the town, I give my parents a shout, hop on my bike, and start out on the winding road that leads into Watch Hill. The town itself seems almost like it is from yesteryear. Completely surrounded by water, the shops and restaurants are quaint. Some appear to be old, renovated cottages. Marinas, docks, and beaches fill up the waterfront. It's a weekday, and although there are some pedestrians wandering the sidewalks, the streets are not bogged down with crowds of people, lending to a laid-back atmosphere. As I walk along a canopy-covered sidewalk, I peer through a window into a place that has the charm of an old-fashioned soda shop. The sign above the door reads St. Clair Annex. Suddenly, I want ice cream.

I'm standing in line, eyeing the menu board, deciding, when I hear—or sort of feel—a fidgety presence behind me. Becoming slightly annoyed by the perpetual wriggling, I am about to shoot the individual an irritated glance when a young girl from behind the counter says, "I can help who's next."

"I'll have a chocolate-peanut butter mixer," I say.

"Hey . . . if you don't mind, there is a special on those—two for one, and I was thinking about getting one too. Do you want to split the difference?" *Huh?* I turn around and come face-to-face with my fidgetor. She has large, brown eyes and chestnut hair pulled back into a tight ponytail, revealing pleasant facial features.

"Ummm . . . I—"

"I mean, you don't have to. But I just thought you might want to save some money." *Who is this girl?*

"Okay . . . *sure.*" I can't really argue with saving money. *But really?* After we pay and split the difference, I go outside to enjoy my ice cream in the fresh air. As I leave the old-fashioned ambience of St. Clair Annex, I feel my fidgetor's presence as she falls in step beside me.

"I'm Kate Owen," she says, extending one of her hands toward me. I switch my mixer into my left hand and awkwardly give hers a shake. She looks at me expectantly.

"I'm Bethany."

"Bethany who?" she asks. *What? Is this an interrogation?*

"Bethany Kuiper."

"Oh. Are you just in town for the day? Or are you staying for a while?"

"We're here for a while." I don't tell her how long. I'm not sure how much information I want to reveal to this overzealous stranger.

Her eyes brighten. "Awesome. Maybe we can hang out some." I glance away, not quite knowing what to say, but she doesn't notice. "I live here year-round. Just up over that hill, in the center of town." My eyes briefly peruse the area where she is pointing. "I'm still waiting for Nick and Emily to come for the summer. They will both be here in a couple of days. Then maybe we can all hang out."

She looks at me, waiting for an answer. I hesitate. "Yeah . . . okay." Her brown eyes glimmer with relief. Wow, I've only been in town a couple of hours, and already I have a new group of summer friends. Who knew how all this would turn out. But what was I worrying about yesterday? Being bored? That is looking doubtful.

Kate finishes her ice cream before me and starts shifting her feet back and forth, playing with her hands. I can tell she's waiting for me to finish too. In amazement, I observe all the bottled up energy she possesses, bubbling just below the surface of her petite frame. *Man, I wish I could borrow some of that.* For a moment I imagine how many miles I could run and how many marathon study sessions I could fit in next year at college. Finally, I scoop the last drop of chocolate-peanut butter into my mouth. *Mmm . . . that was sooo good!* Before I can blink, Kate practically grabs the empty cup out of my hand.

"Here, I'll throw that away for you." She bounces over to the nearest garbage container. I wait for her to return. She eyes my blue bike that is parked in a nearby rack. "You want to go for a ride, and I can show you around a bit?" I contemplate how long she's been following me in town that morning, since she already knows which bike is mine.

"Sure. I'd like that."

Kate grabs her bike, and we head up Bay Street. Very quickly we reach the end of the road, and she points to sign which reads The Flying Horse Carousel.

"It's a historic landmark. The oldest around."

We watch as the carousel circles round and round. Small children are laughing, enjoying the ride, while others hold their parent's hand on the sidelines, licking melty ice cream. The sight is heartwarming, and I think back to simpler times when the Kuiper family might have been here—smiling, carefree, enjoying the same thing.

Next, we turn left onto Larkin Road and head onto Bluff Avenue. There, sitting before us, is a giant, yellow-sided mansion with a stately front porch. Triple-story, white pillars grace the front entrance, adding regality to the wraparound veranda. Young, handsome men in blue uniforms stand ready to valet park expensive cars.

"Dang, I'd like to stay there," I say, as I take in the grand monstrosity before me.

"Yes, you would," Kate laughs. "It has a full-service spa—you would be quite pampered. It's called the Ocean House."

"I could do pampered." We both laugh this time.

"Hey, Jeremy." She yells to one of the boys in uniform. "How's it going?" She flashes him a big smile, and her brown eyes sparkle. *Oh boy, she's not only bouncy, she's a flirt, too.*

Jeremy smiles back. "It's going," he yells back. This seems to satisfy her, and we keep riding. Finally, we reach the end of our tour, and she announces she needs to go home for a bit. I glance at my watch and decide I should probably head back too.

"How about we meet back in town in . . . let's say, two hours, and we go to the beach?" She looks at me with a hopeful expression, and I decide I can't say no.

As I ride away, the exuberant sound of Kate's voice reaches my ears. "I'll show you fun at the beach!" I shake my head. What have I gotten myself in to? But I find myself smiling as I pedal myself back toward the blue summer cottage.

Later, I briefly consider not going back to meet Kate at all. Am I 100 percent sure this is who I want to be friends with this summer? I could blow her off now and that would be the end of it. Then again, who am I kidding; in a town this size, it wouldn't take her very long to find me. Besides, admittedly, she is starting to grow on me just a little. In some ways, she reminds me of Lucy, with her outgoing personality. Making the decision to go ahead with our plans, I throw on my new, brown-striped bikini, a pair of white shorts, lots of sunscreen, and head back into town.

When I find Kate waiting for me in front of the Watch Hill boat docks, I am greeted with warm, brown eyes and an eager smile. She looks very beachy, wearing a short, pink cover-up and silver-rimmed sunglasses. There are a variety of beaches we can go to, but she quickly informs me that the one at the country club is the best. The problem is, we don't have a membership, allowing us entrance. Undeterred by this, Kate beckons me to follow her, and we start walking in the club's direction.

"All right, stay right here. I just need a second." Her brown ponytail bounces back and forth as she heads off in the direction of a young man who is wearing tan shorts and a yellow polo. He appears to be guarding the entrance. I watch as Kate begins talking to him, her arms gesturing in explanation. The next thing you know, he is looking over at me. I feel my face begin to heat up. *What is going on?* He nods his head, and she waves me over.

As I walk to the gate, the yellow polo'd boy smiles and motions me through. "No problem, Bethany," he says. "Kate," he nods. "You both enjoy your day at the beach." I blush and sheepishly smile back.

"What did you say to him?" I demand, once we are well out of hearing distance.

"Oh, I just told him you are William Xavior's granddaughter, and that you had lost your country club membership card while attending a wild party last night. You were too embarrassed, of course, to tell your grandpa. If we didn't get in, other family members would wonder why you were patronizing other beaches today, and then the whole story might get out."

I widen my eyes in shock. "Who is William Xavior?"

"A man with a *lot* of money around this area. Generations of it."

"You are going to get me in trouble, and it's only my second day of vacation."

"No worries. It will be fine." She gives me a wink, and we continue walking toward the exclusive beachfront.

What had I been thinking earlier about Kate being similar to Lucy? I am starting to take that back. She is a lot crazier!

I soon find out that a day at the beach with Kate Owen is not exactly a relaxing, sunbathing type of day. We position our towels, and I settle in on my stomach, eager to start on my tan. Almost instantly, I am interrupted by her enthusiastic voice.

"Let's go in the water."

Most of our time is spent swimming and splashing in the water, walking along the shore, or playing catch with a football—even though we don't own a football. That doesn't pose a problem; she soon finds us one we can borrow.

Finally, as we are lying on our towels taking a brief rest, she props herself up on her elbow and looks over at me.

"Are you a surfer?" Her brown eyes watch me inquisitively.

"What? No. Why?"

"I don't know, you just look like one."

"Well, I guess I could be one. I mean, after all, I am William Xavior's granddaughter. Who knows who else I might soon become?" I roll my eyes at her, and she bursts out laughing. It takes awhile for her laughter to subside. I didn't know I was *that* funny. "Why do you think I look like a surfer?"

"I don't know, you just have that look. Blond, cute, and toned—typical surfer stereotype." *Cute? Huh.*

"Well, I'm pretty pale for a surfer. This is my first time out in the sun this year."

"You'll catch up," she says, and I relax, willing the sun to start working its magic.

Later on my ride back to the cottage, I choose to take a route that winds closely along the shoreline. I am enjoying the quiet after the continual exuberance of my prior company. Blue ocean water laps playfully onto the scattered rocks that are dispersed among the sand. The sky is endless, and the air smells salty and clean. I take a slow, relaxing breath and feel a calm settle over my body. It feels good to unwind. As I'm pedaling along at a casual pace, I hear a sound in the distance that catches my attention. Focusing on the noise, I soon recognize it as music—a guitar. Somewhere across the water, someone is strumming a melody on a guitar. I stop my bike and strain my ear to listen. It is a beautiful, melancholy sound. Almost instantly, I am drawn to the music and have a sudden curiosity to find where it is coming from. Briefly I consider searching it out, but then decide against it as it is getting late. For a minute or two, I continue listening, then begrudgingly drag myself away and travel the rest of the way back to the cottage.

Chapter Two

The next few days pass a little too uneventfully, and it occurs to me that I might need something more to do this summer than sit around ogling the sea and waiting for Kate to text. Randomly, I pull out my laptop and inadvertently find myself researching the ocean. After a couple of Google searches, it doesn't take long for me to discover the havoc we humans can play on its aquatic environment. While I sift through the myriads of online information, periodically my attention is drawn to a program called *Good Mate*. It is an environmental project that is set in place encouraging boaters and marinas to respect the coastal waters around them. Suddenly my mind starts whirling, my eyes brighten, and I have an idea.

My dad is sitting on the front porch enclosure, staring at his mobile computer. His hair is a little disheveled, and his expression is focused as he absentmindedly sips on a ceramic mug full of hot coffee. He looks rather unapproachable, but I proceed through the double screen doors anyway.

"Dad."

There is a pause while he continues to stare at his computer, and I begin to wonder if he is going to answer me. Finally, he holds up one finger in acknowledgement and continues studying the screen. Eventually he turns to me and rubs his dark brown eyes, seemingly clearing his mind.

"What's up, Bethany?"

"I want to do some volunteering while we're here this summer. There is this program called *Good Mate . . .*" I start to lay out my plan.

"Wait. Are you bored already?" He breaks into a knowing grin, and I am overcome with a feeling that it's he that is actually bored. Immediately, I wonder about the implication this might hold for our family.

"Well, no, I just thought . . . you know I like to stay busy, and it's a good way to help the ocean environment . . . and since we *are* staying on the ocean . . ." I hurriedly continue explaining. I don't want him to think I am bored, and I desperately don't want *him* to be bored. I'm not sure what role I play in the whole scheme of things, but I do know I am definitely on team *save the Kuiper family.*

I have spent the last four years of high school volunteering for Key Club, and so now it only seems natural to carry on in that same direction. Besides, it will only help my chances for future scholarships, and I do have a responsibility to care about our environment. My dad looks at me, his brown eyes deep in thought, and I can tell his brain is in motion—he likes to feel needed.

"Let me look into a few things, and we'll see what we can come up with." He gives me a smile and then begins looking at his mobile computer screen again.

Later that day, I receive a text from Kate and drive our LaCrosse over to her place in the center of town. As I cruise slowly down her street, checking the addresses to make sure I have the right location, I am immediately struck with the difference between her tiny bungalow and the other sprawling mansions that are scattered around Watch Hill. Her house is plain with white siding that desperately needs to be painted. No picket fences or flowering gardens decorate the small yard, and the lawn is in need of a good mowing.

"Hey, girl. Come on in." Kate is standing on her compact, wooden front deck that serves as a front porch. Instantly, I am captivated by her enthusiasm and soon forget about the shabby surroundings. She treats me like I'm her best friend, and I have only known her for days. Once again her chestnut hair is pulled into a tight ponytail, and this time she is donning short jean cutoffs and a spaghetti-strapped tank, revealing lots of tanned skin.

"I am sooo excited." Her voice mimics the boundless energy that her body language portrays as she leads me into her kitchen and motions for me to settle in. She gestures toward a swivel bar stool that butts up to the counter. Obediently, I sit and watch as she opens the refrigerator.

"Some juice?"

"Sure."

"Nick and Emily are both coming today." Kate stands on tiptoe, reaching to a high cupboard. She takes out two rocks glasses and pours orange liquid into them. "I can't wait to see them, and I can't wait for you to meet them." She slides my glass of juice down the counter towards me at lightning speed, and I barely catch it in time. Little bits of liquid splash over the rim and soak my fingers. *Whoa.*

"Are Nick and Emily brother and sister?"

"Huh? No. They just both happen to be arriving the same day. They vacation here every summer."

"I take it you all are good friends?"

"Yeah, good friends. They've been coming here for years." Suddenly she bites her bottom lip, and her eyes look dreamy. I can tell there is more she wants to add.

"And . . ." I prompt.

"And what?" Her eyes widen in surprise. "Oh, all right . . . and Nick is gorgeous! He's been my hot crush for years."

"So, are you an item?"

Her face falls slightly. "Well, not yet, but I'm hopeful. What about you? Did you leave a boy crying, missing you back in Philadelphia?"

"No," I laugh, "not even close."

"Well, I have a hard time believing that. Did you date much in high school?" She gulps the rest of her juice and immediately begins playing with her brown ponytail.

"Not really. Just some double dates with my friend Lucy, but that's about it." I finish my juice too, and she motions for me to slide the empty glass back to her across the counter. Hesitantly, I do, hoping that I won't overexert, sending it crashing to the linoleum floor. She catches it efficiently and carries it to the sink.

"So, you've never been in lo-*oove*?" She singsongs the last word. "Well, girl, you are missing out."

"Probably." I shake my head. "There has just never been anyone that really makes me feel that way, I guess." *Whatever way that is.*

"Well, there will be," she winks. "And when it happens, trust me, you are going to love it!"

We wander leisurely through her house and eventually end up in her bedroom. In detail, she describes her summer babysitting job and her hopes for saving up enough money to be able to attend classes this fall at Community College of Rhode Island. Listening to her as she passionately explains her plan for budgeting her earnings, suddenly I feel guilty for going away to Penn State this fall never giving money a second thought. I wonder what her parents do for a living, and, as if she can read my thoughts, she volunteers that she has never met her dad, and her mom is a dental hygienist who works close by in the town of Westerly.

"Well, if I ever need my teeth cleaned while I'm here . . ." I smile, and she smiles back.

We continue talking while sitting on her twin bed—mostly I'm sitting, and she's practically bouncing. Eventually, I share a little bit about why my family is really here this summer, briefly explaining about the fighting and tension around the house, and how I hope my parents won't get a divorce. Unexpectedly, a shiver creeps up my spine as I talk, and I have to swallow away a lump in my throat as I watch the concern that forms in Kate's brown eyes. She grabs my hand and gives it a squeeze.

"I'm going to text you later when Nick and Emily get in town, and you are going to come meet them tonight." Her voice is warm and reassuring, and somehow it lightens the mood.

True to her word, I get a text from Kate early that evening, and I wind back into town on my bike once again; this time, to meet her and her returning summer friends. Apparently her enthusiasm is contagious, I realize as I'm pedaling along, because I feel excited to see Nick and Emily too—and I don't even know them.

Once I'm in town, I scan the boat docks where she told me to meet. At first I don't see any sign of Kate, so I park my bike, head to the shoreline boardwalk, and watch as the sparkling water from the bay laps up against the docks and parked boats. Periodically I glance at the pedestrians passing by, hoping to catch sight of her.

From a distance, Kate recognizes me and waves me over to the group of kids she is talking to, standing by the Narragansett Bay entrance. Suddenly, I feel nervous to meet this new assortment of strangers who could potentially become my new friends. I pick out Nick immediately. Just as she has described him, he is very good-looking with a well-toned physique, tanned skin, and an unmistakable confidence about him. Next to him is a tall, dark-skinned girl with kinky hair pulled into a loose bun. This must be Emily. Another boy that I don't remember her talking about is among the group, and I secretly wonder if Kate has picked up another conquest.

"Everybody, this is Bethany Kuiper." Kate introduces me, and right away I notice that vivacious Kate has been replaced by a subdued, dreamy-eyed Kate. She is giggly and almost shy as she talks to her acquaintances. *So this is what boys do to girls.* I'd seen this happen to Lucy a couple of times before too. I recognized the symptoms. *Amazing.*

Everyone is very welcoming, and I immediately begin to feel at ease. Nick and Emily take turns asking the usual questions. Where are you from? How long are you here for? How old are you?

"Another summer girl," the boy I don't recognize interjects. He is small with shiny, black hair and a high voice—as if he hasn't quite reached puberty yet. His energy seems to be similar to Kate's, and he practically dances around as he talks.

"I'm sorry. I haven't met you yet. You are . . . ?" I question. But before he can answer, Nick answers for him.

"This is Jacqueline, I mean Jonathan," he laughs. Right away I feel sorry for Jonathan, thinking Nick is picking on him for his high voice. But the small, black-haired boy doesn't miss a beat.

"Oh, you wish my name was Jacqueline," he says to Nick with a smirk, then he turns to me. "I'm Jonathan. Nice to meet you, Bethany. By the way, have you met Nick? His name is short for Nicole." Silently I applaud him for his wit and offer him a smile.

"Let's walk toward Napatree Point," Kate suggests.

As the five of us begin nonchalantly meandering down the beach, heading toward the point, I can't help but notice the skillful way Kate eases into place, walking next to Nick. And she seems to hang on his every word, laughing at everything he says, even when it's really not that funny. A real ego booster for Nick, I think to myself, or else annoying—depending on which angle he's coming from.

We all laugh and joke as we walk, kicking up the sand with our heels. Periodically we meander into the water, getting our feet and legs wet and sometimes the bottom edges of our shorts. At times I wonder if we are making a spectacle of ourselves as I notice an occasional affluent pedestrian pass by, eyeing us apprehensively, but no one ever confronts us, telling us to tone it down, and so we keep on walking and laughing.

Finally, our shoreline excursion takes us back to the place where we began. As I hop on my bike, getting ready to head back to the cottage, Emily passes on the news to me that there is a group of kids meeting to play volleyball at Misquamicut Beach the following evening, and am I in?

I don't even have to think about it; I assure her I'll be there and wave my good-byes. As I'm pedaling away, my lips form into an enthusiastic grin. I really like my new summer friends. When I arrive back at the cottage, I pull out my phone and text Lucy.

Making some new friends. This might be fun. Wish you were here to meet them too. *(send)*

The next morning I wake up feeling energized. Rays from the sun permeate the windows, brightening the great room, while I stretch my now slightly tanned legs and get ready for a run. Dad is sitting on a bar stool staring at his computer, and Mom is across the room at the breakfast nook, sipping juice and leafing through a magazine. The room is very quiet. I extend my arms down to meet my toes and hold the position, making myself relax into the pain. Biting my lip, I wait for some interaction between my parents. But as the silence continues, it starts to feel more uncomfortable than the ache in my flexed calves. Silently I wonder if things are going any better between them, because it just doesn't seem like it. Suddenly I long for the old days when we all lived together in a tension-free house. How long ago was that? I can't even remember; and since there doesn't appear to be anything I can do to help solve the problem, I feel an impulse to bolt out the door and run. This morning's sprint is going to feel eradicating. As I'm heading out the side entrance of our cottage, my dad's voice finally breaks the stillness in the room.

"Bethany, are you available this afternoon?" I pause in place and listen while he continues. "I have a colleague who is friends with the owner of Hill Cove Marina, and he may be agreeable to let you do some volunteer work there this summer." Now my ears really perk up.

"Sure. What time were you thinking?" I can't hide my excitement.

"Let's say, about two o'clock."

"Two o'clock . . . I'll be ready." I continue through the door with a motivational spring in my step. As I start down the side gravel drive, I notice Josh's and Jake's sandy blond forms darting around on the lawn as they pass a soccer ball back and forth to each other.

"Hi, Josh. Hi, Jake," I yell. They briefly look up in acknowledgement and resume dribbling the ball. Shrugging my shoulders, I continue on down the drive and onto Foster Cove Road.

Hill Cove Marina sits on Little Narragansett Bay close to the hub of downtown Watch Hill. As Dad and I head toward a tan, cedar shake-sided main office building in search of David Chambers, the owner, I glance out front and notice a flurry of activity on the front docks. Various sizes and shapes of boats are waiting to fill up at the gas pumps or tie up for a reprieve from the big lake. The faint smell of gasoline, mixed with salt from the ocean, pervades the air, and the wake from passing watercrafts gently splashes against the wooden landings. Dad has transformed into a casual businessman, dressed in tan shorts and a polo, but businessman nonetheless. He looks like he has come prepared to make a deal, and I secretly hope he won't seem too intimidating to David Chambers. My worry is soon alleviated, however, when a balding, slightly plump, middle-aged man greets us with a sincere smile, and Dad instantly relaxes.

"So, young lady," David Chambers begins. "I hear you are interested in helping out with the *Good Mate* program. You want to help protect the ocean environment. That is very altruistic of you."

"I'd just like to do my part," I say, hoping he doesn't think I'm trying to be a hero or anything. It just seems like a productive way to spend the summer, and I *do* love the ocean.

"Well, we have implemented some of the program at our marina already, but we can definitely use some help servicing what we already have in place, and hopefully we can use you to put more ideas into practice."

I feel rather energized as David Chambers gives me an impromptu tour of the shop, imagining myself standing behind the counter passing out brochures to patrons or helping out in the back room organizing recycled material. Once we're out of the shop, he takes me down to the service station and onto the front docks, where the hustle and bustle of boats coming and going keeps a steady pace. As we're standing on the main dock where the gas pumps are housed, my attention is drawn to a man appearing to be in his mid-twenties who is imparting orders to some marina personnel. First glance simply reveals a man with light brown hair and glistening copper highlights, and eyes that seem to smile even when he's not. But as we continue walking, I tune in more closely to his voice as he talks to the group of employees, and I notice that it has a gravelly quality, like he'd recently gotten laryngitis and is just now recovering. Instantly, I like the way it sounds.

As we approach, he looks in our direction, nodding in recognition to David Chambers. Suddenly, I feel self-conscious as I realize how good-looking he is.

"Ethan, I want you to meet Bethany Kuiper. She is our summer volunteer . . . going to be working with the *Good Mate* program. Bethany, this is Ethan Vaughn. He helps me manage the marina."

Immediately, I am greeted with a disarming smile. "Hi, Bethany." Ethan reaches out a strong hand in my direction, and I put my own in his, hoping that it won't seem too sweaty. His warm, brown eyes connect with mine in such a way that it makes me feel like I'm the most important person in the world. "It's going to be really nice having you around this summer. I know you're going to like it here." His whole persona exudes charm, and I have the feeling that anyone who enters his presence is left feeling slightly undone.

"Thanks, I'm excited to be here," I say, hoping my voice sounds businesslike and not resembling a floundering schoolgirl.

"Well, when can you start?" his gravelly voice questions.

"Soon . . . any time really." I try not to glance at my dad for approval, wanting to appear independent and grown-up.

"Great, we will look forward to seeing you." Once again he flashes his warm smile, and I am left feeling very welcomed and embraced.

David Chambers walks us back toward our Chevy Tahoe, and we turn to leave.

"Tell ol' Jim Grant I said hi," he says to Dad, and I figure this must be the colleague that is our connection to the marina.

"Will do," Dad smiles and nods his answer, then we jump in the Tahoe and head down the road. While we veer down the now familiar route back to the cottage, I feel exhilarated as I contemplate my new summer volunteering position at Hill Cove Marina. The ocean is our escort as we travel along the winding path leading back to our cottage, and I watch it closely, reveling in its shimmering, blue waves. *I'm here to help you stay beautiful,* I silently tell it half-jokingly, before self-consciously glancing over at my dad to make sure my thoughts are not exposed. But he only continues driving, eyes peeled to the road.

A north wind is coming off the Atlantic, blowing down from Canada, making it a cool evening for playing beach volleyball, perfect sweatshirt weather. I grab my royal blue and white Penn State sweatshirt and pull it over my head, and then shimmy into a pair of white shorts. After drawing my blond hair into a ponytail, I smooth on some strawberry ChapStick, glance in the mirror, and head off to find Misquamicut Beach.

As I approach the long stretch of beachfront, I am greeted with loud, pulsating music and a nightclub type of atmosphere. Jamaican-style cabanas line the street side of the sand, offering fruity drinks, grilled snacks, and the promise of a good time. Even though it's cool outside, girls and boys are gyrating to piercing, techno-style music, barely even clothed. I look beyond all this in search of volleyball nets and a familiar face, and soon find what I am after. Padding through the pale sand, I leave the loudest rhythms to pound behind me and venture toward the quiet, rolling surf where the games are being played.

"Hey. Penn State," I hear a boy shout as I walk past a straw-roofed cabana. I'm not quite sure if he is talking to me, so I keep walking.

"Penn State, in the white shorts," he calls out again. *Okay, maybe he* is *talking to me.* I turn around slowly to see if it's someone I might recognize. Of course it's not, but he and the boy he is with appear friendly enough, so I give a little wave.

"Is that your school?" he asks, and I notice his words are slightly slurred.

"This fall," I answer a little hesitantly.

"Hey, us too. Come sit with us and we can compare class schedules." He slugs his companion in the arm and takes another gulp out of a tall glass. Immediately, I wonder what exactly is in his drink and how many he's had.

"Sorry, I'm headed to play volleyball." I point in the direction I'm currently headed and instantly wonder if I've revealed too much information. I'm not interested in him and his buddy showing up on the court to play drunk volleyball.

"Well, too bad," he calls after me and settles back into his chair. Relieved, I keep walking. I can tell he won't be going anywhere anytime soon.

When I reach the nets, the games are already in play. Sitting on the sidelines, I watch my new friends volley, serve, and spike back and forth. As expected, Kate uses her relentless supply of energy wisely and offers a lot to her team. Nick seems to be naturally athletic, executing each play with ease. Emily appears mostly to avoid the ball, and Jonathan tries his best to disrupt the game in order to cover his clumsiness on the court.

Kate sends me a big wave and a smile as soon as she sees me, before dusting some sand from her knees. "We're almost done with this round, and then you can join in."

"Yeah, you can have my spot," Jonathan quickly volunteers. I nod and smile back at him, knowing he's not just being polite—I can tell it will be a relief for him to be out of the game. On the other hand, I feel a little nervous as I anticipate entering the match; I'm really not that great either. Mostly, I've only played in gym class, and I was certainly no superstar then. Secretly, I hope I won't let my team down.

Ready or not, I step onto the sandy court, dig my feet into the soft granules, and prepare for the oncoming serve. Seemingly in slow motion, the white ball whizzes through the air, veering straight toward me. Uneasily I bend my knees, clasp my hands together in a bumping position, and watch in horror as it lands just to my right, leaving me swatting at only the air. *Oh crap, this might be a long night.*

"Do over," I say, trying to minimize my mistake. Instantly there are groans from the opposing team. *Or not.* Wiping my sweaty palms onto the sides of my white shorts, I concentrate a little harder, and soon I am into the flow of the game—maybe not making lethal spikes, but at least holding my own. After a few rounds, the teams disperse and begin mingling along the shoreline among a couple of scattered campfires.

The evening progresses, and I'm just starting to think about heading home. I see Nick, Jonathan, and Kate standing at the water's edge, conversing with a group of volleyball players, so I wander over to say good-bye. As I come up closer on the group, Nick steps to one side to adjust his sport sandal, offering me a better view of the assembly. Among them is a guy I've never seen before. Almost immediately, I feel my heart pause, and I am frozen in my tracks. It's as if I've come face-to-face with a Hollister model. He stands casually but well-composed, talking with my friends, occasionally running a hand through his tousled, blond hair. His body is toned and well-built, making his tee shirt cling to his chest. Unintentionally, I glance at it, half expecting to read the word *Hollister.* Instead, from my distance, all I can decipher is something about marine biology. His fine facial features and perfectly chiseled jaw are breathtaking. Momentarily I watch him as he talks. When he pauses to smile at someone in the group, white teeth are revealed, offset by the golden tan of his skin. The first word that comes to my mind is *beautiful.*

Unexpectedly, I can't move. I have to remind myself to keep stepping forward. The others turn to look at me as I approach.

"Oh, hey, Bethany," I hear Kate say. But all I can see is him.

As he hears my name, he too glances my way, and we make eye contact for the first time. I can feel myself flush as I try to look away, but what I see in his face catches me off guard. For just a moment, he stares hard at me as if in shock, or as if he recognizes me in some way. Not wanting to appear awkward or insecure, I resist the urge to look over my shoulder to see if his reaction is meant for someone else. But almost instantaneously, his initial expression is replaced with his former, more casual one, and I am left to wonder whether I imagined the whole thing.

"Here is our star volleyball player," Nick playfully offers. I roll my eyes.

"I doubt that." Suddenly I am self-conscious as I talk. I feel like I'm onstage and instantly become hyperaware of the way I'm standing, about whether my hair is half coming out of my ponytail, making me look like a mess, and whether there is still sand stuck to my knees, causing me to look juvenile.

"As I recall, you got a few good points for our team. Not too shabby," Nick continues. Suddenly I am thankful he is painting me in a good light right now.

"Oh, Bethany . . . have you ever met Tristan Alexander? Tristan, this is Bethany Kuiper," Kate interjects. Indisputably I know who she is referring to, and I look up to meet the most intense, sea green eyes I've ever seen. My mouth goes dry, and I feel as though when I speak, my voice might sound cracked and funny.

"Hi, Bethany." Fortunately he speaks first, giving me time to recover. His voice sounds smooth, deep, and self-assured.

"Hi," I say back, giving him a little half wave.

"Sounds like I missed a good volleyball game." His green eyes seem to study me as he talks, making my heart beat a little faster.

"Yeah, it was a lot of fun. Maybe next time." Out of nervousness, I reach up and start playing with my ponytail.

"Why did you have to show up so late, Tristan? The other team could have definitely used your help. They sucked," Jonathan interjects jokingly. I laugh too, appreciative that the spotlight is taken off of me.

The group continues to hang out and chat, and now my earlier thoughts of leaving are far from my mind. Mostly I hang at Kate's side, allowing myself a glance now and then in Tristan's direction. Surprisingly, at times I think I observe him looking at me too, but it happens so quickly that I am never sure if I'm just conjuring up the idea.

Eventually the sun fades behind the western horizon, and the water begins to take on a darker hue. The north wind has turned the evening air downright chilly. My Penn State sweatshirt and white shorts are no longer doing the job. Reluctantly I turn to leave, following the cue of the many others who have now exited the beach. Unobtrusively, I take one more glimpse in Tristan's direction. He is standing several feet away from me, inches from the vast expanse of the darkening water. *Wow, he is sooo hot!* Suddenly, I don't want to leave without saying good-bye. In desperation, I wonder if I will meet up with him again or get a chance to know him at all this summer.

From my distance, I see that he is conversing with a couple of lingering volleyball players. Jonathan is among them. As I'm getting ready to leave, he stops talking and stares in my direction. For a brief moment, time stands still, and I experience an overwhelming sensation that he is contemplating coming toward me. My heart begins to pound. But then he sets his jaw, gives me an indecipherable nod, and looks away.

I hug my blue sweatshirt tighter to my chest, feeling somewhat disappointed and yet very alive at the same time. As I head back toward the sounds of "Party Rock Anthem" pulsating through the outdoor nightclub stereo speakers, my head is spinning with this new phenomenon I am experiencing.

My first day volunteering at Hill Cove Marina is spent listening to David Chambers as he gives me the rundown on what type of environmental projects I'm going to be working on around the facility, mostly involving recycling. I have to work hard to stay focused on what he is saying, instead of letting my mind wander to a certain blond-haired, green-eyed boy I have just met. I only encountered him briefly the night before, and yet somehow my thoughts keep drifting back to him continually. This type of thing has never happened to me until now, and it is a little unsettling. But more disconcerting to me is the idea that our meeting may have been a one-time, chance encounter, and I may never see him again.

"So, after you get the recycling bins organized, I'm thinking you could make signs to alert the boaters to use the best practice methods." David Chambers rubs his balding head and looks over at me. I give him a reassuring smile to let him know I'm listening.

"I really appreciate you giving me this opportunity," I tell him. I don't want him to notice my distractedness and think I'm not really up for the job, after all. Shaking my head to clear my thoughts, I try even harder to stay focused.

It had been a beautiful clear crisp morning, and I had decided to ride my bike to the marina. Now it waits for me just outside the back door of the main office for the return trip. I jump on its black, cushioned seat and drive beside the ocean, letting the salty breeze wash over my face as I ride. The sky radiates a brilliant blue as it disappears into the surrounding sea, and the constant sound of the waves pushing onto the sand and rocks offers a kind of peacefulness to the afternoon excursion.

After many minutes of pedaling, another sound breaks through the tranquility, drawing my attention away from the water—the melancholy sound of strumming guitar music. *There it is again!* This time I am determined to follow the sound. Winding my bike farther down the ocean drive, I pass the usual turn which leads to my street. Finally I run out of road. Carefully, I lean my bike against a bush, hoping it is well-hidden from view, and proceed down a rocky path which leads to a meandering, sandy shore. Just ahead in the distance, I discover the mysterious musician, and I stop dead in my tracks. I can't believe my good fortune! *It's him!* Sitting on an old piece of driftwood with his back turned slightly away, I observe Tristan, lost deep in thought, his strong hands lightly plucking the strings of a guitar.

As if he can sense my presence, he turns slowly and greets me with a surprised look on his face. Instantaneously, the expression is replaced with a smile, and my insides melt.

"Um . . . hi," I say, feeling suddenly silly and rather like a spy. "I just heard the guitar, and I heard it another time the other day, and I just wanted to see who was playing . . ." I begin rambling as I try to explain why I'm here.

The musical sound of his laughter halts my blathering, and I stop midsentence, unsure of what to say next. His intense, green eyes study me as I continue to look at him, and I wonder what he is thinking.

"Bethany, from volleyball, right?" he says, and I have a hard time concentrating; his voice is deep and smooth and completely unnerving.

"Yes, and you're . . . Tristan," I manage to say, like I don't know who he is, like I haven't said his name over and over again in my head one hundred times since last night at volleyball.

He smiles again, and I clasp my hands together, not wanting him to notice how shaky I've become in his presence. "So . . . are you visiting here this summer?" he questions.

"Yes, we'll be here all summer. My family is renting a cottage on Foster Cove Road."

"Well, welcome." He turns to set his guitar off to the side before his green eyes settle back on me. The warmth in his voice gives me the feeling that he is okay with me interrupting his playing, and I feel elated.

"So, I guess that means you are from around here?" I question.

"Yeah," he answers rather nonchalantly, not offering any more information.

I point to the guitar. "Your playing is beautiful." He glances at the instrument that rests beside him on the driftwood, and shrugs without answering. *Oh no.* Suddenly I feel like the conversation isn't going very well, and I don't know how to turn it around.

As if Tristan senses this, he lightens the mood. "When is your next volleyball game?"

"I'm not sure but . . ."

"Well, next time I hope I can get there a little earlier." *Wow! Really?* Suddenly I am breathless. Standing up, he stretches and walks over to stand a little closer to me, causing my heart rate to accelerate. He gives me a disarming smile, and once again I get the feeling that he is studying me for some reason. A delicate breeze ruffles his already tousled blond hair, and I notice for the first time that he is wearing ripped jeans. *Wow! Does he realize the effect he has?* He walks over to the water's edge and then right into the water, up past his ankles—not even caring that the bottom of his jeans are getting wet. Bending down, he picks up a small, flat rock and tosses it skillfully away from shore. It skips perfectly four times over the water's surface.

Not knowing what else to do, I stroll over in closer proximity to him, standing centimeters from the edge of the ocean. The surf laps up over my toes, but I have too much reserve to walk right in and join him.

"That was pretty cool." I motion toward the rock that he just threw, and then I see something flat, round, and black swimming just off the edge of the shore. It is the size of a Frisbee, shaped like a disc, and has a long, skinny tail.

"Oooh, what is that?" I ask, suddenly interested in the aquatic creature that is moving in front of me. Tristan treads through the surf in his ripped jeans to take a look.

"That is a horseshoe crab. We get a lot of those around here." He sifts his hand through the water, and for a second I think he is going to pick it up, but he doesn't.

"I have a feeling I have a lot to learn about the ocean and what lives in it," I say. At those words Tristan looks over at me in surprise, and I become a little confused. I get the feeling that I dumbfound him in some way, and I am not sure why.

"Well, you came to the right place then. There is as much ocean around here as you could ever want."

Speaking of want. I blush at my thought and look away. There is a moment or two of silence, and he shoves his hands in his jean pockets and looks away too.

Eventually, we continue making some small talk. Mostly he asks me about Philadelphia, and I ask him a couple things about Watch Hill. I find out he is eighteen, and I tell him I'll be eighteen soon. By the time I leave to go back to the cottage, my heart is doing a happy dance in my chest, and I want to sing at the top of my lungs. All I know is, Tristan Alexander is all I can think about.

Chapter Three

Lying in my double bed at the cottage, I let the sunlight flood into my room, warming the skin on my face and arms. A cool breeze sneaks in from the open window that tenders my view of the rippling sea, fluttering lightly against my eyelashes and cheekbones. It's morning and I don't want to move. I don't want to get up. I don't want to eat. I don't want to see what the rest of my family is up to. I just want to lie here in my full-sized bed and think about Tristan. Butterflies are quivering in my stomach, and I feel a sensation of a shiver rush through my body. So this is it then. This is what they have been talking about, this feeling that is so hard to describe. They warned me that eventually it would happen, that it would just blindside me out of nowhere. Well definitely, it *had* happened. I'd been taken captive in an unguarded moment, and now I am relishing the unexpected feeling.

I'd had a couple of so-called crushes in high school, but by the time I actually got to know the guy, on any level, I was always somewhat disappointed—it just seemed like something was lacking. That feeling that all my girlfriends talked about—it just wasn't there. I thought maybe I was destined to be single my whole life. It's not that I felt lonely, or at least I didn't realize I felt lonely, until now. Now everything was being revealed to me in a whole new light. The way the sun invades my room seems a little brighter. The way the birds sing to each other outside my window sounds more melodic, and the way the cool morning breeze glides across my face feels like a newfound caress.

Suddenly, I want to share this unfamiliar revelation with someone, so I reach over onto my nightstand and grab my smartphone to text Lucy.

So . . . there's this guy. *(send)*

I lie back in bed, hoping to hear back soon. Even though I am getting to know Kate and the others more and more, I not ready to confide in them the way I can with Lucy. We've been together since elementary school, and I feel safe sharing information with her.

(unlock) What? Who?

I smile thoughtfully as I contemplate her text. Who is Tristan? So far, he is a gorgeous guy that I met at the beach who completely takes my breath away. But other than that, I really don't know much about him—yet. I *so* want to know more about him, though. I do realize, however, that he is not quick to reveal information about himself. The times I asked him questions about himself, he seemed to evasively shrug them off.

I wonder if Lucy is surprised to hear that I have met someone I feel is worth talking about. Thinking back to the double dates she coerced me into throughout the years, I cringe and shake my head. Lucy's vivacious personality and unusual combination of doelike brown eyes along with shimmering, blond hair kept her calendar full of suitors. Occasionally she felt that I too needed a male companion, and she would drag me along to keep the friend of a boyfriend company.

I wince as I vividly recall sitting beside Brandon Johnson in the backseat of Kyle Manning's jeep, while Lucy, bubbly as always, sat beside her then boyfriend Kyle in the front. It's not that Brandon Johnson wasn't cute. By most girl's standards, he was probably okay to look at. But there was just something about the way he sporadically chewed with his mouth open or the nasal quality of his voice that left me repelled.

I remember the speakers blaring Nickelback and him singing

along, slightly off-key, ruining the tune; and how he was trying to unobtrusively inch closer to me while I held my breath and shrunk myself into the tightest space possible, hugging the passenger-side door. He didn't seem to pick up on the usual dating cues, because in spite of this, his right hand eventually reached out in search of mine. When I didn't offer it back, he proceeded to grope my leg instead. *I was going to kill Lucy!* I wriggled in my seat, hoping he would withdraw his sweaty palm, and when he didn't, I pressed my lips together, inhaled sharply, and removed his hand myself. Irritated, Brandon retreated to his side of the car and sulked the rest of the evening.

This new feeling I have about Tristan is so unlike the awkward dates I experienced in high school, I can hardly compare the two.

After eating breakfast, I wander into my favorite room, the screened-in front porch. In spite of the rolling landscape and the cloudless day, the view isn't very promising. Josh and Jake are in a world of their own, playing with remote control boats on the edge of the shore. Mom is sitting in a white Adirondack chair, glancing impatiently at Dad as he paces across the front lawn, speaking into his mobile phone. It must be business. Occasionally he runs his fingers through his brown hair and sends a fleeting look back in her direction, but then keeps right on talking. I notice there is an empty chair next to Mom's, and I have to assume that Dad had been occupying it prior to his call. I watch as Mom jiggles her leg and taps her fingers impatiently. Eventually the look on her face is replaced with irritation. I wonder whether I should go down and distract her with conversation, but decide against it for the time being—this may be a good time not to get involved. At this point I don't want to be the subject of her wrath.

Dad keeps talking, steely eyed, jaw set, eventually turning his back completely to Mom—now he's not looking back at her at all. I imagine he no longer wants to observe the formidable expression on her face.

It appears as though Mom's patience has reached its end. In a huff, she marches to the shoreline in an attempt to drum up some interaction with the boys, but they continue playing without acknowledging her. Scanning the yard one more time in search of Dad, she sends him an insufferable glare. This time Dad does notice.

"Hey, Mark," I hear him say into the phone. "Can I call you back in just a few—" he stops midsentence as he receives yet one last leveling expression from Mom before she exits the yard and heads up to the cottage.

"On second thought, let's just continue this conversation right now." He narrows his eyes and shakes his head.

Dinner is intolerable that night. As silence fills the room, I wonder why we are going through the motions at all. Why not serve us buffet style and let us all eat in our own separate rooms? *I call dibs on the screened porch!* Intermittently, Dad and Mom take turns talking to us kids, but never to each other.

"You are not eating much," I hear Mom say, and I look up from my plate to see a concerned look in her blue eyes. Right away, I imagine she thinks my sudden aversion for food is due to the tension filled home environment. What she doesn't know is that my new thoughts about Tristan have replaced my appetite.

"Well, I'm really not that hungry, but . . ." I start to say, but she shoots me a disapproving look, and I shove some spaghetti in my mouth to keep her happy.

I notice the twins are spending more time playing with their food than eating it. Both of their places at the table appear to have turned into miniature war zones. *How appropriate!* Really, they seem a little too old to be making such messes, but my parents are so preoccupied with their own misery they can't seem to detect it.

After dinner, I help wash dishes and wipe down the granite countertops. All the while my mind is racing, filling with thoughts of when I'll get to see Tristan next. Already, almost a whole day has gone by since I've last seen him, and it feels like an eternity. I feel a little silly as I think these thoughts. I have only had two rather brief encounters with him. I shouldn't be obsessing so much. The fact remains, however, I do really want to see him again, and so my mind plots over and over, all the ways I might be able to make this happen. I contemplate biking into town by myself or maybe even hiking back to the secluded beachfront where I discovered him and his guitar yesterday, but decide against both. The first idea seems obscure enough, but the second seems borderline stalkerish. In the end, I decide to text Kate.

It appears as though Kate is in no hurry to text me back, so I meander down to the water's edge to enjoy an evening with the ocean. Slipping off my sandals, I wade in up to my calves, relishing the feel of the salty liquid on my legs and the grit of the sand between my toes. Walking along the lakefront, a foot offshore, I let the water splash up past my knees. It feels refreshing. I scan the clear expanse beneath me in hopes of seeing one of those creatures I had discovered while I was with Tristan the night before. After much searching, I finally spot a black organism moving slowly by my feet, noting that it reminds me of a flattened turtle. Immediately, I smile as I am taken back to yesterday—to a remote shoreline only miles from my cottage. What was that thing called? *A horseshoe crab.* In my mind, I recall Tristan's voice telling me the answer, and goose bumps begin to surface on my skin.

The next morning, I check my phone and see a text I missed from Kate. Taking a few minutes to clear the sleep from my head, I text her back. After we formulate a plan for meeting up, I grab an oatmeal raisin muffin and head into Watch Hill on my bike.

Our paths cross in front of St. Clair Annex—the ice cream spot.

"Hey, do you want to get some ice cream?" I say, flashing her a smile. "I hear there is a special today. Buy one, get one free. You buy one, and I'll get one free."

Kate immediately bursts into laughter, and I shake my head. I didn't think it was *that* funny, but I kind of enjoy that I can crack her up so easily. It's a talent I never really knew I had before. For some reason, though, I get the feeling that my humor may only have this effect on *her*.

"Seriously, I would like to get some ice cream later. Do you?"

"Yeah, later. Do you want to ride around?" She is straddling her bike anxiously, looking like she wants to keep moving.

As we roam through various side streets, I appreciate each well-manicured yard and the bountiful array of green foliage that lines our path. Each lane we take seems to wind on and on, up and over hills whose peaks offer a glimpse of the surrounding sea below.

"I'm going to show you East Beach," Kate says enthusiastically as we park our bikes. She leads me to a sandy path that is lined with dune grass, and we meander down to the wide-open expanse of sand and ocean that is East Beach. It's early enough in the day that the area is still absent of the hustle and bustle of daily tourists. A warm breeze flows off the lake, blowing wisps of blond hair that have loosened from my ponytail. Kate takes off her hair tie and allows her chestnut locks to stream freely in the wind. I can't help but study this new look on her, noticing how her unruly hair softens her features, giving her a fairylike appearance. She glances over at me.

"What?"

"I don't know, I like your hair like that," I say.

She rolls her eyes. "It's wild!"

"It suits you," I smirk, hoping I don't sound too offensive.

"Ha! What are you trying to say about me, Bethany?"

"You're not really wild exactly . . . maybe a little crazy though." I playfully glance over at her to see how she's taking my remark. She pulls some windblown strands of hair behind her ears and narrows her eyes in jest.

"So, what did you think of my Nick?"

"*Your* Nick is pretty hot!" I tell her, and instantly her face breaks into a wide grin.

"I know, and I have to say, he looks even better this year than he did last year—if that is even possible."

"Well, you can only imagine what next year is going to bring, then." Once again she bursts into laughter at my apparent newfound wit, but then soon recovers.

"Oh no!" She grimaces dramatically. "I'm in trouble."

"That you are, my friend." But as I'm saying the words, I'm thinking of my own recently discovered trouble—Tristan. I *so* want to see him, but don't know where to look. Actually, I *am* looking—unobtrusively looking everywhere; scanning the streets as we ride, scrutinizing the surrounding beachfront as we walk through the sand—but so far I've come up empty-handed.

Eventually, Kate becomes bored with East Beach and wants to head back into town. Secretly, I'm ready to move on too, eager to find a new area to peruse.

We park our bikes beside the public docks on Bay Street and are strolling the water-front boardwalks when I spot him. All at once, my heart pauses and then speeds up rapidly. My thoughts become tangled, and I can't seem to focus—somewhere in the back of my mind I realize Kate is saying something to me, but I can't comprehend the meaning of her words.

Tristan is standing on a dock, engaged in conversation with a middle-aged man. His legs are spread slightly, and his tee shirt is snug, revealing strong arms that are folded over a sculpted chest. His stance is thoughtful, yet confident and—*magnificently beautiful*. His tousled, sunstreaked hair blows lightly in the wind, and he rakes his hand through the strands, seemingly to keep them out of his eyes.

The man and Tristan appear to be conversing about an old, wooden boat that is parked in a slip next to where they are standing.

Tristan's face is serious as he listens to the man, and then he bends down and rubs a hand over the weathered hull of the swaying craft. Momentarily he stands back up, makes some comment to his converser, and—as if in slow motion—looks in my direction.

My heart stops.

As if my being there is unexpected, he appears to do a double take. And then, after his green eyes connect with mine for a flicker of a second, he reengages in conversation with the middle-aged man, and it's as though he hasn't seen me at all.

Now my heart plummets.

Instantly, a million thoughts start coursing through my mind, like, maybe he never saw me at all, or maybe he didn't recognize me, or maybe he is in the midst of a crucial conversation and he'll catch up with me when he's finished, or—I don't want to think about the other *or(s)*.

"Are you ready for ice cream?" Kate's voice breaks through my thoughts.

"What? Sure," I say, shaking my head out of its daze, and we walk over to St. Clair Annex.

As we are sitting at one of the parlor-styled tables, scooping ice cream into our mouths with long-handled silver spoons, Kate eyes me contemplatively.

"What's with you all of a sudden?"

"Huh? I don't know what you mean." I play dumb. Suddenly Kate's eyes widen, and her mouth gapes open a bit.

"OMG! You like Tristan Alexander, don't you?"

"What?" I narrow my eyes and start to shake my head, but she interrupts.

"I just saw him at the docks just now, and you saw him too, didn't you?" She's laughing now. "Admit it."

"Who wouldn't like Tristan Alexander?" I mutter.

"Yeah, but you *like*—like him, don't you?" she continues to question me relentlessly. I shrug my shoulders and look away. I'm not ready to admit this to her yet, and besides, after what just transpired, I'm left feeling a little confused.

"Let's go," she says, practically bounding from her seat. "Let's go talk to him. I need to talk to him about something anyway."

My eyes widen in surprise, or horror, I'm not sure. "I'm still eating my ice cream."

"Well, hurry and finish it up."

I roll my eyes and take my time. She taps her foot, and I smile.

When we head back over to the docks, Tristan is still there, but the man is gone. He is still checking out the old boat when we approach him. My heart is pounding in my chest.

"Hey, Tristan," Kate's voice sings out.

He turns and sees us then, and his jaw tightens ever so slightly. "Hey, what's up?" he answers back, rather nonchalantly. As if I'm not there, his eyes connect with Kate, and my heart resumes its previous sinking. *He doesn't even want to look at me.* Suddenly I am overwhelmed with his obvious disinterest toward me.

"What are you doing with this boat?" Kate is oblivious to my pain as she continues her conversation

"I'm not sure yet. I'm just checking it out." He eyes it appreciatively, and I get a brief opportunity to observe his athletic physique and perfect profile as he turns away from me—but this only leaves me with an unrequited ache.

"It looks like it needs a lot of work." Kate walks over to scrutinize it more closely.

He chuckles and rakes a hand through his blond hair. "Yeah, it definitely does."

"Bethany, does your family have a boat at the cottage?" Kate tries to draw me into the conversation. At this, Tristan finally glances in my direction, but his face is expressionless, not holding any of the warmth from two days ago.

"Um, no, but my dad is talking about renting one, so maybe we'll end up getting one, who knows."

"Well, I hope you get one. We could have so much fun. You'd go for a boat ride with us, wouldn't you, Tristan?" Kate has so much enthusiasm, but she is trying too hard.

"Maybe." Tristan looks uncomfortable, and suddenly I want to just disappear. I look over at Kate and plead silently with my eyes. Thankfully, she gets the cue and comes over to stand next to me, almost protectively.

"Well, let's get going, Bethany. See ya, Tristan."

At this, he looks right at us to nod his head in acknowledgement of her good-bye, and for just a moment, I sense something else in his green eyes besides apathy, but I can't place what it is. Then that quickly it disappears, leaving me with feelings of disappointment and confusion.

We are mounting our bikes when I feel Kate's brown eyes studying me. "Don't be sad."

I glance over at her and scrunch up my nose and forehead. "I'm not being sad."

"There are other fish, you know."

"What?"

"Other fish in the sea . . . besides him. Please don't get all moody over a boy this summer. You are so much more fun when you smile." She waits for a response, so I give her what she is looking for, attempting a halfhearted grin.

"We're going to have tons of fun this summer. You can be sure of that." She leans over to wrap her arm around my shoulder, careful not to tip her bike in the process.

"Whatever you say, Kate, but I'm really not that sad." I hope my tone sounds lighthearted.

"Okay."

We go our separate ways after that, but I'm not quite ready to go home, so I stray in a different direction instead. Soon I find myself at the entrance of a zigzaggy path that leads to Watch Hill Light—the light house that sits on the juncture of Block Island Sound and Fisher's Island Sound. Once again I park my bike. Then I begin the hike that leads to the sixty-one-foot-tall, white brick structure, looming high above the roaring waves beneath.

My eyes encompass the jagged rocks and the pounding surf below as I saunter along, all the while struggling with the ugly thoughts that have invaded my mind. I feel so stupid for letting my heart get tangled up so fast. Really, I can't be mad at Tristan, though. I am the one who jumped to conclusions, but what do *I* know about romance and love and boyfriends, anyway—next to nothing. I am so inexperienced. I wasn't trying to let this happen, it just did.

AsI stand there pondering all this, I feel a buzz in my back pocket, and I pull out my phone to check my text. It's from Lucy.

(unlock) How's it going with that Hot guy?

Ummm. It's not! *(send)*

Once I reach the lighthouse, I stare up at its stately presence and try to recall some of the history I'd read about it. I know it first came in to existence in 1745, during the French and Indian War and the Revolutionary War, but was destroyed and rebuilt several times since—the most recent damage inflicted by the Hurricane of 1938. Presently, it is leased to the Watch Hill Lightkeepers Association and delivers its signal by automation.

My history review is interrupted as my phone buzzes again. It's Lucy once more.

(unlock) Oh well,there's got to be more fish out there . . .

Ha! That's the 2nd time I've heard that line today. *(send)*

Speaking of fish in the sea, I notice several fishermen lined up along the edges of the embankment that borders the lighthouse, enjoying the simplicity of life by the sea. Life doesn't seem simple for me anymore—not like it did for most of my childhood. Maybe that is part of growing up, discovering that life's experiences aren't always so neat and tidy—like all the fighting between my parents, or now this new awareness that I have of boys, created simply by Tristan's existence. Well, I have to try hard to forget about him—he really *doesn't* exist for me. But right now it still hurts; it is a throbbing in my chest that needs to be soothed away. I need something for the pain—a good, long run. Suddenly, I wish that I hadn't ridden my bike into town that day. I crave the feeling of pavement pounding beneath the soles of my shoes for the trip home instead.

I glance back up at the high tower of the lighthouse, contemplating the beacon of safety that it is to the navigators at sea. It sends an alternating red and white flash every 2.5 seconds and flares a warning signal every 30 seconds in the fog. I shake my head, hoping the ships are much better at interpreting signals than I am. Man, was I bad at interpreting signals the other night, because somehow I had the feeling that Tristan was kind of into me too. *Was I ever way wrong!* I decide I'm not very good at this whole boy/girl relationship thing, but what was I thinking anyway? Tristan is *so* hot, the kind of guy girls swoon over, the topic of discussion at parties, the kind of guy that makes you and your girlfriends nudge each other and drop your jaw as he passes by.

And who was I? There was nothing exceptional that stood out about me. I'd rarely had a date in high school and I doubted if I'd ever turned many boy's heads. I had been deluding myself, thinking that a boy like Tristan would ever be interested in a girl like me.

Pulling myself away from my derogatory thoughts, I glance up at the sky and notice the once scattered, white clouds above me have transformed into an ominous black. All my brooding has made me oblivious to the change in weather, and now it appears I may be in for a good soaking. I break into a jog, shortening the hike back to my bike. Jumping onto it quickly, I set my wheels in fast motion, hoping to get home in time to evade the threatening rain.

The first drop splatters against my skin just as I hit Bluff Avenue and round onto Larkin Road, heading into town. After I reach the Watch Hill boat docks and wind toward Foster Cove Road, the rain begins gushing from the clouds, soaking my hair and making my clothes cling to my body. At first I shrink away from deluge, trying in vain to protect myself from the inundating moisture, but eventually I surrender to it, allowing the steady flood to eradicate my earlier pessimistic thoughts. Every droplet saturates my attire, my cheeks, my eyelashes, my sunstreaked ponytail, and my mind. By the time I reach our cottage, I am soaked to the bone, and I am feeling so much better.

Chapter Four

I plunge into my new position at Hill Cove Marina enthusiastically. I am given a uniform to wear: tan shorts and a pale green polo. At first I'm not very excited about this, but I decide that maybe it won't be too bad; at least I won't have to spend a lot of time contemplating what type of outfit to put on each time I show up for work. David Chambers prepares a list of things for me to do on my volunteer days, mostly involving management of the recycling bins and waterfront cleanup. After those things are accomplished, I work on creating signs to post around the marina—reminding the boaters to take proper care of the aquatic environment.

The manager, Ethan Vaughn, comes around to check up on me periodically, and each time I find myself blushing in his presence. I'm not quite sure why this is; he is too old for me. It's not like I want him for a boyfriend, but there is just something about his aura that leaves me feeling shy and unsettled every time he addresses me. I secretly wonder if he realizes this effect he has on younger girls and enjoys toying with them just a little bit.

"So are you making yourself at home here?" I am accosted by the gravelly sound of his voice as I'm emptying a glass recycling bin, and I jump slightly, nearly sending a bottle to its shattering demise on the surrounding cement.

I look up into warm brown eyes and copper highlights that are glistening in the sun. Suddenly I feel self-conscious, hoping he didn't notice how easily I startled when he spoke. He is my manager—what does he want me to say? I don't want to appear too complacent, but on the other hand, I don't want to seem like I'm not fitting in around here either.

"*I* think so. Things are going well." As my cheeks begin to heat up, I chide myself for acting so schoolgirlish.

Ethan's perpetually smiling eyes crinkle up even more as though I amuse him in some way.

"Well, let me know if you have trouble finding something around here."

"Sure," I answer, trying to sound self-assured. "I've been lining up the recycling bins closer to the walkways so they are more noticeable. Is that okay?"

"I think what you've done so far looks great. I like your initiative." *Yes!* His gravelly words of praise make me feel good all over, motivating me to keep up the good work ethic for the remainder of the morning. For some reason, he makes me want to please him.

"Well, it looks like I'm wanted out front." His copper highlights dance in the sun as he turns to face the main docks. I scan the same area and notice a cluster of boats approaching, creating a fresh current of rippling waves that eventually find their way to shore. As he departs to receive the oncoming watercrafts, I become aware of the ease and confidence in his stride as he wanes into the distance. I exhale, shake my head, and face my recycling bins once again.

Later that morning I take a short break and decide to saunter away from the hub of the main docks down to a sandy clearing along the shoreline. The reverberations of the boat motors fade into the background, letting me enjoy the rhythm of the waves gracefully cascading onto the shore. Solitude surrounds me instantly as I am alone with the sea. While I'm walking along the water's edge, I spy something white and shiny sticking out of the taupe granules of wet sand. Reaching down and uncovering it from the grit, I pick it up. Brushing off the grainy substance that coats it, I study the markings. They form a ringlike pattern. *Cool.* Another piece of the aquatic life that I have immersed myself into for the summer. I hold it down toward the flow of the tide and let the water sweep over it, freeing it from the last few granules of sand and seaweed. For the rest of my break, I hold the shell in the open palm of my hand, letting a warm breeze blow it dry. Eventually, I stick it in my pocket to take home.

After lunch I am in the main office, working on updating some signs about how to keep the ocean environment clean, when I hear some commotion at the front door. Looking up from the neon print that is laid out in front of me, I am met with the exuberant smile of Kate, along with Nick, Jonathan, and Emily. I glance around to look for my boss, hoping I'm not attracting too many people for this small space. On the other hand, I am happy they cared to come see me.

"Hey girl, we miss you," Kate's voice sings out as she waves at me. "You are spending far too much time working and not enough time having fun with us."

Jonathan echoes her smile, but Nick and Emily look a little less comfortable in the tiny surroundings, as if they get that their visit may not be appreciated.

"When are you getting off work?" she continues.

Unexpectedly, from around the corner my manager Ethan appears. His eyes scan the group and he nonchalantly strolls over to me. Glancing at my visitors, he offers them a brief smile and then turns to me.

"Hey, Bethany, how is your sign coming?"

Behind him I see Kate's eyebrows lift and her eyes widen in surprise. She is sending me a look like, *Why didn't you mention* HIM?

"Wow," she mouths so only I can see, and suddenly I am horrified that Ethan will discover her silent gestures. I am unable to respond, telling her to quit, so I am stuck hoping she won't be exposed. *Will you please leave?* I beg her telepathically.

"Um . . . so far I think it's going pretty well." I feel my cheeks grow pink as I answer him, but this time it's mostly due to Kate's shenanigans that are going on behind his back.

As if sensing it's the right thing to do, Nick and Emily decide to quietly exit the building, leaving only Kate and Jonathan to accost me. I take this time to address them.

"Hi, Kate and Jonathan. I'll be done here pretty soon. I'll text you later, okay?"

At this, Ethan gives the sign I'm working on one more glance, and offers me an approving smile before he heads out the door toward the boat docks.

"Tough job working here, huh, Bethany?" Kate asks, eyebrows raised, after he leaves.

I roll my eyes. "I'm volunteering here," I remind her. "Plus, whatever! I still have to finish this up for the day, so I'll have to catch up with you guys later, okay?"

"I know, we weren't going to stay very long. We better get going before *plus whatever* has to come back in and kick us out." She gives me a knowing smirk, and Jonathan laughs as if he's in on her little joke.

"What are you working on anyway?" Kate asks, eyeing my printed sign.

"I've been creating signboards to post around the marina to give boaters tips on how to care for the ocean environment."

Jonathan leans over to see what I have printed so far. "Retrieve trash when it blows overboard. Clean up beaches that are accessible by boat only. Plus one boating—bring back everything you take out with you plus one piece of litter."

"This is good, Bethany; you are really going to make a dolphin happy," Kate interjects.

"Really? I'm just doing my part, Kate. You can do your part too, you know."

"Hey, I like what she's doing." Jonathan flashes me a smile, and momentarily, I feel like he's coming to my rescue until he adds, "Maybe someday, when we grow up, we'll be as good as you, Bethany."

Suddenly, I get the impression I'm being picked on, and my face falls. At this Kate reaches out and gives me a big hug.

"You know we love you, girl."

"If we didn't love you so much, we wouldn't be giving you such a hard time." Jonathan's voice echoes Kate's declaration. I roll my eyes.

Right then, Emily pokes her head in the door.

"Hey, have you guys told her about my party tonight yet or what?"

"Oh yeah." Jonathan's eyes widen as if he's just remembering. "Emily is having a bonfire tonight at her cottage. That's why we've assaulted you at your place of employment. We came to give you an invite."

I tell them I'll try my best to make it, and they finally depart from the marina, taking their fun someplace else for the rest of the afternoon.

The sky is starting to cloud up just as I'm getting ready to leave the marina for the day, and I think of Emily's bonfire. I hope it won't get rained out. I am already beginning to look forward to it, eager to get acquainted with other kids in the Watch Hill area. I had driven the LaCrosse into town earlier today and I'm grabbing my handbag, heading toward it, when Ethan approaches. Immediately I think of the earlier ruckus in the shop, and an unsettled feeling starts to form in the pit of my stomach. I really should apologize about my chaotic friends.

"Leaving, huh?" His eyes assess me warmly.

"Yeah." I take a deep breath, getting ready to continue with my spiel, but he interrupts me before I get the chance.

"So, I see your friends have disappeared." He has a speculative grin on his face as he talks, and it's hard to tell what he's thinking.

"Yeah, about that . . ." I try again.

"It seemed like half the teen population of Watch Hill came to visit you here at the marina today. Next time, I just might decide to put them to work." He gives me a little wink, and I groan inwardly. I can't tell if he is kidding or just dressing up a dead serious statement.

"Sorry about that," I finally manage to say. "I'll tell them to stick to the beaches and ice cream shops when they are looking for a place to hang out. Anywhere else, actually, but here."

"Well, hey, if any of them have half the work initiative that you have, I'd be happy to let them spend some time volunteering here this summer too."

How does he do that? He has such a gift of turning a confrontational situation around and making you feel good all over. I give him an appreciative smile. "Thanks."

I jump into the LaCrosse and drive back towards the summer cottage, periodically glancing up at the sky in hopes the clouds will dissipate. Enthusiastically, my mind fills with anticipation as I contemplate the upcoming event of Emily's bonfire.

The evening is cool, and I decide to wear jeans and a blousy, floral top that gathers at the waist. Spending a little extra time on my blond hair, I leave it long, curling it into waves. I take one last look in the mirror and head for the door with a spring in my step. Having fixed myself up a bit, somehow I feel a little less ordinary. Once outside, my eyes scan the sky one more time. So far it's not raining, and I'm determined to have fun tonight. I send a text to Lucy.

Bonfires on the beach . . . sooo much fun! *(send)*

Just as I'm getting ready to exit my driveway, I hear the soft vibration of my phone on the console beside me.

(unlock) I'm sooo jealous!

I smile to myself and wish Lucy was riding in the car beside me, accompanying me to the party.

Emily's family must have a *lot* of money, I decide as I pull up beside her mammoth vacation home. It is decorated in tan and stone siding and seems to go on in every direction for miles. Suddenly, I feel small as I head onto the sprawling front lawn where the party is being held. People are everywhere. Now this really *is* half the teen population of Watch Hill. Or maybe the whole population. I am excited and overwhelmed at the same time. I peruse the area for a familiar face, and no one jumps out at me, so I see an umbrella-covered stand that houses a cooler filled with sodas, and decide this might be a good place to start the evening.

As I head that way, a boy with light brown hair and blue eyes walks slowly past me, deliberately catching my eye. He smiles, revealing dimples. I smile back and hold his gaze for a moment before I continue on. *He's pretty cute.*

Soon after I grab a Coke, Kate spots me and buoyantly comes over to join me. Her brown eyes appraise our surroundings.

"This is great, huh?"

"Definitely. I take it her family is wealthy?"

"I'd say. I know her dad is a bigwig at some company."

"There are so many people here." As I'm glancing in the direction of the ocean which borders Emily's front yard, suddenly my mouth goes dry. Immediately, I lose all train of thought.

Standing at the water's edge talking with a couple of girls is Tristan. He is wearing faded jeans, a tight-fitting polo, and his hair is blowing lightly in the wind. For a moment I am frozen, and I have to remind myself to breathe. *He looks so freakin' good!* Why does he have to look like that?

Momentarily, I exhale just as he looks over in my direction. Purposely, I don't give his green eyes time to connect with mine. I turn away before he can turn away first, as if I don't really notice him, as if I don't really care about him. As if! *Dang!* Why is my heart beating so fast? Why do I feel this sudden ache in my stomach?

Inconspicuously, I glance over to briefly scrutinize the girls he is talking with. *Well, that figures!* They are both dark-haired, glamorous, and curvy, and it looks like they are hanging onto every word he says. Well, why did I ever think he would be interested in me—blond and petite and unpainted? Suddenly, I feel the need to show him that I don't care about him at all. Suddenly, I want to have a *really* good time tonight and prove to myself that he was just a passing phase.

From that moment on, everything I do that night is extra fun. Well, at least I give the appearance that it is. I make it a point to mingle through the crowd meeting lots of people. I laugh extra loud at things that aren't necessarily even that funny, and I attempt to flirt with cute boys—doubting that I'm very good at it, but they don't seem to mind. Most are willing participants who really don't have my full attention, because somewhere in the back of my mind I am always wondering where Tristan is, wondering if he is noticing that I am having a *really* good time without him.

But the truth is—he probably doesn't even care.

Now and then I run into my new summer buddies, and I wonder what they think of my latest effervescent personality, but they never really say. Occasionally, I notice Emily looking at me funny like *what has gotten into you?* Kate, on the other hand, joins in with me, embracing all the fun.

As the night wears on, Nick notices me walking by myself and invites me over to where he is standing, conversing with a cluster of people next to the bonfire. As I set off in his direction, I hesitate for a fleeting moment as I notice Tristan's lean, muscled physique standing among the group. But then, resolutely, I set my jaw and proceed forward, determined not to let him intimidate me. Still, deep down inside I feel very self-conscious as I approach the group.

"Come warm up by the fire," Nick welcomes me.

I begin rubbing my arms, just then realizing how cool it has become throughout the evening. Funny, I hadn't even noticed until now.

"You having fun?" Nick continues.

I don't trust my voice to answer, but when I do, it comes out surprisingly confident. "Yeah, I'm having a good time."

I try hard not to look at Tristan, but when I eventually do, it's just in time to see him turn and walk away from the fire. *Oh my gosh, he can't stand to be in my presence even for a minute!* It's like a knife to the chest. I don't want to care that he practically loathes me, but somehow I still do. I am completely confused. I can't remember doing anything so offensive during one of our very brief encounters that would render such dislike for me. Bemused, I shake my head—maybe he's had a bad dream about me.

Kate joins the fire and begins to warm her hands over the lambent flames. She has donned the dreamy Nick eyes and is tuned in to his every remark. I notice he seems pretty complacent about all the attention, but at least he isn't rude to her.

"Was that Tristan I just saw walking away?" Kate asks.

"Yes, it was," someone else answers. Someone besides me, because I don't want anyone to know that I've noticed him. I don't want anyone to know how hyperaware I was of him standing around the fire, and how hurt I am now that he's gone.

"You know what's weird?" Kate continues. "It seems like I've hardly ever seen him around the area much, and now it seems like I see him all the time."

"You are right," Nick agrees, as if the thought has just occurred to him too. "I've been coming here for lots of summers and have never seen him so much as I have this summer."

Kate glances wistfully in Nick's direction, and I can tell that she is pleased that he has concurred with her line of thinking.

Well, great! He's picked a fine time to start hanging around here more, just in time to make my summer miserable. Mentally I roll my eyes, not wanting the others to see how affected I am by him, or by even just the mention of his name.

As a welcome interruption to my thoughts, loud, souped-up

techno music begins blaring from a far corner of the yard, adding to the partylike atmosphere. My attention is drawn to the new musical commotion, and I note a stone patio sitting midyard has been transformed into a dance floor. Drawn to the music, kids are gathering to mix it up to the steady, beating tempo. Flashing lights circulate, making the venue discolike. *Wow! This is pretty cool. What a little money can't do!*

Suddenly, I want to dance.

As if right on cue, blue-eyed dimples from earlier is walking my way. He is pretty cute, and he has a darling smile.

"Do you want to dance?"

I smile back. "Sure." We head in the direction of the dance floor. By the time we reach it, "Let's Go" by Calvin Harris, featuring Ne-Yo, is filling the air, making it easy to jump into the rhythm. My dance partner leans in close to me.

"I'm Liam, by the way."

"Bethany," I shout back.

I let go of my earlier obsessions and let the pulse of the music take control. Soon I'm carried away into the world of musical gyration, and it feels good and so carefree. It is nice to just enjoy myself and forget about Tristan. Liam smiles at me periodically, revealing his trademark dimples every time. He is a pretty good dancer and appears to be having a good time too. Now and then he leans in toward me and makes snippets of conversation, speaking loudly over the din of the music.

This time as he is talking in my ear, I glance over his shoulder and spot Tristan standing on the perimeter of the dance floor talking with another party-goer. Momentarily he looks my way, and for the first time all night his green eyes connect with mine. *Yep, I am having a good time!* My jaw stiffens, but then I find myself blushing as I turn away from him, continuing to move my body to the grinding beat of the song.

Minutes later, unable to resist, I find myself peering back at him for a second time and am surprised to see him looking in my direction once again. Something in his eyes catches me off guard. It's as if he's examining me in some way, a trace of wistfulness lacing his green eyes. But then the look dissipates into the night as he turns away again. Abruptly, goose bumps begin to form all over my skin. *What was that?* Probably nothing, just my overactive imagination wanting him to want me too. I let it go and keep dancing.

Eventually, I tire of the music, tell Liam thanks, and take a seat by the fire. My body is already warmed from the continual movement on the dance floor, but it is mollifying to watch the flames glimmer and dart and reach toward the sky. The group is more subdued on this area of the lawn, and the conversations come out in hushed tones, contrasting starkly to the pulsating disco club just yards away.

I am quietly conversing with the others that have gathered around the fire, when momentarily my whole body tenses; somehow I can sense Tristan approaching. He nonchalantly takes a seat two down from me, completely unaware that this simple act is leaving me undone. As though nothing has changed, I continue my discussions with those that are on either side of me, but I am hyperaware that he can probably hear everything I am saying. Soon, I find myself clamming up.

When Emily joins the group carrying supplies to make s'mores, the assembly livens up a bit. Everybody likes food, especially chocolate! I am waiting my turn for a roasting stick when I hear a voice that, irritatingly enough, takes my breath away.

"Do you need one of these?"

I look over, and in Tristan's extended hand is a bag of marshmallows.

"Ah . . . sure." I take the bag from him, careful not to make eye contact. As I crouch near the fire to begin the process of roasting,

I feel as though his green eyes are piercing through my back, but I can't be sure that it's not just my imagination. I have to concentrate hard not to burn my marshmallow as I hear Tristan's deep, smooth voice behind me conversing with someone in the gathered crowd.

"That is one heck of a setup they have over there." I assume he is referring to the dance floor.

"I know, right?" a male voice answers. "The only thing that would make it better would be live music. I wonder if anyone around here plays guitar?"

At this, I pause in place, and my eyes become wide. I wonder what Tristan will say to this? I so want to turn and view the expression on his face, but instead I remain facing the fire, realizing that my marshmallow has now burst into flames. *Oh crap!*

"Yeah, live music would be cool." His answer is vague.

"Check out this guy," the male voice continues, changing the subject. "That guy is not right; he creeps me out."

I can no longer help myself; I have to see who he is talking about. As I twist around just a little bit to get a glimpse, a rather gaunt-looking young man with shaggy, brown hair is wandering past. He is dressed in grunge and carries with him an insolent attitude. Instantly I wonder who is really hiding below his seedy exterior, but I hate to jump to conclusions.

"Who is he?" Tristan asks.

"Brian Vega. I'm telling you, if you ever try talking to him, he will not look you in the eye."

"Interesting." Once again Tristan's answer is vague, and I find myself wanting to hear more of his thoughts on the matter.

After I finally get a marshmallow cooked to my liking, I don't return to my seat. Deciding I no longer want to be in Tristan's presence, I finish making my s'more and wander away from the fire. For some reason, just hearing his voice hurts. Just knowing that his beautiful, smooth-sounding voice will never say the things to me that I want to hear, hurts. Instead, I meander away from the party down to the shore. Following a path on the edge of the ocean, I walk through the inching tide until I reach a spot that is secluded. Finding a dry place in the sand, I sit down. Knees folded, arms hugging them, I stare out to sea.

The water is unbelievably calm tonight, not a flutter of movement anywhere. It feels so peaceful. I begin raking my fingers through the fine granules that surround me, and my left hand comes in contact with something small and hard. It's hard to see in the dark, but it appears to be a seashell. I slip it into my jean pocket, deciding to take it home.

As I gaze out into the black, endless sea before me, isolated with my thoughts, I begin to get the feeling that I am not alone. It's an unexplainable sensation. I haven't really heard any unusual noises, but the sentiment passes through me anyway.

I become motionless and listen, but I still don't hear anything strange or out of place. After some time goes by, I relax and decide I have an overactive imagination. Once more I begin to stare at the endless, opaque expanse before me, and suddenly I feel exhausted. All the effort of acting like I was having a marvelous time tonight has left me feeling depleted. Although I did end up having a lot of fun at the party, I don't want to have to overcompensate every time I'm around Tristan. I'll just have to get over that—get over him.

As I allow myself to unwind and contemplate all this, once again the impression that I'm not alone emerges. My eyes begin darting in all directions, but my vision is limited in the dark. I don't detect anything in the nearby proximity, but I can't shake the feeling, so I decide it's time for me to return to the group.

Standing up, I brush the sand from my legs and bottom and begin traipsing back through the unlit beach. As I am walking side by side with the resounding quietness of the sea, a ripple of movement in the water interrupts my thinking. Quickly I glance in the direction of the sound, but by the time my eyes are able to focus on the blackened area, all that greets me is the stillness of the night and the smooth surface of the ocean.

Chapter Five

Josh and Jake are cruising around the cottage great room, darting in and out of my way as I'm trying to get ready to head to the
marina. I want to put in my volunteer hours early today so I can
spend some leisurely time at the beach later. Their little sunkissed
bodies have been transformed into Spiderman and Reptileman,
and the crime scene seems to be everywhere that I am attempting
to be—the kitchen while I'm buttering my bagel, the mudroom
when I am grabbing my freshly laundered work uniform, and the
bathroom where I'm trying to brush my teeth.

My patience is wearing thin.

"Josh! Jake! Will you stop?" They barely miss running into me as
I round the corner by the breakfast nook, throwing me off balance.
I nearly trip and fall to the tiled floor. *Aaagh!*

They both look up at me with startled eyes, as if they are shocked
that I am interrupting their fantasy play, or else stunned that I
would reprimand them at all.

I start to yell at them once more, but bite my lip instead, suddenly
seeing them in a different light—two adjoined souls drifting in a
house filled with chaos. There doesn't need to be one more person
shouting inside these walls.

I take a deep breath. "You guys slow down a little, all right?"

Breaking out of their momentary trance, they both nod, eyes
round. Soon they resume their running, but this time I notice they
are trying a little harder to stay out of my way.

As I stroll along the main boat docks at the marina, I glance up at a vibrant blue sky, taking note of the white, fluffy cotton balls dotting the atmosphere, transforming it into a scene from a Pixar movie. I have just arrived for the day and am completing my daily check of the fuel nozzles, making sure they are hung vertically to prevent spills, when David Chambers advances toward me, accompanied by a now all-too-familiar face.

What? How? Why? Instantaneously my mind is filled with disorder, and I find it difficult to breathe.

David Chambers knows nothing of my distress and proceeds on with an official stance.

"Bethany, I want you to meet Tristan. He is our new employee here. He will be working mostly out on the docks and with the boats." He pauses briefly. "Tristan, this is Bethany."

Disbelief registers across Tristan's perfect features, mirroring my own. He soon recovers from his look of surprise, and immediately a more formal look takes its place. I, however, am not so quick to convalesce. I can't believe my misfortune—every day to have to go to work and be confronted with his beautiful physique, slapping me in the face with unrequited love. It hardly seems fair.

Tristan is the first to speak.

"Hello, Bethany. I believe we've met."

You believe we've met? I've only had to wrestle with myself to stop thinking about you since the first moment I laid eyes on you, and you believe we've met?

"Tristan," I say with a forced smile. Even though his eyes are filled with indifference, they still hold my gaze longer than I like. Immediately a flush begins to spread across my skin.

Wanting more conventionalism from our introduction, David Chambers eyes us expectantly. Detecting this, Tristan hesitantly reaches out to take my hand in an official acknowledgement.

Reluctantly, I put my own in his, and instantaneously it is set ablaze. A tingling, burning sensation sears the skin in my hand that is touching him. It is such an unanticipated, foreign feeling that I almost jump in response.

"We are really enjoying having Bethany around this here this summer." David Chambers interrupts my reaction, giving me a chance to gracefully recover.

"It will be nice working with you, Bethany." Tristan's voice is polite, and I glance at him inconspicuously, searching for any meaning in his words, but his green eyes give nothing away.

Finally, David leads Tristan away to give him a tour of the facility, and I am left with the rest of my daily activities. Irritation consumes me. I can hardly concentrate on the recycling or any other *Good Mate* procedures that I am supposed to be initiating. I continually vacillate between the idea of handing in my resignation at the end of the day in hopes of finding volunteer work elsewhere or sticking it out at Hill Cove Marina in an effort to prove to myself that I just don't care.

Periodically, as I am alone with my thoughts, I am conscious of the tingling sensation that still lingers on my hand and wonder why this is. Immediately, I chide myself. I find myself reacting to Tristan in ways that I never knew existed, and it isn't helping my resolve to move on and forget about him.

Sighing in frustration, I tuck a loose strand of hair back into my ponytail. I won't make a rash decision about whether or not to quit. I'll spend some time mulling it over at the beach and decide what to do later. Happily I vacate the marina and head toward East Beach, where I plan to spend the rest of the day.

It's only after an unhurried afternoon at the beach that I make my decision—I'm going to stay. Anything else would only be cowardly. *And really, over a boy?* So I wake up early the next morning, put on my strong armor of resolve, and text Lucy as a way of confirmation.

Getting ready to go volunteer at the marina this morning.

Going to save a fish! *(send)*

I am getting out of the LaCrosse at the marina parking lot when I feel the vibration of my phone in the back pocket of my work uniform.

(unlock) Proud of you—you little environmentalist.

I envision Lucy's wavy, blond hair and her vibrant, brown eyes as I read her text, and suddenly I experience a wave of wistfulness. I *so* wish she was here in town with me right now. We could go have a soda after work and discuss what an awful day I'd had at the marina, and somehow she'd find a way to turn the situation into something funny, and somehow it would all seem better.

But for the first time in my life, my best friend Lucy isn't at my side—I am all alone, and I will have to figure it out myself.

Glancing around the parking lot and then the boat docks, I make my way into the main office building, seeing no sign of anyone that might start my heart racing. The coast is clear. Maybe this won't be as hard as I originally thought.

As I work making signs for proper disposal of plastic, glass, metal, and paper products, my steadfastness builds. The only people that cross my line of vision during the day are the now familiar patrons of the marina that pop their heads in occasionally, and my manager, Ethan Vaughn.

Ethan's gravelly voice is still captivating, but somehow his copper highlights and enchanting smile don't hold quite as much power, in lieu of the green eyes and tousled, blond hair that I know now lurks somewhere on the premises.

I am just beginning to think that I will be fortunate enough to get off scot-free for the day when David Chambers enters the main office and calls my name.

"How do you feel about washing some boats for me?" He eyes me tentatively, and then elaborates some more. "We have several of the boat owners coming in to town this weekend, and I have a big push to get them out of storage and washed and ready for them to take out on the lake. If you are okay with it, I could really use your help."

Ready for a change of scenery and deciding it would be difficult to say no to the owner, I politely accept and follow him to the back storage units. As we round the corner to the large, steel buildings, I note several boats lined up ready for action.

"I brought you some help," David Chambers calls out. Before I have time to contemplate who he is talking to, Tristan emerges from behind a Four Winds watercraft that sports a navy blue and white hull.

My pulse increases in tempo.

His eyes capture the pale green coloring from his work polo, increasing their intensity—as if he needed that little extra something to enhance his already perfect features. As Tristan's gaze takes me in, his jaw tightens slightly, and a look of annoyance flashes across his eyes. Immediately wounded, my heart plummets, and it takes all my willpower not to look away. Swallowing down the hurt, I quickly become irritated instead. Pressing my lips together, I offer him a fake smile. *I'm so happy to help you!*

Soon David Chambers leaves us, and I am alone with Tristan. Abruptly the air becomes thick and uncomfortable.

"Ah, do you want to grab that green, long-handled sponge? I already have the buckets with cleaner in them on the other side of the boat." His voice comes out deep and smooth, and even though I don't want to be, I am immediately affected.

"Sure." I grab the sponge that he is referring to, all the while trying to avoid eye contact.

"I haven't gotten to that side; you want to start over there?" It's more of a command than a question, but it doesn't come across *too* bossy, and I find some relief in knowing that I will be working alone and not side by side with his lean, muscular frame, which would have completely unnerved me.

I feel like I'm making some progress soaping and cleansing the massive blue and white hull before me when I feel a presence standing disconcertingly close. Glancing over my shoulder, I observe Tristan analytically eyeing my work. Rubbing one of his strong hands along the recently bathed side of the craft, he looks up at me. I steel myself, waiting for him to say something I'm not going to like.

"Nice job. You must be stronger than you look. You are *really* getting this clean."

What is he insinuating? Watching his face in disbelief, I detect a mischievous sparkle in his eyes, and I am caught off guard. Is he being playful with me?

I narrow my eyes in jest. "Apparently I *am* stronger than I look."

He allows a slight smile to escape his lips. "I'm going to help you on the front, so we can finish this one up."

"All right." I shrug my shoulders indifferently, not wanting him to see how unsettling the idea of him working side by side with me is.

As we labor in silence, now and then I take a fleeting look in his direction, thankful he doesn't catch me. Regretfully, I find myself blushing each time I take note of the strong muscles in his arms as they move fluently across the boat, and the way his pale green polo pulls against his chest with the slightest shift in position.

Eventually, my arms and legs ache from the repetitive cleaning motions, and I decide to go down to the shoreline for a stretch. The water extends on endlessly in front of me, reaching for the horizon, and the wake from the boats passing by creates miniature waves that sneak up and lick my bare feet. Wading calf-deep into the water, I notice several black, dotlike creatures swimming around me. I eye them for a second or two before bending down to get a closer look. *Cool.*

"They are periwinkle snails."

I practically jump at the sound of Tristan's voice. I am so engaged in my aquatic surroundings that I didn't hear him approach.

"Well, there sure are lots of them," I finally respond.

"Yeah. It's another thing we have lots of around here." He walks over so that he is standing within a foot of me, and the tingling that I felt earlier in my right hand begins to resurface. This time it starts to spread throughout the rest of my body, as though he carries with him some sort of invisible force field that has ignited from the point of our first physical contact.

"Hey, come see this." He wades right past me deeper into the encircling ocean and points in front of him. I notice that his tan shorts are now partially immersed in the water, but he doesn't seem to mind. If I go out into the lake to meet him, mine will become even more soaked than his. I feel like I'm in a predicament, but somehow I still can't resist.

Hesitating, I roll up the legs of my shorts and head out to join him. He watches me for a moment as I stride through the water, but then, as soon as our eyes meet, looks away. I shake my head, wishing such a simple act would not leave me so unnerved.

Finally I reach him. From my viewpoint, all I see is something large and black.

"What is it?"

"A school of fish," he answers, and for a moment I think he is going to go even farther out into the water. Soon we will both be swimming in our work uniforms. But then he takes a step back again, and I am instantly relieved.

"You must have really good eyes. I would have never guessed that. From where I'm standing, it just looks like one giant *something*."

"I don't know about good eyes, just experience, I guess." His voice is nonchalant.

"I can't even tell they are moving." Leaning forward slightly, I strain my eyes for a better view.

"The way they all move their tails, it makes a whirlpool-like motion, and each fish can use the swirling action from its neighbor to reduce its own water friction. Swimming is a lot easier for them this way. Eighty percent of known fish species do this at some point in their life."

It dawns on me right then that this is what Tristan seems most comfortable conversing about. For once his answers aren't vague, and he doesn't mind sharing his apparent vast amount of knowledge in this area.

"Do you happen to be majoring in marine biology?" I blurt out before I can think.

At this Tristan goes motionless. "Maybe, we'll see." He pauses for a second. "Well, I'm going to head back."

I hug my arms around my chest, continuing to stare at the big, black blob before me. Disappointment floods through me as I hear him retreat through the water—I wasn't ready for our conversation to end.

For the rest of the afternoon, I see very little of Tristan. I try to tell myself that he is not purposely avoiding me, but I can't be sure. He gives some brief instructions about the next two boats that need cleaning, and then advises me that he'll be inside working on other boats if I need him.

The rest of the day I go on working in seclusion and eventually head back to the blue summer cottage.

The next day at the marina I find myself looking for Tristan instead of trying to avoid him. But after several hours of scoping out every direction, I come to the conclusion that he isn't going to be at work that day. Surprisingly enough, I discover that I am disenchanted to find that I won't be seeing him at all that morning—when only two days before, I was infuriated that he had invaded my workspace.

Finally my list of volunteer tasks are completed, and it's time for me to leave. I walked into town earlier this morning with the idea that I would run home after work, but now that I am done for the day, I opt for an unhurried stroll beside the ocean instead. There is a steady northeastern wind blowing through the salty air, and the waves are rapidly cascading onto the shoreline in response. The sand I amble through is pasty, made this way by the continual push of the surf. As I walk, I find myself not only appreciating the tumultuous expanse before me, but also periodically scanning my path for new, unexpected treasures.

Soon, I'm not disappointed as I spot a quarter-sized tan and white ridged object wedged between two coastal rocks. Kneeling down, I pick up my newest shell, brush off the grit from its exterior, and stick it into my pocket.

Just as I am returning to a vertical position, my vision is drawn to an interruption in the pattern of the undulating waves before me.

This time I am *sure* I see something moving.

This time I know it is not my imagination, and so I patiently wait for whatever it was to resurface.

Suddenly, there it is again! *I knew it!* But it is so quick, and before I get a chance to focus, once again it dives below the breakers and disappears.

But I'm not going anywhere. I gather all my staying power and wait, eyes glued to the sea.

When the figure resurfaces a third time, I am able to adjust my vision more clearly. Momentarily stunned, I realize that what I'm seeing is a human—some incredibly brave person who has decided to challenge the surging waves for an afternoon swim. Quickly an unpleasant thought flashes through my mind, and I wonder if that someone could be in distress, submerged in the tumult around him, hence the repeated disappearing and reemerging. I panic at the thought of trying to save anyone—I can barely swim myself. Involuntarily, I reach for my smartphone that is tucked away in my back pocket. I may have to call for help.

Frozen in place, keeping a shaky hand on the rear compartment of my tan shorts, and a steady eye glued to the sea, I watch in relief as the figure appears to be swimming steadily towards the shore, in spite of the pandemonium around him.

As I watch a minute longer, wanting to make 100 percent sure the person will be able to reach safety, my heart starts pounding in my chest, and I am conscious of a weakening sensation that is overtaking the limbs of my body. Recognition sets in. I shake my head, trying to clear my vision, but the sight doesn't go away.

It's him! Tristan is coming toward me, swimming in the direction of the shore. My mind rushes with a thousand thoughts. What are the chances? How can this be? I want to leave, immediately wondering if he has spied me too, but my body doesn't respond to the command, so I stayed glued to the spot I'm in.

I feel embarrassed to have been viewing him without his knowledge, but somehow I can't seem to tear my eyes away. As much as I grasp the understanding that he really shows no interest in me and that I need to release him from my consuming thoughts, my senses stay peeled to his every movement. His gracefulness and beauty as he dives in and out of the resounding surf is breathtaking. Watching for a while longer, I reluctantly turn to journey the rest of the way home.

Trying to get as far away as I can from the shore so as not to be spotted, I round a section of dune filled with grass and head toward the road. Unwittingly, I allow myself one more glance over my shoulder in Tristan's direction, and stop dead in my tracks. My heart rate accelerates, and I become a little breathless as I watch his form emerge from the water. He looks like a Greek god from the sea. As he shakes the water from his blond hair, tiny droplets of moisture glisten over his bare, chiseled chest. I notice that there is no towel in the nearby vicinity with which to dry his skin, so he stands on the edge of the shore, letting the air waft over his body instead. The shorts that he is wearing cling to his legs, revealing strong, muscular thighs.

I turn my head away in embarrassment, having invaded his private moment. Abruptly, I fear being discovered. Easing myself further behind the dune, I hope that I am well-hidden from Tristan's view as I continue heading home, trying hard not to draw attention to myself.

Completely shaken, I resume advancing down the road. I am almost a mile away from where I first discovered him before I realize that I am still tiptoeing and holding my breath.

Chapter Six

The next day I dread going to volunteer at the marina. I can't rid myself of the feeling that Tristan may have seen me watching him on the secluded beachfront. After much procrastination, I finally arrive at the now familiar boat-servicing station. Slinking around, I perform my duties unobtrusively, trying to make myself as obscure as possible. Hiding myself rather well, I am sitting behind the counter at the main office building composing recycling signs when I hear the musical jingle of the front door opening.

Out of habit I look up, then inhale sharply. *Oh crap!* Tristan rarely enters the main office, and so I felt relatively safe in the cocoon I created for myself.

Green eyes pierce into mine.

Oh, definitely busted! I cringe inwardly.

But then his perfect features break into a relaxed smile, and I am tentatively relieved. Maybe he *doesn't* know. I search his face for an expression, a clue, anything that might give his thoughts away, but nothing is revealed. Instead, he holds out a finger that is wrapped in tissue.

"Do you know if they keep any Band-Aids around?"

"I believe they have some in back." Getting up, I circle around the counter and head toward the rear of the shop. His eyes follow me as I walk, and it makes me feel so self-conscious. Silently, I hope that I don't trip while I'm en route.

"So what happened?" I think to ask when I return. By then, I notice his temporarily concocted dressing is filling with blood, and

I feel a wave of dizziness pass through me. I haven't been exposed to bleeding very many times, and I instantly hope I'm not the fainting type.

"Hey . . . you okay?" Concern is written all over his face.

Quickly I get a grip on myself, shaking away the light-headed-ness. "I should be asking you that question." I hand him the package of Band-Aids.

He eyes me a second longer, apparently satisfied that I'm not going to collapse on the floor in front of him. Finally he answers my earlier question. "I cut myself while I was trying to release a gas cap." He mutters something inaudible under his breath.

I work hard to suppress a smile. *My, my,* perfect Tristan is human after all.

Walking into the restroom to rinse his finger, he returns fiddling with a Band-Aid wrapper.

"Uh . . . would you . . . do you mind putting this on for me? I can't seem to get at that angle."

"Oh . . . sure." I flush at the thought of nursing his wound—the act of it seems intimate, somehow.

He interprets this as hesitancy. "Don't worry, I'll make sure it's clean before you get near it. I'll make sure none of my blood gets on you."

"Okay . . . yeah." I watch as he spreads his strong hand out before me, cringing as I eye the gash in his finger. Gingerly I apply the bandage, trying to disguise the shakiness in my own hands as I work.

The instant the skin on my hands makes contact with his, the tingling sensation returns. Momentarily, I inhale and finish what I'm doing. When the application is complete, I glance up at him to let him know that I'm done, and find him watching me. When our eyes meet, his jaw clenches and he turns away. Butterflies begin fluttering in my stomach, and I back awkwardly away.

I sigh, wishing I knew what he is thinking. So much of the time it feels like he practically loathes me, and yet there are moments, split seconds, when I detect something else coming from him, but I'm not sure what it is. It all seems so perplexing.

"Well, thanks." His earlier manifestation of openness is now replaced with a type of reserve. Then he heads toward the door, and just as I think he is going to leave, he pauses and looks at me instead.

"So you are just here visiting for the summer? I'm surprised you wanted to get a job, when you're only staying here for a while."

"Well, technically I'm not actually working. I'm volunteering. I wanted to help out the marine environment a little bit by instigating some of the *Good Mate* interventions that will help protect ocean life in this area."

As I'm earnestly explaining this, he begins to look flabbergasted, shaking his head, literally laughing out loud. *What? What did I say?*

"Well, that figures," he mutters under his breath, running his fingers through his already tousled hair.

Great! Another person who thinks I'm just being a goody-two-shoes by volunteering to help our environment. Well, I'm sick of having to defend my intentions. Quickly I feel my face heat up in anger, and I press my lips tightly together.

"I sure hope your *finger* feels better soon," I say dismissively.

Appearing a little taken aback by my curt retort, he eyes me speculatively. "Okay . . . thanks," he murmurs before heading through the door, back out toward the front docks.

I roll my eyes, not once glancing in his direction. Geez, he pisses me off!

The first thing I notice when I wake up the next morning is the absence of the sun peeking through the windows of my cottage bedroom. It's a rare, gloomy day. As I steal into the kitchen for a drink of water, I have to stop short, just missing a collision with Mom. She's not watching where she is going. Startled, she glances up at me, and I am taken back by what I see. Her ordinarily crystal blue eyes are red and swollen. *Oh no!* Right away I contemplate the implications of this.

What has happened between them now?

Of course I can't be sure an altercation involving Dad caused this, but I strongly suspect this is the case. In answer to my pondering, momentarily Dad comes padding out of the guest room looking like he's been hit by a Mack truck. He squints his eyes to avoid the subdued daylight that pours into the great room windows, and his hair looks like it's been in a midnight tousle with an alley cat.

Well, whatever transpired, it must have been a silent fight, because I don't recall hearing any major outbursts the night before. Swiftly, I glance around the kitchen, the breakfast nook, the great room. Nothing seems out of place—no broken dishes, no knocked over lamps, no pictures turned cockeyed.

I rack my brain and try to recollect last evening. I vaguely remember that they were leaving to go to a get-together at some acquaintances of theirs from back in Philadelphia. Someone who just happened to be visiting Watch Hill for the time being was having a party last night—what were their names? The Sheldons.

I don't remember any unusual commotion during the night, but at times it seems I can't remember or focus on anything anymore. Sometimes, I feel like I'm viewing the world through a thin veil, and the only thing that presents itself vividly to me are the echoes of the most recent conversations I've had with Tristan. Anymore, it seems as though I have ADHD, something I contracted from a certain blond-haired, green-eyed boy who is now driving me crazy—both mentally and physically.

Physically, he is giving me sensations I never even knew existed before. At times I practically ache from wanting him to be mine.

Mentally, I can't keep up with the emotional rollercoaster I've boarded from the first moment I saw him. When he smiles at me,

I'm high. When he ignores me, I'm devastated. When I can't interpret his actions or the transient look in his eyes, I am completely bemused.

I am sitting at the breakfast nook quietly eating Cheerios with Josh and Jake. Glancing up from behind the cereal box, I become aware of Mom lounging across the room. Perched on an overstuffed couch, she is staring through a giant window that overlooks the ocean. Her silky bathrobe is pulled tightly across her body. Knees hugged to her chest, she is desperately clinging to a fluffy, pink blanket that lies across her lap. She doesn't glance to her right or to her left; she doesn't move a muscle—she just stares straight ahead.

The picture that this presents is almost eerie. I blink my eyes wishing for the scene to go away, but it doesn't. Presently a chill sneaks up my spine, and I consider going to my room in search of a sweatshirt. Instead I keep eating, trying to concentrate on the little oats that are swimming in a sea of milk inside the bowl.

I am almost finished when Dad approaches the table, clean-shaven, hair combed into place. The smell of cologne permeates the air. His freshened-up appearance almost disguises the haggardness that is hovering just below the surface of his skin.

He eyes all three of us tentatively, and it becomes obvious that he is about to make an announcement.

My heart thuds in my chest.

Presently, I wonder about the nature of his proclamation. My body tenses, and I prepare for the worst.

He clears his throat.

"It appears like I need to go back to Philadelphia to do some work for a while." *Whew! At least it's only that!*

Mom continues staring out the window as he speaks. I imagine that I see her shoulders shaking, but the motion is so slight, it's difficult to tell for sure.

"I'm going to try to make it brief. I'll return as soon as I can." It seems as though he is nervous as he talks—very unlike my dad.

I nod silently.

The twins don't acknowledge his statement, but start punching each other at the table instead.

"Boys," is his only response to their actions. Then he attempts some half hugs, and I hear the door slam on his way out.

Josh and Jake get up from the table eventually, cereal half-eaten. I finish my own in silence—the normally enjoyable flavor becoming virtually tasteless.

Two steps forward. Three steps back.

I decide to text Lucy.

You might see my dad in town. *(send)*

I lie on my bed listening to my iPod, and eventually I feel a familiar buzz in my hand.

(unlock) **I'm sorry, Bethany. I'll keep praying.**

I try to shrug off the situation at home, but my steps are still a tiny bit slower the next day at the marina. I'm behind the counter talking to some patrons about proper procedure for collecting oil for recycling when Tristan saunters in through the front door. This is the second time this week, and it catches me off guard. As I continue talking with the clientele, he wanders around the office like he is looking for something. I get the feeling there is something he is searching for and probably wants to ask me about it, but is waiting patiently while I finish.

Geez, it's so hard to concentrate with him in the room. I get a glimpse of him from across the room while I'm conversing, observing his flawless profile and his chiseled jaw. Does he even realize the impact he makes? I purposely take my eyes off him so I can effectively continue what I am saying.

Before long, the customers leave and Tristan approaches. He is looking for a special type of wrench. Ethan told him it would be in the office. I know what he is talking about, so I wander to the back room to retrieve it. When I return, I find his piercing, green eyes searching my face.

"You okay?"

Huh? "Yeah, I'm fine." I force my voice to sound cheery. Apparently my countenance is revealing more about last night than I wanted it to.

He studies me for a second longer. "Well, thanks for this." Abruptly, he changes mode and walks out the front door.

After I contemplate his look of concern, I feel warm all over. There was something about his stance that seemed so inviting, making me want to share about the things that have been happening at home. Thank God, I had a safety valve on my mouth, or I could have easily disclosed too much information—scaring him away for good. No guy wants a girl around who blabbers on about the baggage at home.

The recycling bins by the main docks are stuffed full, and I am fastidiously emptying them when I am startled by a chipper-sounding voice.

"Heeeey, Bethany. How's it going, girl?"

I turn around to see Kate's effervescent, brown eyes and her snug ponytail. Right away I hope she hasn't brought the whole summer crew again. My eyes scan the docks briefly, but she appears to have come alone this time.

"Just emptying my bins. What's up?"

"I was close by and I haven't seen you in a while. I wanted to come see you for a quick minute."

Somehow she too detects a note of sadness in my demeanor, and I end up telling her about my dad leaving for Philadelphia yesterday—and how that even though nothing was implicitly said, it resonates trouble. She gives me a hug and then effectively spins the conversation in a new direction. In a short time, our lighthearted laughter echoes off the waves that are pushing onto shore.

Later, I decide to spend my lunch break sitting on the end of a seldom-used dock that sits isolated from the hub of the steady flow of traffic. Hanging my feet in the water, I let the wake from the passing boats curl around my toes, welcoming the soothing feel of it on my skin. The sun is pleasantly warm as it shimmers on my hair and eyelashes.

I am mindlessly watching the boats that are berthed around me sway gently in a steady rhythm, when I hear the sound of footsteps slowly approaching behind me.

I freeze in place, wondering, nervously hoping.

The sturdy resonance of the sound ends. For a brief moment there is silence.

"I'm sorry about your dad leaving." My heart lurches in my chest. *How does he know?* Kate. He must have heard me talking to Kate. Finally I turn around.

I am met with a tender look that emanates from the depths of green eyes. *Oh no!* I don't want to come unglued.

"Thanks." I shrug my shoulders and sigh, resigning myself to the situation.

Unexpectedly, Tristan walks closer and sits down beside me on the end of the dock—only inches away. My heart starts to pound. I hope he cannot hear it due to our close proximity. His strong thigh is only centimeters away from my own, and suddenly I feel fidgety, nervous. I look away, staring out at the ocean, trying to focus on something different.

"Things aren't really the best at my house right now, but I'm still hopeful." I try to sound nonchalant and lighthearted, not wanting to burden him with the troubles of the Kuiper household.

"It's good to stay positive. Maybe your optimism will spread throughout your family."

I laugh then. "That would be good."

"So does your family take a summer vacation like this every year?"

"Very rarely. This is the first vacation like this that I can ever remember. My dad is usually pretty tied up at work, and of course there have always been summer camps and stuff. We've always stayed pretty busy."

Tristan splashes the water lightly with his legs, and I watch the rhythmic motion as we talk.

"Maybe when you were younger then?"

"No." I chuckle self-consciously as I realize how pathetic it sounds. "I don't think so, not even then. We probably should have, though. It might have been good for us."

At this, I feel his eyes studying me, and my heart rate accelerates. I want to look back at him, to read his expression, but I feel so shy. By the time I finally muster up the courage, he is looking back at the sea, and I have missed my chance.

"Well, I know you don't have much to compare it to, but how do you like Watch Hill as a vacation place so far?"

Where do I start? Watch Hill is okay. But with you sitting next to me right now, I absolutely *love* it.

"I like it here." My voice sounds surprisingly casual. "I really *love* all the ocean around here."

He laughs and I glance over at him, trying to read into his reaction. "I can tell . . . miss volunteer to save the ocean environment." *Oh no, not this again!*

I feel myself stiffen, and I squint my eyes defensively. "Why is that so bad?"

His laughter subsides, and a more serious expression overtakes his countenance. "That *isn't* a bad thing. I think it is a great thing that you care so much about the marine environment that you would volunteer to help protect it, Bethany."

I want to ask him why he was laughing then, but the instant he says my name, I lose my train of thought. The sound of it is so nice coming from his lips—it's hard to concentrate on anything else.

"Well, I better get back to work." He jumps up with astonishing ease and exits the dock the way he came. The minute he leaves, his absence leaves a gaping hole beside me, and I find myself wishing he could have stayed just a little longer. I glance at my white, braided wristwatch and sigh. Really, I need to get back too.

The rest of the day passes too quickly, and I find am not ready to leave Hill Cove Marina when the time comes. Just knowing Tristan is still somewhere in the vicinity makes me want to stay there too—just in case. Just in case I get to see him again, or talk with him again, or feel the warmth of his body radiating off his skin while he's sitting only inches away.

Reluctantly I leave.

But I'm not ready to go home, so I decide to wander around town instead. Leaving my car parked by the marina, I begin strolling down Bay Street. While I am walking, I am greeted by a row of quaint shops that are tucked along the waterfront, adding to the charm of the district. Not sure what I'm looking for exactly, I mosey along, eyeing the stores through the exterior of the windowpanes. Finally, something inside one of them draws my attention. I glance up and notice that the wooden sign above the door reads "Halls" .

Entering through the front, I go in search of what had caught my eye on the outside of the shop. A seashell collecting kit—I've officially decided to start a collection. The kit consists of a pail, mesh bag, cleaning solution, and brush. It occurs to me that I might find all the included items separately without too much trouble, but somehow having a kit seems like a lot more fun. Tucked beside it on the shelf, I note some booklets on seashell collecting, and I start thumbing through.

Scanning through the material, I find all sorts of snippets of pertinent information: A good place to find fresh, dead shells is between two big rocks on the coast, or in big rock holes where the tide will not allow the shell to roll. A *gem* shell is flawless, having no defects. A *fine* shell may have only minor defects, such as a scratch. A *good* shell is still intact, but has major defects.

It feels like I have a lot to learn. A little overwhelmed, I spy a pamphlet on Rhode Island shells and start leafing through. The booklet is colorful and filled with pictures. Perfect—just what I need. Right away I recognize some of the shells that I have uncovered so far—slipper shells and quahogs. I note that the Neptune is the state shell, but also hard to find. Well, I enjoy a good challenge.

Grabbing both pieces of literature and the collector's kit, I head for the checkout. A part of me wishes that I wouldn't have driven the car into town today, as I suddenly feel inspired to take an oceanside walk on the way home. Maybe later, after dinner, I'll go for a little jaunt near the shoreline and see what I can find.

After I hand the clerk the money, I slip my handbag over my shoulder and exit the shop. On my way out the door, I stop short as I hear voices engaged in a playful conversation. Clearly a guy and a girl immersed in a type of flirtatious banter. Instantly my radar goes up as I recognize the deep, smooth reverberation of the male voice. Scanning the outdoor area in search of the sound, I observe the owner of the voice along with a glamorous redhead, standing next to the waterfront park.

They aren't close enough for me to hear what they are saying, so I only get bits and pieces of the conversation.

Uncomfortably, I watch as the auburn-haired girl throws her head back in laughter at whatever clever thing Tristan has just said. Her body language is very enticing, and from where I'm standing, it appears as though he is having a good time teasing her. The girl's eyes glisten and dance as she stares up at him, seemingly hanging onto every word he is saying.

Tristan makes another comment to her, but I can only make out the words *smile* and *terrific*. At this, she flips her perfectly waved hair over her shoulder and presses her full lips into a coy pout. Presently, Tristan moves a little to the left, and more of his face is revealed. Now I am able to clearly observe the amused, interested look that is reflected in his eyes.

My heart plunges. Has he ever looked at me that way? The unmistakable answer to that leaves me feeling very disheartened. Quickly, unobtrusively, I look away from the happy couple and walk across Bay Street to the lot where my car has been parked for the day—all the while my heart continues sinking like a ship in my chest.

Chapter Seven

Now my summer roller coaster has just descended another time. Once again I am reminded of how silly it is for me to get my hopes up where Tristan is concerned. The following morning as I'm slipping my green work polo over my head getting ready to go to the marina, the image of the alluring redhead comes flashing back into my mind. She is definitely Tristan's type—glitz and glam—all runway modelish. How perfect they would be together. I imagine the headlines: Hollister model meets cover girl, and they walk happily off the red carpet—into the sunset. Suddenly, I feel nauseated. The thought of morning breakfast seems almost repulsive, but I suffer through a berry-filled dish of yogurt anyway.

I leave on foot for the marina that day allowing myself plenty of time for travel; not because I'm eager to get there, but because I'm quite sure I'll be in need of a good run on the return trip. After I arrive, once again I find myself skulking around the facility trying my best to avoid an encounter with Tristan. Every building I enter, every dock I chance upon, every task I perform, I am jumpy and on edge. *Geez, this is getting old.*

Presently, I am so busy scanning my peripheral surroundings, strategically planning the safest route from the main office to an outlying storage structure, that I nearly miss a head-on collision with the owner, David Chambers.

"Whoa . . . slow down, roadrunner. You look like you are running from the law . . . or trying to escape from a villain—one or the other."

I blush in embarrassment, realizing how unprofessional I must look.

"Sorry about that." I try to think of an explanation, but nothing reasonable comes to mind. Maybe I should just tell him the truth—he's actually right about the villain part. I *am* trying to flee from a criminal—a thief who is trying to steal my heart. Who am I kidding—*has* stolen my heart. Now I am going to have to work diligently to retrieve it.

"So which is it, a villain or the law?" David Chamber leaves my company, and I glance to my right, startled. The green eyes I am trying so desperately to avoid are crinkled at the edges, playfully mocking me.

Tristan's beautiful lips are formed into a smirk as he stands only feet away from me, next to the entrance of the storage unit I am about to enter. His arm is resting confidently on the doorframe, and he is watching me, obviously entertained. *Oh crap!* Evidently, my course wasn't *that* efficiently calculated.

"Pretty sure a villain," I mutter under my breath.

"What?"

"Nothing." This time my voice projects a little more clearly. He continues to block the doorway. "Uh . . . would you mind . . . ?" I motion to the entrance.

"Oh . . . sure." He acts surprised as though he has just realized that he is in my way—but somehow I get the feeling that he knows he's delaying my access and is just toying with me.

Finally he moves and I am left shaken—and annoyed with myself for letting him get to me that way.

After I put in my volunteer hours for the day, I experience a sense of relief. I made it through the rest of my schedule without any more confrontations. Grabbing my backpack, I head toward the employee restroom to change into my running clothes, feeling a little less jittery.

"Hey . . . Bethany," Tristan's velvety voice calls out just as I'm about to step onto the wooden deck that leads to the building where the bathrooms are housed. I freeze in place, and a shiver shoots quickly up my bare arms. When I turn around, I notice the teasing grin from earlier is gone, replaced by a hesitant demeanor. Strangely enough, he appears anxious. *What is this?*

"Are you headed home?"

"I was about to."

"I didn't see your car; did you walk?" Why does he look so much like a nervous schoolboy right now?—and so beautiful at the same time—*omg, I just want to grab him and . . .*

"Yeah, I walked."

"I was about to leave too. I could walk with you, if you want." *If I want?*

"Um . . . sure."

As we fall into step, the more familiar, confident Tristan re-emerges, and I am left to speculate what the shy act was all about. The town of Watch Hill fades behind us as we walk, and soon we are alone with the ocean; the waves cascade onto shore, serenading us as we stroll along. I glance over at their encouraging rhythm, and suddenly I'm glad they are there—like a supportive friend. I feel so reticent being alone with Tristan like this.

The farther we get away from town, the closer Tristan seems to walk next to me—so near that periodically our arms brush. Each time I find myself catching my breath from the physical contact. *Why do I react this way to him?* Every time I experience something new with him—something as simple as being alone with him on a walk—I feel like my eyes are being opened to a whole new world. To something I never knew existed.

"So what do you bring in your backpack when you come to work?"

"Usually my lunch, and sometimes my running clothes." *Like today.*

"Are you a runner?" I feel his eyes regard me as we walk along, but he's so close, I can't bring myself to look back at him.

"Yeah, I like to run."

"But not today?"

"No, not today." I try to suppress a smile, wondering if I've been caught blowing off my run—trading it in easily for his company instead.

From the corner of my eye, I see him start to smile too. *Definitely caught!*

"And you're a swimmer," I say before I can stop myself, suddenly remembering that I wasn't supposed to know this yet. *Oh crap!*

Silence.

Finally, I look over at him. His blond, tousled hair and chiseled profile are only inches from me. I notice his jaw set ever so slightly. From out of nowhere I have a sudden urge to reach out and trace his perfectly shaped cheekbone with my finger. I fold my hands together tightly instead.

"I do swim." He keeps looking straight ahead.

"I mean . . . I assume everyone around here swims with all the water and all." I feel like I'm stumbling over my words.

"You are probably right." Bending down, he picks up a rock and tosses it toward the endless expanse of ocean that is the backdrop for our walk. Skip . . . skip . . . skip . . . skip. It bounces effortlessly along the surface of the rippling waves. "So do you swim too?"

At this I let out a small chuckle. "Not very well. Let's just say I'm a *lot* better runner."

He bends down and picks up another rock. Skip . . . skip . . . skip. "Well, you really should learn . . . I mean with all the water around and all."

From out of nowhere I feel an unexplainable sense of déjà vu.

"I probably should." By now we're almost to my summer cottage, and suddenly I wish I lived farther away. *Many, many miles away.* I'm not ready for our walk to end. "Well, we're almost to my place."

I hesitate before giving into curiosity. "Do you live close by?"

"A little further south, around that big bend in the shoreline."

I strain my head around to see, but nothing in particular grabs my attention. But at least now I know the general direction—at least that's something.

Undoubtedly, I decide to *walk* to the marina the next day. After I said good bye to Tristan the day before, one thought began to consume my mind—will he ask me to walk home with him again? I get butterflies in my stomach with the anticipation. Now it is lunchtime, and I'm feeling so jittery that at first it's hard to imagine eating. But I packed some of my favorite leftovers from the previous evening's dinner, and just knowing that they are in the employee fridge has my mouth watering.

With Dad gone back to Philadelphia, dinners are quieter than they had been around the Kuiper house. But we are all used to that. Before coming to Watch Hill, Dad was hardly around for family mealtimes anyway. Mom still seems sad with Dad gone, but at least she is rallying on some level. The first few days after he left, we pretty much fended for ourselves eating sandwiches, macaroni and cheese, and sometimes cereal. But eventually, some of the familiar dishes started reappearing on the table—last night I was delighted to see one of my favorites, grilled marlin and shrimp cocktail.

Now I sit at a picnic table at the marina that is housed in shade, only feet from the winding shoreline. A warm breeze is blowing in from the waterway, making it a perfect temperature for an outdoor lunch. I am dipping a tiny piece of shrimp into a plastic container filled with cocktail sauce when I feel the weight of the table shift. Looking up, I pause to catch my breath, and my heart starts to beat faster.

"Hey." Tristan's green eyes regard me warmly.

My hand freezes in place. Now the shrimp is completely saturated. "Hey."

"Did you walk again to—" Abruptly, Tristan's voice fades and his coloring turns slightly pale. He eyes the food spread out in front of me. "What are you *eating*?"

"My lunch." I gaze up at him, puzzled. He continues to eye the leftovers from the night before without saying anything, and suddenly I feel like he wants more of an explanation. "It's grilled marlin and shrimp cocktail."

"Oh." His beautiful face has now turned the color of his eyes and the pale green work polo that pulls tightly across his chest. It seems as though he is trying hard not to gag. "You eat that stuff?"

"Yeah?" I answer with uncertainty. *Shouldn't I?*

Indecision crosses over his features, and finally, as if he can't take it anymore, he gets up from the table and starts to back away. *Holy crap, is he going to puke?*

Eventually he gets far enough away and seems to recover a little. "Well, I've got to get back to work. I'll see you later," he manages to call over his shoulder.

Wow! To say he's not a seafood lover would be an understatement. And what was he starting to ask me about walking again? Disappointment floods through me. I have just missed my opportunity.

Later, I change into my black Nike running shorts and a high school track tee shirt, resigning myself to the run home. Today this mode of travel is my second choice—not even close to my first choice. I am bending over lacing my neon green and black running shoes when I detect Tristan approaching from the corner of my eye. Glancing up at him, I notice his coloring is back to normal, and he is looking like his confident, gorgeous self. Immediately, my breath catches in my throat.

"Are you okay? You didn't look so good earlier today."

He narrows his eyes at me, and I can tell he is fighting back a smile. "What? Are you trying to tell me you don't like the way I look?"

I feel my eyes widen and I swallow. Momentarily I don't know what to say. This couldn't be farther from the truth, but how do I answer without giving my feelings completely away?

"No . . . I . . ."

He smiles completely then, and I feel like an idiot. Why do I often stumble over my words when I am around him?

"Are you walking again?" He doesn't give me the chance to remain uncomfortable.

"Yeah." I flush, wondering if he notices the running clothes.

"Do you want some company?"

"Sure."

Once again we walk side by side near the rolling surf of the ocean that incessantly stretches onto shore. Once again I am captivated by the endless beauty of the sea and the vigor of the green-eyed boy who walks beside me. Secretly, I wish that we could stay like this forever.

I glance over at him and unexpectedly flash back to another day when I invaded his privacy and observed him swimming in the ocean. I recall the attraction I felt when I witnessed the water that dripped from his blond hair and his perfectly carved chest as he emerged from the rolling surf. Defenselessly I blush.

"What?" He eyes me speculatively.

"Nothing." I look away, hoping he can't guess my line of thought.

"Well, if you won't tell me, I guess I'm just going to have to dunk you in the water." *What?*

My eyes widen. "You wouldn't."

His green eyes sparkle dangerously, and I can tell he's going to be true to his word. Reflexively, I dash away from him, heading in the opposite direction from the water. Thankfully, I am light on my feet—but not quick enough. I don't get too far before I feel his strong arms scoop me up.

"Wait . . . wait." I am shrieking and laughing at the same time. I am no match for his strong muscles as he holds me, but finally I am able to wriggle out of my backpack. It drops to the sand. "My shoes," I cry out in desperation as he continues on into the water.

He hesitates, then effortlessly grabs each running cleat and tosses them one by one back onto the shore, far from the reach of the surging tide. All the while he manages to grip me tightly to his chest. Any chance for escape is gone.

We continue wading into the wide expanse of the unrestrained whitecaps, and finally he lets go. *Oh my gosh . . . he actually did it!* Instantly, salty liquid envelops me, soaking my clothes. The shock of it startles me momentarily, but my second instinct is to retaliate. I reach out to grab Tristan, and he lets me, easily. I push him completely underwater. Soon he reemerges, and shakes the water droplets from his hair. For a brief second it registers in my mind how sexy he looks, but the deliberation is short-lived as his strong hands press against my shoulders, forcing me completely under as well.

Quickly, I hold my breath, and for a few seconds everything becomes a muted sound. Moments later, I resurface and am greeted with playful eyes and a darling smile. I can't believe this is happening. I can't believe I am swimming in the ocean with this exquisite boy who steals the very breath from my lungs—fully clothed. Never in a million years would I have thought to do something like this.

Eyeing him cautiously, I finally feel safe enough to walk onto shore. He boldly holds my gaze, but never makes a move to recapture me. Eventually, we both leave the water behind us and stand side by side on the shore, dripping wet. My clothes are completely soaked. I hug my arms to my chest, not knowing what else to do—it feels strange not having a towel to dry off with. Tristan's clothes are saturated too, but he doesn't seem too bothered by it.

"Now . . . will you tell me?" *What?* By now I can't remember what it was he wanted me to tell him. How does he do that—leave me feeling completely bemused and undone?

"How am I supposed remember anything after that near drowning?"

He shakes his head; once again I notice his wet, tousled hair. Self-consciously I think of my own dripping strands, and I run fingers through my tangled locks. He watches me while I do this and then chuckles lightly. "I guess you're off the hook then." His voice is quiet.

The air is warm on my wet skin and clothes as we continue walking home, allowing me to dry off more quickly than I expected. We both carry our shoes in our hands as we keep a slow pace side by side. Each time the skin from his arm comes in contact with mine, I get a chill, in spite of the balmy breeze that surrounds us. As the silence stretches out before us, my vision is drawn to the ground, and something about Tristan's feet captures my attention. He has tiny bits of extra skin between his toes.

"So . . . do you like my sexy feet?" Tristan's voice breaks through the quiet before I get a chance to look away.

"Huh? I . . ."

He laughs then. "It's okay . . . it's hard not to notice them. They are slightly webbed. I guess one in every two thousand people are born that way. If it bothers you, I can put my shoes back on."

"No," I blurt out a little too fast. "I mean, no, it's all right. It doesn't bother me." Nothing about this glorious-looking person walking beside me could possibly disturb me—surely not something as small as webbed feet.

He eyes me for a moment or two as if he is trying to figure something out. "Okay."

We are almost back to my house when Tristan speaks again.

"Is your dad still gone?"

"Yeah, but I think he'll be back soon," I reassure him lightheartedly. He nods, and we keep walking.

Surprisingly, I am almost dry by the time I reach my side entrance door, but I realize I must look like a mess. So I sneak into the house in hopes of my mom not asking a million questions.

Successfully, I plunge into my cottage bedroom and shut the door. Throwing myself onto my double bed, I stare up at the ceiling while hugging a pillow to my chest and sigh. *Oh my GOODNESS!* I am falling hard for Tristan Alexander.

Now I want to practically live at the marina. When it's my day to go in, I bound out of bed and spend extra time in the bathroom trying to make myself look okay. I am not going for the glamour-queen look, but at least somewhat okay. I am almost giddy with happiness as I fix my blond hair in the mirror. Owl City with Carly Rae Jepson is cranked in the background. "Good Times" resonates through my iPod home speakers, and I reach over to turn it down a notch. I don't want to wake the boys. On impulse, I decide to text Lucy.

I love webbed feet! *(send)*

I don't expect to hear back from her anytime soon. It's still pretty early in the morning, and it *is* summer. She is probably still sleeping.

Once I'm at the marina, I find myself glancing here and there in hopes of getting a glimpse of Tristan. Was it only a couple of days ago that I was trying so industriously to avoid him? I am researching various types of environmentally friendly cleaning products on the computer when, finally, the front door opens, and I am not disappointed.

He flashes me a smile that feels very personal and affectionate. Instantly, a warm sensation starts to spread throughout my body, reaching to every limb. *Oh . . . wow . . . !* I like this guy. There is a small part of me that wonders if his demonstrative smile is indicative of his feelings for me or is just a part of the charm that he shares with all the girls. Either way, it feels good, so for the moment, I just don't care.

"If you ask me, you are looking a little too dry sitting there at that desk right now."

I smile, then roll my eyes. I peek out the window in the direction of the water and then back at him. "Don't get any ideas."

He hesitates briefly like he's mulling the notion over. "Well, you're in luck, because I don't really have time to throw you in the water right now. I came to ask you what are you doing over lunch break?"

I think of the lunch I had packed earlier that morning and am immediately thankful that there is nothing in it that resembles seafood. "Nothing planned really."

"Well, after you are done eating, there is an antique boat parked at Watch Hill Boatyard, that I want to check out . . . Do you want to come with me?"

Absolutely! "Yeah . . . sure."

His enthusiasm is contagious as we walk along the shoreline toward the marina where the boat is being stored. My small, numerous steps are keeping time with his hurried, longer stride when I feel a buzz in the back pocket of my tan shorts. Reaching behind me, I pull out my phone. Lucy must finally be awake for the day. Must be nice to be able to sleep half of the morning.

(unlock) Webbed feet? What? Girl, you are crazy!

I smile briefly at that and discreetly tuck the mobile device back again. Tristan glances over at me and I bite my lip. *Geez, I really hope I'm not blushing right now.* I don't want to end up in the lake because I'm not ready to reveal my thoughts again. I try hard to look stoic, and he looks away again—his zeal over viewing the boat seems to supersede anything else for the moment.

The weathered vessel doesn't look like much to speak of, but the way Tristan's face lights up as he inspects the exterior makes me think otherwise. I cannot really comprehend the thrill of inspecting the worn, wooden structure, but the idea of him wanting to share this moment with me has me suddenly fascinated by old boats. Maybe Lucy is right; maybe I am starting to go a little crazy.

As he is scrutinizing the 1951 motor, an older man approaches us. He appears to be in his seventies, but it's hard to tell for sure, due to the weathered condition of his face. It is evident he has spent a lot of time in the wind and sun over the years, prematurely aging his skin.

"Well, hello there, young lady." He holds out a wrinkled hand, and in spite of his craggy appearance, his brown eyes twinkle with warmth.

He encloses his calloused fingers around my soft hand, and I smile back. Upon hearing the old man's voice, Tristan shimmies away from the motor and greets him with an enthusiastic grin.

"Mr. Horton . . . this is Bethany Kuiper. Bethany, this is Mr. Horton."

"I believe we were just in the process of meeting." His voice is friendly and unassuming.

"I believe we were." I smile in response.

"Well, what do you think of this boat?" Tristan continues.

"If you like it, then that's good enough for me."

Tristan's countenance resembles that of an animated schoolboy— it is clear that he values this older man's opinion.

"It has a six cylinder engine that supposedly runs pretty well, but obviously the body needs some work."

"I can tell you are very interested."

Tristan nods, eyeing the boat speculatively. "I am."

Later that afternoon, much to my joy, Tristan accompanies me home once again. We are sauntering along the now familiar, ocean-side route when my thoughts take me back to earlier in the day.

"How do you know Mr. Horton?"

Right away, Tristan's countenance brightens. "He is a good friend. I've known him for a long time." It occurs to me that it is a little odd for him to call Mr. Horton a friend, considering their age difference—but if he feels comfortable with the relationship, so am I.

"He seems very nice."

"He is. I'd trust him with anything."

We are almost back to my summer cottage when I make an

impulsive decision. He felt comfortable enough with me to show me the boat that has captured his interest—maybe he'd like to take a look at the shells I've been collecting. I pause for a fleeting moment and then muster the courage to ask.

"Do you want to stop over for a minute to look at some shells I'm collecting?"

His gaze holds mine for longer than I like, and my heart starts to pound. *He's going to say no.*

"Sure."

I bring him into the screened-in porch, run inside the cottage, and in no time, am back outside on the front enclosure—happy that I am sharing my favorite room with Tristan. In a satchel I carry my small but growing collection.

As he thumbs through the various sizes and shapes, secretly I am elated that he is here with me and so attentively examining my personal belongings. Taking a small shell and holding it in the palm of his hand, he studies it. It is swirled with tan etchings and resembles a miniature sand castle formation with an opening on the side.

"I think this might be a Neptune . . . the Rhode Island state shell, but I'm not 100 percent sure because it is pretty flawed. That would be cool, though. Those are hard to find."

"Really." I make a mental note to do some more research later and find out for sure.

When it's time for Tristan to leave, I find it's getting harder and harder to let him go. I just want him to stay here with me. *Forever.* As I stare at the ground, not wanting to reveal my thoughts, everything around us becomes very still. I can hear the sound of crickets chirping outside—and of course the ever-present, mollifying sound of the surf.

Soon I feel Tristan's strong hand gently lift my chin up to look at him, and my heart hammers against my chest.

"What are you thinking?" His voice is soft.

His cheekbones are so striking, and his lips look smooth—only inches away from me.

I can't speak.

His green eyes stare into my own blue ones for a while longer, and I am paralyzed, not knowing what to expect next. Finally he says good-bye, but it is only a whisper.

I try to say good-bye back—it's a barely audible sound.

Then slowly he exits my screened-in porch, and I am left alone, feeling completely undone.

Chapter Eight

I breathe a sigh of relief when Dad returns, hoping that maybe there is still a chance for things to turn around at home. The likelihood of it seems slim, but his presence around the house—as strained as it may be—offers some type of optimism. But it's hard for me to focus on that when my thoughts are consumed with something else. Someone else. I arrive at the marina for my next volunteer shift with baited breath—eyes darting around, constantly looking for Tristan. By the end of the day I walk home in a slightly sullen mood, expectations thwarted. He isn't at work that day.

The next time I go in to the marina, I still walk, but decide to bring my running clothes, just in case, all the while hoping I won't have to use them for the return trip—but I do. The course home seems remote and isolated. As I push myself into a faster sprint, the weighty pattern of my breath keeps time with the undulating whitecaps that are pushing onto shore. Everything else is a distant sound. I chide myself for missing Tristan so easily—I have no hold on him. There have been no promises made, only a susceptible girl that is falling too quickly.

The third time I make my way to the marina, I drive the Buick LaCrosse. Perusing my list of projects for the day, I make short work of anything that holds me hostage to the indoors. Instead, I putter around on the main docks, inspecting the fuel nozzles for proper vertical alignment, not once, but two three four times. I empty the glass and paper recycling bins every time an item or two have been deposited. Unhurriedly, I scan the shoreline that is wedged between the boat slips, looking for washed up debris and litter.

By noon there is still no sign of Tristan.

And I can't help it, I miss him. I wonder where he is right now. I imagine him swimming in the ocean with the grace of a dolphin. Or sitting on a piece of driftwood on a secluded shore, tousled, blond head bent slightly as he strums thoughtfully on his guitar. Or green, animated eyes that sparkle boyishly as he runs a hand over that old, wooden boat. Most of all, though, I wonder whatever he is doing—is he thinking about me?

On a whim, I decide to make a quick truck over to Watch Hill Boatyard to see if he happens to be checking on the antique boat that he so admires. As I approach the white, cedar-sided facility, a quiver of anxiety courses through my veins. What do I say if I do see him? *Oh, I just happened to be in the area.* Even though it's not close by to anything really.

I walk over to the location that berths the aged watercraft—and it's gone. Momentarily, I stare at the vacant boat slip, watching the water lap against the once occupied wooden posts that tied it in place. Strangely enough, the bare surroundings leave me feeling empty inside. An irrepressible sigh escapes my lips as I make my way back to Hill Cove Marina.

It's the last thing I want to do, but eventually curiosity overtakes me, and I seek out my manager, Ethan Vaughn—maybe he knows something.

"Hey, Bethany. What's up?" He is working on a boat motor. Stopping what he is doing, he greets me as I approach. Once again his gravelly voice catches me off guard. Suddenly, I'm nervous. How do I ease into this without sounding too obvious?

"I was looking for someone earlier to help me lift some boxes in the back office. Sometimes Tristan helps me . . . is he . . . is he working today?" *Geez, that sounds pitiful.*

"Looking for Tristan, huh?" Ethan flashes me a knowing smile, and instantly I blush. His brown eyes crinkle at the edges as he studies me for a moment. "He's not scheduled to work today. Actually, he's not scheduled much at all this week. But if you need help, I can be in there in a few minutes. Just let me finish up here."

"Oh . . . I think I already have things pretty well situated now, but if I do need any more help I'll come look for you."

Ethan cocks his head and squints his eyes at me briefly, as if I am confusing him. "Okay." He draws out the word—then flashes me a little grin that is meant to set me at ease. Instead, I'm left feeling exposed.

Resigned to Tristan's absence, I finish my remaining list of duties swiftly and saunter toward the LaCrosse. My steps are leaden. Too many days have passed without seeing him—a depressed mood surrounds me. I am unlocking the driver's side door and am about to slide onto the interior leather seat when I feel the heaviness of the metal door pull away from me slightly. Startled, I turn around.

"Hey."

Beguiling green eyes are gazing down at me along with a smile that emphasizes perfectly chiseled cheekbones. I am unprepared for my reaction. Relief. Joy. Dizziness. I reach for the side window to steady myself. Finally I can speak.

"Hey." *Where have you been, you little twit?*

"Just heading home for the day? I hope you left the life jackets neatly arranged in the boat house. I'm going to be checking next time I go in." His eyes are dancing.

"Well, however the life jackets happen to look, at least *I* go to work. *You* on the other hand . . ."

Tristan is standing less than a foot from me as I am backed against the car. His left arm is resting on the doorframe, lips formed into a playful smirk. He radiates confidence, cockiness, and sexiness all at the same time. *Geez, I am so attracted to him.*

It hardly seems fair that one person could have this type of effect on another.

"Why . . . did you miss me?"

A rush of giddiness rushes through me from his obvious flirtation. *If you only knew.*

I roll my eyes.

"I bought it."

"Bought it?"

"The antique boat. It's a 1951 twenty-foot Chris-Craft Riviera." His enthusiasm is contagious; soon I am grinning too.

"Awesome. I know you really wanted it."

"I'm going to keep it at Watch Hill Boatyard while I fix it up, but it already runs pretty nice." This boyish side to him is so endearing, I find myself wanting to give him a celebratory hug. Instead, I hold the palm of my hand up for a high five.

He reaches his own strong hand up to mine, but instead of giving it a triumphant smack, he rests it against my raised palm for a moment. For just an instant, our eyes lock. My heart rate accelerates. Then he eases his hand away, and suddenly the mood seems different somehow. The playful ambience is now gone. Self-assured Tristan has been replaced by a nervy schoolboy. For an extended moment he appears to hold his breath. Finally he exhales and hesitates. He looks like he wants to ask me something. The silence lingers for a second longer, his jaw clenches ever so slightly, and then as if resigned, he looks at me.

"What are you doing tomorrow?"

My heart starts pounding. Why do I have so little control over myself? "Nothing too important."

"Do you . . ." He swallows and then continues. "Do you want to come over tomorrow and check out the . . . check out my cabin where I live?"

I am confused and elated at the same time. Why was that so hard for him to spit out? "Sure."

"Do you remember that little beach past your house where you saw me play my guitar?"

Do I remember? "Yeah."

"Let's meet there at ten o'clock. Then I'll take you to the cabin."

"Okay." I hope my voice doesn't sound as breathless as I feel.

I hardly remember driving the LaCrosse home. As soon as I pull into the side gravel drive, I text Lucy.

So there's this guy! *(send)*

Lucy must have her phone in hand, because right away I feel a buzz in *my* hand.

(unlock) What . . . another one?

No, the same one. *(send)*

(unlock) Oh him again?

Yes, him again. Again, and hopefully forever. No one has ever made me feel the way I feel when I'm with him, and I can't imagine anyone else ever could. That whole evening at home, I am soaring. I am light-headed with the anticipation of what the next day will bring. Finally evening turns into night, and I force myself to go to bed. After I slide under the covers and tuck my green and purple duvet around my arms, I compel myself to relax, and eventually sleep finds me.

That night I dream.

The ocean becomes my planet. Soon I am swimming, coursing through an endless realm of misty blue. Tristan is by my side. On and on we swim, with no shore in sight. It feels so infinite and peaceful. At times it seems odd to me that there is no land on the horizon, but it doesn't matter, because I am with Tristan—and I feel so safe. The water feels like a silk blanket as it slides over my skin, caressing my arms and legs and stomach. Warmth envelops me, encouraging me to relax my body into the encircling abyss. Each stroke I take through the salty liquid is fluid and effortless. It is easy to imagine continuing on like this incessantly. On and on we remain surging through the vast, muffled depths of the ocean until finally, slowly, the panorama fades away, and I am eased back into the remaining night's slumber.

I dress in cutoff jean shorts and a layered medium blue and light blue tank top. I braid my hair and then unbraid my hair, put it into a low ponytail, and then let it hang free. Finally, I decide on a messy bun. Satisfied, I set down my comb and brush a little mascara on my eyelashes. Leaning into the mirror, I am getting ready to pinch my cheeks for some color when I stop. As my reflection gazes back through the glass, it occurs to me that I am not in need of any additional tinting—my face is already plenty pink from my perpetual blushing at the thought of spending the day with Tristan.

When I reach the secluded beachfront that we'd agreed upon, Tristan is already there, sitting on a piece of driftwood—staring out at the ocean. I pause and take a calming breath. His disheveled, blond hair is so appealing, even from the back. I clench my fingers into a fist at my side. Somehow he senses my presence, because before I can say anything, he turns slowly around.

Green eyes pierce my own blue. *Breathe, just breathe.*

His gaze holds mine for a second longer before he shakes his head faintly, seemingly to clear it. The motion is so brief, I'm left wondering if it happened at all.

"You made it." He smiles at me warmly.

"Yep."

"Well, let's go." We head through a long, winding, not-so-cleared path in the woods, just yards from the shoreline. If he didn't know where we were going, in minutes I would be lost. But he seems well-acquainted with the surroundings, so I'm not concerned. As we begin walking, it appears as though he is going to reach his hand out for mine, but then changing his mind, he shoves his into the front pocket of his shorts instead. Once again my fingers tighten into a fist.

His cabin is secluded, sequestered by the forest, and oddly enough, the driveway looks as though it is almost unused and unapproachable. The exterior is worn and unpainted, but the structure looks sturdy enough. Immediately, I recall the boat he is so taken with and realize that aged things must offer a type of appeal to him.

He leads me inside, and immediately I am captivated. It reminds me of something out of a dated storybook. The floors are wooden, and the furniture is old and sparse. Even the appliances are from yesteryear. Instantly, I am impressed with how quaint it is—and how clean. Not a speck of dirt to be found, or a dish out of place anywhere. I can't help myself—I grin without restraint.

"I love it."

"Really?" Tristan's whole demeanor relaxes. I hadn't even realized how tense his stance had been as he stood at my side.

"It is so . . . charming. It has to be so peaceful living here." Spinning slowly around, I take in every detail. I want to memorize everything about this place that is home to him. "Did you grow up here?"

He shoves both hands into his front pockets and looks away uncomfortably. *Oh no. Don't pull away.* I want to know everything about him, but still, I don't want to push too hard. At times he seems so mystifying. Not having had much experience, I wonder if all boys are like this.

"Not here at this cabin exactly, but I've grown up close by, off and on my whole life." Well, that's a start. Next, I find myself wanting to ask what school he went to and about his family. Instead, I walk over to the fireplace and run my hand over the masonry.

"I love this stone fireplace. I don't know if I've ever seen one so beautiful."

The tension in the air is relieved at that, and Tristan walks over to join me. "It *is* really well made; I like it too." I love that he is smiling again. "Do you want to walk down by the water?" he asks.

"Sure."

The segregated nature of his cabin does not offer a view of the ocean, so we take a narrow, zigzagging path that leads us through brush and onto a sandy shoreline. We round one more curve in the slender trail before the magnificence of the vast waterway is revealed. Waves pound to shore. We walk down to the ocean's edge and eventually a ruler's length into swelling surf. A whitecap reaches up and skims the bottom of Tristan's tan shorts—by now I know this doesn't bother him at all. I take a step back, not ready to get wet. My move does not go by unnoticed. Tristan turns around and eyes me speculatively before moving his hand slowly through the water toward me, as if he is going to give me a splash—all the while his gaze holds mine, waiting for a reaction.

I shake my head—not this again. Then he laughs and I relax. Suddenly he points out toward the measureless expanse before us.

"Hey, did you see that?"

"What?" I move closer to him and strain to look where he is pointing.

"That . . . way out there. There it is again." He takes his arm and rests it on my back, still pointing with the other hand, as if to guide my vision. Warmth immediately floods through my blue tank top and onto the skin of my back—his touch feels so good. "It's a dolphin."

"Really . . . how do you know?" This is exciting. I've never seen a dolphin in the ocean before.

He shakes his head and gives a small chuckle. "I just know." Finally he takes his hand away from me, and suddenly I feel like something is missing—the phenomenon that was created by his simple touch.

"I hope I can see it too. I don't know how you can see out that far. I should carry a pair of binoculars when I'm with you. You always point out the coolest things."

"Yeah?"

"Yeah."

I study the water for a while longer, but still don't see any movement. As I survey the undulating seascape, I'm reminded of last night's dream, and I decide to tell Tristan about it, hoping he won't think I'm strange. Surprisingly, as I recall the particulars of the endless ocean swim out loud, Tristan listens intently. Periodically he asks me for extra details, and I try to relay everything I can, verbatim. As I talk on, I detect his countenance becoming more and more serious, and at times I notice his jaw tighten. Well, I didn't have to worry about him laughing me to scorn over a silly dream. But what is this? At times I feel so bewildered by him.

Eventually the dream is forgotten, and playful Tristan reemerges as we wander farther down the shoreline. Momentarily I see him watching me from the corner of my eye as we saunter along, and I have to fight back a blush.

"What?" I narrow my eyes slightly.

He keeps looking at me, but he's smiling a little now too. "Nothing . . . you're just so . . ."

"Just so what?" *Do I want to know the answer to this?*

He exhales and shakes his head. "Nothing." But he holds my gaze for an uncomfortable moment, and now I *am* blushing.

I look away. Why does he make me feel so shy?

As we are ambling down the sinuous shoreline, we come upon some dark sludge and debris that plunders the otherwise impeccable coast. I scrunch up my nose in disgust.

"Ooh, what is this?"

Tristan appears livid. "It's from waste that is dumped into the ocean by shipping companies. It's destroying life in the ocean."

Suddenly, I'm listening. Isn't this what I've been volunteering all summer for—to protect marine life from things like this? "This looks awful; what do they dump to make it look this bad? Aren't there laws against this?"

Clearly, this has hit a nerve. Tristan looks really pissed. "Well, yeah, there *are* laws against it, but obviously some companies think they are *above* the law. They dump the oil residue from the engines.

Some even hook up something called a magic pipe that bypasses the separation equipment they are required to have. The separation equipment is meant to divide the oil, to incinerate it or store it until they reach port. Instead, they just pump the oil overboard, and the shipping crews fudge the logs to make it look like they didn't."

"Wow, with all we know today, that seems so ignorant. Even before today, you would think it would be obvious that this type of thing would be destructive to ocean life."

Tristan's jaw is rigid, and even in all his anger he looks so beautiful. I can't take my eyes off of him. Suddenly, I wish there was something I could say to make him happy again—but I can't think of anything.

"You would think," he mutters, then leans down and scoops up a decayed-looking creature into the palm of his hand. "This is a lobster that has lobster shell disease. It has a rotting, black shell that was created by invading bacteria from chemicals generated from industrial waste."

My eyes widen as I inspect the unrecognizable organism. "That is disgusting . . . unbelievable."

Silence stretches around us as Tristan looks lost in thought. Eventually it appears as though his adverse mood has reached its limit. He looks over at me and attempts a smile. "Do you want to head back?"

Just like that the conversation is over, and I find that I'm a little relieved.

The charm of the cabin reaches out and touches me the minute we walk back through its weather beaten door. "Time for some lunch, don't you think?" Tristan questions as he opens the outdated refrigerator. Abruptly, I realize how famished I've become.

"Sounds good."

"Turkey sandwiches?"

"Perfect." Soon we are sitting at his small, butcher-board table eating turkey and tomato on rye. I glance up at him in admiration. Not bad. This dazzling boy in front of me can make a pretty mean sandwich. Is there anything he can't do, I secretly wonder?

We are almost done eating when something in the remote corner of the cabin catches my eye. It is the guitar that played the mysterious, melancholy sounds that had originally drawn me to find Tristan on his secluded beach. It almost looks forlorn as it rests against the worn, clap-board paneling that covers the walls. I glance at Tristan and then back at the guitar. Perceptively, he doesn't miss the meaning in my look.

"Oh no," he shakes his head.

"What? Yes."

"No, Bethany, I shouldn't."

"I think you should." I eye him expectantly. "Please?" My voice is soft, barely audible.

Tristan lets out a big sigh and closes his eyes momentarily. Then he opens them and holds my gaze. "Okay." He seems resigned. I hope I haven't pushed him too far.

Pulling a chair away from our lunch table, he rests the guitar on his lap. His rumpled, blond hair falls over his eyes slightly as he bends his head. I hold my breath. His strong hands are splayed over the strings as he plucks the first couple of chords—as if he is getting reacquainted with an old friend. He pauses and looks up at me. I am watching attentively. He hesitates as if he is struggling with a thought or a decision. Finally, his beautiful face turns away from me again and back to the instrument on his lap—and he begins to play.

The sound is exquisite. I am instantly captivated. It's like nothing that I can compare it to—soothing, enticing, and thrilling all at once. Immediately a warming sensation starts to spread throughout my veins. I am delighted that he has finally agreed to my request. Gaping at the unadulterated musician before me, I become newly aware of an ache that has been created inside me. I am completely under his spell. All these thoughts and sensations are rushing through my mind and body as I continue to listen to him play, when finally Tristan's green eyes look back up.

Abruptly he stops.

No.

He seems almost irritated as he hastily exits his chair. Depositing the guitar back into the original remote corner of the room, he turns and faces me.

"I think we should go."

"Okay." My voice is barely a sound. I am so confused. Why did he quit playing so brusquely? Why does he appear vexed? I'm having a hard time recovering from it all. I sit for a minute longer, not trusting my legs to hold me. Shaking my head, I try to clear the light-headedness that wants to claim me.

Tristan waits patiently by the door, looking away from me— silent.

Finally, I am able to go join him. "Ready."

Steadying myself, I head through the cabin door, following Tristan. As we begin the branch-covered trail that took us here, there is a part of me that now wishes he didn't know the way quite so well. I'm not ready to leave him. Will I ever be ready to leave him? The trip back is quiet. The exploding sound of the surf reminds me of its presence just beyond the tree line. Everything else fades into the background.

I sigh and get a glimpse of Tristan's profile as he walks beside me. He doesn't look quite as displeased anymore. I want to ask him what happened, but I'm still so unsure about him, about us, about everything. So I bite my lip and stare at the narrow passageway in front of me instead.

We are nearing the beachfront that lies just ahead of the cottage's front lawn before I realize that we have bypassed Tristan's secluded beach where we had originally met up for the day. *So he is walking me all the way home.* I've barely contemplated this new idea when just ahead in the distance, I notice two figures next to the dock that belongs to our cottage. Mom and Dad. I glance over at Tristan and then back at them.

Is he ready to meet my patents?

"Hi, Bethany," my mom calls out. *Well, ready or not.*

"Um . . . hi."

We continue approaching until finally we are all face-to-face. One more time I look over at Tristan to see if he is uncomfortable with the situation, but if he is, he doesn't let on. My parents eye me expectedly.

"Ah . . . Mom and Dad, this is Tristan. Tristan . . . Mom and Dad."

There is a note of caution in my dad's brown eyes as he reaches out to take Tristan's hand. But a warm smile lights up my mom's face, and I can tell she is mesmerized by his looks.

"So are you a Watch Hill vacationer, or are you from around these parts?" my dad questions. I hold my breath, hoping the conversation won't turn into a full-blown interrogation. Thankfully enough, the interaction is kept short, sweet, and polite. Finally my parents excuse themselves and head back to the house, leaving us alone once again. We wait in silence, watching them retreat. When they are out of sight, we turn and face each other. His eyes pierce mine for many moments, and I struggle to find my voice.

"I'm glad you took me to your cabin," I eventually say, but the words come out raspy and breathless.

Tristan blinks and shakes his head briefly. "Me too," he murmurs. Seconds, minutes go by, I'm not sure which—but I can't look away from him. He takes an escaped strand of my blond hair and tucks it gently, slowly behind my ear. His fingertips lightly graze my cheekbone as he does. I suck in a breath while my heart hammers in my chest. Involuntarily, I feel myself lean towards him. What do

I want? I eye his soft lips and watch as an almost inaudible groan escapes them before he tightens his jaw. He looks away and then finally back at me again as he blows out a long, slow breath.

"Well . . . good-bye, Bethany."

No. Not yet. Don't go yet. Once more I eye his mouth. Then in effort to fend off the shakiness that wants to claim my body, I hug my arms tightly to my chest.

"Good-bye, Tristan." I say against my will, before turning reluctantly to follow my parents' trail back to the cottage.

Chapter Nine

The next time I go to the marina, once again Tristan is not there. Disappointment like fire spreads through my veins. The main reason I started volunteering at the marina in the first place is now lost. My sole purpose for reporting in to work each time is only to see him, talk to him, be anywhere near him. The next couple of days are repeats of the same—he is nowhere to be found. The hours drag. I can't wait to leave the boat works behind and look for him—but where? I rack my brain; does he even have a phone? I don't recall ever seeing one. If he does have one, why hasn't he gotten my number to text me?

There is a part of me that believes he might be caught up in the excitement of his new boat and is most likely working on it at the boatyard. But how to just show up there without being completely obvious? I'm not ready to do that. Instead, I find myself wandering to what I've come to think of as his secluded beach. I scan the entire, protected shoreline in search of him, but all I find is a hungry seagull screaming impatiently at me to toss him an edible morsel. Ignoring the screeches and the wings flapping around me, I stare speculatively at the sea. The water is calm with only an occasional ripple of water trickling in to moisten the scattered pebbles on the shore. My eyes skim the unreachable horizon and the teal expanse in between, hoping. But Tristan's ardent form never breaks through the surface. I walk away feeling rather silly. Really, how often does he go for a swim anyway?

I think of asking Ethan for Tristan's schedule, but immediately nix that idea. I'm not ready to withstand any more of Ethan's taunting gazes or perceptive grins. Now as I leave the marina for a fourth time in a row without seeing Tristan, my mood is dismal—matching the increasing clouds that are gathering in the sky. I arrive back at the summer cottage and deposit my mode of transportation for the day in the shed, my bike.

In accord with my own disposition, the atmosphere is heavy with pent-up moisture. Finally the clouds can no longer hang on, and tiny snippets of drizzle begin to spread through the air. In spite of all of this, I am not ready to go inside for the evening. So I wander down to the waterfront and follow the shoreline aimlessly, not caring that my hair is becoming damp and my clothing is beginning to stick to my skin. As I mindlessly stare out at the blackened sea, becoming more and more sodden as I do, I notice a far-off movement among the waves. The motion is so outlying and obscure that I have to strain my eyes to determine if it is anything more than a rolling surge of water. *I need to start remembering my binoculars.* By the time I am able to focus my eyes, the isolated activity has been swallowed up by the seething whitecaps that are increasing in strength. It was probably nothing.

But still I wait, eyes glued to the sea. Hoping, wanting it to be Tristan. But of course it's not. Whatever it is, *if* it is anything at all, it isn't a human. It was almost touching the horizon—it was so far offshore. Maybe a dolphin, or a shark, or a—? Who really cares? If it wasn't Tristan, I know *I* don't really care. Giving one more fleeting glance in the direction of the tempestuous waterway, I sluggishly head home.

Against my own better judgment, I end up making my way over to Watch Hill Boatyard the following day in hopes of finding Tristan. I'm practically shaking with nervousness as I follow the shoreline to the place where Tristan is storing his boat. A million thoughts are streaming through my head with each step I take on the path that is leading me closer and closer to the possibility of finding him. Why am I chasing him down—shouldn't he be coming to find me if he is remotely interested? The way he looks at me, the way he talks to me—it *seems* like he likes me, no, he *definitely* acts like he likes me. But then, why hasn't he tried to come see me lately—he knows where to find me if he wants to. Is he going to think I'm stalking him? Maybe I should just turn back around.

Still I keep walking.

Finally, I reach the boatyard, but Tristan's boat is not there. My eyes dart around anxiously scanning the vicinity. He probably moved it to another part of the facility in order to begin working on it—possibly a boathouse or a storage unit. Unsure of where to begin looking, I hear a high-pitched, whirring noise coming from two buildings over, and decide to follow the sound. *Maybe.*

As I enter the rear of the large, metal building, the din increases in intensity, making it difficult to think. Adjusting to the light, my eyes rapidly peruse the interior of the structure, finally focusing on the noise. My shakiness is instantly overpowered by the force of my heart pounding against my chest. The source of the defining shrill belongs to a sandblaster—and the person holding the high-powered machinery is Tristan.

My breath catches in my throat as I stand there watching him lost in his work. He is wearing ripped, faded jeans and a tattered tee shirt that pulls tightly across his chest with each movement. Safety glasses cover his perfect cheekbones, and blond hair waves rebelliously over the straps. An ache instantly forms in my stomach. He is ridiculously beautiful.

As he continues to electronically smooth his boat, I stand frozen in place, unsure of how to get his attention. I don't want to interrupt his task, but I didn't come here to just observe him from across the room. The noise continues to whir as I wait for the right moment. For an instant, I think I notice him glance fleetingly in my direction as he balances the machinery in his strong, muscled arms—but then I decide I must have been wrong as the blaster drones on and on, and he never looks my way again.

Seconds turn into minutes, and I begin to feel like I'm in a dilemma. Do I interrupt him or wait for him to take a break? Am I imagining things, or did he already notice me and actually doesn't *want* to see me? I become horrified as I contemplate the last thought. Still the piercing sound fills the air without stopping. Making an impulsive decision, I take a step in his direction. I wave my arm in an attempt to get his attention. Still he continues to work without looking at me, and my heart begins to take a slow dive in my chest.

Finally, he glances up and meets my gaze. Briefly, he gives me a nod and then resumes his previous undertaking. Confusion, embarrassment, and devastation consume me at once. Feeling like an idiot, I turn to leave.

The noise stops.

I freeze in my tracks. Should I turn around or just keep walking? What was *that* all about? I should have never come here! My chest feels heavy; I don't trust myself to breathe. This is all so stupid, I just want to run a million miles away.

Finally, I turn back around.

"Hey," he says as he sets down the blaster and slowly pulls off his safety glasses. His green eyes regard me rather coolly. *OMG! What happened to the warm eyes that couldn't take theirs away from mine? What happened to the affectionate smile that felt like it was meant for only me?* "What brings you here?"

A lump begins to form in my throat. I work hard to swallow it down. "Well, I came by to say hi, but . . ." Suddenly I feel so hurt and stupid. If only there were such things as redoes, I would never have come here. In fact, I would never have allowed myself to fall for someone like him, someone who could turn on a dime and leave me feeling so injured and absurd.

"Since you are here, come see what I've done with my boat." His voice is cordial, but something is missing—the tone holds none of the sincerity of our previous time at the cabin. *I'll tell you what you can do with your damn boat!*

My legs are like rubber as they make their way over to where he is standing. "I've stripped off several layers. I'm almost down to the original wood." He runs a hand over a smoothed area of raw lumber, and I can't help but notice the flexed muscles in his arm that pull against the sleeve of this tee shirt. This only compounds the hurt in my aching chest. I don't trust myself to speak.

"Nice" I finally mutter. I want to take a nail and gouge his work so he too is in need of a redo. I take a step back. I have nothing more I want to say right now. Suddenly, I need to get out of the enclosed area.

"You didn't have to volunteer at the marina today?" he continues on like nothing has passed between us—like we are two strangers that have had brief, casual encounters in the past and are now just making niceties with each other.

"Nope," I exhale and shake my head. An hour ago I desperately wanted to ask him about *his* hours at the marina, and now I hope I never have to see him there again. I can't look at him. "Well, I gotta go." My jaw is clenched, and my cheeks are burning with anger.

"All right, good-bye," he offers back with polite indifference.

I deliberately slow my steps in order to stop myself from sprinting to the door. When I finally exit the building, I gasp to fill my lungs with air as my heart explodes in my chest. His obvious rejection hurts so bad. I should have known when he didn't come to see me after our excursion to his cabin that he had changed his mind about me—that he wasn't interested in me anymore. Was I only imagining that there was ever something between us? No. No, I couldn't have imagined *everything*. I mean, he did ask me to his cabin, and he did show me his boat, and he did walk home with me several times, and he did pick me up and throw me in the water, and—and I can't breathe—it hurts so bad, now that he doesn't want me anymore.

Thankfully, I make it home and into the safety of my own bedroom before I succumb to the endless outpouring of tears that have welled up inside of me. By the time dinner is served that night, I am able to freshen my face effectively enough in order to avoid unnecessary questions from my parents. By the time I go to bed that night, I am numb and exhausted. I sleep without waking until morning.

When I do arouse the following day, the sun flooding through my cottage bedroom window does nothing to alter my mood. I am pissed. How did I think I was ever going to compete with the beautiful redhead and brunettes I'd seen Tristan with before? I had been *so* stupid to fall for his seductive looks and boyish charms. Well, now he can save his efforts for the other swooning ladies in his life, because I sure will not be succumbing to this type of stupidity again.

As if right on cue, I receive a text from Kate, who unknowingly offers me the type of moral support I need right then. She informs me in no uncertain terms that she misses spending time with me, and that I need to quit spending so much time with *blond lover boy* and spend an afternoon with her instead! She includes a smiley face to soften the bossiness, and I can't help but smile in response.

The plan is for me to meet Kate and possibly Nick, Emily, and Jonathan at St. Clair Annex after I volunteer at the marina that day. Instead, Kate shows up prematurely at the front office building as I'm getting ready to finish up.

"Hey, girl. Where have you been? I've missed you." She bounces in and surprises me by wrapping her arms around me in a big hug.

"I've been around. Where have *you* been?" It's so nice to see her and her supply of interminable energy. I feel the tension in my shoulders fade away as I subject myself to her smile. "I'll be done here in a minute."

As I put away the supplies that I've been working with and finish straightening the front counter, Kate is chatting incessantly about what all she's been up to in the last couple of weeks. Alerted to Kate's arrival by her animated conversation that fills up the office interior, Ethan Vaughn saunters out of the back storage room and makes his way over to where we are. *Oh no!*

"Leaving for the day, Bethany?" At the sound of his gravelly voice, Kate turns around to face him. Her eyes instantly become large, and I know what she is thinking. *Be good, Kate!* "What are you girls up to this afternoon?" His brown eyes regard us both warmly and then end up resting on mine.

I'm getting better at this—I'm not quite so undone in his presence anymore. "We are about to head to St. Clair Annex. I haven't seen my friend Kate in a while; we have some catching up to do."

"You can come too, if you want," Kate interjects before Ethan gets a chance to respond to me. He looks over at her and gives a small chuckle.

"Thanks, but I'd better stay here. Someone might need to run this place." His brown eyes glance back in my direction. "Another time though?"

Kate is quiet for once, and I realize it is up to me to reply. I clear my throat; suddenly it feels dry. "Sure, you are always welcome."

When we step out into the fresh oceanside air, Kate punches me in the arm.

"Hey, what was that for?"

She purses her lips and shakes her head, eyes dancing. "He so wants you."

"What? Uh-uh!"

"Uh-huh!"

"That is so not true." I can feel my cheeks starting to burn. "He is just like that. Plus he's too old for me, *and* he's my manager."

"Oh girl, but it *is* true and I don't care who he is or how old he is, I saw the way he looked at you."

I roll my eyes, wanting the conversation to end. Anyway, that is *not* true. *Is it?*

When we arrive at St. Clair Annex, Nick and Emily are already inside sitting across from each other at one of the parlor-styled tables. They both look up and wave when we walk through the door.

"Miss Bethany Kuiper. We thought you went back to Philadelphia—you've been nowhere to be found." Nick smiles playfully. "You've been spending all your time with that football player boy." *Football player?*

The look on my face registers confusion. "You know, Tristan," Nick clarifies.

I am still confused. "Does he . . . I didn't know he played football."

"Well, I don't know if he *plays* football, but he sure looks like he does."

"Oh." *Oh yeah, him.* I secretly grit my teeth as I feel a flash of anger spread quickly through my veins at just the mention of his name. I so want to leave the memory of him submerged. I want to focus on my fun group of summer friends today and try to have a good time. *Try!* It's going to be *so* hard. "Well, I'm here now. It's so good to see you guys." I muster a smile.

Kate takes the seat next to Nick, and right away I notice Emily press her lips rigidly together. She pushes a strand of her tight, curly hair behind her ear, and a look of irritation briefly flashes across her face. *What is this?* I'm not around for a couple of weeks, and seemingly the group dynamics have changed. I take a seat next to Emily.

The ensemble chats animatedly for a while before getting in line for ice cream and sodas. Emily doesn't want anything, so she saves our seats while we order. Kate is still clearly mesmerized by Nick's presence, hanging on to every word he says—reaching out to touch his arm periodically as she talks to him. But what is their status? Are they an item now? Nick does make a lot of eye contact with her, but then he makes a lot of contact with Emily, and really me too—he is pretty friendly in general, so it's hard to tell. Eventually Kate will let me know, I'm sure.

By the time we get back to our table, our arms filled with bowls of creamy delectables, Jonathan extravagantly announces his presence as he bursts through the front door. His smile fills up the room as he enthusiastically springs toward us. We resume our previous seating arrangement. All the while Emily is regarding Kate coolly. *Uh-oh!*

"Hey, sweet thing," Jonathan's soprano voice sings out as he reaches over to pinch my cheeks. " Good to see that your cute little tushy has decided to grace us." I blush at his phraseology—his vocabulary knows no limits. There aren't any more seats available at the table, so Jonathan motions me over and squeezes in beside me to share mine. "You've missed a couple of good volleyball games. God knows I could have used your help."

I smile then. I'm quite sure he's right about that—he's no volleyball player. "Next time I'll be there, I promise."

He squints his eyes at me and massages my back for brief moment. "You better." I glance at the slim, black-haired boy who is crowding me and then over at the rest of my companions who surround me at the table, and a measure of comforting warmth encloses my shoulders. I feel safe and welcomed in their presence. The pain of Tristan's rejection is eased just a little.

As I watch the group in front of me, I am reminded of someone else I want to include in this circle of friends, someone I miss desperately. While the others are talking spiritedly on either side and across the table from me, I pull out my phone to text Lucy.

Ice cream with friends. I wish you were here too, BEST friend!
(send)

I am continuing to playfully converse with my companions when I feel the familiar buzz of the phone that is resting on my lap.

(unlock) **I miss you too! LOTs!**

Unexpectedly, a sentimental tear begins to form in the corner of my eye. I wipe it away discreetly, hoping it goes by unnoticed.

I find myself hoping that Tristan has resigned from his job at the marina, brief as it was. Each day that passes that he isn't there, I experience a sense of relief. Today David Chambers has me running an errand for him, carrying a stack of papers to the front boathouse, and I am enjoying the saltiness in the early morning air. The sun is still relatively low in the sky, birds are soaring above the surface of the ocean, calling to one another, and the wake from a passing Boston Whaler laps gently against the docks. I am mindlessly strolling toward the open water when something in my peripheral vision catches my eye, snapping me out of my reverie. My heart lurches in my chest. Tristan is back. He has a hatch propped open on a boat motor and is leaning over it, working. His physique is painfully exquisite even from this angle. *Dang him!* I keep walking, looking straight ahead—making my steps as quiet as possible. Maybe he won't notice me.

As I near the place where he is, I pass next to him—only feet from him. He is still bent over, face buried in the traplike door. *If only I can be discreet enough, he won't hear me.* I'm practically walking on tiptoe, holding my breath, when I realize in horror that my heart is pounding so loudly it is sure to wake even the dead. *Crap, crap!* I keep walking, eyes focused on the boathouse.

Exhaling in relief, I walk through the side entrance and wait for my vision to adjust to the darkened room. I've made it. I complete my task and search for an alternate exit, but there is none. No matter which route I take, eventually I will have to circle back by him in order to get off the main docks. So I sigh, and as unobtrusively as I can, retrace my steps the way I came.

This time I am not so lucky.

Soon after I leave the shelter of the building, I detect movement over the motor of the boat that I traveled by earlier. Momentarily,

I freeze in place. I have nowhere to go. I could literally sprint, that may be the only way. Slowly, Tristan stands and stretches, wiping his hands over the front of his shorts. Unhurriedly, he glances in my direction. For a split second, shock registers across his perfect features, then he blinks, and immediately the look is replaced with indifference.

The hurt that I'd been working so hard to keep at bay comes rushing back. Seconds pass and I am paralyzed with the pain. He nods at me politely and raises his hand in a halfhearted wave. Pressing my lips together, I swallow back the discomfort that is forming in my throat. I attempt an impassive nod in return, but am not sure if my head actually moves at all. Amazingly, my legs continue to carry me the rest of the way off the dock. Each step that takes me farther from Tristan, the more my cheeks burn. By now, the pain that has overtaken my body is being replaced with anger.

For the next hour, I complete each task I'm assigned at the marina with fervor, fueled by the infuriating force of Tristan's apathy. Who does he think he is, anyway? Toying with a naive girl's heart and discarding it so easily. *An unequivocally gorgeous guy who completely takes my breath away each time I look at him, who captivates my heart and soul each time I'm with him, who used to make me laugh and embrace life in a way that I have never known before.* I shake my head in defeat. Somehow I need to repress all these uninvited feelings. Anger and irritation seem like the best way to cover them up.

Later I'm in front of the main office getting ready to set up a new type of recycling station meant for oil filters and other items that contain metal or chemical components, when I perceive Tristan's athletic form occupying a nearby dock. Without trying, my shoulders tense. Momentarily, I glance in his direction, but he doesn't return my look. But I *know* he sees me. Impulsively, I react.

Out the other corner of my eye, I am aware of Ethan's frame

approaching, and I think back to Kate's comment from the day before. *He so wants you.* Before I know it, I stop what I'm doing and flash him a big smile.

"The ice cream was pretty good yesterday; you should have come," I call over to him. *Seriously? What am I doing?*

"Really?" His brown eyes regard me almost amusingly. "Maybe next time you can give me a little advance notice." As he answers, I am only vaguely aware of his gravelly voice; I am so hyperaware of Tristan in my peripheral vision. Tristan becomes very still the moment Ethan's and my exchange begins. *Good. I hope he is listening. I hope he gets an earful.*

"Maybe next time I will." *Who is this girl talking?*

"All right, I'm going to hold you to it." His brown eyes continue to be playful. Then his vision expands, encompassing Tristan standing in the near distance. As comprehension registers across his face, he chuckles lightly and shakes his head, his copper highlights glistening in the sun.

"Show me what you are setting up here."

I take one more peek in Tristan's direction before leading Ethan over to the recycling bins I'm setting up. Almost imperceptively, I detect Tristan's jaw tighten before he continues on with his previous task. Coquettishly, I proceed to explain each container and the reasoning behind it, all the while hoping Ethan isn't taking my brazen flirtations the wrong way. But he doesn't seem to mind—somehow I get the feeling this is all very second nature to him.

I am inside the main office, and my day at the marina is winding to a close when I detect some movement outside the east-facing window. Mr. Horton, the older man I'd been introduced to at the boatyard, and Tristan are standing in close proximity to one another, having a conversation. Unwittingly, I find myself staring out the glass pane, watching them. The earlier look of apathy is wiped clean from Tristan's features, and a type of affection is conveyed instead. He really likes Mr. Horton. I can't help it; in spite of everything, I am intrigued by their relationship. Tristan's green eyes light up as he listens to whatever his older friend is saying to him. Mr. Horton reaches over and pats him on the back, and Tristan laughs. As I take in this endearing picture, I experience an aching tug at my heart. But before I can be drawn too deeply into the scenario, I snap out of the reverie and shift my gaze away. Mr. Horton has left Tristan's side and is now heading toward the main office.

Right on cue, the musical sound of the front door opening fills the room.

"Hello there, Bethany. How is the marina's favorite volunteer doing today?" Immediately I am reminded of why Tristan likes his older companion so much.

I smile at Mr. Horton warmly.

"I'm doing okay." I don't want to lie and say I'm doing terrific or anything. His darling friend took care of that for me. Suddenly something occurs to me. "Word must get around . . . I mean about me volunteering here."

Mr. Horton's brown eyes sparkle. "Indeed it does. I have a pretty reliable source." *Tristan? Tristan talks about me?* Reliable indeed! I can't keep up with his mood changes and his unpredictable behavior. "Carry on with the good work, and, Bethany, don't get discouraged." The weathered skin on his face displays a thoughtful grin before he exits the way he came.

I am caught off guard, barely nodding to him as he leaves. What did he mean by *don't get discouraged*? Discouraged about what—my volunteering to help save the marine environment? Don't get discouraged about Tristan? Surely he didn't mean that. It was a pretty confusing statement.

As I leave the main office building, finally heading home for the day, I spot Tristan once again. This time he is sitting on the edge of a dock, feet dangling into the salty water below. He is now accompanied by an assortment of besotted female friends: the glamorous redhead I'd seen him with on an earlier occasion, a petite brunette, and even a blond. *What do you know, I'm not the only blond he pays attention to.* The girls are clearly delighted to be in his company. As female laughter rings through the air, my stomach turns. I can't stand to be in his presence for another second. I have to mentally restrain myself from physically running away. Just before I take the final turn on the sidewalk which will mercifully take me out of his line of vision, Tristan looks away from his girly fan club, and his green eyes pierce my own. For a split second his expression becomes very still and unreadable. Then he turns back to face his admirers once again. I take a sharp breath and keep right on walking.

Don't get discouraged indeed!

Chapter Ten

I've always been a relatively happy girl, so having to fight this new melancholy mood is inconvenient and irritating. It is hard to believe that such inner turmoil could be created from a few weeks spent with a boy. I often find myself moody, wanting to spend time alone. On occasion I meet up with my summer friends for a few moments of hilarity, but don't feel as though my temperamental disposition offers much to the gathering. It is so much work hiding my wounded spirit from my lively chums. It is summertime—the season of fun; time for frolicking on sandy beaches, splashing carefree in the ocean, exchanging stories over ice cream, congregating around the dancing flames of a bonfire as the sun fades behind the horizon—I in no way want to destroy that evanescent rush for anyone.

Instead, more and more, I find myself spending the unoccupied hours of my day with my ever-waiting companion, the sea. It is always there, available, only feet away from anywhere I am—calling me to its shore. As though sensing my angst, its thundering waves swell from the distance, aspiring to swallow up my sorrow. And so I let it—I let the relentless sound of the pounding surf and the tepid, salty, ever-reaching tide calm my vexing spirit and soothe my wounded pride.

If my eyes aren't busy scanning the generous expanse before me, they sort through the pale granules of sand that crumble between my toes as I amble down the shoreline. Periodically, something catches my attention and I reach down and scoop it up, deciding whether it is a shell worth adding to my compilation.

On this particular afternoon, no collection-worthy shells cross my path, but something else captures my attention as I stare at the endless, distant horizon. An object, black and round, peeks above the relatively calm surface of the sea. I am instantly elated—this time it doesn't disappear as before. Quickly, I grab the small bag that is strung over my shoulder and pull out my binoculars. It takes me a second to focus. Now more objects have risen above the surrounding ripples of water. I squint my eyes in concentration—two black, flattened forelimbs accompany what I can now tell is a head. *Yes! I know what this one is!* I peruse my mind, recalling the marine life of the Atlantic I've been recently researching. Just as the answer comes to me, a teardrop-shaped body arises from the midst to join the other body parts. The absence of a checkered shell confirms my notion. I feel a ripple of excitement flow through my body as I watch the large, grayish-black creature amble through the sluggish tides. A leatherback sea turtle. *This is so cool!*

Immediately, I want to share this experience—with Tristan. Like a knife to the chest, the memory of my recently unrequited love comes flooding back to me. In a split second, my elation of discovering the turtle is replaced with dejection. The hurt I've been struggling with for the past few days resurfaces with a vengeance. *Geez, this really sucks!*

With some effort, I work to push the thought of the green-eyed, golden-haired boy from the forefront of my mind. Suddenly, I resent him for looking so dang good. If only there was something unappealing about him, it would make it so much easier to get over him. If only his eyes weren't so beguiling. If only his facial features weren't so perfect and his hair so sexy, making me want to run my fingers through it. If only his physique wasn't so impeccably formed and athletic. If only his deep, smooth voice didn't take my breath away each time he spoke to me. Then maybe—maybe this wouldn't be quite as hard. My shoulders slump in defeat. I shake my head to free my thoughts. Readjusting my binoculars, I center my focus back on the leatherback, making a mental note to report the sighting to the authorities—what if there are eggs in the nearby vicinity that need to be protected? I study its strong, muscular form lumbering above the surface for a while longer, before it finally disappears again.

As I continue wandering down the shoreline, a type of down-heartedness sets in. For some unexplainable reason I feel homesick. Even though my family is all here with me in Watch Hill, something is tugging at me, making me want to go back to the safety of my home, back in Philadelphia. I miss Lucy. I recall her wavy, blond hair and warm, brown eyes and the way she always has my back. We'd shared so much together over the years, most of it good, but sometimes disappointments too. Either way, I felt like I could always count on her.

Unwittingly, a smile begins to form on my lips as I recollect the time our freshman year that I was bound and determined to try out for the swim team. I had never been a swimmer, but for some reason, I thought I needed to try something new my first year of high school. I needed a challenge, needed to overcome an obstacle, or some crazy notion like that.

"You are doing what?" Lucy's brown eyes regarded me incredulously as I told her the news. "Do you even know how to swim?"

"Well, I'm in good shape from running, so I think I can do it. I will just apply the same concept for endurance training on land to the water. I can do this."

Lucy's eyes were round. "Okay." She exhaled the word slowly, as if in disbelief.

A week later, Lucy found me staring dejectedly at the bulletin board outside of the girl's locker room. My name wasn't included on the list. I felt her presence as she sided up next to me. For a few moments no one said a word.

"I didn't make the team."

Lucy's arm slid around my shoulder, and I leaned into her briefly. "I'm sorry," she spoke softly. Quiet surrounded us momentarily before she spoke again. "Hey, why don't you come over for a while this afternoon? I just got a new iTunes card. We can download some songs."

While we were sitting on her bed drinking strawberry milk-shakes that she had talked her mom into picking up on the drive home, she suddenly tossed a pillow at me. "Girl, I love you, but the swim team, what were you thinking? Do you not even remember that you can't swim?"

In spite of everything, I couldn't help but smile. She was so right. What was I trying to prove?

"You are a superstar track runner—the envy of all your competition. You need to stick to that." She tucked a wisp of wavy, blond hair behind her ear before she continued. "Why does this give me a feeling of déjà vu? Do you remember back at summer camp when we were nine? Remember how you were so determined to pass the advanced swimming test so you could swim out past the deep raft?"

I squinted my eyes and shook my head in recollection.

"You must have tried three times before you finally accepted that you weren't going to be able to do it. You were so upset."

"And as I recall, you stayed inside the beginners ropes with me the entire week, even though you passed the test easily." I glanced over at my best friend who was seated only feet from me, hoping my look was conveying the appreciation that I felt for her unwavering friendship.

"That was no big deal; the water slides were better inside the front ropes anyway." *But not nearly as fun as the deep raft with the diving board that you missed out on all week.*

"You're a good friend, Lucy."

She shrugged her shoulders and began twirling her hair into a bun as she glanced away. "No big deal, nothing you wouldn't have done for me. By the way, you need to give up on your obsession of swimming. Why do you have these bouts of sudden determination to be a swimmer anyway? You know it's not your thing."

I chuckled then, "You know, I'm not sure." Unexpectedly, my giggling escalated, eventually evolving into snorting laughter. Before long, Lucy had joined in, and we both laughed until we had tears in our eyes. Soon I was feeling so much better.

Even now, I find myself laughing out loud at the memory. Momentarily, I glance up and down the shoreline making sure the coast is clear. I imagine the picture I'm presenting might seem rather odd—a solitary girl rambling aimlessly along the lakeshore, lost in thought, laughing as I go.

On a whim, I pick up a rock and give it a toss toward the liquid, blue, fading skyline. Not expecting any results, I am surprised when the flattened object skips playfully, momentarily ruffling the tranquil surface of the sea. *Hey, not bad. Maybe Tristan wasn't as talented as I thought.* I try it another time with no outcome. Now I am determined—three, four more times. Still nothing. Then, finally on my fifth try, skip . . . skip . . . skip. *Yes.* Once again I smile, and then decide it's probably about time to head back to the summer cottage.

That night I dream again. As warmth envelops my body, I recognize this place right away. Immediately the hazy cloud of liquid that surrounds me feels familiar. I easily relax into its comforting temperateness. Stretching my limbs, I allow them to move effortlessly through the safety of this underground realm which makes up the sea. The gentle pressure from the encircling water caresses my form, and it feels so mollifying. I submit myself to the moderate current that flows around me. Coursing on and on, I part the space in front of me fluently with just a simple stroke of my reaching arms.

Presently, just ahead of me through the dimly lit water, I notice a darkened form. It too is swimming—surging on through the liquid deep without effort. Suddenly, I have an inherent need to reach this enigmatic figure. The more I try, the more it is always just out of reach, just beyond the grasp of my seeking fingertips. Who is this being? Why can't I reach it, touch it? Instantly, my mind becomes completely preoccupied with this notion, and I keep striving to find an answer. On and on I swim, always just short of the grasp of this new need that is consuming me. Now the caressing that placated my frame is being replaced with an ache. Just when I think I cannot stand another minute of this refutation, the configuration turns its head to gaze back in my direction. Helplessly, I am paralyzed, my whole body melting into liquid as sea green eyes penetrate through my own.

The next morning when I wake in the confines of my own room, I am somewhat troubled. As I clear my mind from the sluggishness of sleep, thoughts of the previous night's dream and my current standing with Tristan come flooding in. Groaning, I pull the covers over my head. I don't want to get up.

My hiatus is short-lived, however, as Josh and Jake come bursting in my room—their little nine-year-old bodies besieging my bed with no thoughts as to what space I might be occupying beneath my covering.

"Hey . . . ouch! Watch where you are jumping." I peel the layers of protective wrapping down from my head, revealing blond, flyaway hair.

Two sandy blond heads and two pairs of eyes are eagerly regarding me.

"We need breakfast," Jake says.

"Yeah, we need breakfast," Josh echoes.

"Where are Mom and Dad?" I am not keen on the idea of getting out of bed.

"Dad is on the computer. Mom left in the car."

"What do you mean Mom left in the car? Did she go to the store?" I glance at the clock on my nightstand—8:30 a.m. It's too early for a trip to the store. "Oh, all right." I drag myself out of bed and pad into the kitchen.

Two hours pass, and finally I notice Dad taking a break from his computer and phone. He is pulling a carton of juice out of the refrigerator.

"Where's Mom?" I ask.

"Not sure." His answer is complacent.

"I mean did she say she was going to the store or had a hair appointment or something like that?"

"Like I said, I'm not sure. She didn't really say. Why don't you call her cell phone and ask her yourself?" He rakes his hand through his dark brown hair, obviously irritated.

I don't reach Mom by phone, but before another hour passes, I hear the LaCrosse pulling into the gravel drive. When the door slams, my heart sinks. The rest of the afternoon unfolds in uncomfortable silence at the Kuiper household.

I am lying on my bed in the early evening leafing through a magazine when the distant rumble of voices makes me go very still. The sounds I hear coming from the upstairs suite are not pleasant. Mom's distraught vocalizations are resonating through the upper-level walkway, increasing in decibel as she descends the stairs. Dad's deep voice follows close behind. Impatience and anger are exhibited in his tone. I want to get up and shut my bedroom door, shut out their hostility from my mind. But I freeze in place instead.

Josh's and Jake's forms whiz past my room like a flash of lightning. The banging of their door as it closes leaves a reverberating echo.

"You never really change, Kevin. You always say you are going to change, but you never really do. I am so sick of it . . . sick of you."

"Well, guess what, I'm sick of you too," Dad retaliates, then mutters, "sick of your whining."

"What?"

"I said, get off my ass!"

"How can I get off your ass, when you're such an ass*hole*?" Mom's outraged voice is a precursor to the sound of shattering glass against the wall.

I cringe inwardly and mouth a little prayer.

"When are you going to grow up and stop throwing things, Lisa?"

"Maybe when you grow up and stop being married to your work."

"This again." Dad's voice is forced, like he's speaking through gritted teeth. "You know maybe I wouldn't be so *married* to my work if you didn't spend so much time flirting with the boy's soccer coach."

Silence.

"Yeah, don't think I don't notice the way you are always hanging around talking to him all the time. Before the games, after the games. Before practice, after practice. I can't make you smile any more, but you sure laugh at everything he says. It's always, 'Michael does such a good job with the boys'. 'Michael showed me how to check my oil when the engine light came on today'. "

"What do you know about the boys' games or practices or anything else? You're hardly ever there. How many games did you make last year? Five if you're lucky. And don't say anything bad about Michael. He's never been anything but nice. You should be thankful a positive male role model is spending time with Josh and Jake. You sure don't." Mom's tenor is shaken; frustration and hurt are evident.

"Oh nice . . . talk him up some more. What . . . are you sleeping with him?" *I don't want to hear this. I really don't want to hear this.*

"You know, why don't you ask your secretary, Melissa? I'll bet she knows all about sleeping with someone."

"You *little* bitch!"

The sound of a door slamming ricochets off the vaulted ceiling in the great room, before a momentary hush falls over our summer cottage. Then the subtle click of the television being turned on interrupts the quiet. Soon an anchorman's voice fills the air. *Dad must be the one left in the living room.*

I'm not sure how much time passes before I hear movement again, some type of commotion in the other room. This time it is closer, coming from the kitchen.

"Where are you going?" Dad sounds annoyed.

"I'm leaving." I can't believe the words coming out of my own mother's mouth. Mom doesn't leave. Suddenly I feel panicked. Then I hear the muted sound of footsteps approaching.

Josh and Jake run into the hallway and into the arms of my mom. "I'm going back to Philadelphia for a while, but I'll call you every day and I'll be back." *Be back? Be back when?*

The muffled cries of two nine-year-old boys pressing their faces into their mom's chest follows. Every part of my body goes rigid.

Soon my mom's tearstained but resolute face appears in my doorway. "I'm sure you've heard."

I attempt a nod.

She reaches for me, attempting to give me a hug. "Good-bye, Bethany. I love you. I'll be back. I'll call. Call me."

I swallow a lump in my throat. Jaw set, fists clenched at my side, I don't move a muscle.

In the surrounding quiet, I strain to hear the sound of the car ignition rolling over. So that's it, that quickly she's leaving? *NO.* No, she hasn't thought this through, maybe if I ask her to stay—On instinct I bolt out of bed and run through the side entrance of our blue sided cottage. When I reach the gravel drive, all that greets me is the disintegrating trail of fumes from the LaCrosse's exhaust.

Feeling numb, I close my eyes and sink dejectedly onto one of the steps on the cement porch. My first impulse is to text Lucy. Thankfully, my phone is with me, tucked into my front pocket, because for now, I'm too stunned to move.

My mom and dad had a big fight. Mom just left. (send.)

With an enormous amount of relief, I feel a vibration in my hand almost immediately.

(unlock) Left for where?

Philadelphia *(send)*

(unlock) I'm soooo sorry!

I'm scared. Keep praying! *(send)*

What now? Dad usually comes and goes as he pleases—where does this leave me? Am I responsible for Josh and Jake now? I don't cook; who cooks now? What if Dad decides he needs to go back to Philadelphia too, for business? Does this mean the end for our family? Will we all have to move out of our house I grew up in? I'm going to college anyway, but what about the twins?

The undulating thoughts are overpowering.

Maybe she'll change her mind. Any moment the LaCrosse is going to pull back into the drive. She has never really been apart from us for very long. She's going to rethink things through while she's driving down the highway and realize she can't do this. She's going to come back any minute now.

Staring at the gravel in front of my feet, I wait. And wait. Finally, it becomes apparent she isn't *going* to return. I try her cell phone, but all I get is voicemail.

Dolefully, I go back into the cottage. Josh and Jake are wrapped in a blanket nestled close to one another watching a movie in the great room. Dad is on his computer, staring intently at the screen. Already back to work, as if nothing ever happened.

Suddenly I am overwhelmed.

I just want to get out of here. I need to run. I exit through the side door, leaving the screen door to slam behind me. As I'm heading toward the shoreline, somewhere in the back of my mind it occurs to me that I am shoeless, but I just don't care. When I hit the sand, I begin running with all my might alongside the crashing waves of the ocean. I want to escape the pain, the agony of *everything!*

I am one hundred feet up the coast before I feel the first sting of liquid seep from my eye. The tide flows over my bare feet as I run, even as the tears flow down my cheeks. I sprint along the meandering seashore as daylight fades to dusk, hoping that sheer speed will erase the recent memory of all that has just happened. But even my lightning quick pace can't quite conceal all the hurt I've been assaulted with lately. The tears continue to come, eventually turning into sobs. Blinded by my relentless weeping, I become oblivious to my surroundings. Still I run. As I round a bend in the winding landscape of the shoreline, unexpectedly, breathlessly, I collide into a lean, muscular chest.

Stunned and frightened, I almost trip backwards, but immediately, strong hands reach out to steady me. In a fraction of a second, recognition sets in, and I realize in horror that it's the *last* person I want to see right now. The look of shock and concern that gazes down at me belongs to Tristan. *Oh no, oh no, oh no.* I shake my head.

I try to pull away, but he holds me firmly in place. "Bethany . . . Bethany, what is wrong?"

I can't speak. The sobbing continues and all I can think is—*this can't be happening right now! This can't be him seeing me like this right now!* I look away, trying to control my tears. When I don't answer, he wraps his arms around me and gently pulls me to his chest. *No!* He smells so good, like fresh soap and salt mixed together. It's intoxicating. His hands begin to stroke my back and my hair as he holds me fitted against him. And I can't help it—it feels so good. I surrender myself to his comforting touch. I need this so bad right now.

Finally, my tears subside and he eases me away. Realizing I must look like a mess, I motion to the water, and he nods his head faintly. Walking down to the ocean's edge, I bend down and scoop up some of the emerging tide to wash my face. When it is cleansed to my satisfaction, I hesitate, knowing that when I turn around I'm going to have to face Tristan's empathetic eyes. I don't want to come undone, *again.*

But I don't have to turn around. While I am deliberating, Tristan soundlessly approaches me. Strong arms slowly turn me to face him.

"What's the matter?" His voice is soft.

I sigh. How much do I want to share with him? After all, he is a big part of my problem too. "It's my parents. They had a big fight today. My mom left."

"Come here." He keeps one arm wrapped around my shoulders as he leads me to a dry spot in the beach. "Let's sit. I think you need to talk."

His arm rests lightly across my back, hand curved onto my shirtsleeve protectively as we sit cushioned on a blanket of sand. In spite of everything we've been through, all the hurt I've undergone from his changing dispositions, I feel so safe right now with him here by my side. I find myself easily opening up about the upheaval and insecurities of my home life. He listens intently, occasionally offering bits of counsel and reaffirmation. It is all very cathartic. The more I talk, the more comfortable I become in his presence. Suddenly I have an overwhelming need to know something from him, but I'm too timid to ask. Still, there are some answers I really *want* from him. I clear my throat, then stop.

He squeezes my shoulder. "What?"

I take a deep breath. *How do I say this?* "There is this boy . . . that I like. And . . ."

"And . . . ?"

"And he confuses me. Sometimes it seems like he is interested in me too. But then other times he's so cold and distant, like he doesn't know I exist." Tristan removes his hand from my shoulder and goes very still. My heart plummets. More pain.

Finally, he sighs. He is sitting knees bent, arms resting across them, staring out at the ocean. "Well, I think that boy should be shot—made to walk the plank."

I glance over at him. How should I take *that* answer? He looks back and smiles. My heart rate accelerates. Suddenly, his eyes brighten as if an idea has just occurred to him. "How would you like to get away for a day? I really think you could use some fun."

"I'm listening."

"There is place I love to go to . . . an island. How would you like to go there with me for the day? My boat isn't done yet, but I could get another one."

How could I say no to him? In spite of everything, there is no one else I would rather spend the day with. "Okay, sure."

"Tomorrow?"

Tomorrow? What did tomorrow hold? Would I have to watch the twins? Go to the grocery store? Attempt to cook dinner? I make a decision. "Tomorrow works fine."

His green eyes dance in response." Meet me at Watch Hill Boatyard at 10:00 a.m."

Chapter Eleven

When I arrive back at the cottage, Dad is waiting for me at the door. *This is a surprise.*

"You okay?" He seems uncomfortable.

"I'm fine." My mind is going a million miles a minute. Dad is still focused on the earlier commotion of the evening, but now I have something else that is consuming my mind. Tristan. And what it's going to be like spending a whole day alone with him tomorrow on some island. To say I have butterflies in my stomach would be an understatement. "I just went running."

"Without your running shoes?"

"Barefoot running is popular now." Dad seems rather subdued, and while I have him in this mood, I decide to continue. "I've made plans for pretty much the whole day tomorrow with friends." *One friend actually. One drop-dead gorgeous friend of the opposite sex.* "Is that okay?"

He studies me for a moment. " Okay." It occurs to me the—then looks so tired. Worn. Older.

It still hurts that my mom left—the unknown of what will happen to our family now is still unnerving. But my prospective date with Tristan is devouring my thoughts, softening the blow.

I awaken in the middle of the night, and elation surges through my veins as I remember how I'm going to spend my day. After I lie in bed for some time without being able drift back to sleep, I get up and quietly retreat to the front porch. A cool breeze flows through the screen, gently caressing the skin on my bare arms. I wrap myself in a hug, soothing away the goose bumps that have surfaced. In the distance I can see the ocean. I watch, mesmerized, as the waves placidly roll to shore. It is calming and exciting at the same time. The moon reflects on the darkened water, creating a path to nowhere—or somewhere? The island that I will be accompanying Tristan to in less than seven hours?

A warming sensation sweeps through my body as I hear a loud splash in the water, breaking the monotony of the rolling tide. Once again I find myself willing Tristan to emerge from the depths. But of course, he doesn't. Once again I chide myself for being so whimsical and silly. If he only knew I had these recurrent notions of him arising from the fathomless abyss, godlike, taking me in his arms.

The next morning I dress in jean shorts and a sleeveless, blousey top. Leaving my hair long, I take a few strands and twist them together, barretting them away from my face. After applying some mascara and ChapStick, I head for the door.

I arrive at Watch Hill Boatyard at promptly 10:00 a.m. There is no sign of Tristan. I wait five minutes. Five minutes feels like five hours—still no sign of him. I am getting a bad feeling in the pit of my stomach when I notice his athletic form approaching me from a distant dock. He smiles and I lose my breath, then he waves me over.

He studies me for a moment. "How *are* you today?"

I smile sheepishly. "Better, thanks."

He leads me to a shiny, newer-looking, fiberglass teal and white speedboat. It's gorgeous. "Well, this is ours for the day. I know it doesn't hold the charm of my *wooden* boat, but I think we can get by."

I step into the passenger front seat and wait as he easily pushes us off from the docks. The boat motor hums softly as we troll through the bay area, leading us toward the open water. Tristan looks over at me and bites his lip. For a brief moment a conflicted expression crosses over his perfect features. Then it disappears, and he smiles.

I watch him back, my heart hammering in my chest. He reaches over, tweaks his finger lightly on my nose, and then turns back to face the front of the boat. We enter the wide, blue expanse of ocean, and he increases our speed, causing the engine to roar.

We are skimming the surface of the blue, glistening water at breakneck speed, our hair whipping through the air. The sun shines down generously, warming my skin. The boat motor is loud, leaving little room for conversation. But we don't have to talk in order for me to understand there is something between us, something electrical, drawing us together. It's in the occasional look he sends my way as we ride along. It's in the way I hold his gaze when he does, because I can't bring myself to turn away. Every inch of my body is tingling. This whole experience is so new to me, I can't fathom the unexpected rush that it is bringing.

Once, as we are riding along, I intend to steal only a glance in his direction—instead, unwittingly, I find it hard to peel my eyes away. I am mesmerized by his handsome profile, his perfectly sculpted cheekbones, his blond hair that is disheveled in the wind.

He catches me looking, gives me a wink, and keeps driving. *Like he knows. Like he knows he's hopelessly good-looking and realizes I can't keep my eyes off him, and he's okay with it. Like he understands.* He is so confidently sexy. My heart melts as I turn my head away, blushing.

Eventually, he leans in my direction slightly and places one of his hands on my arm to gather my attention. He doesn't even try to speak over the din of the motor; instead, he points to something in the distance. My vision is drawn to a body of land that has emerged from the water. I shake my head back at him to let him know I get it. This must be his island.

Right away, I am drawn to its splendor. As we approach the tree-lined, sandy shoreline, he cuts the engine. Suddenly, everything seems so quiet. The natural dwelling looks uninhabited. It's just us then. The butterflies in my stomach resume their fluttering.

"Well, what do you think?" His voice breaks through the stillness.

"I think I like it."

"Yeah? I think I like it too." He beaches the boat and I climb out. Grabbing a duffle bag, he throws it over his shoulder and walks around the side of the boat to join me. "Lunch." He points to the bag.

"Okay." I am breathlessly nervous. "Well, where to?"

"I'll show you. I know the perfect spot on this island." As we begin strolling through the warm sand, he reaches over and takes my hand in his. I inhale softly—immediately liking the way it feels. Sensing this, he gives my fingers a little squeeze. We continue walking, away from the beach, over a section of rocky terrain, through a sparsely wooded area. Finally, we round a corner, eventually stepping into a secluded cove. It is a picture out of a postcard. The shoreline is covered in pale, almost white, sand. The water that eases onto shore is a sparkling turquoise. I glance around, taking in my surroundings—half expecting to discover straw huts and coconut trees. I have to remind myself that I'm still in Rhode Island.

Tristan pulls a blanket out of the bag and we position it in the sand, only feet from the reaching tide. We sit down side by side, our bare arms periodically coming in contact with one another from the slightest movement. Each touch is electrifying. He asks me how we made it through the first night of my mom being gone. I ask him how his boat is coming along. We talk about the marina and about some of the humorous characters that patronize it. Sometimes we sit quietly, each lost in our own thoughts, staring at the magnificent display of turquoise before us.

It's during those times that I'm afraid he can hear the thundering sound of my heart in my chest. But he never lets on if he does.

As we are sitting only inches apart, silence surrounding us, Tristan turns to face me. Everything becomes still. I suck in a breath. I know he wants me to turn to face him too. I can't move. He takes one of his fingers and traces my cheekbone down to my jaw. "You're *so* pretty." His voice is just a whisper. *What? Really?*

I slowly turn to face him, then. I try to speak, but my voice is cracked. Clearing my throat, I try again. "Really?"

His green eyes pierce my own blue. He shakes his head. "Geez Bethany, you really don't know, do you?" *Know what?* "You are so beautiful and you don't even know it." He seems dumbfounded. My heart is pounding. My mind is spinning so fast with this newest revelation I can hardly keep up. He closes his eyes momentarily and opens them again. "You are too good to be true. You are intoxicating." His last statement is just a whisper.

I am overwhelmed. I had never really thought of myself as pretty—not really ugly either, but *beautiful?* Never in a million years had I imagined a boy like Tristan calling me beautiful, *intoxicating?* I am so inexperienced at all of this. What do I say back?

"I've always loved your long, blond hair," he continues. *Always?* He studies me with an intense gaze, and I get the feeling something is going to happen, got to happen, to ease this new transfixing tension between us. I should say something, anything. But I'm lost in the spell of his green eyes. My heart is pounding.

Seconds pass. Finally he leans slowly toward me and gently kisses my lips. At first I am paralyzed with the newness of the feeling. Then instinctively, I begin to kiss him back. A sensation spreads throughout my being like nothing I've ever experienced before. I feel utterly connected to him. The kiss continues, and the gentleness is replaced with something else, a type of urgency.

Suddenly, Tristan pulls away, seemingly stunned. Right away he shakes his head and apologizes. *Don't. Please, don't be sorry about this, about us.* I work hard to recover my breath. He gets up and walks away from me to the water's edge. He looks pissed.

I follow him, my whole body trembling. What is going on? He won't look at me.

"Bethany . . ." He takes a deep breath. "I can't do this . . ." *What? No! I can't do this either!*

"What . . . what do you mean?"

"I can't be with you, have a relationship with you." His voice is resolved. Abruptly, *I* am pissed too.

"Well, you are not the only one, Tristan. You're not the only one who can't do this. I can't play these stupid games with you anymore." At first my voice sounds shaky, a little breathless. Fueled by anger, determinedness soon takes over. "I'm really tired of you leading me on and then, minutes later, dropping me flat. It's all so cold." I begin walking in the direction of the boat, hoping that I remember how to get back to it. I don't want to endure the humiliating task of having to ask him the way. I keep walking, wanting to get away, *far* away from him. Infuriation quickly turns to devastation, and I have to fight back tears. *Oh no! Not now!*

I hear the sound of hurried footsteps behind me. Soon, Tristan reaches me and turns me around to face him. *What now?* His jaw is set. The look in his eyes is so intense, it's almost frightening. He looks at me without saying anything. Finally he exhales, looking defeated.

"Bethany, there is something I have to tell you . . ." He stops, like it's too hard for him to continue. He studies me momentarily, his expression almost pained. I wait patiently for him to finish. "There is something I have to tell you about myself, and I don't think you are going to want to hear it." He clenches his jaw again, looking so troubled and serious. Unexpectedly, I am overcome with his beauty, even in all of his intensity.

He exhales again, looking right at me as if to determine if I'm ready—ready to hear whatever it is he is about to say. My gaze does not waver. "I shouldn't be here with you right now . . . shouldn't be around you at all." He kicks a small piece of driftwood away in frustration. "God knows I tried to stay away." He stops, as if it is all too much—turns his head away.

Now it's my turn.

I reach out to gently touch his arm. "What is it, Tristan? Whatever it is, *please* tell me." My voice is soft.

He looks up at me then and takes a deep breath, looking resigned. "I'm not from around here really. Well, kind of, but not like you think—not from Watch Hill, actually." My heart is beating rapidly. What is he about to tell me? Whatever it is, I can't imagine that I won't be able to handle it. I brace myself for whatever is coming.

"I've been coming to Watch Hill ever since I was a little boy. When I first came here, I met this little girl with blond hair who was vacationing here with her family. We spent a lot of time together on the beach. Every day that she was here, really." He pauses and clears his throat. "I became pretty infatuated with her . . . kept hoping every summer that she would come back. It seemed like a pipe dream. She was probably never going to return, but I couldn't let go of it. And now . . . she's here . . . finally."

My mind is whirling. What is he trying to tell me? Is there someone else? Then why does he keep having these run-ins with me? Why did he just kiss me?

"Who is she?" My voice sounds bitter. His head snaps up quickly, and he looks me directly in the eye.

"Bethany . . . it's you." I am instantly confused. It can't be; I would remember coming here.

"How can it be? I don't remember vacationing here when I was little."

"It *is* you. I can't really explain it in your terms but I'm 100 percent sure it's you." I am instantly relieved. I desperately *want* it to be me.

"Soooo . . . I really don't see the problem then." I am still bewildered.

Tristan takes a deep breath and closes his eyes as if it's hard for him to continue. He looks so scared, almost as if he might cry. *What? What is this . . . what is going on?* I just want to take him in my arms and tell him it's going to be okay. Whatever it is, it's okay with me—really—I can handle it.

"Before I tell you this, I just want you to know, when you want to leave . . . *if* you want to leave the island right away, I will take you back—safely. So, don't ever be scared, okay?" *Scared?* I begin to feel a little nervous, but only slightly. The only thing I'm really scared of is that he doesn't feel the same way about me as I feel about him. "When I say I don't live here, I mean *here* on land." He pauses again, looking straight at me. "I live in the water."

What? "What?" I am completely confused; there is something I'm missing. I'm quite sure it has something to do with my inexperience—there is some hidden meaning here that I am just not getting. I am embarrassed to reveal my ignorance on the matter. Finally, I continue. "I don't get what you mean."

His beautiful face looks solemn. "I *mean* that I am not a human like you, Bethany. I don't live on land, I live in the *water*." He glowers at me unwaveringly, waiting for my reaction.

I turn away from him for a second or two, then whirl back to face his green, piercing eyes. "Is this your idea of a cruel joke? Because if you don't like me, just tell me. You don't have to go to such lengths to make a fool out of me. I may be naïve, but I won't get played *that* easy. You'll have to get your kicks somewhere else . . ."

Tristan quickly bridges the gap between us and grabs me by the arms. "I know how this seems to you, but I would never play you, Bethany. Oh Geez . . ." He lets go of my arms as he puts his face in his hands, groaning. "I should have never told you this, but I wanted you to understand what I was fighting, why I was trying to stay away from you. I should have never fooled myself into believing that you would believe any of this."

I am stunned. My thoughts are in a complete jumble; I can't sort through anything. I feel like I have stepped into the twilight zone—nothing is real anymore. Everything has become faded and distant. The only the thing that does seem authentic is the green-eyed, magnificent boy standing in front of me. His voice is speaking to me, but I can't process what he is saying—all I can see is him. I continue to stare at him, speechless.

Finally, his voice breaks through my befuddlement, and I focus on what he is saying. "I know this seems incredible, but just watch . . . I couldn't do this if I was human . . ." His tone is desperate as he leaves my side. Ripping off his shirt and discarding it in the sand, Tristan runs into the turquoise blue water. Paralyzed, I watch his muscular back and the rear of his white shorts as he dives beneath the surface, disappearing from my sight.

Oh no! What is he going to do now? What is he trying to prove? Just like that, he is gone, and I am left alone with my thoughts.

Webbed feet. Discovering him swimming in the ocean, seemingly out of nowhere—how often would a human be actually doing that? Still they *could* be doing that, it's not impossible. My reoccurring dreams with him in the ocean. His keen familiarity with sea animals. I try to sort out my considerations. None of them are unexplainable from a human point of view, really. But they *could* steer one in the direction of what he is saying.

Fighting through the perplexity of the situation, I make a decision. I am *going* to believe him—the way I feel about him, I *have* to.

Seconds turn to minutes, and still Tristan is gone, swimming somewhere beneath the surface of the deep. *Okay, Tristan, I believe you. You can come back now.* All that answers my silent beseeching is the repetitious movement of the glistening waves.

My eyes begin darting in all directions, frequently returning to the infinite liquid landscape before me. Time slows to a standstill. A panicky feeling begins to overtake my limbs. Where is Tristan? I *want* to believe that what he is saying is true. At least I *think* I do. *Yes,* I do. But the logical part of me can't wrap my mind around the idea that he's been out in the water this long. It's not humanly possible. Not. Humanly. Possible. My head is swirling—anxiety increasing. What if the information he's disclosed to me isn't really true, though? What if he is out there somewhere—? He couldn't survive this long. *Geez, Tristan, where are you?*

I am quivering, entranced in my jumbled thoughts, when a dripping wet Tristan emerges from the lightly cascading waves in front of me. His green eyes lock onto mine, and I am frozen in place. He is not gasping for breath. There is no visible struggle for air. The indomitable look in his eye dares me to deny what I have just witnessed.

"I believe you." My voice is a whisper.

He studies me momentarily and begins advancing toward me slowly—relief instantly spreading across his features.

"I know it doesn't make sense. I know it doesn't seem possible, but I believe you."

"Really?" A tentative grin makes its way to his perfect lips, and my heart increases in tempo. He watches my face as if to read any doubts into my expression before eventually taking my hand and leading me back to our blanket. We sit down side by side. I am very conscious of the water dripping from his tanned skin, only inches from me. Finally, he sighs and looks in my direction.

"This all is a lot for you, isn't it?"

I nod my head.

"Are you scared . . . of me?"

I look over at him quickly. "No." I half breathe, half laugh. "No, I'm not scared of you. I just . . ." I hesitate, trying to collect my thoughts. "I just have a lot of questions."

"Ask them."

"So . . . I don't understand how it's really possible. I mean, is it just you?" I pause. "Are there more . . . um people, or whatever, like you?"

"To the human mind, it seems pretty impossible. But your mind is capable of understanding and doing much more than what you actually do. All you know is what you see right in front of you. There is a whole world that exists in the depths of the sea, but because it hasn't really been discovered—to you, it's not there." I watch him, listening intently, trying to process everything he is saying. He continues. "Over the years, occasionally people have spotted us. Some believe; others have turned us into myths."

Finally I interrupt. "Are you saying you're a mermaid, I mean, a merman then?"

Tristan laughs at that. "If that's what you want to call us. No, wait, that *is* what you want to call us. Mostly, we think of ourselves as the same as you, only we live in the water."

There is something else I want to ask him, but suddenly I feel shy. I don't know how to quite pose the question. Unwittingly, my face begins to heat up.

"You are blushing, Bethany; what is it?" His look is teasing, making it even more difficult to organize the words.

"So . . . are you the same as humans pretty much . . . I mean human boys . . . or do you have a tail . . . like when you go in the water?"

I can tell he is trying hard not to laugh. "No tail . . . if that answers your question." He looks me right in the eye. "We're . . . just . . . like . . . humans. Does that make you feel better?" *OMG, now I am really embarrassed.*

"Okay." I glance at the ground beside me. Finally, I look back up at him. Something about the way he is regarding me makes my pulse accelerate. I exhale quietly before I can continue. "How do you stay underwater so long?"

"Well, our DNA is very similar to humans, but we carry an enzyme that converts the chemical makeup of water so that is compatible with air and blood. It is cleansing to our systems. We actually *need* to breathe water to purify the toxins from our body—just like you need your liver and kidneys."

After he finishes telling me this, he becomes momentarily quiet, as if a thought has occurred to him, causing him distress. "The problem is . . . we're not supposed to expose ourselves to humans. Potentially there could be big trouble if we do." He sighs resignedly before looking up at me with a sheepish grin. "I guess I'm not doing very well in that area when it comes to you, am I?"

My heart soars as he reveals his inability to stay away from me, but there is something I have to know. "Is that why you don't come around me sometimes? Or . . ." I pause, feeling awkward. "Or act indifferent—" *cold.* "—toward me sometimes?"

He faces the ground, not looking at me. "Yeah, that's why." His answer is more or less muttered, and I immediately get the feeling that it is a topic he doesn't want to discuss. I really want him to expound on that, but I'm not willing to press it.

Suddenly it occurs to me that I'm famished. With all the commotion, we haven't taken time to eat. "That lunch you brought sounds pretty good right now."

His eyes light up. "You are right, I'm starved." He gathers the duffle bag and pulls out an assortment of fried chicken, grapes, and cheeses. Laying out the food on plates in front of us, he looks at me and smiles. "Eat up."

I smile back at him and hold his gaze. "I could get used to this."

"What?"

"The good lunches you make."

"Oh." He shakes his head as if it is no big deal and chuckles.

As we are eating, the memory of an earlier lunch crosses my mind, and I burst into laughter.

"What is it?" Tristan eyes me suspiciously.

"I think I finally understand why you looked so sick that day at the marina when you saw me eating seafood."

Immediately, he scrunches up his nose. "For us, that's practically cannibalism."

After we eat our lunch, he takes me by the hand, pulling me up off the blanket. "Let's walk."

We stroll along the shoreline, allowing the growing tide to wash over our feet in a soothing fashion. The sun transitorily hides behind a cloud, leaving a slight chill in the air and I shiver briefly. Noticing this, Tristan reaches over and puts his arm around me.

"How are you doing with all of this?"

"I'm okay." *Better than okay.* Being here with him like this is *way* better than okay.

We stop walking, and both turn to face each other. His green eyes penetrate my own. His lips are so close. "You sure?" His voice is barely audible.

I nod. I can't speak. I can barely breathe. He leans towards me slowly and then kisses me for the second time that day—for the second time ever. So much has passed between us since that first kiss—a lifetime of revelations and commitments. My body becomes liquid. He pulls me to his chest and I find myself pressing into his damp body. His wet shorts are getting me wet too, but I don't even care. Our kiss deepens, the intensity of it a testimony to the bond that's been created that day.

Finally, he pushes gently away from me. "Bethany." He speaks my name reverently as he pulls my head to his chest. I can hear his heart pounding. I wrap my arms around him, holding on tightly. I never want to let go. "Bethany, baby." His voice is barely audible as he whispers into my hair. Did I hear him right? *Oh . . . wow . . . , I like the way that sounds.* We stay that way for a lot of minutes. I want to stay that way for an eternity.

Reluctantly, we separate and head back to the boat. The ride back is subdued, our ensuing glances holding a new understanding of each other. The reverberation of the motor stills as we are only yards from the Watch Hill Boatyard docks. The realization that we have to part soon fills me with an unspoken dread. Tristan's voice breaks through the newfangled silence that surrounds us.

"Well, after all you learned about me today, one question remains. Are you going to love me or leave me?" His smile makes my heart rate accelerate. This playful side to him is so charming. He is simply breathtakingly beautiful to look at.

I laugh. "Love you." *Definitely!*

He winks at me. "Good answer."

I mull over his question as I walk away from him, heading back to my summer cottage. Certainty grips every part of my being. It doesn't matter to me if he resides in the depths of the ocean, or if he resides in a distant galaxy, or if he resides directly across the street. Regardless of those menial details, regardless of anything at all—the realization hits me, I am completely in *love* with Tristan Alexander.

Chapter Twelve

I hardly recognize the girl that is staring at me in the mirror the following morning. Her hair is a little more sunstreaked. Her cheeks are an enhanced hue of pink. Her eyes are a vibrant shade of blue. *Were my eyes ever that blue before?* She is radiant from the inside out. I can't restrain the smile that lights up my face as I recall everything that happened less than twenty-four hours before. Tristan Alexander. *Geez, even his name drives me crazy.* Being on the island with him. Kissing him. *Kissing him!* I get chills all over. *Oh . . . my gosh, that was the best thing ever!* He is the best thing ever. The way he looked at me, the way he held me in his arms. *I love, love, love his sexy smile!* I bite my lip and wrap myself in a hug—remembering. I feel warm all over.

Then, my thoughts shift slightly, and my body stills. Tristan Alexander lives in the sea. *Tristan Alexander lives in the sea!* An electric thrill courses through my body. This is so hard to believe. My brain can barely wrap around the thought. I want to push the idea to the back of my mind. It shouldn't really matter—it *doesn't* really matter. But there it is, making its presence known with a vengeance—shocking me with each renewed jolt of memory. I am the only one he's revealed this significant information to. At least I *think* I am the only one—only girl. Yes, I'm sure I am. Who would go around telling people something like that? Word would spread too quickly. I have to believe I'm the only one who knows. Goose bumps resurface. He must really like me to confide in me like that!

I want to text Lucy. In my mind I play out a thousand different ways that I can tell her the news. In the end I realize there is very little about Tristan that I am going to be able to share with her. For the first time ever, our relationship is going to be divided by a secret. I decide to send her a generic text.

So I really liked my date I went on yesterday! *(send)*

It's not long before I hear back.

(unlock) OOOh. Tell me more! What is his name?

Tristan *(send)*

Even texting his name gives me chills.

I had received a text from Kate the night before, after my island excursion. Now we are meeting in town for breakfast before she has to go to her babysitting job for the day. I ride my bike into town, reveling in the feel of the wind blowing against my face. Taking a calming breath, I prepare to walk into Bruna's Café. Will it be written all over my face? This new love-rush that I'm experiencing, will it be evident to Kate? Will I be able to evade the myriads of questions that she will assault me with if she figures it out?

"Bethany, Bethany." I hear my name being called the minute I walk through the door. "Over here." I turn to the sound of the voice and see Kate waving enthusiastically at me. Her chestnut hair is pulled into her famous, snug ponytail, causing her brown eyes to explode with animation. When I reach the booth she is sitting at, she pauses momentarily, perusing my face. *Oh no, here we go.* "You look great. Did you do something different?" She continues to study me.

"Not really." Well, let's see, since I saw you last—I went on a hot date to a secluded island, kissed a boy, fell in love—fell in love with boy who lives in the *sea*.

"Well, you look great. Sit down."

I slide into the seat across from Kate. "You are looking pretty chipper yourself for this early in the morning."

Kate smiles at that and bites her lip reflectively. "Yeah, I had a fun night last night. A bunch of us went over to Jonathan's. Where were you? I texted you."

I evade her question. "I didn't get your text until late. So who all was there?"

She taps out her nervous energy on the table with her fingers as she talks. "Lots of people. I swear half of Watch Hill. Jonathan, of course, and Nick."

"Emily?" I watch her face.

"No, not Emily."

We make our requests to the food attendant, and soon our steaming hot short-order meals are staring up at us. I have no appetite. With much effort I stab some eggs with my fork and shove them into my mouth. I glance at Kate from across the table. She is futilely pushing her hashed brown potatoes around on her plate. Apparently breakfast wasn't such a good idea for either of us today.

Kate barely touches her food, chatting spiritedly about the previous night's events at Jonathan's instead. I want to share about my island adventure with Tristan, but am afraid everything I say might reveal too much information about him. I don't want to betray his confidence in me—so I say nothing.

We are still picking at our food and continuing our conversation when Kate's vibrant chattering quiets. Glancing around the homey café interior, I seek out the cause of her sudden change in temperament. *Ah, Nick.* Before I have time to get a glimpse of the expression on Kate's face, Nick is at our table.

"Hi, girls." His brown eyes are warm, glancing at me briefly before they rest on Kate's. "You're up early."

Kate blushes. I smile to myself—how quickly Kate transforms. "You too. You're up early too." Her voice is subdued. A look passes between them. Well, any doubts I had about them earlier are quickly dissipating. There is definitely *something* going on. Nick slides into the booth next to Kate. Kate doesn't move an inch, allowing them to be wedged in snugly together.

I have finally finished poking at my food and am about to excuse myself from the intimacy of their conversation when Nick jumps up. "I gotta go. I promised my dad I'd help him move some stuff today. We're cleaning out our storage shed."

Soon after he leaves, Kate and I exit the building too. We are ambling down the sidewalks of Bay Street, watching as one by one, the store owners are emerging from their business interiors to unlock their front doors. The sun shines its approval on the freshness of the morning as the nocturnal shadows are beginning to recede into the street-lined shops . The charm of the tourist town is awakening. I am lost in the newness of the day, the newness of my thoughts, the newness of everything, when suddenly my heart stops.

Standing on the sidewalk on the other side of Bay Street, only feet from the downtown municipal docks, is Tristan. He is conversing with someone who looks to be close to our age—a boy I vaguely remembered seeing at a previous party. The jeans that he is wearing are hanging perfectly—slightly low on his hips. The tee shirt that adorns his body is pulled snugly across his chest—accenting the strength of his arms. My breath catches in my throat. I am instantly undone.

Inadvertently, anxiety arises in my throat. So much has passed between us, I feel like we really have something, but I'd thought *that* before, and then he'd done a 180, leaving me flat on the floor, cold and alone. Suddenly I'm terrified of what *the day after* is going to bring this time.

I'm only given a few short moments to wallow in my trepidation before Tristan's captivating, green eyes glance in my direction. Instantly, recognition sets in. I hold my breath in anticipation of possible rejection. Then, my pulse skyrockets as all the warmth of the previous day at the island comes flooding back. Lifting one finger to indicate *hold on one second*, he retains my gaze as he finishes talking to the boy.

Soon, he is crossing the street toward me, and I almost forget that I still have Kate by my side. She nudges me in the arm. "Hey, look who's heading your way."

"Yeah, I noticed." My voice comes out softer than normal, and Kate shoots an inquiring look in my direction.

"Hey." Tristan finally reaches us and looks me directly in the eye. All the memories from yesterday come rushing back. I find myself blushing as I remember the warmth of our bodies pressed together and the way his lips felt on mine.

"Hey," I manage to say.

He holds my gaze a moment longer before turning toward Kate. "Kate." He nods a greeting. "So, what are you girls up to this early?"

"We could ask you the same thing," Kate retorts.

"We just ate breakfast at Bruna's Café," I interject.

He smiles then, and my pulse quickens. The simple act of him standing close by, talking to us, leaves me feeling shaky. His stance is so self-assured. *He is so hot!* "Mmm, sounds good. You got home okay last night then?" His question is directed right at me.

"I got home fine." And I had the best time ever with you yesterday, and your secret is safe with me, so don't worry about that, I tell him with my eyes.

"Soooo . . . that's where you were at. You didn't answer my text because you were with *Tristan*," Kate teases me. "You know, you could have taken her to Jonathan's party last night. You don't have to be so exclusive," she continues, playfully reprimanding Tristan.

"Nope. Sorry, Kate, but it wouldn't have been the same." He catches my eye, reading all sorts of meaning into his gaze, and I can't help myself—once again I find myself blushing.

Finally, after glancing at our watches, we all realize it's time to go our separate ways. We all have things we have to do, responsibilities for the day. We part, and reluctantly I begin walking toward my parked bike. Every portion of my being is begging to turn back and get one more glimpse of Tristan, but I don't want to be so obviously smitten, so I keep walking, trying to restrain myself. Finally, when I reach my bike, I am able to position myself at just the right angle to look back without being completely blatant.

And he's still watching me.

Instant goose bumps. He gives me a little grin and I lift my hand, imparting a half wave in acknowledgement. I bite my lip. *Oh. My. Goodness!*

Later that evening, the sun is getting ready to set, and I feel an overpowering need to walk down by the ocean. Somehow, just the thought of being by the ocean makes me feel closer to Tristan. As I'm moseying toward the shoreline, a curious thought grabs my attention. Since I've come to Watch Hill, since I met Tristan, it seems as though I've been constantly drawn to the ocean. It's like I can't stay away. If I think about it, it's where I've spent most of my free time. Was it possible—did I intrinsically know that Tristan was connected to the ocean in some way all along? I shake my head; how could I have known? I mean there *were* signs, little clues. But still.

As I'm pondering these thoughts, I become aware of the direction my steps are taking me. I am almost to Tristan's secluded beach. Rounding a familiar bend, I eventually reach the sheltered clearing that unveils a wide expanse of iridescent liquid. Sidestepping the dune grass, I am making my way toward the increasing tide when I detect movement several feet offshore. I stop moving, holding my breath.

It's him.

Immediately I want to run into the water, sift through the waves, dive into the sparkling fluidity, and join him for an evening swim. Instead, I take two steps back. *This is his home!* In awe, I watch from a distance as Tristan's powerful, agile physique dives effortlessly in and out of the cascading whitecaps. My heart tightens in my chest. I love him.

Lost in awe, I continue observing him for a few moments before gradually turning away. He deserves his privacy. I leave my heart on the shoreline as I retrieve my steps and slowly make my way back home.

In the days that pass after Mom leaves, surprisingly, Dad learns how to cook a few things. Even more remarkable, the food he prepares actually tastes pretty good. I wonder how exactly he is able to balance his perpetual work schedule with this new role of caregiver. But amazingly enough, with his back pressed against the wall, we all find out he is actually *quite* capable. If Mom could only see him now.

On one occasion I have to do a double take as I pass by the great room front windows. Who *is* that guy outside playing soccer with Josh and Jake? *What? Dad?* I stare, dumbfounded with the discovery. Peering through the windowpane, I find myself smiling as I watch the joyful expressions of two nine-year-old boys who are delighting in the simplicity of kicking a ball around with their dad. I soundlessly applaud him. Who knew? Who knew you could be that lithe, Dad?

Silently I implore Mom to come back and witness this scene too.

Two days later Mom comes home.

Things are a little awkward around the cottage on Mom's first day back. Conversations are polite and strained. It's like each of us has to rediscover our role in the family. It seems every time Mom is in close proximity to me or one of the boys, she grabs us and gives us a hug—as if one of *us* are going to be leaving soon.

Dad doesn't appear to interact much with Mom. But at times I notice him watching her from across the room—as if she is a stranger in the house and he is perplexed, yet intrigued by her at the same time.

Mostly, it feels good to have some semblance of a family again.

I am settled in for the night, snuggled into my covers, hovering between wake and sleep, when I hear a light tapping on my bedroom window. I strain my ears briefly, trying to decipher the sound. Everything is quiet. Deciding it was either my imagination or an act of nature, I pull the blanket tighter around my shoulders and prepare to begin the process of drifting again.

"Bethany . . . Bethany." The instant I hear my name being whispered, I am wide awake. My heart is pounding. I pinch myself to make sure I'm not dreaming. *Holy crap, Tristan is outside my window!*

Taking a deep breath, I pad in the direction of his voice, very conscious of my nighttime attire—a tank top and Penn State pajama pants. "Tristan?" My voice sounds cracked, having been awakened out of my semi-state of sleep.

"Hey," he murmurs. "Can you come out?" My mind races briefly—can I come out, can I come out? No, of course not.

"Umm . . . sure." I pause, looking around the room, trying to think of a way.

"I think this screen will come out pretty easily." His deep voice is still just a whisper.

"Okay." I grab a hoodie and begin my escape.

Once I'm through my newly discovered exit, Tristan grabs me gently and pulls me to his chest. He smells so good, like soap and salty water. I breathe him in—the scent is so fresh, like he just got out of the water. My fingers come in contact with his skin just above the collar of his shirt. He is slightly damp. I pull back and glance up at his hair through the dark shadows that surround us. Even through the obscurity of the night, I can detect traces of recent moisture in his hair.

"Were you just in the water?"

He laughs lightly. "I'm *always* in the water. Come on, let's go." He takes my hand, and we head away from my cottage.

My head is spiraling with the novelty of the situation. I can't believe I have just snuck out of my bedroom window and am walking beside this unbelievably gorgeous guy in what is practically the middle of the night. My body is pulsating with exhilaration. Suddenly a thought occurs to me.

"Hey, do you ever text?"

"I've considered it, but I'm pretty sure phones don't do too well in the water, so I nixed that idea." Even in the dark, I detect a smile on his face.

I nudge him with my elbow. "Smart mouth . . . It would just make things easier."

"I don't think anything is easy when it comes to us, Bethany. But I have to believe we were meant to find each other." His last statement causes goose bumps to surface on my arms. I squeeze his hand to let him know that I believe that too.

He returns the squeeze.

"My mom is back," I tell him as we walk along.

"Really? How is that going?" Concern is evident in his voice.

"We'll see. So far it's hard to tell, but I'm glad she's back."

When we reach the nearest beach, we stand side by side staring out at the vastness of the blackened sea. It is a cloudless night, and the stars are dancing in the sky. The moon provides a dreamy ambience as it glistens on the darkened water. I turn toward Tristan as he stands contemplating the perpetual ripple of the surf that is pressing toward us. The light from the moon extends beyond the water to illuminate the tousled strands of his blond hair. I fight the urge to run my fingers through it.

He senses my stare. "What is it?"

"Your hair. I love your hair."

"You mean my messy hair?" He smiles in the moonlight.

"Yes. I think your *messy* hair is very sexy." I surprise myself—I'm getting braver around him.

His eyes widen. "Well, in that case, I'm never going to comb it again."

"So, what is it like . . . living in the sea?" It's such a comfort to finally be able to ask him questions about his home life. It's the part that's been missing between us, the part that I've been desperately wanting to know, the part that he's been so evasive about.

His green eyes instantly come to life. He leads me to a worn piece of driftwood, and we sit side by side, thighs touching. He tells me about the relief of breathing water after being in the open air for long periods of time. He explains about the adaptability of his body temperature to the various depths of the ocean, and his ability to adjust to the maritime lighting and the lack of it. He describes in detail the various types of underwater vegetation that are his food source and how the nutrients they contain keep him and his people healthy. Hospitals are for humans.

"What about coral reefs? Do you love swimming on the coral reefs . . . are they beautiful?"

"I probably take them for granted, but yeah, they are beautiful." He pauses, and even in the dark I can feel his eyes on me—so close. "They are beautiful." His voice is husky. "But they don't come close to being as beautiful as you."

I suck in a breath. His eyes are still on me, I can feel them. Slowly I turn to meet his gaze. Darkness surrounds us, but in the trickling light of the moon I can see his green eyes, his perfect cheekbones, his beautiful lips. We are only inches apart. My heart rate accelerates. Unhurriedly, inches turn to centimeters. Then I feel the softness of his lips on mine and that new, growingly familiar sensation begins to claim every inch of my body.

Instantly, we wrap our arms around each other, pressing together as our kiss deepens. Becoming more brazen, I reach up to run my fingers through his hair. *Omg. He is so hot!* The kiss continues until Tristan finally eases us apart. Leaning back from me, he holds my face in his hands. We are both trying to catch our breath. It's amazing—I'm in such good shape from running, yet the simple act of a kiss with him leaves me completely breathless. With a pained look, he stares into my eyes, his thumbs gently running along my cheekbones.

"I can't get enough of you, Bethany." I know what he means. I know *exactly* what he means. It's like I can't get enough of him either.

"Me too," I whisper. He pulls me to his chest, and we stay like that for a long time.

"I promise I'll take you swimming on a coral reef sometime, okay?" he murmurs into my hair.

I nod into his chest.

After much time passes, I pull away from him. There is something I want to know, but I'm a little nervous to ask. Finally, I forge ahead.

"So . . . are we . . ." I begin shyly. Tristan reaches over to rest his arm across my back in encouragement.

"Are we what?"

I try again. "Are we like . . . an item, now?" I can't look him in the eye. I feel a little silly for asking, but I just want to know where we stand.

"Do you mean, are you my girlfriend now?"

"Yeah?"

"Well, I think you've *always* been my girl." He squeezes my arm. *So I guess that means yes?* I feel like his answers are a little vague sometimes, but I decide to go with it for now.

As we are quietly sitting side by side, I notice the reflection of a glistening object to my left. I glance toward it. Leaning on another piece of driftwood, only yards away from us, is his guitar. I look back at Tristan.

"You brought your guitar?"

Tristan sends a fleeting consideration towards the piece of drift-wood. "Yeah, I like to play in the evenings sometimes. It's relaxing."

I think back to our excursion at his cabin—how much I enjoyed his playing. Then I remember the way he reacted, ending the session so abruptly. I want to ask him to play now, but I don't want to cause a big problem. What *was* the problem, anyway?

"Will you play for me . . . now?" I proceed bravely.

"That's not a good idea, Bethany."

"I don't understand."

He sighs reluctantly before continuing. "When we play our music, it tends to put people in a trance. It gives us a lot of power over them. Dangerous things can happen when humans become entranced by our music. People have been known to fall off ships, never to be seen again. It's not a good idea for me to . . ." He pauses. "I don't want to have that type of power over you."

I sit silently, once again having been handed an unexpected piece of information from Tristan. I could handle it. I could handle Tristan. I love him—I *would* handle it. I would handle anything Tristan sends my way.

"Too late. With or without the music, you already hold a type of power over me, Tristan. I can handle it."

"What?" He looks momentarily dumbfounded. He gazes at me speculatively, and I am undone by his beauty. "No . . . I mean, yes, I know what you mean." He pauses thoughtfully, as if something is just dawning on him. "I *do* know what you mean . . . because you hold that same type of power over me."

The breath exits my lungs. I swallow to keep light-headedness from claiming me. "So play then."

Tristan watches my face for a few moments, then silently gets up and walks to the piece of driftwood, returning with the guitar in his hands. He settles in on the sand in front of me, cradling the instrument in his arms. He looks back up at me, challenging me to withstand him, withstand what he's about to do to me.

I hold his gaze unwaveringly.

Finally, he looks back down and begins to play.

The next morning I pad into the kitchen for breakfast and glance around the room. Does anyone know? Did anyone realize I was gone last night? Mom is cooking chocolate chip pancakes for the boys.

"Good morning, honey. Sleep good?"

I nod sleepily and stretch. "Yep." *No clue.* My eyes turn toward Dad. He is sitting at the breakfast nook, sipping coffee from a yellow, ceramic mug. The newspaper is in his hands. He is so engrossed in the article he is reading, I don't even think he recognizes that I'm in the room.

Suddenly he clears his throat. "Listen to this . . . we all need to be careful . . . Bethany, Lisa, boys, don't go out alone anymore. It says here there was a girl found dead down by the boat docks in Watch Hill last night . . . they are thinking it's a possible homicide."

Chapter Thirteen

Dad insists on driving me to the marina to volunteer the next day, himself. The thought of a homicide in the nearby vicinity is rather unnerving, so I really don't mind. The ocean passes by in a blur as we travel the winding roads that take us into town. A thousand different possible criminal scenarios take a voyage through my mind as the car meanders along. Each new thought leaves a chill across the surface of my skin. It's all very creepy.

"Don't leave the marina on your own for any reason today, okay?" Dad's concerned voice breaks through my thoughts. "And call me when you are ready for a ride home. I'll come pick you up."

"I'll call you if I need a ride, but if Tristan is working today, I'll probably walk home with him."

Promptly, I feel Dad's scrutinizing eyes on me. "Tristan? Have you been spending more time with that boy lately? I've only met him once. I don't know him well enough to say I feel comfortable trusting him to walk you home. How well do *you* know him?"

Inwardly, I roll my eyes. *Very well, actually!* I take a breath, trying not to blush. "Yeah, I've been hanging out with him quite a bit lately. He's a good guy." *Better than good!* "I'd feel okay with him walking me home. He's pretty strong."

"I'll bet he is," Dad mutters under his breath.

"What?"

"Well, call if for *any* reason you need a ride home . . . Stay safe."

The Chevy Tahoe pulls up to entrance of Hill Cove Marina. My eyes stay peeled to the neighboring boatyard as I approach the front office building. A large section of docks filled with high-end yachts is sequestered by yellow tape. People wearing official-looking attire are scattered everywhere around the nautical landscape.

The whole exhibition slaps me in the face—the crime scene is so close by.

Momentarily, I shudder as a prickling sensation travels across my arms. A girl was killed here a night ago—a girl, possibly even close to my age. One minute she was breathing air into her lungs, her heart beating to the rhythm of life, and the next, she was forever gone. I had already texted Kate. I knew her and Emily were both okay.

The marina was abuzz with the news. It was rare for something like this to occur in a small, elite, summertime, community like Watch Hill.

I overhear Ethan Vaughn talking to David Chambers throughout the day. As a frequenter of the twenty-something nightlife scene in the area, Ethan had a bit of the lowdown on the victim. To hear him tell it, apparently this girl enjoyed visiting the party scene quite liberally herself. Megan Shaffer was her name. She was twenty-one years old.

Although yesterday's paper omitted a photo of the quarry, today's reveals an opulent, auburn-haired beauty with a buoyant smile. Instantly my stomach turns queasy as I recall seeing her around town. Although I hadn't actually spoken with the girl, having visualized her firsthand makes the murder seem that much more real. Someone has just lost a daughter, a best friend, a girlfriend, a sister. It's all very sad—and scary at the same time.

It's hard to focus on my tasks at the marina when little snippets of information about the homicide keep floating through the air. Each new detail reaches out and assaults my ears as it reveals itself. Megan Shaffer had been staying on a yacht for the summer—one of those coveted luxury liners that has now been seized by the local and state authorities.

The morning passes by quickly, and the first chance I get, I step outside and meander down to the marina's main dock. Deciding to take a short break, I sit on the edge of the wooden structure and stick my toes into the tepid water below. Instantly, I relish the soothing feel of it as it laps up over my feet and onto my calves. Recalling my dad's admonition to *stay safe*, I glance back at the office. I haven't gone too far from the security of the building, and besides there are lots of people milling around—curious onlookers, luxuriating in the flurry of the transgression, as gruesome as it may be. Unwittingly, my eyes, too, keep drifting to the property next door.

Bits of speculative evidence from conversations heard earlier in the day begin to waft through my mind. Word is, there had been evidence of a struggle. A rope was used—to strangle. The deck of the boat was wet, littered with bits of sand and foliage from the surrounding lake—had it been a lover's midnight swim gone bad?

Reluctantly, I pull my feet from the lightly cascading surf and begin to make my way back to resume my previous duties inside.

I am guiding a couple of tourists through a Watch Hill brochure, enlightening them about the local shops, places of interests, and favorite eateries, when my attention is drawn to the front door.

My heart jumps.

It's Tristan. He is wearing his pale green work polo along with tan shorts. The green in his shirt makes his eyes pop. *He is working today, then.* I have to catch my breath before I can continue with my quick-guide tutorial.

Now where was I?

Instantaneously, there is a type of energy in the room that wasn't present before.

I glance back down at the brightly colored booklet in front of me. "Now if you are looking for an enjoyable place for dinner, the Olympia Tea Room is nice. Or if you are looking for something more formal, you might want to check out the Ocean House on Bluff Avenue."

Tristan begins to walk in my direction. Pausing, he stands a few feet behind the out-of-state travelers that I am conversing with. His sunstreaked hair is freshly tousled from the wind. *He looks so hot!*

"Hey," he mouths to me. My heart pounds in my chest. I send him a little smile back, trying to concentrate on the captivated customers in front of me.

Now where was I?

"Which road did you say we should take if we want go to Misquamicut Beach?"

Which road? Where? Tristan has his back to me, nonchalantly perusing a shelf. He reaches for something in front of him, the movement emphasizing the breadth of his shoulders. His whole back side is so strong and fit. I swallow and look away, trying not to blush.

The female tourist eyes me with a confused expression on her face.

Misquamicut Beach? "Um . . . if you take . . . ah . . ." Misquamicut Beach. *Concentrate.* "If you take Ocean View Drive and follow it around, it will take you there . . . or . . ." *Don't look back up. Don't look back up.*

I look back up.

Tristan is leafing through a booklet on boating care. I have a perfect view of his profile. His perfectly sculpted cheekbones cause my body to practically ache.

"Or?" The female's counterpart breaks through my thoughts.

Crap! "Or you can take Watch Hill Road out of town and turn right onto 1A."

"Okay . . . well, thanks." The tourists shoot each other a bemused look before retrieving their brochure and heading for the door.

I sigh and fight the blush that is rapidly heating up my face. I'd really like to disappear through the floor.

Hesitantly, I glance in Tristan's direction. He is approaching me with a knowing smile on his face.

"So . . . *how* exactly do you get to Misquamicut Beach?"

I roll my eyes. Oh yeah, he heard me blundering my way through the instructions, all right. I'd like to wipe that smirk off his face. *On second thought, I'd like to kiss it off.*

"Not much work around here to keep you busy today?" My tone feigns sharpness.

He looks right at me. His green eyes are still dancing playfully, but there is a serious edge to them too. "There's plenty of work, but I wanted to come in here and see *you*."

My heart rate accelerates. "Oh." I hold his gaze for a moment before continuing. "Well it's probably hard to get any work done today, with all that commotion outside anyway."

"Yeah, what is that all about?"

"You really don't know?" It's unfathomable to me that someone could not have heard the breaking news in such a small town. "A girl died on one of the yachts a night ago. They think she was murdered." I think back to a night ago. A night ago I was sneaking out of my window, walking on a moonlit beach with Tristan, kissing him underneath the stars, listening spellbound as he strummed lightly on his guitar. I shake my head, trying to bring my mind back to the present.

A look of shock and confusion briefly registers across Tristan's perfect features. I hand him today's paper. As the picture and the print jump out at him, his countenance becomes expressionless. The only movement I detect is a slight twitching in the hollowed area above his set jaw.

I wait quietly while he reads. Finally, he sets the paper aside.

I search his face. "Terrible, isn't it . . . scary."

"Yeah." His voice is quiet, his expression unreadable. Soon, David Chambers approaches and begins talking to him, and I turn back to my work. Periodically, I overhear them discussing the theoretical elements of the homicide. It's hard to concentrate on the task at hand when each rehashed detail I eavesdrop on keeps stinging my ears.

I glance over at Tristan as he is deep in conversation with the owner of the marina. His countenance is completely stoical, not a hint of his thoughts on the matter being revealed.

I am walking only feet away from him, as I'm heading to the back room in search of a new pack of pens, when he stops me on the way.

"How did you get here today?" His face is solemn.

"My dad drove me."

"Good. When you are ready to leave, come find me. I'll walk you home." It feels more like a command than an offer, but I'm okay with that. I certainly won't turn down a chance to walk home with him.

It's late afternoon when I find a stopping point for the project I'm working on. I am making a contact list of other local marinas that I can implement the *Good Mate* program at. The agenda is running successfully at Hill Cove Marina, and David Chambers has suggested trying the interventions at the nearby harbors as well.

As I step outside of the main office building where I've spent the majority of my day, once again my eyes are drawn to the neighboring boatyard. Immediately, I get a stab of uneasiness. This time the air is filled with silence, and the absence of patrons and personnel leaves me feeling skittish. Has it ever been this quiet around the marina before? My eyes dart in all directions in search of Tristan— there is no evidence of him anywhere.

I hug my arms to my chest. Do I just have a case of the post-murder jitters? The enveloping stillness in the atmosphere magnifies the sound of the water lapping up against the boats, making them creak as they sway back and forth. Back and forth. Back and forth. A seagull caws ominously as it soars directly overhead. I think back to the morning conversation I had with my dad. Suddenly, the safety of the Chevy Tahoe sounds pretty good. Where *is* Tristan?

I am descending on the central docking system, thinking that it may be a good place to start looking for him, when I detect a shadow looming behind the side entrance to the front boat house. Instantly, panic courses through my veins. I cover my mouth to stifle a scream. My fight or fight mode surfaces quickly as I prepare to encounter a potential perpetrator. I don't know whether to continue advancing forward or turn around and run. Fleetingly, the thought occurs to me that I'm thankful that I'm a fast runner.

Just as I'm about to turn back toward the main office, the owner of the shadow steps out from the obscurity of the building. My whole body begins to tremble.

"Tristan . . . you scared me!"

"What . . . Bethany. It's okay." He reaches for me. Rapidly his voice grows stern. "You shouldn't be down here alone."

"You told me to look for you."

He pauses. "You're right, I did. Next time I'll come find you though. Are ready to go home? I'm ready, if you are."

I nod as the shaking begins to subside. Suddenly I'm more than ready to get far, far away from this place. Far away from the crime scene next door. Tristan reaches out to take my hand and we begin the journey, oceanside, back to my summer cottage.

Walking next to his well-built frame, my small hand enveloped by his strong one, I feel safe and protected. With him by my side, I could take on a miniature army.

It's a blustery day, and the wind stirring up the ocean causes the waves to explode recklessly toward the shore. At times their roar is almost deafening, making it hard to carry a conversation without shouting loudly over the thundering din. Speculatively, I wonder if this is the cause of Tristan's lack of conversation, or if it is due to his consternation over the recent murder.

Glancing up at him as we walk along, I try to read his thoughts. He smiles down at me and squeezes my hand. I smile back, suddenly feeling the need to lighten the mood.

"Hey, do you want to help me look for some shells?"

"Sure."

His grip on my fingers loosens, and we separate in order to begin the search. Now we walk side by side, eyes glued to the sand. Periodically, I notice an object making an appearance through the shifting, taupe granules as we traipse along. But each time, it is a rock, a piece of debris, or a repeat of something that already exists in my collection. I am almost home before we finally discover two shells worth keeping. Tristan seems particularly impressed with one, describing it as a flawless conch.

As we near my cottage, a familiar ache begins to surface—I am not ready to leave him. Thinking back to the last time I was alone with him, I sigh as I recall his guitar playing. I wish he had it with him now. Momentarily an idea occurs to me. I look over at him spiritedly.

"Do you sing?"

"What? Where did that come from?"

"Well, you play guitar . . . I'm thinking that most likely you can sing too."

Tristan laughs at that and shakes his head. "Is that how it goes? No, I don't sing."

I eye him suspiciously.

"What?" He is trying hard to fight back a grin.

"You are lying."

"I'm not lying." He won't look at me. I won't look away. We keep walking. "What?"

"You *do* sing."

Resigned, he shakes his head. "Okay, maybe I can sing *a little*, but that doesn't mean I'm any good."

I proceed ahead undauntedly. "You know what I'd really love? I'd really love it if you would sing a song for me sometime."

He finally looks over at me. His eyes are so green, practically piercing through my soul. "You would, huh? Well, I doubt it . . . but we'll see."

My heart soars.

The next two days drag by. I don't hear from Tristan, and I'm not supposed to go anywhere alone, so I don't really have an opportunity to look for him. Each day I report in at the marina to volunteer, I wait with baited breath for him to make an appearance through the main office door. Every hum of a boat motor that pulls up to the docks for servicing causes me to snap my head in that direction. All to no avail.

At night, I lie motionless in my bed, straining my ear for a light tap-tap-tap on my window. The most minute sound causes my heart to jump. But in-spite of my best efforts to wish Tristan into existence, I am never able to conjure him up out of the midnight shadows of the moon.

Kate and Emily come over one afternoon to discuss the most popular topic around town—the murder of Megan Shaffer. Secretly, I wonder how they are able to hang out together if they both have their eye on Nick. After breakfast at Bruna's Café, I now have to assume that Emily has conceded victory to Kate. I glance back and forth between both of their faces as they animatedly confer about the gruesomeness of the strangling, and the speculative opinions around town on who could possibly be responsible. On the surface they seem to be getting along, but I do notice that Nick's name is never brought up.

By the third evening of not seeing Tristan, I can't stand it another minute. I decide to take my chances and head down to the ocean to search for him—alone.

It feels like forever since I've walked anywhere unaccompanied. The minute I reach the shoreline, I realize how much I've missed my solitary, oceanside strolls these last few days. The sea seems to welcome me, sending its frothy whitecaps sweeping into shore as a greeting. As I wind my way over to Tristan's secluded beach, I become spellbound by the unremitting cadence of the surf.

Occasionally, I remember to scan my surroundings to ensure my safety, but mostly I am lost in the sights and sounds of the maritime ambience.

My heart pauses, and then immediately accelerates when I spot Tristan's strong, lithe form diving through the waves. The beauty of the resounding breakers quickly fades into the background the second his powerful figure makes an appearance through their rolling proliferation. *He is so beautiful!*

I gaze unapologetically, captivated by his strength and effortlessness. Minutes pass while I deliberate on whether I should interrupt his swim, or simply walk away, leaving him to plunder the waves in peace. I have almost convinced myself to retreat, when I notice his form become still in the water. He stands motionless, staring in my direction. My breath catches in my throat.

He sees me.

As he approaches slowly, wading through the water, heading toward the shore—toward me, I detect something in his green eyes that makes my body cringe with worry. What *is* that look splayed across his perfect features—tension, apprehension, *anger*? *Crap! He looks pissed off!*

He reaches the beach where I am standing. His feet are planted in the sand, water dripping from his skin, shorts clinging to his body—I have to remind myself to breathe.

"What are you doing here, Bethany?" He doesn't give me a chance to answer. "Did you come here alone?"

Oh . . . I came here alone. I sigh in acquiescence to his anger. "Don't be mad . . . I just . . . missed you. I haven't seen you . . ."

He closes his eyes briefly and shakes his head almost unperceivably. Little droplets of liquid fall from his saturated hair. Running his fingers through the disheveled strands as if to clear his mind, he looks right at me and sighs. "Come here."

I quickly close the gap between us, walking effortlessly through the sand. The moment I reach him, he pulls me in to his chest. Wrapping his arms around me, he holds me securely in place. As my own arms encircle him in return, I revel in the feeling of the strong muscles on his back beneath my fingers. Once again, I realize that I am becoming completely soaked by the leftover water from Tristan's evening swim. Once again, I don't even care.

"I've missed you too," he murmurs into my hair. The soapy, clean smell of him is so heady, I breathe him in completely. Much too soon, he pulls away from me and holds me at arms length as he stares into my eyes. "You can't be going around by yourself, though. You apparently don't understand how dangerous it is, with a murderer on the loose. I worry about you, Bethany. Don't you have any self-preservation?"

I bite my lip contemplatively. *Apparently, not much when it comes to wanting to be around you.* A thought comes to me. "Well . . . if *you* would come see *me, I* wouldn't have to come looking for *you.* Then, this wouldn't be an issue at all."

Silence.

"Right?" I watch his face closely, searching for an answer.

For a brief moment, he appears apprehensive, as though he is struggling inwardly for a reply. Then his features relax, and his lips form into a smile. "Yeah, you are right," he pauses. "Can you stay here with me for a while, now?"

I nod, feeling the tension between us ease away. He puts his arm around me and leads me to a dry spot on the sand where we sit together. It feels so safe and peaceful sitting this way beside him, looking out to sea. As I contemplate the way he looked swimming in the ocean, I glance up at him. I have so many questions about him living in the sea; it all seems so mysterious—but one question in particular has been burning in my mind. It's like a type of sixth sense I have about him—an intuition.

"So . . . before I knew about you . . . about you living in the ocean, there were times I would be walking beside the water and I would hear a splash . . . a pretty loud splash. And it would always get my attention. I always wondered what it was, but every time I looked in the direction of the splash, there was nothing there. I would wait, but nothing would happen, again. I was just wondering . . . was that ever . . . you?" I feel silly the instant the words leave my lips. Some thoughts are just better left unsaid.

Tristan stares straight ahead.

I bite my lip—does he think I'm crazy? Momentarily, I notice a sheepish grin working its way onto his face, slowly replacing his previous stoic expression. Finally he looks over at me. "All right, maybe it was me sometimes."

My eyes get wide. I'm not crazy after all. I punch him in the arm. "It *was* you, then?"

He is laughing by now as he pulls me close to him, his arm tightening around my shoulder.

"How many times have I been walking by the ocean, thinking I'm alone, but I'm not really alone?" I pull away from him slightly, narrowing my eyes in jest.

"Not many . . . *really*, not many." He sounds as if he is trying to convince me. "I don't want you to think I've been stalking you or something like that."

I laugh, remembering the times that I'd watched him swimming without him knowing.

"You know, I have to tell you, there were a couple of times I watched you swimming, and you didn't know."

"Really?"

I scrunch up my nose guiltily. "Yeah."

"Does this mean we're even?"

I ask him questions about life in the sea, his family, his people. How often does he see them? Do they always swim around this area? Do they sleep?

I feel like my questions are endless, but he doesn't seem to mind. He answers them patiently and I listen intently.

His people and family always reside in this area, deep in the ocean, so as not to be discovered. Sometimes they travel, but they always come back to their place of dwelling. Their residence is not like human houses, but a type of shelter nonetheless. He sees them regularly. It doesn't take him long to get from place to place when he swims, so he can visit land and return home fairly easily. Yes, they sleep. They have wake/sleep cycles just like us.

I am overwhelmed as I try to sort through the information he is telling me. I try to picture his home—dwelling, and life with his underwater family. It just doesn't seem real or possible. I don't want him to know what I am thinking, so instead, I plunge ahead with more questions.

"How long can you be out of the water?"

"Four to six hours, safely. Then I feel myself begin to weaken and become short of breath. Don't worry, though, I never go far from the water."

"Well, that's good." I gaze at his well-built physique. It's hard for me to imagine him in a state of frailty. I shiver involuntarily.

Tristan notices this and rubs my arm. "You sure you're okay hearing all this?" His voice is soft.

I swallow. The look in his eye has changed somehow. I feel my own body responding, becoming liquid in return. "I'm okay," I breathe.

His hand leaves my arm and reaches for my face instead. Gently he rubs his thumb along my cheekbone down to my jaw. Every part of me begins to tremble. "Because the last thing I want to do is scare you or . . . or anything like that." His voice is barely audible now.

His other hand reaches up to tuck a wisp of my blond hair behind my ear before he cradles my face in both of his strong hands. My heart is pounding. My breathing is noticeably louder.

Slowly he leans toward me and gently kisses my lips.

As I answer the kiss, the original tenderness of the union, rapidly fades to an overwhelming need to be as close to him as possible. Soon our bodies are pressed tightly together. I am consumed by him, by every part of him. It's like I just can't get enough of the kiss, can't get enough of him.

As usual, Tristan ends the kiss, easing me into a hug instead. My head is buried in his chest. I am shaky and breathless as I inhale his scent, feeling the strength of his body as I burrow into him.

We stay this way for some time.

"Tristan?" I begin, uncertainly. "Is it . . . is it easy for you to stop kissing me, every time?" I swallow before I continue. "Or . . . do you feel like you want more . . . want something more from me?"

He wraps his arms tighter around me. Finally he sighs, almost groans. "No . . ." He stops, taking a breath. "No . . . it's not easy for me at all, Bethany."

I proceed ahead bravely. "I never knew what it was like to want someone, before you." I pause. "Now I know."

Chapter Fourteen

Relief from the dark cloud of the murder and from the tension around our household comes in the form of an impromptu visit from good family friends, from back in Philadelphia.

The Callahans.

We have known the Callahans forever. I had gone to preschool, and every grade since, with Tyler Callahan. He was like my brother, but even better, because we rarely fought.

The minute the longtime family friends pull into our side gravel drive, the Kuiper residence transforms from a segregated entity into a unit. The strained hostility that occupies our quaint summertime structure instantly dissipates, and laughter begins to resonate from the interior walls, instead.

Mom and Dad are immediately at ease with Mr. and Mrs. Callahan, and soon the conversation between the four of them becomes integrated, forcing Dad and Mom to ask each other questions to keep the dialogue flowing. Questions such as: What are the names of the beaches in the area, Kevin?—Or—How many years have they been renting out this cottage to vacationers, Lisa?—Or—What night are they having Music on the Green in Watch Hill this week, Lisa?—Or—How long is the ferry trip to Block Island, Kevin?

It's the most I've heard my parents speak to each other in weeks.

I haven't communicated with Tyler since graduation, but the moment I see his playful smile and his teasing, blue eyes, we are instant buddies. It doesn't take long for the familiar back slaps and the frequent punches in the arm to resurrect between us.

"Geez, you really have it rough here this summer, Bethany." Tyler scans the picturesque landscape as he comments.

We are hanging out on the sandy shoreline in front of our cottage. Mom and Dad are sitting, shaded, under a canopy, talking with Mr. and Mrs. Callahan. Tyler's ten-year-old brother, Phillip, is playing with a remote control boat in the water, along with Jake and Josh.

I glance over at the twins' sandy blond heads and their little, tan bodies as they scoot along the shoreline, trying to make their boats perform up to their expectations. They are laughing and chatting animatedly, not only with each other, but with Phillip as well. A warming wave of gratitude passes through me as I watch them. It's so nice to see them interacting with others, instead of remaining in the exclusive, enigmatic duo that they have become.

"It is great here, isn't it?" *Better than great.* I think back to yesterday: kissing Tristan, being held in his arms. My body becomes Jell-O just remembering it. Will I tell Tyler about Tristan? I glance over at him as he saunters along the shoreline. He seems older than the last time I saw him, more filled out. My heart melts. It's nice having a piece of home so close by. Out of nowhere, I get a pang in my chest. I wish Lucy could have come too. I miss her so much.

"Do you ever see Lucy around?"

"I've seen her a couple of times. I think she's ready for your year at Penn State."

Penn State—something I hadn't thought about in quite a while. I had been so focused on Tristan, I hadn't been thinking beyond when would I see him next, or whether he feels the same way about me that I feel about him. A panicky feeling shoots through my veins as I contemplate leaving Watch Hill, leaving Tristan, and going away to college this fall. I shake my head to clear my thoughts. I'm not ready to think about that right now.

"So, how about you, are you ready for Temple University?"

Tyler's blue eyes sparkle. "Definitely. Have you been training for cross-country?"

"Yeah, I run, but I'm not sure I'm going to do cross-country in the fall. I haven't decided."

Tyler's face registers surprise. "Really, miss runner USA? I figured you would be preparing to blow out the competition."

I watch his bemused expression momentarily. I had always thought that too. I guess a girl has a right to change her mind. So many things were changing for me this summer, my head was practically spinning. Tyler was a runner too. We had spent years running together in meets. I had the feeling I was disappointing him.

"Well, I haven't decided for sure. Either way, I will be mentally cheering you on while you're running for Temple."

He looks temporarily relieved at that. Picking up a handful of sand, he lets it sift through his fingers until all that is left in the palm of his hand is a small shell.

"I've been collecting those."

"What?"

"Seashells. Do you want to come inside and see my collection?"

As we are walking side by side heading back toward the cottage, leaving the lightly cascading waves in the distance, I decide to broach the subject of Tristan.

"So are you breaking many hearts this summer?" I smile over at him.

His head snaps quickly in my direction, a playful grin on his face. "Not many . . . Okay, maybe some."

"Meany."

He shrugs his shoulders, his eyes wide. "I don't really try to; sometimes it just happens."

I punch him in the arm and he laughs. He looks over at me imploringly. "What about you?"

I swallow, here it goes. "There *is* someone." My voice is quiet.

Tyler scans my face, unbelievingly.

"What? Did you think it would never happen?"

He shakes his head, seemingly at a loss for words. "No . . . I just . . . No, I knew you would, it's just . . . What's he like . . . He better be—"

I cut him off. "Don't worry, he's great." Why do I feel like it's my dad giving me the third degree?

"What is his name?"

"Tristan." Suddenly, I want to change the subject again. Suddenly, I'm afraid of a question that I won't be able to answer. Would my eyes be able to hide the truth—the truth about who he really is?

After I show Tyler my shell collection, I decide to text Lucy.

Tyler's here. Where are you? . . . I miss you so much! *(send)*

It's not long before I receive a text back.

(unlock) HEY! He forgot to give me a ride. I want to be there too!!!

"Lucy says you forgot to give her a ride." I throw a pillow at Tyler to get his attention. He is sitting across from me on the living room sofa, his head buried in his own phone.

"What?" His eyes become wide." Well, you tell her if she would start going to some of the summer parties, I might run into her and have the opportunity to invite her along, to go places like this. I've only run into her a couple of times since you left . . . You just tell her to get her arse up here. She knows how to drive."

I roll my eyes and start typing into my phone, secretly wishing she *would* get her *arse* up here; I'd love to see her.

Later that evening Tyler and I are walking oceanside, heading to a bonfire volleyball party. Nick's cousin is hosting the festivity, and all my summer friends will be attending. I'm so excited to be able to introduce Tyler to the group. Momentarily, my thoughts drift to Tristan. I wonder if he will show up there too. I have no way of getting ahold of him, and I hate it. I really wish he would get a waterproof phone, *if something like that even exists.* Or at least keep one at his cabin, so that he could check on it once in a while, to see if he has a message—*from me.*

I think of all the times he has just shown up at events. How does he even know when something is going on around town? I feel frustrated and nervous too. I really want to introduce Tyler to him, but there is a part of me that is a little apprehensive about how they would respond to each other, and I am not sure why.

The undulating surf is pressing relentlessly toward the shore as we amble along. We are lost in conversation, the beauty of the effervescent sea accompanying us as we trek through the sandy, winding terrain.

Out of nowhere, the surrounding landscape assaults my senses, breaking through our playful bantering. Suddenly, I realize we have reached Tristan's secluded beach. My heart accelerates unexpectedly, and my eyes begin darting around. I don't see Tristan anywhere. Does he see *me*? See us? Precipitously, I quicken my pace. I want to hurry through this area. Somehow it doesn't feel right sharing this place with someone else, not even for a few moments. Somehow it feels like sacred ground, belonging only to Tristan—and now to me, too.

Finally, we arrive at the party. My summer companions greet Tyler warmly, and he integrates into the group easily. But I wasn't worried about that. His outgoing, pleasant nature usually affords him friends effortlessly. Will introductions go that smoothly with Tristan—should Tristan even show up? I try to enjoy the get-together, laughing and chatting amiably with those around me, but there is a small part of me that is always a little on edge, wondering.

Soon volleyball teams are formed, and the informal, competitive rounds begin. I am immersed in the game, focusing all my efforts on helping my team pull ahead, digging, setting, and serving, when in my peripheral vision I notice someone standing only yards from the court.

Intuitively, my blue eyes turn in that direction, and my heart leaps in my chest.

Tristan.

I remind myself to breathe. He is wearing black and white athletic shorts that emphasize the strength of his body. His sunstreaked hair is gloriously disheveled. His perfect cheekbones are lightly tanned. *Geez, will I ever cease to be amazed by his beauty?*

"Hey," I call over to him.

"Hey," he says back, his green eyes never leaving mine. Suddenly, I can't wait for this round of volleyball to end.

It's hard to concentrate with Tristan spectating from the sidelines, but somehow, much to my joy, I am able to execute some pretty good moves, secretly hoping I'm impressing his watchful eyes in the process. Finally, the round ends and my team wins by a narrow margin. Dusting the sand from my knees, I walk over to him.

Why do I feel so shy, suddenly?

His green eyes are all over me. "Hey, baby, I'm impressed."

I smile. "Yeah?"

He pulls me into a hug and kisses me lightly on the cheek. Well, if anyone wondered about our status, it's evident now.

I am elated.

Withdrawing from him slightly, I look up into his face. "I was wondering if you were coming."

Before he can answer, I sense Tyler's presence approaching from the side. "So, this must be Tristan." Tyler's voice is resolute. I almost jump at the sound. Where did my playful buddy Tyler go?

I turn to stand between Tristan and Tyler. "Yes, Tristan, this is my friend Tyler from back in Philadelphia. His family is close friends of ours. They are staying with us, visiting for a little while. Tyler, this is Tristan." *My boyfriend?* "The guy I was telling you about." I glance up at Tristan. *But not too much about.*

Tristan's jaw sets ever so slightly, his expression stoic as he reaches out his hand. "Tyler."

Tyler's countenance is daunting as he meets his gaze. He nods marginally, and takes his hand in greeting. "Tristan."

Geez, who are these guys? There is too much tension filling the air. I cough, suddenly finding it difficult to breathe.

Volleyball teams reconvene. Tristan joins the team opposite of Tyler. I decide to sit out, taking a place beside Kate on the sidelines. This time the players consist of guys only. Soon, shirts come off and are discarded into the sand. *Crap.* I swallow. *This is getting serious.*

Tristan and Tyler eye each other from either side of the net. Somehow, I get the feeling this is not going to be a friendly little game.

Each time the ball is served by either of them, it appears as though it's struck with an extra surge of power—amazingly, directed at the one-of-the-two-of-them, who is left receiving. Each serve, dig, or spike seems like it's targeted at the other with a vengeance, as if it's just Tristan and Tyler on the court.

I cringe inwardly as I watch them face off against each other on separate sides of the net—so much competitive testosterone in one place. *Could someone get seriously hurt by a volleyball?* They are both standing in the front row, feet from each other, separated only by the thin rope of the mesh. The look in both of their eyes is formidable. Muscles are flexed, rippling across both of their backs. Tension fills the air as they wait for the ball to be served.

Finally I can't take it anymore. I get up and walk away, leaving them to finish their ruthless duel un-spectated by me.

After the games, Tyler mingles easily with the others at the party. Tristan finds me staring into the fire. He comes over by me and stands really close. His hands are shoved in his pockets; our arms are touching. Once again I experience a thrill from the contact, as diminutive as it is.

Silence unfolds between us. Finally I speak.

"You finished with your little volleyball game?"

"Yep."

"Well, good." I sigh in relief.

"Don't you want to know who won?"

I shake my head with a forced laugh. "No . . . no, not really."

The quietness resumes as others chatter spiritedly around us. We both stare into the fire. Arms touching. My body tingling.

"So you have some houseguests for a while?" Tristan's deep, smooth voice finally breaks through the restrained calm.

"Yeah, my family is good friends with the Callahans. They are staying for a few more days. I've known Tyler since preschool—we are practically siblings." Somehow I feel like I'm trying to reassure him, which seems preposterous to me. Who would have ever thought this breathtakingly gorgeous guy standing beside me could ever be jealous over me? I move a half-of-an-inch to my left. Now I am leaning into Tristan. The same fire that I'd been assiduously staring at begins to burn through my veins.

Tristan, too, warms to the touch between us, and the tension that is hovering like an early morning fog begins to dissipate. The conversation lightens, and a playful repartee interjected with moments of visceral attraction brought on by prolonged eye contact or just the right physical exchange begins to emerge.

"Hey . . . Bethany." An enthusiastic intonation reaches my ears, breaking through our private rendezvous. Before long, the body that belongs to the voice reaches the fire. It is Tyler. "I found this really cool shell for your collection."

He holds out his hand. In the light of the fire a tan and white ribbed casing is revealed, dotted with bits of bluish-green markings. Tyler's eyes sparkle. I take it in my fingers, inspecting each crevice. Tristan is looking at it too. His jaw is set, almost imperceptively.

"I'm pretty sure you already have one like that." Tristan's voice is bored.

Tyler's face falls slightly. I look up at Tristan and then back to Tyler's rejected, blue eyes. "I'll bring it home anyway and check it out for sure."

That answer seems to satisfy him, an element of relief spreading across his features.

The rest of the evening unfolds painlessly, and too soon the crowd begins to dwindle, making me realize that I too need to start heading in the direction of home. I contemplate the idea of walking home in the dark with Tyler. As innocuous as the situation might be, somehow I have the feeling that Tristan will be less than thrilled with the idea. A solution occurs to me, and although my plan is going to make my return trip knowingly awkward, I make a decision.

I find Tristan standing at the water's edge. His back is to me, the moon illuminating the blond strands of his hair. I pause momentarily, biting my lip, fighting the ache that is trying to overtake me from just simply observing him at this distance.

"I'm getting ready to leave . . . Do you want to walk home with us?" My voice is soft, barely heard over the swelling sound of the surf.

"Us, meaning you and Tyler?"

"And you . . . if you will come with us too."

The waves swallow the silence around us. The moon sheds a spotlight on only us.

"You know . . . my boat is almost done, and there are a couple of things I want to go check on it tonight, so I'm going to pass."

"This late?"

"Yeah, the owners of the boatyard don't mind . . . so yeah."

"Oh."

The tide continues to grow, stretching out toward us, as the seconds of quiet seemingly unfold into minutes. Finally, I reach out and take his hands in mine. My blue eyes search his face. I have to resist the urge to reach out and trace his perfectly chiseled cheekbones.

"I have known Tyler forever. He is like my brother. Nothing more."

Tristan's green eyes reveal nothing of his thoughts, but somehow

I feel the need to lighten the mood anyway.

"You are not jealous, are you?" My tone is playful.

"I don't really get jealous."

"Because I kind of like it that you'd get jealous over me," I continue, offering a grin.

"Well, if that's what you want, then okay, I'm jealous." He smiles back, but it doesn't quite reach his eyes.

I watch his face as he holds my gaze for an uncomfortable moment. I begin to feel restless, waiting for him to make the next move. My eyes are drawn to his lips, then back up to his green eyes. My heart rate accelerates. I feel my body begin to tremble.

He regards me an instant or two longer.

"Well, you probably want to get going . . . Good night, Bethany. See you soon?" His deep voice is muted, his tone definitive.

No, I don't want to get going. I want to stay here with you, and kiss you, and love you . . . forever.

I swallow and press my lips together. Disappointment floods through my body. "Okay . . . well . . . good night."

I pause before I turn and walk away, slightly breathless, hugging my arms to my chest, trying to combat the shakiness that wants to overtake my limbs.

When it's time for the Callahans to return to Philadelphia, I am not ready for them to go. They have magically transformed the Kuiper household with their visit. Mom and Dad are gracious hosts, escorting them around town, entertaining them at all our favorite hangouts and restaurants. Even mealtimes around the cottage are more animated and festive. Dad shows off his ever-growing grilling expertise, and Mom produces mouthwatering dishes from the stovetop and oven. Affectionate laughter is shared among all the guests, including my parents—at times I find my jaw dropped, as I gaze openly at their unfamiliar joint amicability. One thing I realize with incredulity: Mom and Dad sure have the art of keeping up appearances down pat.

Even Josh and Jake appear happier. With Phillip Callahan in the house, what once was a set of twins has now turned into a group of triplets. But not an exclusive group of triplets: the three of them together gallivant about the house and yard, playfully interacting with the adults and Tyler and me as well.

When the Callahans pull out of our side cottage drive, the sound of crunching gravel reaches my ears, and I wipe away an escaped tear. Secretly I hope that the joviality of the Kuiper household will linger for just a little while longer.

Chapter Fifteen

The next time I see Tristan at the marina, he asks me out on a date—not a go to his private island or isolated cabin or secluded beach kind of date, but a real live go out to eat at a restaurant, human type of date. I am so excited—and for some reason nervous too. I am getting comfortable with him on our oceanside walks, always close to the water. Everywhere I'd been with him so far had included a horizonless view of the undulating sea. He was clearly relaxed in this nautical environment, in *his* environment. Somehow, for me too, it was easy to feel mollified and safe with the sound of the rolling surf befriending you in the background. Now we would be taking a few steps away from that comforting landscape and having a grown-up, non-sea creature type of date. In some ways I feel like Tristan is making a real move in my direction. This concept sends a rush of warmth through my body, leaving goose bumps as it fades. The mystery that has continually surrounded him is slowly disappearing, and I am able to tentatively consider some type of possible future for us.

I put on a pale blue sundress and take extra pains, curling my hair into cascading waves. Pulling a few strands off of my face, I wind them into a side barrette. Spinning slowly in front of my full-length mirror, I become giddy with the thought of spending the evening with Tristan. I stare at the girl in the mirror. Her eyes are bright in anticipation of what the next few hours will hold.

I meet him in front of the Olympia Tea Room, and he takes my hand as we are led to our seats. I feel the closeness of him as we skirt around the tables in the dimly lit dining room, his body periodically brushing up against mine. Tingling sensations devour me with each touch. We settle into our chairs and begin to look at the menu.

"I promise I won't order seafood." I look up from the pages in front of me and smile at him.

He laughs. "I appreciate that."

We place our orders with our waiter who is adorned in solid black. Tristan holds my gaze frequently as we talk across the table. I am glad the room is darkened so that he can't detect the blush that perpetually tries to sneak its way onto my cheekbones. *Why does he make me feel so shy?*

The candlelit room, the white linen tablecloths, the sultry, soft music in the background—it all seems so romantic. I get butterflies. By the time our dinners are served, in spite of the mouthwatering dish set in front of me, I find it difficult to eat. I compel myself to swallow each bite that I bring to my lips. I don't want Tristan to discover the tumult of nerves that are playing havoc with my stomach.

Halfway through dinner, I glance up from my chicken and sautéed mushrooms to see Mr. Horton making his way over to our table. Tristan immediately smiles.

"Hello, Mr. Horton. This is a surprise."

Mr. Horton chuckles. "Us old guys occasionally make it out for a nice meal, too. I'm having dinner with a friend." He nods his head toward the rear of the restaurant, where he's left his mealtime companion seated in a booth.

He places his hand on Tristan's shoulder affectionately. Tristan's green eyes radiate warmth in return.

"You young kids enjoying a night out on the town?"

Tristan's gaze wanders to me with a slight grin and then back to his older gentleman friend. "We are."

"Well, I see you found a lovely young lady to accompany you." The weathered skin on Mr. Horton's face crinkles at the corner of his eyes as he regards me pleasantly. "I approve."

Tristan looks pleased. I am secretly pleased too. I am really starting to like Mr. Horton's kindly, good-humored nature. And for some inscrutable reason, he seems to like me too.

After we finish dinner, Tristan takes my hand once again as we linger on the sidewalk just outside the front of the restaurant. Cars travel by us on Bay Street only feet from where we are standing. Pedestrians weave around us on the cement walkway, only inches away from the very spot we are residing. But all this is lost to me—all I can see is Tristan. All that exists is him and me, in this moment in time.

Tristan is more dressed up than usual. He is wearing pale tan, almost cream-colored pants. A lavender pinstriped, button-up shirt is fitted snugly against his chest with sleeves rolled to his elbows, revealing strong forearms. His tousled, blond hair rests marginally on the back of his collar.

He is breathtakingly good-looking.

I swallow and look away momentarily.

"Would it be okay if I walk you home?" His voice is subdued, his green eyes piercing. My heart rate accelerates.

Would it be okay? "I'd like that," I answer.

We begin walking away from the heart of Watch Hill, taking a sandy, shoreline path that leads to my cottage. The sea is unusually calm, periodically dotted with tiny ripples of movement. Bright white sailboats litter the horizon. An occasional light breeze softly caresses the skin on my face, lightly disheveling the strands of my and Tristan's hair.

One of those disturbances in the tranquil, liquid landscape reveals a swordfish as it pierces the sky, airborne, before once again penetrating the still, blue waters and disappearing.

My mouth gapes open as I exclaim in surprise. "Did you just see that?"

The sound of Tristan's musical laughter fills the air. "Yes. Pretty cool, huh?"

"A swordfish?"

"Yep. There it goes again." He lets go of my hand as he points to the ocean. "He's showing off."

Now I laugh. "It appears as though he is." Momentarily a thought occurs to me. "Do you ever show off?"

Tristan shrugs his shoulders before draping an arm around me as we continue walking. "Maybe . . . sometimes."

Out of the corner of my eye I can see he is grinning.

I nudge him in the ribs with my elbow. "Did I ever tell you about the time I saw a leatherback swimming in the water?"

"No, you never told me. Lately?"

"A few weeks ago." I feel a little stab of hurt as I recall a few weeks ago when I longed to share my turtle discovery with Tristan, but he was being purposely evasive.

As if sensing this, he gives my shoulder a little squeeze. "That's very awesome. I like to swim with leatherbacks."

I glance over at his chiseled profile and his perfect lips. "Really? *That's* awesome."

As we are lost in conversation, it dawns on me that we have passed the path that leads to my summer cottage and are now heading further down the shore. *On purpose?* My heart hammers in my chest. I easily recognize the shoreline trail we are taking. We are heading to Tristan's beach. A thrill courses through my veins as I consider spending time alone with him there.

"Um . . . we passed my cottage," I mention softly, secretly hoping that it wasn't just an oversight.

I feel his eyes on me. "We did . . . are you okay with that?"

I nod, slowly exhaling the breath from my lungs.

When we reach the secluded alcove that has begun to feel like home, I fight to calm the butterflies that are fluttering around restlessly in my stomach. Walking to the water's edge, I regard the muffled refection of a blond girl that is staring into the liquid, crystal glass. Soon another blond reflection materializes, standing next to the girl. A boy—his ardent physique swallowing up the presence of the tiny, rippling image of the girl.

I try to subdue my wildly beating heart. I don't need a mirror to know Tristan is standing beside me. I can feel his strength and the warmth radiating from his body as he stands only inches away from me, just as sure as I inhale the air that I breathe.

As we stand facing the water, side by side, I begin to detect a type of restlessness coming from Tristan. I feel the sand loosen below me as he shifts back and forth on his feet. Out of my peripheral vision I notice him shove his hands in and out of his pockets. *What is it, Tristan?*

Finally he turns to me.

"Come over here and sit down." He takes me by the hand and leads me to a blanket that's been laid out in a sheltered nook on the beach. *Where did that come from?*

I situate myself on the protective covering, relishing its warmth on the skin of my legs. Tristan kneels in front of me. His shirt is untucked by now, giving him a more sexy, casual appearance. He pulls something out of the back pocket of his pants before sitting back.

"I got you something." He acts somewhat nervous as he hands me a small, white box. I feel my heart pounding against my chest as I take it in my hands. *He got me a present.* I glance up at him before I remove the lid. In his green eyes is disclosed a type of uneasiness and eagerness at the same time. I watch him inquisitively. There is something else I detect there too, something I can't quite put my finger on—but it makes my already accelerated heart rate quicken.

I open the box.

Inside is an exquisite seashell. It glistens with vibrant shades of orange, brown, rust, and cream. Perfectly shaped, with tiny smoothed ridges and an intricate pattern of color, it practically illuminates the container it is in. I pick up the slim leather rope that it's been attached to and hold it in front of my face, eyeing it reverently. It is flawless. I have to remind myself to speak.

"It's beautiful." My voice is breathless.

"Do you like it?"

"Love it." Turning it around slowly, I inspect each miniature crevice. "Is it . . . is it a Harpa costata?" I remembered learning about that shell in one of my new books.

Tristan's green eyes are dancing. "It is."

"They are rare and expensive . . . aren't they?"

The momentary silence causes me to look up from the shell. Tristan is watching me. Our eyes lock and I can't look away. "You are worth it," he murmurs. *OMG!* My body goes weak.

"I had it made into a necklace for you." He reaches over and gently takes the roped shell from my hands. "Here, let me help you put it on." He gets up and kneels behind me on the blanket. I feel myself begin to tremble. "Can you lift your hair for me?"

I obey, and he reaches around to the front of me, resting the shell on my chest, and then proceeds to fasten the clasp, his hand barely grazing the back of my neck as he does. My body tingles with shivers.

Realizing I am holding my breath, I force myself to exhale as he slowly turns me around to face him. His green eyes scan me. "It looks nice on you," he says softly.

As his gaze becomes more intense, my heart explodes in my chest. He leans in toward me slightly—and then unexpectedly jumps up.

What?!?

"Stay right there. I have one more thing for you, but I have to get something first." His countenance reveals the look of a zealous schoolboy.

My head is spinning. I have gone from excitement to nerviness to disappointment—and now back to expectancy, all in a matter of moments.

I am completely breathless.

After what feels like forever, he reappears with a big smile on his face. He is holding his guitar. I freeze in place as I watch him, my expression is inquiring. *What is he going to do now? He said he wouldn't sing for me . . . would he . . . is he going to . . . ?*

There is a piece of driftwood close by. He perches on it directly across from me as I'm sitting, legs curled up on the blanket.

"Remember how you said you would like it if I would sing a song for you sometime? Well, here it is. It's something I wrote . . ." He pauses for a second and then tries again. "It's something I wrote for you."

Holy . . . oh wow! He . . . wrote . . . a song . . . for me? I suck in a breath.

He settles in, cradling the guitar in his arms. Staring down at the instrument in his hands, he begins to strum a few chords. From where I am lounging, I take in his impeccably carved cheekbones, the relaxed position of his strong legs, the way his disheveled, sun-streaked hair falls over his face, shadowing his eyes. I wonder if I will even be able to decipher the musical reverberation of his words over the thundering sound of my heart.

Soon the preliminary individual thrumming of chords transforms into music, and I am instantaneously tuned in to the sound.

The minute I hear his voice, every other noise fades into the far, far distance.

TRISTAN'S SONG
Can't seem to make it go away
This need I found for you the other day
Was it just the other day
I want to swim inside your soul, breathe you in so close

I don't want to exhale, find out it wasn't true
Shake the water from my lungs
So much I never really knew
I never really knew

Chorus:
I feel it all slip from me
My heart, my life, my reality
Just like the sand to sea
Please take me where I want to be
'Cuz the sand keeps slippin' out to the sea
And with you is where I need to be

Let the water go away
I just want to stay

As the song begins, my eyes stay glued to Tristan, while he remains looking down, concentrating on the instrument in his hands. Even then, almost immediately I feel something begin to stir inside me, drawing me in—taking over my senses. All sights, sounds, smells, sensation of touch, become focused on him, on the song. Nothing else exists outside of this. I am caught completely off guard by how beautiful his voice is—perfectly tuned, breathy, and husky, all in one. The words of the song infiltrate every ounce of my mind; I can't fathom that he is singing it to me. It's as if I'm being pulled into a trance that I can't break free from, don't want to break free from.

Then he looks up.

His green eyes pierce inside my soul.

Immediately I begin to tremble. He is so beautiful, his voice is so beautiful, the words of the song that he wrote *for me* are so beautiful. Helplessly, tears begin to fall down my cheeks. I am completely lost in the melody, lost in his gaze. He has taken my breath and my heart—and I know in that moment, that without a shadow of a doubt, I will never get them back.

After Tristan strums the last few chords of the composition, he becomes very still—watching me.

"You like it?" His voice comes across gently, breaking the silence.

I can't speak. I can't answer. I can only nod my head in approval.

He moves toward me slowly, sliding in next to me on the blanket. In a caressing motion, he begins to wipe away the tears on my cheeks. All the while his gaze remains on my face.

"Bethany . . . I love you," he tells me reverently.

I feel myself begin to shake. Once again, he has stolen my words. I want to tell him how I feel in return, but I am having trouble finding my voice. As if sensing my overwhelmed state, he steps in to rescue me from the silence. In slow motion, he brings his face to mine, lightly covering my mouth in a kiss.

His lips are so soft.

And warm.

Immediately I respond. The inches that have separated us quickly dissolve. I can feel my body intuitively press into him, but no matter how hard I try, I just can't seem to get close enough. An overpowering need surfaces. The kiss deepens. A floating sensation overtakes my being, reminding me of the dreams I've had recently of swimming through the depths of the ocean with him by my side.

My hands push against the strong muscles of his back, drawing him to me. My senses melt into liquid as I experience the touch of Tristan's hands running through the strands of my hair, up and down my back.

Finally, remorsefully, breathlessly, we break apart. We both sit staring at the reaching tide of the ocean, willing our bodies to reach some type of impasse. Moments or minutes vanish, I'm not sure which. He has bared his soul to me today. *He loves me!* I am stunned and overjoyed by this new revelation.

I turn unhurriedly to face him. His face is flushed, his eyes bright. Reaching out to take his hand, I swallow before I attempt to speak.

"Tristan . . ." He turns to meet my gaze. His face is an open book. *Oh my—wow!* I want to melt. "I love you too."

The tenderness in his green eyes makes me want to come undone. His strong arms reach out to envelop me as he pulls me to his chest. We stay this way for a long time.

"You know, I've been praying for you for the last few years," I murmur into his chest.

He becomes very still. "What?" We are both quiet. Finally, he speaks again. "So you *do* remember me, then?"

"No, I don't remember you . . . I wish I did . . . really I do. But I prayed for you anyway. I knew I would find you someday . . . the person that I would love forever. And I prayed that God would keep you safe for me . . . until we would meet."

I can feel Tristan's breath as he exhales slowly into my hair. "Wow." He seems awestruck and a little overwhelmed by what I've just revealed to him. Wrapping his arms securely around me, he fits me more tightly to him. "Well . . . keep praying."

The sun sets and daylight fades to night. Darkness is not my friend. I realize that very soon I will need to leave Tristan and go back home. But it feels so good to be here under the temperate caress of the maritime breeze, lying together, our bodies tangled. I snuggle in closer to his warm, hard body and tell him I don't want to go back to the cottage. I want to stay here with him all night, sleeping under the stars, with the sound of the ocean waves drifting rhythmically to shore.

"I know, baby," he whispers into my ear before he kisses me one more time.

In the end, regrettably, we separate, and I do go reluctantly back home.

The minute Tristan is gone from my side, I miss him terribly. But I'm not ready to go to bed, so I text Lucy.

I'm in LOVE!!!!!!!! *(send)*

I am lying in my bed staring out the window, my mind racing as I watch the stars twinkle in the night sky, when I feel the familiar buzz of my phone beside me.

(unlock) Tristan?

Yes!!!!!! *(send)*

(unlock) Yea!!! I'm so happy for you. I better meet him some-day.

The next morning I awaken and pad into the kitchen for break-fast. I am feeling deliciously warm all over from the memories of Tristan and last night. I glance around the room. Can anyone detect all the stars that are dancing in my eyes? It seems no one is paying any attention. Instead, my cloud nine dissipates with lightning quick speed as reality comes crashing in with a vengeance. Suddenly I experience an intense feeling of déjà vu as Dad reads me the headlines of the morning paper.

A second murder has been committed in Watch Hill.

Chapter Sixteen

A dark cloud resettles on Watch Hill as we are reminded that a murderer is still on the loose. A murderer that is actively killing. The thought of it is bone-chillingly disturbing. I fight down the queasiness that is festering in my stomach as I ask my dad about the details.

He sets down his ceramic mug filled with coffee as he focuses on the black and white print in front of him. His eyes are serious. "The paper isn't saying too much, except that once again the victim was found on a yacht. This time it was a person in his upper forties."

"Have they found the killer yet?" Even as I speak the words out loud, I realize how credulous and fanciful they must sound.

"No not yet." Dad's voice is solemn.

He asks me if I am planning on volunteering at the marina today. When I tell him yes, he promptly informs me that once again he will be driving me. I don't argue. Puttering around the kitchen, I pull open the refrigerator and then the cupboards as I search for something to eat. At this point, nothing sounds good. The unsettled feeling in my stomach has progressed into a full-fledged churning, causing a sour taste to ascend toward my throat.

Why did this ominous turn of events have to occur just when my summer was becoming so enchanted. Last night had been so beautiful, almost fairytale like. Remembering the seashell that rests around my neck, I raise my hand to it, confirming that it is still there. I don't let go. I can't let go, as I stand, suspended motionless, recalling the events of last night. Experiencing a bout of breathlessness, I think back to the song that Tristan wrote and sang for me.

Goosebumps spread across my skin as I envision his green eyes and the way he looked at me while he sang, like I was the most important person in the world.

OMG! I shake my head and groan inwardly. He is so ridiculously hot, and I love him so ridiculously much. Why did something stupid like a homicide have to occur, trying to overshadow what I shared with Tristan last night? I just want to spend the day basking in the afterglow. Now I will be forced to face the particulars of a gruesome murder instead.

I send a quick text to Lucy to let her know what's going on.

There was another yacht murder in Watch Hill *(send)*

She responds quickly.

(unlock) What?! You better come home right now!

I can't leave . . . *(send)*

(unlock) Tristan?

YES! *(send)*

(unlock) BE CAREFUL!!!!

As dad pulls the Chevy Tahoe up to the marina's front office, once again my vision is drawn to the neighboring boat works. Its parking lot is besieged with police cars and other official-looking vehicles. Once again it has become a crime scene, interrupting the touristy feel of the quaint, summertime community. A sinking feeling takes its residence in my chest.

"What time do you need to be picked up today?"

"Oh, I probably will just walk home with Tris—"

"I will be picking you up today." My dad's voice is unyielding.

I sigh. "I'll only be here for a couple of hours today. I'll call you."

The front office is practically humming with most recent news of the homicide next door. It seems like we have more patrons than ever, all trying in their own discreet way to get as close to the crime scene as they can without actually crossing the threshold of disturbing the police. It's as if they think that because we are the neighbors of the felonious venue, we must have some inside information on who the perpetrator is. I secretly wonder if David Chambers and Ethan Vaughn are getting irritated with all the unexpected attention. Maybe they will end up needing to put up a sign to keep all the extra people away—or maybe even hire security.

I vacillate between wanting to know details and just willing the whole thing to go away. Little snippets of information keep drifting into ear-range, and unwittingly I find myself tuning in to the speculations every time I hear something new. *The victim was a forty-eight year old man named John Dawson. There was evidence of him taking a blunt object to his head. Repeated stab wounds littered his body. From all appearances, it was a crime of rage.*

I go about my work quietly, fighting the somberness that wants to overtake me. Ethan notices this and offers me a chance to escape by asking me to sort some inventory in the back room. Relieved, I wander to the rear of the office and shut the door, grateful for some respite from the hullabaloo of the investigation. I feel somewhat guilty. Is it so wrong for me to not want to share the splendor of last night with thoughts about the newly deceased?

Too soon, I find myself in need of a box slicer, and once again, I make an appearance in the front as I search for the required tool. Immediately I am re-assaulted with specifics and hearsay. *John Dawson was Megan Shaffer's stepdad. It's safe to assume the murders are related. At least we can be sure it's no random serial killer. John Dawson was the CEO of Alantrop Sea Shipping Company. Oh, that company is huge . . . what a shock! Talk about giving a small town a big name!*

I sort through the shards of data that infiltrate my ears. *Alantrop Sea Shipping Company. Alantrop Sea Shipping Company.* I search the forefront and the recesses of my mind trying to decipher why that name sounds familiar to me. It does ring a bell, somehow, but try as I might, I am unable to think of why.

Trying to block thoughts of the murder, my eyes stray to the boat docks every time I pass by the office's front window. I keep hoping I'll get to see Tristan today. The hours tick by and each time I sneak a peek, he is nowhere to be found. Still I keep hoping. Finally, this time as my eyes graze the nautical landscape through the glass pane of the window, I notice a pair of tan shorts and a pale green polo belonging to a body that I've become very familiar with. *Yes!*

I practically sprint to the front door.

Tristan is helping to guide a boat into the docks, getting ready to gas up at the pumps. He pulls on the watercraft's rope, causing the muscles in his arms to flex. His blond hair blows recklessly in the wind. I exhale slowly and wait for him to finish assisting his customer. At last the transaction is completed and I approach him quietly, suddenly feeling shy.

"Hey, Tristan," I call to him. My tone is breathlessly quiet.

He turns the minute he hears my voice. Immediately, I am greeted with all the warmth and love from the night before. "Hey, Bethany."

My heart soars.

"How are you doing?" His green eyes are all over me. Instantly, I read meaning into his words. *How are you after last night when I gave you the seashell, and sang the song I wrote for you, and you came completely undone, and I kissed you until you were crazy? How are you doing now?*

I feel my cheeks heat up.

"I'm good."

As if right on cue, he closes the gap between us and pulls me into a hug. Right out on the main docks at Hill Cove Marina. Right in front of everybody. It's like announcing to the whole world that I'm his.

And I love it.

After we ease apart, the amorous look is gone, replaced by

something else. Concern? Fear? Infuriation? *Oh no.* Immediately I want to drag him back into my arms, erasing any negative thoughts, exchanging them with all the love I saw reflected in his eyes only moments before. Instead, I sigh, resignedly.

"I'm sure you heard about the murder."

He nods, seeming to hold his breath. His jaw is set.

"Oh well, I'm sure they'll catch the person. I'm not going to worry about it." Determinedly, I try to lighten the mood.

Tristan's eyes become fire. "Well, don't you think you *should* worry about it a little bit, Bethany? I don't think it's wise to be so relaxed about the whole thing."

I am taken back by his intensity. I pause momentarily. "Okay . . . yeah, I'll be careful." My voice is subdued as I watch his face. "Ah . . . my dad is picking me up today . . . soon."

A semblance of relief crosses over his flawless features. "That's good."

I can't hide it, my countenance falls. *A better choice would be— for you to take me home.*

Sensing my disappointment, Tristan reaches out to take my hand. "Hey." He searches my face imploringly. "You have a couple minutes before you have to leave?"

I nod my head as I glance at my watch. "A couple."

"Let's walk."

He continues to hold my hand as he leads me over to an unoccupied dock. We take a seat on the wooden structure, hanging our feet over the edge, inches away from the cascading rhythm of the surf. He sits very close to me causing, his arm and thigh to burn into mine. Our conversation takes on a carefree tone in opposition to the worrisome topic of the murders. But I have a hard time concentrating with our physical proximity. I try to listen to everything he is saying, but my mind keeps slipping back to last night. Instinctively, my hand reaches for my shell.

Tristan's eyes follow the motion. He stops talking midsentence. His eyes return to my face, regarding me unwaveringly. My heart beats fast. He looks as though he might kiss me, like he *wants* to kiss me—but here we are, sitting out here in front of so many people on the unhidden docks of the marina.

I swallow before I let out a slow breath. The Chevy Tahoe is pulling up to the front office entrance. "My dad's here, I better go."

Tristan glances back toward the direction of the vehicle. "Yeah, okay." He takes my hand and squeezes it. "Be careful, Bethany," he murmurs.

I nod and exit the dock, en route to my transportation home.

As I approach the Tahoe, I notice Dad standing just outside the driver's side door, talking with David Chambers. I am about to position myself shotgun, when I hear a bustle of familiar voices.

Kate, Nick, and Jonathan are hastening toward me, faces flushed, all talking at once about the recent flurry of the murders. The news is pulsating through the town. *Who could it be? How unusual for a town like this? How can we all stay safe? We should all be sticking together. Yes, the homicides seem related, but you never know what a crazed murderer might be capable of.*

I am immediately sucked into the conversation, inserting my animated observations here and there, but there is a small part of me that wishes this would all just go away, allowing me and Tristan to have our new romance in peace.

"They are suspecting that the killer entered the boat from the rear ladder," Kate announces. "They think he *or she* could have been hanging out in the water for a long time, just waiting for the right moment. Doesn't that just creep you out?"

I scrunch up my face, trying to stifle a shudder. *Yes, that does creep me out.*

"Makes me want to stay away from boats for a while," Nick interjects.

"It gets creepier though. They found seaweed and sand on the deck again . . . this time mixed in with the blood of John Dawson. I hear it was quite a blood bath." Jonathan's eyes are bright as he tells the story.

A wave of nausea threatens to overtake me. Where are they finding out this information from anyway? It's far too soon in the investigation to have all this information leaked. It is like playing the game of telephone. Who actually knew how much of these details were reliable data, and how much had become a spiraling myth?

"Ooh, that sounds so gross!" Kate's brown eyes are narrowed.

"Hey? What's for dinner?" Jonathan laughs, carrying it a little too far. "It sounds like a vampire's casserole."

Kate punches Jonathan in the arm. Nick laughs. "More like spa material. Bloody—seaweed special. Anyone for a massage?"

I notice Kate does not punch Nick, but the look on her face is still less than pleased.

I feel a chill creep up my spine. It all sounds tragic and horrific to me. Solemnly, I excuse myself and slide into the passenger seat of my dad's car.

When I arrive back at the cottage, I begin to experience a type of restlessness. I hate having to be cooped up all the time because I'm not supposed to go anywhere alone. Nonchalantly perusing the interior rooms to see what my family is up to, I make a determination. No one is paying any attention; it's time for me to escape, escape for a much-needed walk along the seashore. Slipping down to the waterfront, I am immediately captivated by the vast, blue engulfment opposite of me. The waves are rolling pompously, majestically displaying their white frothy caps. Their roar is deafening, drowning out my melancholy mood that is threatening to surface. I smell the salty air and inhale deeply.

My insides turn to Jell-O as my thoughts are intrinsically pulled back to last night with Tristan. I get butterflies as I mull over the song he sang for me. It had completely taken my breath away. I gulp a lungful of seaside air, realizing that it is *still* taking my breath away. It is such a special sentiment shared between only the two of us. I sit staring at the whimsical pattern of the waves, wondering how long ago he had written it. Does that mean he spends time thinking about me when he's alone? *Oh—wow, obviously he must!*

I want to pinch myself. He is so absurdly gorgeous. I still can't really believe a guy like him spends his free time thinking about *me*.

I focus on the song, trying to remember the words. I am surprised by how many I actually *do* recall. *I want to swim inside your soul. Breathe you in so close.* A warm, tingling sensation begins to spread across my body as I sing the words in my head.

Something about *sand to sea.* I muse on those words momentarily, but I'm not able to quite remember that part. Unobtrusively, my thoughts switch to the word *sea. Sea . . . sea . . . Sea Shipping Company.* The name of that murdered CEO's company again. Momentarily I become irritated with the mental block that won't allow me to recall where else I've heard that phrase lately. I kick a tiny piece of driftwood with my foot.

Then it dawns on me. On my Yahoo account—I was opening my e-mail the other day, and it was on a news blurb. The Alantrop Sea Shipping Company was recently indicted for dumping waste into the ocean. I feel some semblance of satisfaction in finally being able to figure it out. I tuck a strand of hair behind my ear to keep it from straying across my face, blocking my vision of the ocean. Alantrop Company has certainly had its share of trouble lately.

The reverberation of the undulating surf begins to lull me into a relaxed state. Moments like this make me feel like I could just stay this way out here forever—alone with the ocean. Except that I would *definitely* want Tristan to join me. And then eventually, I'd start to miss everyone else too. I smile contemplatively. Well, at least for now, it sure seems nice.

Absentmindedly, I begin sifting my hands through sand. As I idly run my fingers through the pale granules surrounding me, my thoughts reflectively go to my parents. There had been no big outbursts lately. Since the Callahans had left, they actually, at times, appeared to be getting along. Not in a warm, loving way, really. But more in a cordial, professional manner—as if they are two business associates. Was that good? I shake my head, trying to free my mind from the burden of the thought. I didn't know enough about relationships to make that determination. It sure was nice not having to listen to the hurtful accusations and the frenzied skirmishes lately though.

In the recesses of the dark that night, I startle from sleep.

My heart is pounding.

I am awakened by a phrase that has emerged into the forefront of my unwanted thoughts. Out of nowhere, it keeps playing over and over in my mind. My forehead scrunches tensely as I picture Tristan's disturbed countenance as he spews the words heatedly while we walk the beach together, the day he took me to his cabin. Plain as day, I visualize the black sludge that laces the shoreline.

It's from waste that is dumped into the ocean by shipping companies. It's destroying life in the ocean . . . it's destroying life in the ocean . . . shipping companies are destroying life in the ocean.

A breeze drifts in through the open window to the right of my bed. Shivering involuntarily, I snuggle deeper into my covers. Making myself relax, I take a few deep, slow breaths, pushing the obtrusive thought to the recesses of my mind. Finally, I am able to subdue the deliberations that are running through my head, and I find myself drifting back toward sleep.

Chapter Seventeen

I awaken the next morning with the bright rays of the sun invading my room. I open my eyes and then close them again in protest to the glare. In a few moments, I give another attempt. This time I keep my lids open long enough to focus on the filtered light that falls across my white, antique bedroom furniture. Sleepily I peel back my warm covers and stretch, getting ready to embrace the day.

With the force of a runaway freight train, all the disconcerting thoughts from the middle of the night return, bowling me over, taking my mind captive. Running my fingers through my already mussed up hair, I attempt to brush away their unwanted intrusion. Why was I even allowing these ludicrous notions to penetrate my brain?

Stealing into the kitchen, I begin sifting through the cupboards in search of breakfast food. Finding some granola and fruit, I settle in to the breakfast nook and begin slicing a banana into a bowl. As I stare at the cereal box in front of me, tiny tidbits of uncertainty over troubling notions keep plaguing me.

Could? My mind pauses. Would—Tristan hate so much? *Omg!* I close my eyes momentarily. *What is wrong with me?* How can I even think this way? I keep shoveling food into my mouth, concentrating on the black and white print covering the cardboard granola container behind my ceramic cereal bowl. Surely he loves his heritage, where he lives—the ocean, his family. It's the very essence of who he is. The victims, especially John Dawson, had strong ties to a shipping company. And *some* shipping companies *were* destroying the ocean. John Dawson's shipping company *had* been destroying the ocean. Destroying Tristan's world. Destroying his family's world.

I swallow and exhale the breath from my lungs. I do know for a fact it was hate I saw reflected in his green eyes that day when he discussed the black debris littering the shoreline, and then when he told me about the shipping companies. A shudder vibrates through my body as I connect the dots—as far-fetched as they might seem. Is it possible? Would he stop at nothing to protect his environment?

I stop myself before my mind can go any further. Instantly I recollect him holding me so tenderly in his arms, the caring way he looks at me, his green eyes piercing my soul. It's just not possible. *He* couldn't have any connections to the yacht murders. Relieved at this newest enlightenment, I relax and finish eating my cereal.

And then out of nowhere I hear Megan Shafer's laughter ringing in my ears.

I picture her luxuriant, auburn hair and her flirtatious smile as she tosses her head back coquettishly. And then I envision the intrigued look in Tristan's eyes as he watches her. How many times had I seen them together? I had never really thought *too* much of it, other than experiencing a momentary stab of jealousy. Was their connection of any importance? He obviously knew her. Why wouldn't he open up and say anything regarding the matter? Once again I dismiss the preposterous thought. If every person holding a remote association to a murder victim was considered guilty, prisons would have to be the size of an ocean to hold all the convicted.

Once again Dad drops me off at the marina. I carry out each assigned task while continually peering out of the corner of my eye for Tristan. How will I react when I see him? Will my latest dismal thoughts about him be written across my face? I press my hands together nervously. Did it really matter anyway? The ache that is consuming my body from wanting to be near him is outweighing anything else.

Halfway through the day, David Chamber approaches me. Tristan was on the schedule for the day and he didn't show up. Did I know where he was? I freeze in place. No, I didn't know where he was. *But I wish I did.* This is when the cell phone thing would have been helpful. There is still so much about Tristan that I don't know. Every time I am with him I am learning more and more, but there is still so much that remains a mystery. I really want to know *everything* about him. Briefly, a shudder besieges my shoulders and arms. *Don't I?*

At the end of my volunteer day, I fleetingly consider calling for a ride home. I know this is what I'm supposed to do. Should do. Instead, I find myself heading on foot toward Watch Hill Boatyard in search of Tristan. As I approach the large, steel buildings designed to store local watercrafts, I experience a sensation of déjà vu. Once again I am advancing toward the boat works facility while trying to ward off a type of nervousness that is threatening to overpower me. This time for a different reason.

This time I don't have to search for Tristan indoors. Right away my vision is drawn to his lean muscular body standing down by the docks. I stop and stare. The yearning I'd been fighting all day increases as I view his perfectly chiseled cheekbones and tousled, blond hair. I am overwhelmed with longing for him and yet apprehensive over my newest thoughts about him at the same time. Slowly I approach. As I get closer, I notice he is working on his boat. It's in the water. And it's beautiful! But it's not the boat's beauty that has me spellbound.

At last, Tristan turns and sees me.

I am not at all prepared for the intense gaze that he sends my way. It's a powerful force field that wants to swallow me up. My heart rapidly accelerates. I can't look away.

"Hey, Tristan." My voice is subdued, held captive by the magnetic pull that he is drawing me in with.

He shakes his head slightly, as if to break the bond of our trance. His hands clench at his side, forming tight fists. Finally he smiles. A warm sensation immediately spreads throughout my body. He motions toward me. "Hey, baby, come here."

Without hesitation, I go to him, and he pulls me into his strong arms for a hug. My hands press into his back. I want to devour him. I close my eyes together tightly, trying to shut out the unwelcome thoughts that are trying to play havoc with my mind. This is the Tristan that I love—*and no one else*. Before I'm ready to, I remove myself from his embrace and look up at him.

"You missed work today. They were looking for you."

"Oh . . . yeah . . . ," he pauses, looking slightly uncomfortable. "I thought I told them I wouldn't be in . . ." Breaking our eye contact, he glances away. I wait for him to offer something more for an explanation, but he doesn't, so I decide to let it go. Stepping even farther back from him, I peer over his shoulder. His old, previously battered boat is sitting in the water tied up to a docking post. It has now been transformed into a shiny, wooden masterpiece. The metamorphosis is remarkable.

"Holy cow! Your boat . . . it looks great!" My mouth gapes open in awe. "Is this even your boat?"

He laughs at that. "That good, huh? Yep, she's mine. Do you like how it turned out?"

"Do I like it? I love it. Oh my gosh, Tristan, it's beautiful."

He looks like a proud father. A really *hot* proud father. "Come here and check it out."

I step up close to the boat and run my hand over its smooth, glossy, mahogany finish. Edging around to the front, I eye the blond, wooden stripe that graces the bow. "Wow. All I can say is wow. You did all this, Tristan Alexander?"

His green eyes are dancing. "I got some help with a few things. But yeah, mostly I did it all myself."

"Well, heck, and here I thought when you left me, you went to sleep at night. This is what you've been doing."

For a moment a look of confusion or something else indiscernible crosses over his flawless features. But then, very quickly, the look of exhilaration returns. "Step inside." He pats the front seat.

Obediently, I climb into the cream-colored leather interior and place my hands on the steering wheel. "This so rocks!" I eye the pale, pristine-looking material that makes up the seating inside the vessel. Glancing over my shoulder at Tristan, I notice that he is still smiling, reveling in my reaction to his prize possession. I just shake my head; no words can describe this magnum opus adequately.

I hop back out and proceed to the rear of the watercraft, checking out the stern. Painted in ocean blue cursive lettering is the word *Blue.* "You named it *blue.*" I point to the immaculately written word. "Is that because of the color of the ocean?"

Silence.

Quickly I glance over at him, expecting an answer.

"No, not because of the ocean, Bethany." He pauses, looking directly at me, almost as if he's studying me. Finally he offers a tentative smile. "I named her *Blue* after the color of your blue eyes."

Once again he has stolen the breath from my lungs. "Oh." My voice is raspy. I want to say something more. I feel like I *should* say something more, but I am completely tongue-tied. All this time I've spent riveted by his green eyes, and he had been obviously captivated by my own blue ones as well. *I never knew.*

As if to help me with the awkwardness of not knowing what to say, he reaches out and gently traces my cheekbone with his finger. I feel myself begin to tremble beneath his touch. *I love him so much.*

Finally, he steps away from me and gestures toward the boat. "So you like it, huh?"

"Yeah, I really do." I clear my throat, trying to find my voice.

The moments that pass after that are slightly uncomfortable, and

I get the feeling that according to him our impromptu get-together is now over. Somehow I feel like our conversation is finished, and I'm being politely dismissed.

But I'm not ready to go yet.

At last he sighs. "Well . . . I'm getting ready to take *Blue* out so . . ." *So? So what? So I can leave now? I don't think so.*

I look over at him expectantly.

He studies me for a long moment, mutters something under his breath that strongly resembles a curse word, and then sighs again. "You . . . do you want to come with me?"

"Sure." I can't hide my smile. "Just let me make a quick call first."

I dial my mom's cell phone and tell her I'm spending the afternoon with Kate. I feel a little guilty for not relaying the truth, but I'm sure she would not approve of me spending an afternoon alone with Tristan out in the middle of the ocean, due to all that has gone on around town lately. But I just can't stand the thought of *not* going, either. I glance over at Tristan's athletic, powerful frame while I'm talking on the phone. He is preparing the boat for departure. Once again, those old creepy speculations from the night before begin to wriggle their way into the forefront of my mind. What if something *were* to happen? I would be floating over the depths of the sea, and my parents would think I was safely at Kate's—and no one would ever know the facts. I swallow down the anxiety that is rising in my throat.

Tristan glances over his shoulder and smiles at me.

My heart melts.

I wave and smile back while I continue speaking into the phone. My heart is pounding in my chest. Adrenaline mixed with anticipation. *Seriously!* What is wrong with me? Because I just *want* to go with him.

No matter what.

The immaculately recreated wooden vessel pulls slowly away from the boat docks. As I am nestled into the front seat of Tristan's

Chris-Craft Riviera, I take note of the dark clouds that are accumulating in the distance. Right now I am enjoying the brilliance of a sunny day. The glossy sheen of his newly refurbished boat picks up the intermittent rays of the sun, causing them to dance and sparkle off of its smooth surface. Leaving the no-wake zone, we pick up speed and begin flying across the open waterway at a breakneck momentum. I feel a mixture of warmth from the sun on my cheekbones and the rush of the wind as it collides against my face. Tucking a strand of hair behind my ear, I try to tame it into place uselessly, as it whips all around me.

I glance over at Tristan. His hair is being whipped too. Gloriously. He catches me looking and sends me a little grin in return. But his eyes have taken on a distant hue as we travel along, just like the gathering clouds. A wall of silence seems to separate us somehow. It's hard to decipher if the lack of interaction between us is due to a type of aloofness that is emanating from him or just due to the impossibility of talking over the loudness of the boat motor. I have to wonder if I've pushed too far—did he really want to take this ride by himself, and I interrupted his solitude by insisting I come along too?

Then at times I catch his eyes studying my face with a type of longing that steals my breath away. *What is this?* Inside, I experience that same type of longing and want to share it with him, telling him that whatever it is that he is feeling, I am feeling the same way. But with the uncertainty of the moment I'm not sure how. So I just swallow it down, causing an ache to fester instead.

When we have driven far enough away from shoreline that the land has become just an indistinct slice of the horizon, the Riviera begins to slow unexpectedly. Soon, I feel a jerking motion as the boat sputters, lurches, and eventually stalls.

"Crap." Tristan's voice is loud and clear, in stark contrast to the absence of the boat motor.

"What is it?"

"I'm not sure. I thought I had this thing running perfectly." A note of irritation is easily detected in his deep voice.

The wooden watercraft sways back and forth aimlessly in the restless waves. Water slaps loudly against the sides of the boat. The shrill of a seagull's caw fills the air as it circles and swoops, eyeing our drifting vessel. I raise my eyes to the sky, feeling like something is missing—immediately I realize that it's the sun, which is now completely covered by dark clouds. The once sparkling, blue water has transformed into a dull shade of gray.

Tristan shimmies to the center of the boat, lifts the hatch, and begins checking out the motor. I too transfer to the middle seat, ready to offer my help should he need it. His face is shoved into a compartment that houses the engine while he fiddles around, looking for the problem. His strong, muscled legs are only inches from me as he works, and once again I feel the familiar pull of wanting him close, of wanting to reach out and touch him. I sigh and look away. He is completely unaware of my desire for him as I sit, watching. Finally I move to the edge of the seat, far away from where he is tinkering, far away from him—focusing my stare on the ebb and flow of the waves instead.

Eventually I hear movement behind me, and I turn around. Tristan is standing now. His green eyes meet my own blue ones as he raises a pair of crossed fingers.

"Well, here goes. I'm going to try to start this thing."

He situates himself back into the front seat and turns the key.

Nothing.

"Damn." His hand pounds the steering wheel and I wince. For a moment he is silent.

"Looks like I'm going to have to go in the water. I think something might be stuck in the opening to the inboard motor."

Pulling off his shirt, Tristan prepares to go in the water, revealing well-built arms and rock-hard abs. Once again I turn away to watch the waves.

I hear the splash of liquid behind me as he descends into the surrounding ocean. Minutes go by with him gone from my presence, while he works on the boat from somewhere beneath. Occasionally a clunking noise reaches my ears followed by a lurch or vibration in the watercraft, and I realize he is still searching for a solution.

Finally he emerges from the stern of the boat. Climbing the rear ladder, he enters the back of the silently swaying watercraft, dripping wet. Drenched, tan shorts cling to his legs as droplets of water roll off of him, while tiny, disseminated pieces of green foliage adhere to his skin.

Seaweed.

They are suspecting the killer entered the boat from the rear ladder . . . the rear ladder . . . He could have been hanging out in the water for a long time, just waiting for the right moment. They found seaweed on the deck mixed with blood.

Seaweed.

Doesn't that just creep you out . . . ?

My body begins to tremble. Inadvertently, I wrap my arms around my chest to comfort myself. The realization of how isolated we are, drifting out in the middle of the open sea, hits me full force. I take a calming breath—*isn't this what I want?* Where else would I rather be than alone, somewhere, anywhere, with Tristan? I hug myself tighter in an effort to subdue the shaking.

Tristan is drying off, running his hand through the soaked strands of his hair, when he stops and looks at me. Everything becomes very quiet while his eyes take me in.

"What is it, Bethany?"

"Nothing I . . . I just think I'm cold."

His gaze continues to scrutinize me, and my anxiety increases along with sentiments of guilt over feeling this way.

Still his eyes never leave mine. Slowly he gets up and reaches for something on the front bench. I swallow as I watch his every move. He comes close to me, and I sit motionless as he drapes me in his sweatshirt and pulls it together securely around my front. Stepping back from me, his eyes search mine tentatively, silently imploring me for an answer. Confusion over why I am shivering is written in them.

"I'm pretty sure I fixed the problem. I was able to find what had gotten stuck. It was filled with seaweed. We must have driven through a bad area."

Seaweed.

Nervously, I snuggle deeper into his sweatshirt.

Tristan hesitates before continuing. "We'll have to wait awhile though, because I flooded the engine earlier when I tried to start it." He stops. "Bethany . . . are *you* okay?"

Holy crap . . . what is wrong with me? I hug his sweatshirt to my body, and it begins to warm me, soothing away the tension. The salty, soapy smell that permeates it reaches my senses, calming me—the smell of him. I think back to a time, not very long ago, when I was so sure I could handle anything Tristan sent my way. I *had* handled everything he had sent my way—so far. But this. If there even was a this. Could I handle this? What implications would it hold for me if there was? Who *was* he really? Guiltily, I avoid looking at him.

"Really . . . I'm okay. Maybe I'm coming down with something." *Lies. How many lies have I told today?* How many lies has he told me? Maybe none. Maybe he was just omitting the truth about the kind of person he actually is.

Finally, I look up at him. He looks so innocently charming. A SoCal model. *My* Hollister model. I shake my head. All my ugly thoughts just *can't* be true.

"So . . . have you been thinking much about Penn State this fall?" *What?*

His question catches me completely off guard. My thoughts are so far in the opposite direction, I hadn't even contemplated confronting this topic right now.

"No . . . I haven't been thinking about Penn State much at all." *Finally I'm telling the truth.* In one way or another, he alone has been completely consuming my thoughts lately. A lump begins working its way up into my throat. The idea of leaving him to go to college this fall sweeps through my body like a wrecking ball, making me feel completely devastated. What a confusing dilemma I am in. One minute I am quivering in fear of him being a potential monster, and the next I am quivering in fear of being away from him.

I swallow away the threatening tears and try to speak. "Wha . . . what about you? What will you do this fall?" My voice sounds raspy and cracked, not at all like my own.

He sighs. "I'm not sure; we don't usually go to college. There is a big part of me that would really like to. But there is the big matter of applying . . . with no ID and all. It begins to get complicated."

My ears perk up. Maybe he wants to go to Penn State with me.

"If I did, it would have to be a college on the ocean." My heart sinks. That answers that question. "My people naturally have a high IQ, and we spend a lot of our time gaining knowledge, but we have resourceful ways of obtaining information in order to avoid too much contact with humans and the risk of exposing ourselves. Still . . . I think about it."

I survey his pensive, green eyes. "Would your family approve?" I question.

"I'm not sure. Probably not. Maybe if I could convince them it would benefit us if I attended a university to study more ways to help save our marine environment. Just recently a study was conducted on water found in the depths of the ocean, and there was a high percentage of plastic particles found in the water."

I wait for the anger to surface as it had before when he breached this topic, but instead I watch as his shoulders slump in defeat. Immediately my heart melts.

Instinctively, I reach for his hand.

His strong fingers wrap around my own hand as he pulls me in to his chest. Holding me close to his body, he strokes my hair and kisses the top of my head. Very quickly my tumult of emotions begins to fade away. Right now there is only him and me and nothing else. I ease out of his gentle caress and look up at him. Our gaze locks. *I love you,* I tell him with my eyes. He groans and leans in toward me slowly. My heart pounds. Finally, his beautiful face reaches mine, and his lips press softly against my own.

Instantly, unwittingly, my body responds. My hands reach for his blond, disheveled locks. I want him closer. I can't get close enough. His arms encompass me, fitting me tightly to him. Not tight enough. As the kiss continues and we become melded compactly together, it occurs to me that I am completely helpless against him. Some time ago, I had become irrevocably his, and nothing would ever change that.

This time it's me who pulls away first. "Tristan . . ." I murmur. My body is pure liquid in his arms. I can hardly breathe.

"What is it, baby?" His green eyes devour my soul. What is it that I see emanating from them? It almost appears to resemble pain. But why?

"I . . ." I start, then stop. There is so much I want to ask him. There is so much I need to know. I feel so close to him right now, so connected. Maybe now would be a good time to ask about all the bits and pieces of evidence that seem to tie him to the yacht murders.

But I just can't.

I snuggle back into his arms and lay my head against his chest. "Just hold me."

When I arrive safely back home, I text Lucy.

Tristan named his boat after me. BLUE—after my eyes. *(send).*

Right away she texts back.

(unlock) I knew you were going to reel a guy in someday with those blue eyes of yours.

Peering at the screen on my phone, I laugh to myself. Little did she know how literal her words were, how I had literally reeled this boy in from the sea.

That night I dream.

Once again I am swimming through the ocean, this time stripped and exposed. Tristan is close by. The surrounding water envelops me, caressing my skin like petals of silk. Warmth floods through my veins like an addictive drug. The continual flow of salty liquid soothes every part of me—my eyes, my arms, my legs, my soul.

On and on Tristan and I plunge through the mystical haze of the underwater world. The myriads of marine life that accompany us are present and yet distant at the same time. It feels as though we are all alone—everything else has become a muted sound.

Time passes, minutes, hours, I'm not sure which. Eventually as I'm swimming along, an unfamiliar sensation begins to surface, breaking through to my senses. I have a subtle awareness that something has changed, but I can't quite put my finger on what it is. Furrowing my brow, I concentrate, trying to sort out this new phenomenon.

Then it occurs to me—I am slowly losing my ability to breathe.

The oxygen that once filled my lungs is gradually being replaced with water.

I am drowning.

Unsure of what to do, I turn to Tristan for help. But he remains apart from me, idly watching. At first I am confused by this, desperate for him to come to my aid. But finally I come to accept it. *He probably wants me to breathe water like him.*

So I just keep swimming.

And losing my ability to breathe air.

Finally I awaken, gasping for life, sustaining oxygen—never really discovering if I was going to be able to sustain or if I was actually going to drown.

Chapter Eighteen

I feel the need to run.

I know I shouldn't run alone, so on a whim I text Kate and ask her to accompany me. But Kate's not a runner, and it takes a lot of convincing to talk her into it.

"I'll go slow. I promise. And besides, I can't go without a chaperone . . . so please."

Finally she says yes.

She arrives at my house with all her usual energy, and I have to wonder why she's *not* a runner. Certainly with all her vigor, she could race for an Olympic gold medal and win. Her chestnut hair is pulled back into her favorite ponytail style, and it swings back and forth as we begin our jog. Animatedly, she chitchats as we trot along the winding pathway of Foster Cove Road. Soon, it becomes evident that she's losing her breath. Gently, I try to advise her to save her lungs for the run, but I can tell it's hard for her to quit talking.

The charm of the picturesque, summertime community passes by us as the soles of our shoes make contact with the pavement. Massive cottages with grand front porches. Quaint bungalows with cedar-shake siding and pristine, white trim. Picket fences and flower gardens. Large, leafy trees. Immaculately landscaped yards with trimmed hedges. Rolling, green lawns with breathtaking views of the ocean.

The salty sea air filters up onto the street, and I take in a deep, cleansing breath. This run is going to be so cathartic—if only I could run faster. I try my best to keep Kate's slow pace, but even then, less than a mile into our jog, she becomes completely winded. Breathlessly, she motions for me to go on ahead of her. I hesitate briefly, but the resolved look in her brown eyes tells me she means business, so I assure her that I'll meet up with her on the way back, and continue on.

Within seconds I break into a faster clip. Soon, the fresh ocean air pounds into my lungs at a cleansing rate. The feel of the wind on my face is invigorating. The muscles in my legs stretch and reach out, to go faster and faster. Turning onto Browning Road, I continue my galvanizing tempo.

I am rounding a bend in the road, surveying a large bird that is soaring through the air above me, questioning whether they have eagles in these parts, when I fail to notice a pothole embedded in the blacktop. At once, I feel my ankle twist as it makes contact with the uneven ground.

Pain shoots through my ligaments, causing me to stop abruptly.

Immediately, I chide myself for not paying closer attention to my footing. An experienced runner knows better than that. Gingerly, I make a couple of attempts to put weight on the affected foot. Each time I wince in acute discomfort. No way around it—I'm not going to be able to continue running. Calling to mind the spot where I said good-bye to Kate, I try to calculate the distance between us. How long will it take for me to walk back to her? I don't want her to worry. I reach toward the rear of my shorts. They are running shorts, without any back pockets. I didn't bring my cell phone.

As my breathing slows, the sounds of my surrounding environment become more evident. I am instantly reminded that I've been warned not to go out alone. But here I am, anyway. I haven't been paying too much attention to reason lately. This time, I hope it won't prove to be trouble. I glance all around, taking in my newly acquired habitat.

Nothing but trees and winding road.

Involuntarily, I shiver. Each snap of a twig sends my heart racing. Each gust of wind that propels the leaves into a swirling frenzy causes the hairs on my arms to stand on end. Anxiously, I attempt to pick up my pace as I limp back toward Kate, toward home. With every quickened step, I try to tune out the unnerving sounds of nature. My eyes continually dart to the right and to the left in search of a summer cottage, any summer cottage. But there are none in sight. Funny, I hadn't noticed how secluded the area was on the way here.

Suddenly I feel very vulnerable without my ability to run.

Somewhere nearby, I hear the panting sound of loud breathing—instantaneously, my heart begins to hammer in my chest. I begin hobbling even faster, my psyche verging on full-fledged panic. Then I consider that what I'm hearing might actually be my own frightened exhalations. *Slow it down. Breathe. Be calm.* I try to de-escalate myself.

Still, I can't stop myself from glancing over my shoulder. Each time I peruse the waning trail behind me, I see no one. Why does it feel like someone is there? Another rustle of leaves comes from somewhere nearby, and my fight or flight mode begins to surface with a vengeance. In my terrified state I become aware of a car approaching, and my mind wrestles with the idea of flagging it down. Am I in grave danger—or is my brain just playing tricks on me, and I'm making too much out of nothing?

The car passes by.

Once again, I'm alone.

Or not alone.

In desperation, I make a hurried decision, turning my stride into a steady jog. My injured ankle screams out in argument as I amble along. By the time I reach Kate, sweat is pouring off of my skin, and I am pale as a ghost.

Kate's brown eyes are round. "Bethany! What happened? What is wrong?"

I wince in pain. The relief of being in her presence brings me close to tears. "I twisted my ankle. I think it might be sprained."

"You shouldn't be running on it then," she chides me. "Look at you . . . you look like you are ready to pass out."

"I know, I . . ." As I begin to explain the creeped-out feeling I was experiencing, being alone in the secluded territory of Browning Road, another pain rips through my nerve endings. I close my eyes briefly, trying to ward it away.

"Come here." Wrapping one arm around my shoulder, she leads me over to a grassy area that sits a safe distance from the shoulder of the road. "Sit down."

With Kate's help, I ease onto the ground.

"Let me look at that." Her take-charge attitude has her quickly rolling down my sock to examine the injury. A swollen, bruised ankle pops into view. "I'm texting Nick to come pick us up. You need to stay off of this and get some ice." She proceeds to punch me in the arm, and not lightly, either.

"Ouch." I rub the spot where she hit me. "That's going to be bruised worse than my ankle."

She laughs exuberantly at that. I'd forgotten just how funny I was to her—a regular comedian. But soon I'm laughing too. Mostly in relief from being safe from the frightening solitude of the woods— and also from the realization that reprieve from my throbbing ankle is soon on its way.

While we are waiting for our ride, Kate broaches the subject of Nick. "So, I just have to tell you. Nick and I are officially a couple."

I glance over at her. "Really. I figured you were heading that way. So . . . how's it going?" Attempting a smile, I keep my eyes on Kate while gently trying to soothe away the tenderness in my swollen limb.

Instantly her eyes become dreamy. "It's going *really* good!" She describes in detail about how they finally came out with their feelings for each other. "Oh my gosh." She reaches out to squeeze my leg just above my knee, *really hard*. "He is so freaking hot!"

"Ouch. Will you stop? Now I have three injuries."

This time she laughs only a little. "Sorry. I kind of get carried away when I talk about him."

Approaching the subject carefully, I inquire about Emily and her obvious feelings for Nick. How was she handling the whole situation?

"Well, at first I think she was pretty pissed. She wouldn't talk to me or Nick. But then she decided *to* talk to Nick, and she spilled her guts about how much she likes him and how it was breaking her heart to see him with me."

My eyes get large. "What did Nick say?"

"Well, he felt bad, but what could he do, he doesn't like her, he likes *me*. He did his best to ease her down gently, I guess."

"And now?"

"Emily's finally coming around. She's not super friendly, but she's speaking a little. What can I say? Love hurts."

"Ouch."

Kate raises her eyebrows. "Ouch is right. She's going to have to get over it. *Back off, bitch*, he's mine."

I grin and bite my lip. Kate was very forthright and also very right. Emily would have to move on.

"What about you and Tristan?"

I can't hide my smile. "Yeah, Tristan and I are good."

I watch as Kate once again moves her hand in my direction.

"Stop . . . keep your hands off me." My voice is brisk, but playful at the same time. She freezes in midair and folds her fingers together.

"So . . . tell me everything." Her brown eyes are dancing.

What could I say? There was so much to tell, so much I couldn't share.

"Have you kissed him? I'm telling you kissing Nick is like . . .

Omg! So . . . have you?" She pauses, eyeing me. "You have, haven't you? Do you like it?"

Have I kissed Tristan? I get light-headed just thinking about it. *Do I like it?* Goose bumps start to surface across my skin. *Like* is not the word I would use to describe what I've shared with Tristan. How can I begin to describe to Kate what Tristan and I have experienced together, how I feel about him this very moment? Somehow it feels sacred.

A sheepish grin unwittingly spreads across my face. "You love it, don't you. I told you, you would. Didn't I tell you?" Kate's voice is so enthusiastic. That's what I love about Kate. I don't have to reveal a thing. She just fills in all the blanks any way she wants to, and all I have to do is smile and nod.

"Lucky girl. Tristan is very good-looking . . . and how do I say this . . . in some ways, almost mysterious."

I suck in a breath. "How so?" I wait for her answer with baited breath. Does he seem mystifying due to his true heritage of living in the ocean, or is there more to it? I hold back an involuntary shudder as I contemplate the perplexity of him. I think back to my dream from the night before. I was drowning, and Tristan was just standing by watching it happen. It was only a dream—but did it mean anything?

"I don't know. It's like, he's around sometimes, and then he's not. I guess I just don't know a lot about him. I do know one thing, however. He is drop-dead gorgeous, and you are one fantastically lucky girl."

When I get back to the cottage, I lie on the plaid couch in the great room, icing my ankle and texting Lucy.

Why do things have to be complicated? *(send)*

By the time my bag of ice is almost completely melted, I receive a text back.

(unlock) Trouble in paradise?

Yes! *(send)*

(unlock) The yacht murders? Tristan?

Yes and I hope not. *(send)*

Tristan doesn't show up for work two more times. By now it's obvious he isn't employed there anymore. David Chambers and Ethan Vaughn eventually stop asking about him. But I don't stop questioning about him. In my mind, I inquire about him all the time. Why would he quit the marina without notice? This just isn't like him. When he was here, he had such a good work ethic. He was a good employee—the managers loved him. Something is definitely going on with him.

Each new day that I don't see him, I begin to feel a void. Each night I go to bed I wait to see him in my dreams, but instead my nights are restful, but empty.

On this particular night I am ensconced in a deep slumber when I am aroused by a light tapping on my bedroom window.

I startle awake.

At first I am disoriented. I wipe the sleep from my eyes. The tiniest threads of daylight have begun to make an appearance through my window pane, and I wonder what time it is. Have I already slept through a whole night? It feels like I just went to bed. Without hesitation, I pad toward the direction of the sound. My heart is beating loudly in anticipation—I have such high hopes.

I'm not disappointed. I see Tristan outside my bedroom window, and my heart soars.

"Tristan." I state the obvious.

"Can you come out?" he whispers.

Of course! "Sure . . . give me a second." I slip my arms into a hoodie, run my fingers through my sleep-tangled hair, and gulp down a big drink of water.

This time I know the drill. Pulling off the screen, I slip through the open glass and land on the ground. Once outside, my eyes meet

Tristan's in the transcendental early morning light. Pools of green, doorways to his soul, transfix on my own, and it becomes evident in that moment how much he's missed me too.

I close the gap between us, falling into his arms. He holds me tight—so tight I can barely breathe. But I don't care. I squeeze him back. *I've missed you so much. I'm so glad you're here. I love you.* We stay that way for a long time. Finally, he loosens his grip and leans back to look at me. His eyes search my face. For just an instant I imagine that they are edged in anguish, but the outdoor lighting is so obscure I can't really know for sure.

"What is it, Tristan?"

He shakes his head slightly. "Nothing. Let's walk." He takes my hand, and we head toward the water.

As soon as our feet come in contact with the sand, my mind begins racing. There are so many questions I want to ask him. So many nagging doubts that I need laid to rest. Where have you been lately? What do you know about the yacht murders? Tell me you're not involved. I glance over at him. The pale morning light falls softly across his cheekbones and the bridge of his nose. No, I *know* you are not involved. I give his hand a little squeeze. *Tell me everything is going to be okay.*

Finally I speak. "I've missed you, Tristan."

In my peripheral vision, I see Tristan close his eyes briefly, as if it pains him to answer. "I've missed you too." He squeezes my hand back.

I pause before I trudge bravely ahead. "And . . . I've missed you at work too." I hold my breath. How is he going to answer that?

Silence.

I anxiously wait.

Finally he exhales a long, slow breath. "I know . . . I . . ." His free hand clenches into a fist and he sets his jaw momentarily before he continues. "I just . . ." He sighs. "Yeah, I know."

Disappointment floods through me as I realize that's all I'm going to get from him right now. But I will wait. When he is ready to tell me, I'll be ready to listen.

We stop walking, and I take in my surroundings. I hadn't even realized we'd been heading in the direction of his beach. We stand side by side staring out at the lightly cascading waves that are advancing toward the shore. The sun begins to make an appearance over the horizon, dividing the ocean from the sky. Tristan leads me over to a sheltered nook, away from the reach of the stretching tide, and we both lie down on a soft blanket of sand. The same place where we'd been before—many times before.

Together we lie, fingers intertwined, the length of our legs touching, eyes fixed on the dimly lit heavens. Daylight gradually erases the darkness from the sky. At times long moments of silence stretch out between us. Then periodically the stillness is broken as we chitchat about the most menial things—the weather, the uncountable grains of sand, how quickly or slowly the clouds are passing by. Carefully, we avoid any topic that could lead to the discussion about the elephant that is draped between us.

Eventually, Tristan lets go of my hand and gets into a sitting position, knees bent, arms situated on them, staring out to sea. I prop my head on my hand, elbow wedged into the ground, while I lie on my side—watching him. There is a far-off look in his eyes as his gaze rests on the wide expanse before him. At one point I detect an expression passing over his perfect features that strongly resembles hate. Momentarily I shiver, but I can't look away.

He notices me watching him and looks back over his shoulder. I go to talk, but silence holds me hostage. Time passes while I sit riveted by his gaze. Finally I find my voice.

"I miss you every minute we are not together," I tell him.

He sighs, a long, hard expulsion of breath from his lungs. He appears almost angry. "It's just the song, Bethany. You just *think* that you want me so much, that you miss me that much. That's what it does, it just makes you *feel* that way."

"No." My voice sounds desperate. "No, I know that's not true. Why do you want to push me away, trying to make me think that all we have together, all that we have shared is just because of a song?" I work hard to push back the tears that are threatening to overtake me. "I love you. I want you . . . I will always love you."

For a moment or two he looks uncomfortable, as if he is struggling with something, struggling with what I just presented to him. Then the previously evident anger drains from his face, and his shoulders sink in defeat.

He closes his eyes before opening them again, holding my gaze. "You're right. It's not just the song. I love you . . . I always have . . . And I know you love me too."

There it was. The absolute truth between us. Nothing else mattered.

When he walks me back home, we stop just before we reach the view of my cottage. Facing each other, we stand an arm's-length apart while he gazes into my eyes. What I see there catches me off guard. Ensconced deep in their green, oceanlike depths, I see more than love—I see something almost resembling pain and loss. *What is it, Tristan, please tell me* I silently beg him.

He answers by pulling me to him and kissing me with an unexpected urgency. Instantly, any questioning thoughts I might have disappear. I am completely overwhelmed with my need for him. My body responds to him in every way. *I love you, I want you, I need you.* The kiss continues. Our bodies press tightly together, our hands trying to pull each other closer. Devouring each other, we kiss like there will never be another tomorrow, like there will never be another chance to kiss again. Soon my limbs become weak, and I find I can no longer stand on my own. Slowly I collapse into him. The strength of his arms holds me in place. My head spins. My body is liquid. I am consumed with want.

Finally, he breaks us apart.

We both stand breathless, looking at each other. My heart is beating so fast, I can't concentrate. He looks so beautiful right now. I just want more of him. I reach for him again, and this time he pulls me to his chest in an embrace. I feel his heart beating rapidly against my face.

"I love you, Bethany." he murmurs into my hair.

I hold on to those words for a long time.

Eventually, my breathing slows and his slows too. We continue on like this, relaxing into each other, until our heartbeats mesh into one tempo.

"I love you too." My voice is soft as I speak into his chest. "No matter what," I add in a barely audible whisper.

At this he pulls back from me, and looks questionably into my eyes. All is quiet around us except the crashing sound of the waves. For a fraction of a second, time stands still.

Then we breathe our good-byes.

And nothing more is said before I quietly turn to leave.

Chapter Nineteen

"Let's go shopping." My mom's voice breaks through my concentration as I'm flipping through the TV channels, lounging in the great room. Setting down the remote control, I glance up at her. Her blond hair is pulled back into a sophisticated ponytail. She looks chipper, dressed in crisp, white capris and a blousy, peach top. The strain I've come to recognize in her blue eyes seems somewhat faded.

Why not? I extricate myself from the reclining position I'm in and sit on the edge of the couch. "Sure, when are you thinking?"

"As soon as you can be ready. The shops in Watch Hill are already open."

I jump into the shower, slip on a sundress and a chic pair of flip-flops, then pull my hair into a messy side braid. Grabbing a pair of sunglasses and my favorite shoulder bag, I present myself in the kitchen—I'm ready to go.

The air is light and breezy as we meander on the downtown sidewalks. The sun is warm on my arms, and the water that ensconces the touristy area sparkles as it reflects the penetrating solar rays.

We begin to hit the shops. A Summer Place, Diane's Beachwear, Gabrielle's Originals. Shopping with Mom. Something I hadn't done in a very long time. So much had been going on this summer—for both of us. I'd been consumed with Tristan. She'd been consumed with misery from her fights with Dad. And now everyone was consumed with the ugly murders that were painting the quaint community in a murky pallete of colors.

"Nothing like retail therapy to get your mind off everything, right, Bethany?"

I nod in agreement. I'm not sure what all she is referring to, but in my mind her statement speaks volumes. If she only knew the troubling thoughts that have been running through my mind lately. If she only knew who I have involved myself with this summer. From all appearances, her daughter is having the very first real crush of her life, with an attractive, lifeguard-looking, summertime boy from the local community. *How cute.* If she only knew how much more involved it is. The question is, *how* much more?

I shiver, trying to rid myself of that last thought. I have already resolved that quandary in my mind. Tristan, *my* Tristan, couldn't possibly be entangled in the yacht murders. And yet there are so many coincidences, and now by him quitting his job with no notice, and the most frustrating yet—his lack of confiding in me, the truth of *why*.

I sigh and walk to the rack where my mom is eyeing a display of Vera Bradley totes. She glances up at me. "Which pattern would be the most versatile?"

Shaking my head to eradicate the complexities of my continually invading speculations, I begin sorting through the colorful exhibition of purses. She was right—whimsical, mindless decision-making is just what I needed.

The following day I am hanging out oceanside with my brothers while they wade knee-deep in the water, searching for horseshoe crabs. It has been three days since I've seen Tristan, and I miss him. Trying not to think about him and all the discouraging questions I have about him, I get up and join them.

The water splashes around us as they scoot about, starting and stopping, lunging and scooping.

"Hey, Bethany, come see this one." Josh's voice is filled with enthusiasm as he calls me over.

"Yeah, it's a giant one," Jake echoes.

Salty liquid sprays up around my knees as I tread over to where they are standing, pointing animatedly into the water. I am greeted with a horseshoe crab on steroids—much bigger than any I've seen before. Much bigger than the ones I'd seen with Tristan. *Tristan.* How easily my thoughts drift back to him.

I blink. "This is so cool. It's ginormous."

"Yeah, ginormous," they repeat in unison.

Finally the twins tire of their hunt, and we begin heading back to the cottage to get some lunch. Just as we reach the front lawn, we are greeted by the sound of a car door slamming. Dad is home and heading toward the house also. There is an unmistakable spring in his step. We all meet up near the side entrance.

"Hey, some news," he announces rather zealously. "They believe they have the yacht murderer in custody."

My heart hammers in my chest.

Suddenly I can't get enough air.

It hits me full force that I am terrified to hear the next words that will come out of my dad's mouth.

"Apparently it was the *son* of John Dawson, himself. How tragic is that? Supposedly he has given a full confession."

A flood of relief crashes over me like a tidal wave.

I have to fight the emotional deluge of tears that is trying to well up in my eyes. I swallow. "What? Who? Why?" My questions come out in a breathless rush.

My dad stares at me, startled. Then he lets out a soft chuckle. "You were really shaken over this whole thing, weren't you, honey?" He brings me into his arms for a reassuring hug. "I think we are all glad it is finally over," he continues on soothingly. "Maybe now we can all go about enjoying the rest of our summer."

I have to stop myself from coming undone with joy as I listen to my dad relay all of the details. I take a deep breath and force myself to concentrate as he tells me the story. My mind is a jumbled mess, but I don't want to miss a single word of the truth that will extricate Tristan from the horrible, horrible crime.

The offender's name is Liam Vega, the twenty-year-old son of John Dawson. The tip-off came from Liam's neighbor, who resides next door to him in his apartment complex. She had always seen him as strange and reclusive, but lately his behavior had become more erratic. Recently, she had heard him talking in an almost agonizing voice through the paper-thin walls that divide his space from hers. She kept wondering who he was talking to. Keeping an eye out, she watched to see if anyone else was coming or going from the place, to see if he had a new roommate or visitors. But there never *was* anyone else. Then she started getting really nervous, suspecting he might be holding someone hostage inside.

When he was taken in for questioning, Liam's mental state was so fragile that he easily confessed to killing his dad and stepsister.

I am completely elated.

I want to scream at the top of my lungs. Tristan is innocent! *My* beautiful Tristan is innocent!

As quickly as I can, I excuse myself. I just have to go find him.

I hobble back down to the lakeshore as fast as my healing ankle will allow. Keeping my eyes peeled on the ocean, I search for any sign of him. The slightest ripple of water catches my attention. Surely, he has to feel my excitement somehow and know I'm looking for him. Surely he will emerge from the depths at any moment now and come walking up to me, dripping wet, and I can throw myself into his arms.

After what seems like forever, I finally decide he is not going to appear, and so reluctantly I follow the trail that leads from the sea back to the cottage for the second time that day. I am somewhat discouraged, but still hopeful as I revel in the knowledge that he had no part in the yacht murders.

That night when I crawl under my covers, I take extreme comfort in knowing that very soon I will be able to see Tristan again and look him in the eye without having any misgivings about him.

It seems like tomorrow will never come. But when it does, I awaken with renewed vigor and jump in the LaCrosse, heading over to Watch Hill Boatyard. My ankle is still tender, and long walks are out of the question, so I drive instead. The music is cranked, windows down, allowing the ocean breeze to pelt across my face. It feels so good to leave my house unchaperoned. Although at times I'd broken the rules in the last weeks, it feels good to finally have no restrictions. Once again I am free.

My heart is pounding as the tires of the LaCrosse crunch against the gravel drive of Watch Hill Boatyard. Stepping out of the vehicle, my eyes begin searching in all directions. My first glance toward the harbor reveals nothing, so I continue my quest inside the large, metal storage buildings. Still nothing. Slightly discouraged, I walk back out to the waterfront. The faint smell of gasoline mixed with marine life filters through the air. Scanning the maze of docks that fills the shoreline, I find myself practically willing Tristan's lean, muscular frame to appear. I bite my lip, squinting to see beyond the bright reflection of the sun. Finally I swallow down my disappointment. He's not here.

Then my attention is drawn to a remote slip. Shining like a beacon in a storm, *Blue* sits rocking back and forth in the slow wake of the boats that are coming and going from the marina. Hesitantly, I draw near to the watercraft. Tristan's prize possession. The mahogany wood exterior glistens its welcome as I approach. I look in all directions, but the owner is nowhere in sight. My eyes land back on the boat. It truly is a magnificent creation. Pride fills my chest. Tristan did such a good job. Unable to resist, I step into the front portion of the vessel. The crème-color interior is so classy and inviting. I run my hand over the seat beside me—it feels smooth to the touch. Leaning my head back, I sigh. *Where is Tristan?*

I sit there for some time, swaying gently in the waves, feeling the warmth of leather against the back of my legs.

Finally, grudgingly, I remove myself from the comfort of the antique boat and leave the premises.

As I drive back through town, I get a sudden craving for something sweet. Parking the car in front of Bay Street Deli, I enter its anterior doors in search of some fresh pastry. Once inside the entrance, right away my attention is drawn to a flat screen TV that is mounted in the far right corner.

Breaking News. An informal interview is being held with two of Liam Vega's former college acquaintances. In an attempt to gain some insight on the motive of the troubled boy, the anchorman is making an inquiry on the earlier thoughts and actions of the confessed killer. What kind of person goes about murdering his stepsister and father? The former associates, a redhead and brunet with a goatee, take turns speaking into the camera.

"He was *always* rather melancholy," the redhead lets us know. "But he seemed to take it very personally when his dad left his family and remarried. He had a really hard time with it. That is when Megan Shaffer came into the picture. She became his stepsister."

The camera shifts to the young man with the goatee.

"She was like the exact opposite of him . . . very outgoing, a party queen. You could gather he wasn't very fond of her . . . but I would have never dreamed of this." The brown-haired boy shakes his head, clearly flabbergasted.

After the interview clip, the anchorman continues on. "Other sources close to the Dawson family say a lot of hatred was harbored for some time on the part of Liam Vega . . . even going so far as disassociating himself from the Dawson name. After dropping his college classes less than a year ago, he had been residing in the Watch Hill area. John Dawson, CEO of Alantrop Sea Shipping Company, had been bringing his yacht to the Watch Hill Boat Harbor for years. The question remains, knowing this, did Liam move into the area and premeditate the murders for some time?"

Toward the end of the broadcast a photo of the criminal is posted to the screen, an under-nourished young man with scraggly hair and haunted eyes. I stare at the picture momentarily, trying to place him. Then I call to mind a beach party from earlier in the summer when someone had pointed him out—had denoted how creepy he was. I remember feeling a touch of sadness for him even then. It was evident that he was a loner. Had anyone known the thoughts he was struggling with?

And now—now, I feel a bigger sadness for the whole tragic situation.

I purchase my apple pastry and hang my head as I leave the deli. I am overjoyed that Tristan is not involved in the yacht murders, and yet grieved over the idea that two people have lost their lives this summer, taken so unexpectedly and unnecessarily by someone who knew them well.

Before sliding back into the LaCrosse to head back home, I pull out my phone to send a quick text to Lucy.

Yacht murders solved! *(send)*

I am pulling into the cottage driveway when I hear the soft vibration of my mobile device on the seat beside me.

(unlock) Bethany . . . I am so glad!

I know! I'll call with details later. *(send)*

Sighing, I sit staring out the front window of the LaCrosse for a moment or two before tucking my phone into my pocket and heading into the house. My printed text can't really convey the assortment of emotions I'm feeling right now.

The next morning I get up early. I can't sleep anyway. I'm still bursting with the news I want to share with Tristan. Well, it's not that I'm going to walk up to him and tell him that I'd been having some serious uncertainties about him. That I questioned whether or not he was capable of murder. Suddenly I feel rather silly. Would he tell me to get lost if he knew what I'd been thinking?

Once again I hop in the LaCross in pursuit of him. This time I go to his secluded beach. Finding a small turnoff where I can park the car, I amble the rest of way on foot through the wooded path that takes me to his hidden coast. Right away I experience a pang of hurt when I find he's not there. Dejectedly, I position myself in the sand and stare at the ocean waves that are rhythmically drifting onto shore. *Tristan, where are you?*

Rewinding time, I contemplate why I was having so many doubts about him anyway. Sure there were a lot of coincidences, like his loathing for the shipping companies, his access to the yachts via the water, and his personal tie to Megan Shaffer. But that wasn't enough to make me feel the way I did. There was more to it. It was in the way he acted when the murders were discussed—angered, troubled, closed-off. What was that all about? And why had he quit work without notice? Why was he not coming to see me? In the past, he'd gone days without coming around, but never this long.

This time, when he comes back, I swear, I'm going to tell him he can't leave me hanging like this anymore. *No more.*

With a pang in my chest, I think back to the last time I was with him. There was something about the way he held me—so tightly, the sad look that was in his eyes. Did he sense what I was feeling about him? Did he suspect my distrust? Did my actions betray my thoughts?

I focus my eyes back on the undulating whitecaps in front of me. An unexpected rush of panic surges through my veins. Why isn't he coming back—*is* he coming back? *No!* I won't let my thoughts go there.

He told me he loved me. The way that he kissed me. I get breathless even now as I think about it. But how much do I really know about relationships? It feels so genuine—what Tristan and I have. But this is my first real relationship; is it possible that he just led me to believe it all?

I close my eyes and reach for the shell that hangs incessantly around my neck. I recall the expression on his face when he sang the song that he wrote for me.

No, that isn't possible at all.

Chapter Twenty

Desperate for answers after not seeing Tristan for several days, I rack my brain for a solution. I'd been making myself very available to the ocean lately. I was spending hours a day next to its nautical land-scape, watching, hoping, waiting. But he wasn't turning up. Finally I decide to pay Mr. Horton a visit. I think back to the times I'd seen Tristan and Mr. Horton interacting. It seemed as though they had a connection that went beyond a casual friendship. Tristan clearly revered his older companion—and in turn, Mr. Horton's eyes and actions were filled with fatherly love.

I recall Mr. Horton's words to me when he had been visiting at the marina. *Don't get discouraged.* I never *did* figure out what he meant by that. But he *did* let it slip that Tristan confided in him about me. And he *did* help to get Tristan a job in the marina, in spite of him trying so hard to stay away from me. Had Mr. Horton known that I was already volunteering there?

Somehow I just had the feeling he was in *both* of our corners— mine and Tristan's together.

It takes some asking around town and some Googling on the Internet, but finally I have his address and directions to his house in hand, and I am ready to set off in search of the coveted informa-tion I'm after.

I'm a little nervous about how the whole quest is going to unfold, so before I leave, I text Lucy for a little moral support.

I haven't heard from Tristan in days. *(send)*

There it is, in print. Just getting it off my chest feels good. But it scares me too—somehow it makes it seem more real. *Tristan is avoiding me.*

It doesn't take long before I hear back.

(unlock) What is going on?

I'm not sure. Trying to find out. *(send)*

(unlock) Oh Bethany . . . it will all work out for good . . .

It has to! *(send)*

It just has to! I close my eyes momentarily before pulling out of the side gravel drive.

I glance up at the sky as my car hums along Watch Hill Road. It is a cloudless day, and the glistening rays of sun, reflecting on the blue ocean waves, encourage me to keep driving. I take the first left past the Cooked Goose restaurant and wind down a secluded, wooded lane that is thought to lead me to his house. At first I have a hard time locating his property, but then I spot a hidden drive with a wooden sign that matches the numbers in my hand.

I take a deep breath. This must be it. His driveway is long and narrow, snaking back through a densely forested area. Finally I reach a clearing that houses a gray-sided, cabinlike structure. There are a couple of deteriorating outbuildings and a large pile of chopped wood that occupies the vicinity as well. The home of an aging bachelor.

Trying to soothe away my nerves, I pause briefly before knocking on the weathered screen entryway. I suck in a deep breath as the door slowly opens. Mr. Horton's craggy, brown eyes fleetingly register surprise before a warm smile spreads across his face, making me feel instantly at ease.

"Bethany . . . come on in." His arm gestures behind him." Welcome to my humble abode. I'm surprised you were able to locate me. It's pretty remote out here in the sticks."

I smile. "Yeah, I did have a little bit of a hard time."

"Well, make yourself at home. How about a glass of lemonade?"

I nod. "Sounds good."

He leaves the room, and my eyes are drawn to a display of model ships that sits in the far right corner of his entryway. Heeding his advice, I make myself at home by meandering over to the exhibition. I am standing in front of it, taking in the intricate details of each miniature creation, when he walks back in, holding a glass filled with shimmering liquid.

"What you see there is lifetime of hard work." His voice is filled with pride.

"I'll bet. It's a stunning assembly. So much elaborate detail. Did you collect them or create them?"

"I made each one myself." He hands me the lemonade. "Each one has a story to tell. Each replica is of a ship that sunk in the ocean." Running a hand through his thinning, gray hair, he continues pensively. "I guess I just didn't want them to be forgotten."

"Wow . . . that is something."

Momentarily, he snaps out of his reverie and eyes me with a compassionate smile. "But you are not here to talk about my ship display, are you?"

I nod, exhaling a breath of relief. *He understands!*

"Tristan's been gone for days now," I sigh. "I wondered if you would happen to know where he is."

Mr. Horton presses his lips together, watching me as I talk. Motioning me into his front room that offers a hidden view of the ocean, he points to a stuffed chair.

"Have a seat." I sit down. He sits down too, then clears his throat. "I always believed there was life in the ocean. Not just fish and marine life and such, but real live beings like you and me. Communities of people that exist in the far-reaching depths of the sea." His eyes take on a far-off look as he talks. "One time when I was a much younger man, I was out on my sailboat all alone. I had strayed off course, and for a while I was a bit disoriented, trying to figure out which direction I needed to go to find my way back. Then I saw one emerge from the depths. A real live sea-person swimming on the surface of the water, miles from anywhere. I remember thinking I was probably just shaken from being lost and going a little wacko from my nerves being stretched, so I brushed off the vision and worked on getting my boat back on track."

Taking a small break from his story, Mr. Horton gets up and walks across the room. Bending down, he picks up a crumpled wrapper and deposits it in a small trash can in the corner. Then he sits back down.

"Shortly after I got my bearings, I was steering my boat in the direction of home when it appeared again. A lady . . . swimming, only yards away from me. I called to her, but she vanished before I could establish any real communication. But I knew right then and there that my suspicions were right . . . there *were* humanlike creatures living in the sea. I'd just seen a mermaid, not once, but twice."

I lean forward, sitting on the edge of my chair. Straining my ears, I tune in carefully to Mr. Horton's narrative, wanting to hear every word he has to say. I have a strong feeling that I am on the brink of learning volumes about Tristan's world, and I don't want to miss a thing.

I stare at the wrinkles that are etched into his face as he begins again. But it's not really the furrowed lines that I'm looking at. My mind is peering beyond them, focusing on the mental picture that he is creating of a realm that exists in the sea. A world that belongs to Tristan.

"I started researching all I could about sea creatures . . . mermaids and mermen if you will. I started collecting things . . . magazines, newspaper articles, anything that spoke of underwater life. And . . . I started watching the sea."

He stops and looks right at me. "I think that is why Tristan showed himself to me."

My heart pounds. Finally, he's gotten to the part I've been waiting to hear.

Mr. Horton watches my face carefully. He knows he has my undivided attention. "He must have known I could be trusted . . . that I believed. I met him when he was a young boy. Probably soon after he laid eyes on you."

I suck in a breath. Now he *really* has my attention.

He grins in remembrance. "He sure was a cute little fella. Little blond-haired kid. Bronzed skin. It didn't take me long to figure out that he was spending time above the water. You didn't get a tan like that on the bottom of the ocean. After meeting you . . . that is when it began for him. When he couldn't stay away from Watch Hill, couldn't stay in the depths of the sea where he belonged."

Folding my hands tightly together, I recall my trip to Tristan's island. He had told me he couldn't stay away from the little blond girl he had met so many years ago—that I *was* that little blond girl. Now I am getting to hear more of the story.

"His family told him he *had* to stay below the surface, so as not to reveal himself to humans. If he didn't, he would risk exposing his people and there would be consequences . . . possibly severe. But by now, he couldn't stay away, so he would come around now and then, every summer. And he would hang around my place, watching me tinker on things, helping me . . . and asking me questions . . . asking me lots of questions about humans. Over the years, I watched him grow from a curious young waif to a confident, strapping, young man. A handsome one too."

At this, I feel a blush spread quickly across my face. *My sentiments exactly.*

I am relieved when Mr. Horton carries on without glancing in my direction. "I came to think of him as the son I never had . . . Then came the summer of 2012, this summer . . . and that little blond-haired girl had finally arrived back in town. It seemed to

Tristan that destiny had been set in motion years ago. Like the waves that set their course toward the shore, it couldn't be stopped . . . and yet he was trying so hard to fight it."

Inwardly, I cringe. This is the part I hate, that he was trying so hard to stay away from me. But I thought we had covered this, and he had decided he was going to come around anyway. That he loved me so much, he *couldn't* stay away. A little stab of hurt makes its way into my chest. Had he changed his mind and now he had gone away for good? *Well, why the heck couldn't he have told me good-bye?*

I take a calming breath, trying to focus on Mr. Horton's story. Somehow, I have the feeling he wants to tell it to me in his own orderly fashion, and he might quit talking altogether, if he has to deal with a hysterical girl.

"So this summer, even though you knew he was trying to stay away from me, you got him the job at the marina? Did you know I was volunteering there, or was it all a coincidence?"

Mr. Horton's weathered, brown eyes take on a mischievous sparkle. "*He* thought he needed to stay away. But for years I witnessed the eyes that lit up whenever he spoke of that little blond girl, whenever he spoke of you . . . I thought to myself, love can overcome the largest of obstacles, why should this time be any different . . . So, yes, I did knew you were there."

A feeling of warmth floods through me. *He is in our corner!*

"As soon as he started getting to know you at the marina, he began fixing up that old cabin so he would have a place to show you . . . a place to call home. He was scared to tell you the truth about himself, thought you would run for sure if you only knew who he really was. I own the property with that old, rundown shack on it, and he asked if he could use it. I would go over there and watch him hard at work. I'd say he did a pretty darn good job sprucing up that old thing."

My head begins to spin. My heart throbs with the realization of what Mr. Horton just said. He did that for me? *I didn't know.* More than ever I want to find Tristan, wrap my arms around him, and never let go. *The cabin,* another place I can look for him. But first I need to find out what all Mr. Horton knows. I feel like I'm on the verge of becoming unglued in my seat, but Mr. Horton continues on as though my mind is not a jumbled mess.

"The first time he played his guitar for you, he worried that he was holding you hostage with his power. But the longer you were together, the more he knew different. As your relationship grew, he realized that the bond you shared was stronger than the influencing control he could create with his music."

I don't want to exhale, find out it wasn't true. Shake the water from my lungs, so much I never really knew . . .

The image of Tristan perched on the driftwood, pouring out his heart to me with his breathlessly beautiful voice makes my entire being ache. I've got to find him soon. First though, I have to know *why* he disappeared. Mustering up the necessary courage, I ask my next question.

"Tristan acted so strange about the yacht murders. Whenever they were brought up in front of him, he became very closed-off. Do you know why?" I hesitate, ashamed to utter the next words I'm about to say. "When he quit his job at the marina without notice . . . I even considered . . . I even wondered if he was involved somehow." I hang my head in embarrassment. "I wonder if he sensed my doubt and that is the reason he left."

Mr. Horton leaves the comfort of his chair and walks to the front window. As he stares out at the limited view of the ocean peeking out of the apertures between the trees, I wonder if my admission of doubt is too much for him. He clearly holds a fondness for Tristan; have I crossed the line?

Finally, he sits back down.

"The more Tristan came around this summer, the more he was

falling for you, but there was always something holding him back . . . He wasn't supposed to go around humans or there would be consequences. It wasn't his own safety he worried about . . . it was yours. He was never really sure to what lengths his community would go to sever a tie created with a human, to destroy evidence of any connection that would threaten their existence. He was continually struggling with the notion of staying away from Watch Hill and you. Every time he tried to tell himself he was going to disconnect himself from you, he saw that he was hurting you, and it tore him apart . . . He wished he could be stronger."

As I take a swig from my glass, I notice that my hands are trembling. Promptly, I set the lemonade back down and lace my fingers together in an effort to disguise how shaken I am from this conversation.

"What about you? He visited you all these years; weren't you afraid for your safety?"

"At times I've toyed over that question, and I've never come up with an exact answer. But remember, Tristan wasn't the first one to reveal himself to me. Maybe they just regard me as a crazy, old man who lives in the woods at the edge of the sea. Nonthreatening. Sometimes I do wonder if anything will ever happen to me, I know so much . . . but it never does. Either way, Tristan never seems concerned about my safety, so I don't worry either."

He pauses, takes a large breath, and adjusts his legs before continuing.

"There was a particular young man, a sea-creature if you will, that Tristan spoke of over the years. Someone he didn't trust. Someone who harbored jealousy and hatred . . . a type of evil that lurked just below the surface. He grew up with him. They were close comrades, by all appearances best friends, and yet worst enemies . . . his cousin, Keuran."

Keuran? I furrow my brow together. This is news to me, the first time I've heard utterance of him.

"There is a part of Tristan that knew that if trouble would ever come his way, it would manifest itself in the form of Keuran. Only one year apart, his cousin's resentfulness became evident very early on. Keuran, being the older relative, deemed that he should be bigger, stronger, faster. Problem was from a very early age, he was outdone by Tristan in every walk of life. Tristan didn't plan it that way, it just happened. Schooling, relationships, athletics. Although most of Keuran's reactions to Tristan's successes were expressed passively, the younger cousin sensed that his kin's jealously ran deep."

The hairs on my arms stand on end. Where is this story going to go? As I run my hands over the exposed skin below my shirtsleeves in a soothing fashion, Mr. Horton watches me. *Go ahead, tell me everything. I can handle this,* I tell him with my eyes.

"And then the yacht murders took place."

Finally. The part I'd been waiting for.

"Tristan became concerned. All the signs, all the evidence, seemed to point to the water."

Relief spreads through me. I'm not the only who had had that train of thought.

"Tristan's concern became focused on you."

Me?

"He was worried about your safety. He didn't trust Keuran. Keuran was always so obsessed with him, he figured now he was following his activity on land. Tristan wasn't sure how far Keuran's fixation would go, but he was growing more and more confident that he was either trying to frame him or leave warning signs for him." *Sick, twisted warning signs.* "After all of these years, Keuran had finally found Tristan's one weakness—you. Tristan knew he needed to leave you and get Keuran off your trail. He tried so many times . . . but couldn't stay away. And now . . . ?"

My mind becomes a speeding train running in reverse as I try to recall all the times I'd been with Tristan and was confused by his actions and behaviors. The aloofness. All the times he didn't come around. The momentary agonized expressions that would cross over his beautiful face. *He loves me, but our relationship is a torment for him.* The taste of panic begins to rise in my throat.

"And now . . . ?" My voice sounds breathlessly desperate. "And now, does Tristan know the truth? That I am safe . . . that the killer was caught? That it wasn't Keuran after all. It's okay for him to come back now. Does he know he can come back now?"

My body begins to tremble as I work hard to fight back the tears that are threatening to surface.

Mr. Horton shakes his head, looking a little uncomfortable. His voice is subdued and he avoids eye contact with me. "I haven't seen him lately . . . If I had, I would have let him know."

"But he will be back soon . . . right? So we can tell him the truth?"

Again Mr. Horton shakes his head. "I do know that in the past he couldn't stay away. But if the situation is tied directly to your safety . . . I'm just . . ." He hesitates, his shoulders hunching in defeat. "I'm just not sure."

What? No!

I can't hold back the tears any longer. "No . . . no . . . he will come back. He promised he'd take me swimming on a coral reef . . . I've never been . . . and I told him that it was something I've always wanted to do . . . He *will* come back . . ." My face becomes a canvas of streaked, salty liquid. Even as I'm saying the words, I realize how despondent and stupid they must sound.

Transitorily, I close my eyes tightly together. Taking a deep breath, I try to control my emotions before I begin to sob. "He has to come back . . ." My voice is barely louder than a whisper.

I glance back up at Mr. Horton. His weathered face is downcast. His signature twinkling, brown eyes look sad. He is at a loss for words.

Finally when he speaks, his tone is hushed and mollifying.

"He loves you, Bethany. Please never doubt that. He really *does* love you. For both of your sakes, I hope there is a way to work this out. I really hope he *can* come back."

Chapter Twenty-one

Now that I finally understand Tristan and his struggle, I am even more frantic to find him. I just want to tell him about the solving of the yacht murders, and that I get his distress over our forbidden relationship and his malevolent cousin Keuran—and that we can find a way to work it all out. If only he had confided in me. If only he would have told me about his concerns over Keuran. I know he probably thought that if he did tell me, I would have tried to stop him from leaving. And yes—I would have. But now, as it turns out, he didn't need to leave at all. I heave a deep sigh and run my fingers through the disheveled strands of my long, blond hair. This whole thing is all such a mess.

After I leave Mr. Horton's house, I immediately go to Tristan's cabin. The last time I'd been there, the only time I'd been there, I'd taken a hidden trail along the lakeshore. This time I have directions via the road entrance, courtesy of the original property owner. As I pull into the brush-covered drive, I am reminded of my earlier visit—I remember thinking it was odd that the driveway looked un-used and unapproachable from the road. How much my world has changed since then. Back then I hadn't known that Tristan didn't actually *need* a driveway. The only transportation he required was his arms and legs, and some water. And actually, he didn't really *need* the cabin either. He had only created the illusion of having a home on land, for me.

I knock, but there is no answer.

I try the doorknob, but it doesn't turn.

My heart lurches in my chest as I peer through the windows, eyeing the tidy interior, the stone fireplace, the small butcher-board table where we had shared lunch. He had fixed this up just for me. My soul fills with longing and love.

Hiking the perimeter of the property, I call his name, but there is no answer.

Reluctantly, I maneuver back through the concealing over-growth of the driveway and crawl into my car. Disheartened, I rest my head on the steering wheel. *He really is gone.* Was this it then? The end of my summer relationship? The end of Tristan and me? Shaking away the feelings of despondency that are trying to over-take me, I put the keys in the ignition and drive back to the cottage without once noticing the road.

Later, I spend a despairing, sleepless night in bed. Tossing and turning, mind racing, fighting an oppressive gloom. By the time daylight fills the room the following morning, I know what I'm going to do.

Feeling a little light-headed from lack of sleep, I stumble out of bed. Apprehension surrounds me as I shower, dress, and fix my hair. But determination overrides my fear, and so I grab what I need and resolutely leave the house.

Nearing the Watch Hill Public Boat Docks, I spy a white sign with red lettering that reads "Boat Rentals". Taking a deep breath, I proceed to the small booth that sits twenty feet from the shoreline.

I clear my throat. "I would like to rent a boat."

What am I doing? No, I *know* what I'm doing.

My hand is shaky as I hand the attendant my license, credit card, and boater's safety certificate. I try to recall the last time I'd driven a boat. It seemed like a long time ago, and it hadn't really gone all that well. My mind feels scattered. As a young man reviews the op-erating and safety instructions with me, I work hard to focus on the meaning of his words. I need all the help I can get driving this thing.

The watercraft chokes and sputters twice before the engine finally reaches a steady hum. The attendant eyes my face uncertainly as he pushes me off from the docks. I set my jaw purposefully, hands tightly gripping the steering column, and concentrate on the endless body of water ahead of me. *I can do this!*

I *will* do this!

For a brief moment I consider texting Kate, letting her know the general vicinity of my excursion, but then decide against it. She would probably try to talk me out of it, and I had already made up my mind.

The greater task still lies ahead of me—finding Tristan's island. I think back to the glorious day I'd shared with him in his hidden paradise. Distracted by his beauty, I hadn't paid very close attention to the nautical route he had taken. I scan the horizon searching for familiar landmarks. The lighthouse. It was definitely somewhere to the left of Watch Hill Light. Staying outside the buoys, I aim the fiberglass bow of the boat toward the juncture of Block Island Sound and Fisher's Island Sound. Once I pass the towering, white brick beacon, I am face to face with nothing but open water. From there, I decide to keep the boat heading in a northeasterly direction and hope for the best.

The sea is endless. I glance behind me at the portable gas tank that sits in the far back corner of the boat. I don't remember Tristan having to refill the main line on our trip, so the island couldn't be farther than one tank away. But then I suppose it's possible he could have filled it once we reached the island, and distracted by other things, I just hadn't paid attention.

It is a bleak, cloud-covered day, and there are no rays of sun sparkling on the water, urging me along on my quest. But I don't need reassurance. The growing ache in my heart is telling me what I need to do. *I need to find Tristan.* Once he sees me, he will be reminded that his desire to be with me is stronger than his resolution of staying away.

I keep my eyes peeled on the sweeping display of interminable gray liquid before me. On and on I speed over the surface of the water. Occasionally, the smooth, aquatic plane is broken up by choppy disturbances that jerk the boat, causing me to white-knuckle my grip on the steering column. Presently, I feel a vibration in the rear pocket of my shorts. The ride is rather calm at the moment, and I am able to effectively reach behind to pull out my phone. It's Lucy.

(unlock) **Hey girl!**

Nonchalantly, I toss my mobile device down on the seat beside me. I will answer her later.

Just as I'm beginning to doubt my ability to find the island, I detect a tiny portion of land protruding from the surrounding abyss. My heart hammers. Maybe this is it. On closer approach, I become more and more convinced. It isn't until I have the boat completely beached that I know for sure. My eyes scan the area, soaking in every inch of the miniature landmass. It's the sandy path, wedged between two pieces of horn-shaped driftwood, that finally makes me certain—the start of the trail that will lead to the Mediterraneanlike setting. I remember it distinctly.

Grabbing my bag of supplies, I start out on foot toward paradise—one step closer to Tristan. Crossing through the driftwood entrance, I wind my way through a rocky terrain, followed by a sparsely wooded area. Somewhere in the back of my mind it all seems vaguely familiar. Finally, rounding the corner that will lead me to where I want to be, I peruse my surroundings.

Nothing is as I remember.

Dune grass is everywhere, hiding the sand. There is no protected inlet. The water that sweeps onto the rocky shore is dull and colorless. Momentarily, panic courses through my veins. *Where am I? Did I take a wrong turn?* I spin around in all directions until I find the path from where I came. I was so sure about where I was going.

Taking a deep breath, I fight the confusion that tries to overwhelm me. Suddenly I feel so alone. Trying to comfort myself, I reach for the shell that rests just below my collarbone. I can't concentrate. I know I need to focus.

Take me where I want to be
'cuz the sand keeps slippin' out to sea
and with you is where I need to be.

The words of Tristan's song play over and over in my head. Over and over again I sing them. At last I feel my body de-escalating. Retracing my steps, I curve back to the rocky terrain near the start of the trail. I glance around. This part I *was* sure about. Girding myself with bravery, I decide to try again. This time when I reach the lightly forested area, I pay closer attention. Once focused, I notice another possibility. Maybe this was the turn I was supposed to take. This time as I round the intended corner, I am greeted with the familiar feel of a tropical getaway.

Weak with relief, I collapse into the velvety, white sand.

In spite of the dismal sky, the water suggests a turquoise hue, boasting frothy, white crowns as it cascades onto shore. Just like I remember, the cove is picturesque and protected. Swiftly, my eyes take in the whole image, expecting Tristan to materialize at any minute, making the postcard complete.

But he's not there. Momentarily my heart plummets. But not for long. I am convinced that I am in the right place—now all I have to do is wait.

My gaze is centered on the sea, hunting for an interruption in the pattern of the waves. Periodically, I take out the binoculars that I packed, along with some food and water. Expanding my line of vision, I search for anything that could be interpreted as movement. One time, unexpectedly, I detect a dolphin. I watch, riveted by each jump and flip that takes it beyond the reach of the undulating surf.

But this is only a momentary distraction. As much as I want to be entertained by the friendly, aquatic animal, I am impatient to find Tristan.

Minutes turn to hours, and still Tristan does not come to be with me. Taking out my small, green cooler, I eat the slices of fruit, roast beef, and cheese I brought. Still I wait. By now I have an uneasy feeling growing in the pit of my stomach. I was completely convinced that if I could just make it here to this island, I would find him. Now with each hour that passes, I am less and less sure. With each minute that passes, I feel tiny pieces of my heart disintegrate into the salty ocean air.

Thoughts of not finding him, of never seeing him again, overwhelm my mind, and the mental effort it takes to keep them at bay leaves me physically drained. But still I hang on to a miniscule thread of hope as I wait.

Midmorning turns to afternoon, and eventually early evening. The only thing that does arrive are dark, ominous clouds, swiftly covering the sky, carrying with them the threat of a storm.

It takes every ounce of emotional strength I have to talk myself into departing the island. I have a menacing feeling that if I leave, I will be leaving Tristan and the chance of ever seeing him again. But as I watch opaque vapors invade the atmosphere, the small bit of reasoning that is left in my brain tells me that I can't stay.

Surprisingly, the boat slides easily off the sand and back into the water. Once in the rocking watercraft, I eye my surroundings. The sea is now liquid steel. I shiver as the wind whips around my shoulders. Then I look up to the blackening heavens nervously. I hope I can make it back to Watch Hill before the storm is in full swing.

I point the boat back in the direction I came.

The engine starts without trouble, and I begin the race against time. As I'm hydroplaning along the now choppy surface of the water, my heart becomes heavier and heavier like the moisture-filled air that threatens to release its fury at any moment. My mind is spiraling with ideas of Tristan being gone and never coming back. Fighting to reach the surface of my thoughts, I try to break free from their dark reverie in order to focus on steering the boat.

Eventually it becomes an all-out war with the water as the waves grow to new heights, now producing foaming, white crests that glow in stark contrast to the contiguous, black sea. I glance at my watch. It is only 6:00 p.m., but it might as well be midnight.

Then the first drop of liquid hits my skin. Minutes pass before several more follow. Soon it becomes hard to differentiate between the raindrops and the outpouring of tears that are blinding my eyes. Somewhere in the back of my mind it occurs to me that I'm losing the race. My rented boat fights desperately to survive in a now severe storm, with a sinister ocean that seems all too willing to swallow it up.

As the wind and the breakers swirl around me, I detect a faint flame in the distance, splitting through my oppressive sphere of despair. I must be coming up on Watch Hill Light. I'm getting closer.

Closer to what? Life without Tristan?

My depressive thoughts are interrupted by a sudden torrent of rain and hurricanelike winds. A wave beside me becomes a wall. Before the impact of fluid devours me, I have a microsecond to know I won't survive. Unsurprisingly, my boat instantaneously capsizes, sending me swirling into a tumultuous world of seawater. All around me the tide surges. I gasp and choke, one minute trying frantically to fill my lungs with air, and the next getting sucked into a chaotic abyss. Fighting for subsistence, I surface. Several feet away I see my upturned transportation being tossed and thrown about. It seems there is no escape.

I feel the fight being sucked out of me, and intermittently I begin to drift in and out of consciousness. Very soon, I accept that this is how it will end for me.

And what a better place to be than in Tristan's ocean. *Forever with him.*

As everything becomes muted and distant, I experience a diminished sensation that something is grabbing ahold of me. I'm not sure what it is, and I really don't care. Is it some type of marine life? Possibly even a shark—*could be.* Or maybe my life vest is caught on something and I am being held in place, *underwater.* At this point does it matter?

Whatever the source, it carries with it an electrical current, a burning phenomenon that rushes through my veins, making me feel warm all over. I relax into it, feeling oddly at peace. I am suspended in limbo, floating.

Next, I feel movement, snapping me out of my abstraction. Now I am coursing through the ocean at a lightning quick speed. Flying. Whether I'm in the water or in the sky, I'm just not sure. But either way, I am soaring. Going away.

Far, far away.

Minutes pass, or light-years. The next thing I perceive is stillness. I am no longer buoyant and free. Instead, a gritty hardness rests below me, scratching the skin on my arms and legs. I recognize the sensation, like I've felt it before, but somehow I just can't put my finger on what it is. No longer pacified, I miss the layer of warmth that had once enveloped me. *Who took away my blanket?*

Out of nowhere, an intoxicating fragrance captivates my sense of smell. *So familiar.* Every inch of my nerve endings becomes heightened. I try to breathe in the scent that is now shooting through my veins like a narcotic, wanting to inhale it deeper. *Salty and clean.* Desperately, I try to open my eyes and find its source. But my lids are so heavy, and they won't follow my command.

Surrendering to the placidity, I lie very still, waiting to find out what will happen to me next. Stillness. A new tranquility. I begin to drift and fade. Then something balmy fills the air directly over me, like a warm breeze landing on my skin, my cheekbones, my eyelids. A breath. Next, a drop of water hits my face. One, two, three, I lose count. Now I have to wonder if I'm back on the boat after all, and the rain has begun again. One of the beads of liquid slides down to the corner of my mouth, and I swallow its warm saltiness. *Not rain after all.* But not really the temperature of the ocean either.

Before I have time to contemplate the cause, I experience an unhurried, soft, sensation of something sliding down over my hair, onto my cheek, in the form of a barely palpable caress. *It feels so good.* I struggle to press into it, trying to intensify the feeling, begging it to continue, to strengthen. But just as quickly as it began, it is gone again, and I feel myself slip back into unconsciousness.

Chapter Twenty-two

My name is being called. Somewhere, someone is beckoning me, pleading. Many people. Through a long, hollow tunnel I hear voices. My body is quivering all over. Someone is shaking me. I try to open my eyes. With effort, this time I am able to. Everything is distant and fuzzy, unfocused. Where am I? The murky haze that is impairing my eyesight begins to lift. I am on a beach. Napatree Point. Several people are standing around me, kneeling next to me—Mom, Dad, David Chambers, Kate, and others that I don't recognize.

Dad eases me onto my side and I vomit water. My mom's arms go around me. She is crying hysterically. "My baby, my baby . . . Thank God you are okay." Over and over again she repeats this phrase.

I am so tired.

It is hard to say when the recovery from my near drowning fades into a depression, but it is an easy transition. What begins as a weakness of the body, from being ravaged and waterlogged at sea, soon turns into a weakness of the mind—and the solution for both is to stay in bed.

I gather bits and pieces of information from those that hover over me, first at the hospital and then in my bedroom at the cottage.

My parents had been worried sick. *Where did I go?* They involved friends, management from the marina, and anyone else they could to help look for me. My mind is numb, and though at times I try to remember how the whole thing went down, I have a hard time recalling the exact details. There was a bad storm. A really big wave—and then, water everywhere. My rented boat. What had become of the boat? I had been drowning. I *knew* I was drowning. And yet somehow, I had made it to shore.

Where had I gone? It isn't hard for me to play dumb about that. My mind can't comprehend that I had gone to Tristan's island, and he wasn't there, and I was never going to see him again. The synapses that are supposed to be firing in my head are now dead. There really is nothing to say, nothing I *can* say. I don't have thoughts to form into words. I don't *want* to form words. I am just lying in my bed—in limbo. And I am *so* tired.

At some point I hear my parents standing outside my bedroom door.

"I know this whole thing has something to do with that boy she is seeing this summer." *Was.* My mom's voice sounds irritated. "And I mean, where was *he* when push came to shove, and we were searching for her? Why wasn't he helping to look for her? I'll tell you why, because he was involved somehow, that's why."

Dad sighs. "You are probably right. There is something fishy about him, anyway. You never see him over here sitting at the dining room table playing monopoly with Bethany or anything like that."

I turn over on my side to stare at the corner of my room. I have no thoughts on the matter.

Days pass, and I begin to sense that my parent's sympathy over my near-drowning incident is waning. When I insist on leaving my blinds drawn to block out the light, they pull them up anyway. When I say *no* to taking a shower, they say *yes, it's time.* Instead of continuing to bring my meals to my room on a tray, they require that I join them at the table.

"You should go sit out on the screen porch for a while. Enjoy the fresh air."

"Come on out of your room and watch this movie."

"We need some help with these dishes, grab a towel."

It takes all of my effort to complete the smallest task, and I find any excuse I can to go lie back down. It takes all the energy I have to put my mind in neutral, shutting out everything and everyone—and the fact that Tristan is gone.

I have very little left for anything else.

"What is it, honey?" My mom is sitting beside me on my bed, while I lay looking in the direction of the window. I have just politely declined to go for a walk with her down by the lakeshore, and concern is evident in her voice. She is lightly rubbing my arm in a soothing fashion. "Is it Tristan?"

Tristan who? I want to pull the blankets over my head and go back into oblivion. Instead I nod.

She waits, but I don't offer anything more. "Well, whenever you are ready to talk, I am ready to listen . . . And I don't know if I ever told you this, but back in college, I had a black belt in karate. I may look small, but if you ever need me to kick someone's butt, you just say the word."

In spite of everything, I glance up at her and give a little grin.

One afternoon I am lying in my near-vegetative state when an image comes seeping forward from the recesses of my mind. A little girl of age six, crouching on the sand, surrounded by an endless stretch of beach. Beside her, a little boy with blond hair and intense, sea green eyes sits looking over at her, playfully smiling.

My heart hammers in my chest. Taking a deep breath, I press my eyes tightly together, willing myself to relax into the vision, urging it to continue.

Now, clear as day, I see the sand that is pasted to their small bodies as they travel in and out of the water, scooping it up in buckets and carrying it back to the shore, where they are making sand castles. The girl looks so young and happy and carefree. She smiles and giggles, clearly mesmerized by everything the boy does. The sun dances on the boy's skin, and at times he has to push wisps of hair out of his eyes in order to see. Even at such a young age, there seems to be a type of longing written in those eyes as he intermittently glances over at the girl.

My eyes spring open, and I gasp for air. I remember.

I remember!

Why now? After all these years, why do I finally remember being with Tristan on the beach as a young girl? Our family had been on vacation with Aunt Judy. I had asked my parents about it awhile back, and they had confirmed that we had indeed vacationed here all those years ago. I was too scared to tell them I couldn't remember it. What was wrong with me? Even now, was I just picturing it through their eyes?

No. The details are so real. The image of Tristan as a young boy—so real.

Completely bemused, I lie on my bed staring at the ceiling, my thoughts reeling, searching for any possible answer. Finally, I open up my laptop and Google memory loss. Then, childhood memory loss. A multitude of information pops up. Narrowing it down, I single out the term **repression**. *The defense mechanism that protects you from ideas that would cause anxiety by preventing them from becoming conscious.*

Had I been gripped by Tristan even as a young girl, and even back then it was too hard to say good-bye? So instead of facing it, I lived without the memory of him. It seemed so extreme. But knowing how strong my feelings are for him are now, it did seem plausible.

Conjuring the vision of a seven-year-old Tristan once again, I hear him call out to me, *don't forget to practice swimming.* Is that why I had been so determined to learn how to swim throughout my growing up years? I had kept trying, failing miserably. I never knew why it mattered so much to me. Now it finally made sense.

A sudden, impulsive thought shoots through my mind. I want to tell Tristan. I want to share the news with him that I finally remember. Then, just as quickly, reality curbs the notion, as I am once again faced with the truth—this doesn't change anything. Tristan is still gone, and I *won't* be able to tell him.

Once more, depression reaches out to grab me.

Not only am I currently obsessed with Tristan, I had been obsessed with him all along. But I had chosen to let him go—through repression.

I would never be able to do that again.

Day by day I go through the daily motions of life. Sometimes I wonder what day it is. Is summer coming to a close? I realize I've lost all track of time, but I never bother to ask and find out. I just keep going, putting one foot in front of the other, doing all that is required from me by my parents. Mostly though, I try to avoid life by staying in my own little part of the world, my bed.

Somewhere amid all my wallowing, an image of Tristan's immaculately renovated Chris-Craft passes through my muffled thoughts, and I wonder what he is going to do with the boat now that he is gone. Surely, he at least had to come back and take care of that, had to put *Blue* away for the winter. Maybe someone has seen him. I have to know. Dragging myself out of bed, I throw on some presentable clothing and walk into the bathroom. For the first time in a long time, I take a quick glance in the mirror. The girl that is staring back me is a paler version of myself, almost ghostly in appearance. It occurs to me then how sick I've really become.

My parents are hesitant at first to let me leave in the car, but they finally decide it is a good sign that I want to get out of the house. Down at Watch Hill Boatyard, I slam the car door and practically run to the section of docks where I will find *Blue*. Once the boat slip comes into view, I slow my high-speed walk to a turtle's pace. Oxygen is sucked from the air around me. Instead of finding the brilliantly shiny, wood-crafted machine, all I see is an empty space. Water hungrily laps up around the posts of the vacant dock. *It's gone.* Blue *is gone.* Where did it go? One more thing swallowed up by the ocean. I feel bereft.

Panic sets in, and I begin running through the maze of docks to find someone, anyone, who might know where the boat is. The workers I run into only seem confused and startled by me. They don't have any answers. Next, I run to the front office. Pausing outside the main door, I take a deep breath, trying to calm myself. I know I need to speak clearly so people will understand what I am trying to ask. But it is so hard when my mind is a jumbled mess.

Once inside, it seems all I'm going to do is hit another dead end when a man steps from the back room. Wiping his hands with a grease-laden cloth, he eyes me questioningly. His gaze makes me aware of the pale, frantic mess that I've become. But I can't make myself care. *Where is* Blue?

"Are you talking about the 1951 Chris-Craft? *Blue?*"

"Yes." I hold my breath.

"That boat was sold by the owner to an antique boat dealer awhile back."

"Where? Who? When?" It is useless for me to try to hide the desperation that is in my voice.

The man's eyes narrow slightly as he continues to regard me skeptically. "I can't give out that information, miss. But I can tell you it was to an out-of-state dealer in Ohio."

I take a step back as the information registers in my brain. So that was it then. *Blue* had disappeared into thin air—just like Tristan.

"Thanks," I manage to say before I turn to leave.

All I want to do now is go back to bed.

"You are going out with your friends. They will be here in an hour to get you," my dad announces as he walks into my room.

"What?"

"Kate and the rest of them. Better jump in the shower so you will be ready by the time they get here."

"I'm not really feeling up to it."

My dad presses his lips together and runs his hand through his hair. I can't quite tell if what I see in his brown eyes is sympathy or irritation. "Yes . . . you are feeling up to it, Bethany. Now get up and get going."

I heave a sigh. "Okay." I don't even have the energy to roll my eyes.

An hour later, just like he warned, I hear voices in the great room, and I know my friends have arrived.

I walk out of the bathroom freshly showered, my wet hair pulled into a ponytail. No makeup. My clothes hanging loosely on me. I know I've lost weight.

"Hi, guys." I attempt a smile.

Kate, Nick, Jonathan, and Emily all stare back at me wide-eyed. I should wonder at their troubled expressions, but I'm too exhausted to care. "Hi," they all murmur at once.

Finally Jonathan's high-pitched voice breaks through the awkwardness. "Well, hey, I say let's go out and have us some fun, kiddos."

Kate shakes her head momentarily and then forces a grin. "Let's do it."

We head to St. Clair Annex for ice cream. After settling into a booth, we begin talking about when and what we want to order. Kate looks over at me. "Hey, Bethany, I'll buy one and give you the other for free."

"Sounds good to me." I know my voice is subdued, but she seems to like my answer. Kate and Nick are sitting close together, across from me, and I am wedged in between Jonathan and Emily. It is hard for me to watch the intimacy shared between Kate and Nick, so mostly I avoid looking them in the eye.

Emily, Kate, and Nick go to the counter to place our orders, and Jonathan stays back with me, talking incessantly in order to fill in the silence. I appreciate all the effort he is putting in to cheering me up, but all I can muster back are one-word answers. I can't be much fun to have around. Soon the others arrive back at the table.

"Chocolate-peanut butter mixer." Kate slides my ice cream over to me, and in spite of the depressive haze I'm in, my reflexes still work. I catch the dish just before it topples into my lap. I smile up at her. *She remembered.*

"Thanks."

She smiles back. "You are very welcome, dear."

Briefly, I study her brown eyes and chestnut hair that is hanging loosely around her face. Where had her ponytail gone? She looks lovely, so vibrant, and alive. And in love. I blink. We had had some good times this summer. She was so crazy and so much fun. And sometimes trouble too, but in a good way. Was the summer almost over? I really had lost track of time.

I notice the subject of college is carefully avoided by Nick and Kate, and I am glad. I can't begin to think about that right now. At times Emily and Jonathan go back and forth discussing their plans, but unless directly approached, I enter in very little on the topic.

Upon Nick's suggestion, we all go for a walk along the shoreline of Napatree Point. I don't want to go with them, but they are my ride home, so I really don't have a choice. Jonathan does his best to entertain by using his insatiable energy, performing backflips and all sorts of other antics as we meander along. Careful to avoid eye contact with the ocean, I keep my eyes peeled to the sand. But I can't help myself; when Jonathan tells his silly jokes and carries out his circuslike acts, I lift my eyes from the ground and laugh. He quickly picks up on this, and misbehaves to the nth degree.

When we arrive back at our cottage, I can tell by my mom and dad's imploring eyes they want to know how it went. The summer gang is inside the door, chatting animatedly among each other and with my parents as they tell me good-bye. I smile and try my best to interact too. Judging from the expression on my parents' faces, they seem satisfied.

Good, I think to myself. I hope this placates them for a while. Then I return to my bedroom, shut the door, turn off my light, and crawl back into bed.

The long days of brooding continue. Deep, depressive thoughts. Hours in bed. Where was the old me? What was she even like? And would she ever return? I am lying in bed wrestling with these thoughts when a shadow crosses my bedroom door, blocking the light that would be otherwise filtering in. I furrow my forehead. Squinting my eyes, it takes me a moment to focus on who it is.

Then recognition sets in.

Lucy.

"Bethany." Her voice is an anguished whisper as she crosses the room to me. As she approaches, I ponder the worried look that consumes her features. She stops just short of my bed and watches my face for a moment or two. Unobtrusively, she wipes her eye with her hand. *Is she crying?*

"You stopped texting," she says as she pushes her wavy, blond hair over her shoulder. It occurs to me then just how doelike her brown eyes really are. I'd forgotten how pretty she is.

"I'm sorry." I have no explanation to offer her, nor the strength to think about what one would actually be.

"I've missed you."

I nod and offer the ghost of a smile. *Why don't I tell her I've missed her too?* All summer I've missed her, and now I have nothing to say? She eyes me tentatively before gingerly sitting down next to me on the bed. I don't move. I know I should move over and give her room, a comfortable space. My best friend, who I've been longing to see for months, travels all the way from Philadelphia to see me, and this is the best greeting I have for her?

But I'm so tired.

Using the little bit of oomph I have, I turn away from her, facing the wall, ashamed. Lucy edges closer. Without saying a word, she reaches out to me and begins stroking my hair. We stay that way for a long time, neither of us saying anything.

Finally she whispers, "It's going to be okay, Bethany."

I don't answer. I can't answer. The tears that have lain dormant since my near-drowning incident are beginning to swell, trying to break through the shell of numbness I had shrouded myself with.

My throat aches.

Still she continues, soothing the back of my head compassionately. Then she stops, and I know she's sensed the change in me. Gently she turns my shoulder so that she can see my face. And the tears that are plastering my cheeks.

"Ahhhh . . . Bethany." Pulling me up to her, she wraps me in a hug while I sob. "Go ahead . . . cry. Cry it out."

And so I cry a summer's worth of tears.

Finally, she jumps up. In minutes she returns with a box of Kleenex, something I haven't needed until now. She shoves a wad into my hand. "It sucks, doesn't it?"

I wipe my reddened face and blow my nose repeatedly. "It hurts so bad." There. I'd finally admitted it to someone, out loud.

She furrows her brow and sticks out her lower lip in a sympathetic pout. "I know . . . and I'm sooo sorry for you." For a moment she is quiet. "Tell me all about it. Talk to me."

She's right. I know I need to talk, but what do I say? It is so complicated. There is so much I can't share without exposing Tristan and his people. Besides, would she even believe me? It would all sound so preposterous.

"Tristan's gone," I begin. It is a start. From there I proceed to tell her anything I can safely share about him. Our summer story. And how in the end, to make it simple, he dumped me. Prudently, I don't share all the myriads of reasons why.

She listens like the best friend that she is, interjecting little comments that are meant to boost my resolve on the road of getting over him. Intermittently, we hug and cry, and I am reminded that I still have feelings inside of myself, in spite of my self-imposed detachment from the world. After hours of therapy, she looks at me long and hard. I tuck a strand of hair behind my ear self-consciously. I know I must look like a creature from a scary movie.

"Well, let's get you all fixed up. You need a good meal and some fresh air and exercise." Her exhortation is an echo of what my parents have been saying to me over the last while, but somehow, coming from Lucy, it seems much more receivable. She snaps me with a rolled up sweatshirt she finds lying beside her on my bed. "Come on now . . . time to get up and get going."

"All right . . . all right." Setting my feet on the floor, I rise to a standing position. Taking a moment to clear the light-headedness that swims around me, a result of staying in bed too much, I pad over to my closet in search of something to wear. I still don't have a lot of energy. But the oppressive gloom that was holding me hostage in my bed is lessened just a little.

Chapter Twenty-three

My visit with Lucy was much needed. Such a comfort. She was a piece of back home. The piece I needed to grasp onto with all of my might. The piece that could pull me back to normalcy. Reality. Back to life as it was before. Back to Philadelphia. Back to before I had eaten from the apple. Back to when I was happy. But there is still a part of me that is holding on to Watch Hill. Holding on to the ocean. Holding on to everything I'd learned and felt in three month's time. Holding onto Tristan. Lucy helped me to realize that I need to let go. But I just don't know if I can.

I am up walking now. But I am still walking around in a fog.

It is late evening, and I am preparing for bed when an incredible feeling of sleepiness settles over me. Groggily, I situate myself in my bed and pull the covers up around me. Lethargy weighs heavily down on me, and I can hardly keep my eyes open. Momentarily, I try to contemplate the reasons why I could suddenly be so tired, but it is hard to concentrate, and my mind immediately lets go of every thought as soon as it enters my head.

Finally, I resist the urge to fight, and I succumb to a deep, drugged-like sleep. It is such a peaceful feeling. Almost like floating. Then it occurs to me: I *am* floating. Drifting through a warm, salty blanket of ocean water.

Here it is, another dream.

It had been so long since I'd had one. I begin using my arms and legs to help guide my body through a ceaseless expanse of effervescent liquid. It is so healing—soothing to my muscles. Satin sheets are being wrapped around my skin. I revel in the gentle ocean current that encompasses every inch of me. Repeatedly I plummet up and down through the flux of fluid around me. I am buoyant. Each movement I make is effortless, gliding through a world of misty blue.

On and on I go, coursing among the underwater oceanic abyss. Soaring, diving, coasting. After much time, as I am basking in the encircling ambiance, I become aware of another presence. I am no longer alone.

My heart pounds in my chest.

In slow motion, I turn.

Face to face, I encounter the one that dominates my mind, body, and soul. Time stands still. The beating heart, the breath that fills the lungs does not exist. Only this moment in time. Sea green eyes pierce my own blue. A bond of intensity locks our gaze, and it doesn't waver, even for a second, as we swim in slow motion toward one another. With every movement, the rippling water that surrounds our bodies is saturated with longing and love.

As I reach Tristan, somewhere in the back of my mind I vaguely remember that there are so many questions that need to be asked. So much I want to tell him. So much that needs to be said. And yet, I can't quite form the words into sentences. Somehow, the thoughts are there, but they don't seem to be of any real importance. Being here right now with Tristan is all that matters. I am consumed with happiness. Joy wells up inside of me, so much so that I feel as though I must keep moving in order to keep it from overflowing.

He senses my need. We smile at each other and begin gliding through an endless nautical void together, side by side. On and on we travel silently. Although we are never physically touching, an electrical current holds us together, connecting us. It is the phenomenon of skin on skin, and yet we are inches apart.

Somewhere close by, I hear the sound of music being played in stereo. Beautiful, melodic chords, touching my ears. I strain to listen and soon realize that it is not just any song, it is Tristan's song. I turn to watch him sing, but his lips aren't moving. Still the song rings out, captivating me, reaching for the depth of my being. I am so happy to be able to hear the sound of his voice. I thought I would never get to hear him sing his song again, my song again—the song he wrote for me. But here it is, being played over and over, as if on CD, etching itself into my mind.

After endless stretches of swimming, we come upon an area that, even upon approach, fills the water with a rainbow of color. A region overflowing with dramatic, underwater scenery. The vibrancy and hues surrounding us illuminate the ocean floor. Deep purple. Bright yellow. Vivid orange. Subdued green. An artist has painted, and the sea is his canvas. *A coral reef.* I glance over at Tristan. He is watching my face for a reaction. Instantly, I break into a smile. His eyes dance in return. Together we begin exploring the stunning marine sanctuary. The reef shimmers with color and energy. Schools of fish dart in and around us, disappearing and rematerializing among the coral. A neighborhood of diversity reveals a plethora of marine wildlife. Spirited fish with loud stripes and polka dots. Subtle gray species with lackluster movement. Eels. Starfish.

Together we pass through long, rippling strands of sea grass. Just ahead, I notice a large, aquatic creature circling the perimeter. *A shark!* Eyes large, I glance quickly in Tristan's direction. With a serious face, he motions me behind him protectively. Upon his direction, I become very still. The large-bodied animal loops around us, yards away, open mouthed—revealing sharp, fanged teeth. A shiver courses through my body. Silently, I pray that it won't sense my panic. The shark passes by one more time before finally swimming away.

I sigh in relief. For a brief moment the electrical current heightens. Eventually, we too leave the colorful, underwater domain and once again begin gliding through an interminable expanse of warm, salty water. Side by side, on and on. It is during this time that I can feel Tristan watching me. Slowly, I turn to find penetrating, green eyes that seem to devour my soul. My heart rate accelerates. I am riveted by his gaze. Starting from my toes, an exhilarating buzz is initiated. It begins to work its way up through my body, leaving me tingling, trembling, and wanting. Suddenly, I experience an overwhelming sensation that I want to be connected to him in a way that words can't describe. The knowledge that we are two entities hits me full force. Swiftly, I experience a compulsion to correct this. *We need to become one!* With a sudden urgency, I struggle to think of a way to convey this to him. Momentarily, he watches my face with a new awareness. Eyes locked on mine, he bites his lip and shakes his head just one time. I watch him back, waiting for another answer. He doesn't waver. Finally, taking my cue from him, reluctantly I let go of the feeling and slowly the hum in my body begins to dissipate, along with the desperate ache. In its place, a feeling of peace emerges.

Soon we are swimming again, and everything feels right and good. A warm, silky blanket of ocean once again begins sliding over my skin, making me feel satiated. On and on we swim, until finally, slowly, the mollifying coverlet is eased away, and all that is left is a cool breeze that leaves goose bumps on my arms and legs.

I awake with a start and realize the cold air I am feeling is coming from the cracked window to the right of my bed. Instantaneously, my dream comes flooding back to me, socking me in the chest. I feel like I just spent the whole night with Tristan, and now I miss him greatly. Involuntarily, I begin to shiver with the fresh memory of him—his hair, his eyes, his skin, the vigor of his body, his disarming smile. It all seemed so real.

Pulling back my covers, I pad across the floor to shut the window, and my heart pounds.

My body is soaking wet.

Something feels gritty on my feet, and I reach down in the twilight of my room to discover bits of sand and seaweed clinging to my legs and toes. I start shaking. I don't know what is real and not real any more. In an attempt to subdue the shivering, I hug my arms to my chest. What I experienced last night, I want so badly to be real. I want it so bad I can taste it. Licking my lips, I taste salt. *Salt from the ocean!* Lying back down on my bed, I close my eyes. If I can just fall asleep again, maybe I can go back. I want to go back—*forever.* Want to go to sleep forever.

The more I try to find slumber, the more it eludes me. I feel restless instead, tossing and turning in bed. With that restlessness comes a type of energy—energy that I haven't experienced in days, maybe weeks. Then it occurs to me that the energy is forming something else inside of me.

Strength.

The strength I need to go on.

Chapter Twenty-four

Bit by bit the fog is lifted. I am not quite Claritin clear, but I begin to notice things that I hadn't in some time. The way the sunshine sparkles on the blue, frolicking water, viewed from the cottage front yard. The cool morning ocean breeze drifting onto the screen porch. The smell of bread toasting and coffee brewing upon first waking in the morning. The delicate medley of birds chirping outside my bedroom window. My brothers' laughter as they chase each other around the house, roughhousing, once again brings a smile to my lips.

But the thing that catches my attention the most is Mom and Dad. I emerge from my self-imposed cave that I call my bedroom, and my gaze wanders to the great room where they are lounging on the overstuffed couch. They look very relaxed. My mom is leaning into Dad while his arm lightly circles her shoulder. I stand undetected, mesmerized for a moment, as Dad says something apparently humorous to Mom, and she looks up at him and laughs. He takes a stray wisp of her blond hair and brushes it off her face. For a second or two they hold each other's gaze. I turn away and walk into the kitchen.

How long had it been since I'd seen that look on their faces? Had I ever? Had I even paid attention before? I know for sure I had noticed the fighting—the constant upheaval in our home. The yelling outbursts, name-calling, slamming doors, silent, tension-filled dinners. But what was it like before then? It was something I always took for granted—a peaceful home.

Where had I been this summer, missing the transformation of

my parents? Absorbed in my own thoughts and feelings, I had failed to notice life around me. I grab a banana-nut muffin from on top of the refrigerator and begin shoving it in my mouth. *It tastes good.* I had experienced multitudes of emotions this summer, and right now what I feel is unadulterated hurt. I still miss Tristan with a raw ache that I doubt will ever go away. But after last night's dream, *or experience*, or whatever it was, somehow, I am ready to slowly move forward. By grasping tightly to the tiny thread of strength that Tristan has passed on to me, I believe I'm capable of taking baby steps toward living life again. A waft of ocean air comes flooding in through the open window in front of me. Opening my lungs wide, I breathe it down.

There is so much I still don't understand, like did he know who the yacht murderer really was? If so, why isn't he coming back to me now? It is a struggle to keep the pain and confusion of that thought alone from consuming my mind. There was so much I could have asked him in my dream, and yet not a single word had been spoken between us. I was only able to share his presence and nothing else. At the time, it had seemed like enough. But now—*if wishes were stars.*

And the song. Tristan's song, that had played over and over again throughout the whole night. I would never have it recorded on CD. I would never be able to download it onto my iPod touch. But somehow, now, it was etched into my mind forever. Every chord on the guitar, every soft, breathy sound of his beautiful voice as he sang the words that came straight from his heart—it was going to be replayed for me again and again with just a touch of a thought. It is this very tune that is running through my mind when my dad walks around the corner into the kitchen.

"Oh . . . hi . . . Bethany." He studies my face for a moment or two, his own registering surprise. "You are up . . . having a little breakfast?"

Glancing up from the glass of orange juice I am pouring, I send him a sheepish grin. "Yeah."

He hesitates, obviously elated by my resurrection, but not wanting to be too overzealous, sending me running back to the exiled life of my bedroom. It is as though he is trying to tame a wild dog, and the dog is now on his turf and unless approached cautiously, the wrong move could send her running away. "Would you like me to cook you something?"

Dad, really? I give a small chuckle. "No, I'm okay, thanks. This muffin is tasting pretty good."

"Well, all right, but let me at least cut a grapefruit up for you."

"Sure." Clearly, it was going to make him feel better to be able to do *something*.

Mom hears our voices and soon joins us. A shocked smile lights up her face as she regards my presence. Swiftly, she crosses the room to me and wraps me in a hug. "It is so good to see you up . . . and eating too."

She takes a seat on a bar stool next to mine as I continue working on my food. Dad leans casually against the cupboards, arms crossed, directly in front of me. This is clearly a party for them. I am definitely feeling the love. *Feeling.* Something I hadn't experienced in days. They both do their best to make lighthearted, unobtrusive small talk, and I do my best to smile and answer back. Occasionally, even asking *them* questions. The biggest one—when are we leaving to go back to Philadelphia?

"In two days." My mom's voice is soft. It is as if she is scared she might frighten me with her answer.

I take a deep breath, nod resolutely, and glance around the room, noticing for the first time all the scattered boxes that are bursting with transportable household items. *Soon then.* I get up and carry my dishes to the sink. I need to help with the packing. I need to keep busy.

I am carrying a box of towels into the mudroom when Josh and Jake discover that I am up and in the land of the living.

"Hey, are you packing up your bedroom too?" Jake's eyes are sparkling with warmth as he takes in my activity.

"We can help you carry stuff," Josh interjects zealously.

"Yeah, we can help you," Jake echoes. "We have our room all ready to go." I'd never seen them so eager to offer their assistance with anything. Their young faces look so happy and filled with relief that I have to wonder whether they had thought I was going to stay here in Watch Hill and mope for the rest of my life. Or maybe they'd just grown up that much this summer, and I missed out on that too.

The boys stay right by my side as I unload my drawers and jam my suitcases full of summer clothing. They chitchat animatedly as they dart in and around me, offering their mostly-unneeded assistance. At times I sigh and bite my tongue to keep from reprimanding them, reminding myself that this is good—a much-needed distraction. All of their enthusiasm leads me to believe they are definitely ready to go back to Philadelphia.

Back to Philadelphia. Back to the routine of daily life for my family. Mom and Dad, Jake and Josh, they all seem so happy now. But will they be able to sustain their newfound restoration? Experiencing a protective pang in my chest, I swallow and eye my nine-year-old brothers who are flitting about the room. For all that is involved, I sure hope so. Back to work for my parents. Back to school for the boys.

And on to college for me.

I suck in a deep breath. The thought seems so overwhelming. Somehow it doesn't hold the thrill that it once had. Silently, I reach up and grasp the seashell that rests on my chest. *Strength.* Somehow I would make it.

I text Kate and arrange for the summer gang to meet in town tomorrow afternoon for a concert in the park. It will be one last hurrah and an exchange of good-byes. I think Kate is in shock when she hears from me. She returns the text so quickly, my phone practically smokes.

"Hey, girl." She sprints toward me and crushes me to her chest. "I'm so glad you texted me." The whole gang is here with relieved looks on their faces, glad to see me out in public, even if it is for the last time this summer—possibly for the last time ever. I try to brush that last thought away from the forefront of my mind. I want to try to enjoy this last bit of time I have with my summer friends.

Picking out our spot, we situate our blanket on the lush, green covering of Watch Hill Waterfront Park. Mostly though, we abandon our blanket and are up walking around, mingling among the large gathering of people. The atmosphere is festive as we wait for the musicians to begin. In the background, sailboats litter the bay, swaying gently back and forth in the shimmering inlet of blue water. Momentarily, my gaze shifts to Hill Cove Marina. From where I am standing, I can see their familiar wooden sign and the cedar shake siding on the front office building. I need to go say good-bye to the staff. Excusing myself from my friends, I tell them where I am going and that I'll be right back. Kate watches my face closely, her eyes narrowed.

"I *will* be right back," I reassure her.

"Okay. You better never leave this town without saying good-bye or I *will* hunt you down."

"I've been warned . . . Seriously, Kate, I will be right back, and then we'll have a whole afternoon for good-byes."

Kate forms her lower lip into a pout. "And that won't be long enough."

I sigh softly. "I know."

I find David Chambers right away. His voice is filled with admiration as he speaks to me.

"I wasn't going to let you leave without telling you thank you for all you have done this summer . . . for all you have done for us around the marina, and more importantly, for all you have done for the environment. Future generations thank you. When you need letters of recommendation, contact me right away."

I tell him thank *you* for giving me the opportunity, then proceed to make my way around the office, telling the other employees that I encounter good-bye also. Finally I walk back outside, my eyes darting in all directions. There is one more staff member I need to see. Ethan Vaughn. I am just about to give up on finding him when I notice his copper highlights glinting in the sun. He is standing on a dock down by the main boathouse. Taking a deep breath, I head in his direction. I haven't seen him in so long, and all of a sudden I feel shy.

"Hey, Bethany." His gravelly voice reaches out to me as I approach. "You are not saying good-bye or anything, are you?" His warm brown eyes hold my gaze, unwaveringly.

I smile apologetically. "I am."

"Well, then . . . off with you." He grins playfully, then his expression grows more serious. "No really . . . I know you had a tough end to your summer, but if you ever come back to Watch Hill, look me up; I'm pretty sure you still owe me a date."

I laugh nervously and shake my head. "Okay."

For a brief moment his eyes rake me up and down, and a shiver crosses over my limbs. He *really is* hot. But I'm not so sure I could handle him. And anyway, I really don't feel anything for him besides some type of innate attraction. But standing here now watching his alluring face, I wish I did.

Back in the waterfront park, I find my friends not far from where I left them. The band is playing now, and the sound of reggae music fills the air. Kate and Jonathan are dancing around, and Nick is laughing at them. Emily motions me over. Once I reach them, Jonathan links his arm in mine and starts bumping me with his hip, encouraging me to start moving. Soon the beat of the music takes over, and I am dancing too. The afternoon carries on lightheartedly, and it begins to feel like old times—almost. Periodically my eyes scan the horizon watching for any movement in the water. But my glances always come up empty. Each time I have to fight the swell of depressing thoughts that want to take my mind captive. Instead, I focus on the good time that I'm having with my companions.

Finally the afternoon fun dwindles down, and I know it's time for me to leave. Nick and Emily take turns giving me a hug. Stepping back from each of them, I exhale softly. *This isn't so bad. Two down, two to go.* Then Jonathan looks at me, eyes wide, and slugs me in the arm.

"Well, you haven't been so hard to have around." His high-pitched voice offering me a backhanded endearment causes a lump to form in the back of my throat. I have really grown to love this squirrelly guy. *I'm not going to cry. I'm not going to cry.* I can't look him in the eye.

"Good-bye, Jonathan. You're a good guy."

"Aw . . ." He pulls me into a hug, and when we separate again, I have to wipe an escaped tear. "You better keep in touch."

I smile and wipe away another droplet of fluid that is stinging my cheek. "I will." I look over at Kate, and she is looking away. Vivacious, self-assured Kate won't look at me. Now the tears flow freely. "Kate?"

She looks up, and instantly we wrap our arms around each other. I can feel her liquid good-bye as it spills onto my bare shoulder. "I'm going to miss you, Bethany."

"You too." Finally, we pull back from one another, and I wipe my eyes with my fists. "I'm glad you offered to split the price of that first ice cream."

She laughs through her tears. "Me too." Then, as though she can't help herself, she begins to laugh harder. I shake my head and join in.

I'd forgotten how funny I was.

I am walking away from my friends, back to my car, when I detect a gray-haired man clad in a plaid jacket farther up Larkin Road. Mr. Horton is coming out of Sherling's Hardware. He has a small package in his hands, and he is heading toward an alleyway that leads to rear of the building. I pause, watching him. He doesn't see me. I could just leave now and that would be that. But deep inside I know this is one more good-bye I need to say, so I fill myself with resolve and cross the street.

"Mr. Horton," I call out to him, stopping him in his tracks. He turns to face me, an empathetic look in his weathered, brown eyes.

"Well, hi, Bethany."

I hesitate. Suddenly there is so much I want to say. "Well . . . we're leaving town."

He nods knowingly.

"Tell him . . . if you see him. I mean . . . you'll tell him all that happened with the yacht murders and all, won't you?"

Once again he nods.

I clear my throat. "Do you think he would come inland . . . to um . . . look for me . . . or something?"

He furrows his forehead, and the wrinkles that are etched into his skin become more evident. "I'm not sure he can. He can't be away from water that long. No . . . don't wait for that to happen."

"Well . . . tell him . . ." I stop and then begin again. "Tell him I love him." A lump begins to form in the back of my throat, and immediately I will it to go away. It starts to swell instead. "Tell him . . . tell him I *hate* him." Liquid is now forming in my eyes. Mr. Horton is paralyzed, looking slightly uncomfortable. But the compassion that is lying just below the surface of his discomfited expression manages to shine through anyway, causing me to come further undone. A well of tears begin to flow down my cheeks.

"Tell him I hate him for leaving and not coming back . . . for not talking to me about everything . . . he could have talked to me. Tell him I hate his green eyes and his messy, blond hair and the way he looks when he first comes out of the water . . ." I pause, trying to catch my breath.

"Tell him I hate him for making me fall in love with him." My shoulders are shaking now, and Mr. Horton takes a step closer, putting a hand on my arm in a comforting gesture. Reaching in his pocket, he pulls out a tissue and hands it to me.

The tears finally subside.

"Tell him . . . tell him . . . I love him," I whisper barely loud enough to hear. Mr. Horton presses his lips together before he nods, and I turn to walk away.

When I get back to back to the cottage, I text Lucy.

I'm coming home. *(send)*

Surveying my bedroom, I scan every nook and cranny for any stray pieces of clothing that still need to be put into suitcases. In the far corner, my seashell collection sits on the white antique dressing table, looking isolated and forlorn. Solemnly, I gather every unique piece of the assemblage and pack it away in a box. At one time, not long ago, I had been so excited about the markings and crevices on each one. Now it just seemed like an extra thing to try to fit into the car. My phone buzzes and I reach for it, knowing that it is most likely from Lucy.

(unlock) Hugs to you girl. I can't wait to see you!

A wistful smile crosses my lips. Very soon I *would* be seeing Lucy again. Tomorrow we were leaving.

Tomorrow comes unexpectedly quickly, and we are loading the last of our things into the LaCrosse and the Tahoe. The cottage keys are returned to the caretaker, and we begin the slow drive out of Watch Hill. I sit with my head resting on the back of the leather interior seat, face turned, watching the town disappear from the passenger-side window.

This is it. Good-bye to a place that now holds so many memories for me. My eyes peruse the other cottages that are also closed down for the winter, boarded up and empty—lifeless. Sadness fills my chest. Rounding the corner, we approach Bluff Avenue. The Ocean House sits on top of the hill, its grand front porch filling up the yellow-sided exterior. From this point the pounding waves of the ocean can be viewed on all three sides. To the left and to the right endless stretches of beach are visible. I can almost feel the tiny grains of sand as they shift below the soles of my bare feet, like they did for most of the summer.

Just ahead in the distance, sitting proudly like the beacon that it is, I spot Watch Hill Light. Even in broad daylight its reappearing flash is detectable. Remembering the last time that I'd seen the historic structure, I experience an involuntary pang through my heart. Returning empty-handed from Tristan's Island, caught in a ferocious storm, the lighthouse had been the last thing I'd seen before my boat capsized. Ironically, the tall structure represented safety, and in spite of the deadly, perilous sea, somehow I *was* brought safely to shore. Although I'd never be sure how.

As we turn on to Bay Street, I eye the long line of shops that are being patronized by a revolving door of tourists—carrying on as if my summer were not ending. Tucked in among the myriads of stores, I see the front door of the Olympia Tea Room. Vividly I recall the date I'd had with Tristan, and how he'd held that very door open for me. He had looked so handsome, all dressed up for the occasion. And then later that night. A blush finds its way to my face as I think about what had happened later. Very quickly though, the flushing in my cheeks disappears, and in its place a desperate hurt emerges.

One by one the buildings of Watch Hill disappear, and all that is left is the ocean, which from all appearances, seems to be accompanying us on our ascent out of town. Frantically, my eyes scan the vast expanse beside me, willing any ripple of movement to break through the rhythm of the waves. Over and over the relentless whitecaps crash onto shore. Unblinking, I stare into the blue until the last drop of water disappears.

Well, that's it then. The sea is gone.

Immediately, a fountain of tears begins to form in my eyes. An unquenchable ache begins to pulse through my body with a vengeance. To prevent hyperventilation, I take a deep breath and slowly exhale. *Strength.* Instinctively, I reach to my neck in search of my seashell. Tenderly I cradle it in my hand, almost surprised that it is still there and not vanished like the now-faded sea.

So much has happened this summer. My family is now a unit again, and I am genuinely happy for that. But for me, love has swallowed my heart in the space of a few months, and I will never be the same. All that I have gone through, every encounter that I've let pierce my soul—will I be able to hang on to those memories, or will they eventually just fade into nothingness? One more thing swallowed up by the ocean. The possibility of that almost hurts more than the loss I am now experiencing.

As I clasp the shell between my fingers and hum the tune that is now a staple in my mind, it suddenly occurs to me—all that I have gone through, all that that I have loved and lost—decades of time in the interval of one summer, all I *really* have left to show for it is . . .

A song and a seashell.

Epilogue

Four years have passed since that Watch Hill summer of 2012. Now I find myself on a road that hasn't felt the weight of my tire treads in all of that time: Highway I-95 North. After my recent graduation from Penn State University, my life feels a little stymied. I'm floundering for direction, searching for the next path to take. Indecision holds my hand. I finally realize that what I'm lacking is closure. Somewhere in the back of my mind there is a story that's been written about a boy and a girl who fell in love on a sandy beach in Rhode Island. Before moving on with my future, I need to reopen that book and write the final chapter. I know the ending is going to be painful, but hopefully redeeming as well. It is time to say good-bye to one of the main characters in the book—the blond-haired boy. It's time to say good-bye and lay him to rest in the Atlantic Ocean forever.

My first semester at Penn State was rough, passing by in some-what of a blur. And the following semester was only slightly better. I missed Tristan with a heart-wrenching passion. I would never encounter another drop of water again without being reminded of him. He was not only in the ocean that I worked so diligently to stay away from. He was in every lake, every river, every early morning shower that touched my bare skin, every glass of spring-fed liquid that I pressed to my lips. I couldn't escape him. But somehow, I used the strength I had borrowed from him and kept pressing on. My second and third years of college, I focused on academics with a vengeance, four-pointing my way through. This helped to challenge my mind, but more importantly, kept it very occupied. By the time my senior year rolled around, after much encouragement from my roommates, I was able to try dating. But I had such high standards and I felt like there was always something lacking in my suitors.

Namely, blond hair, green eyes and webbed feet.

Now graduation had come and gone, and here I am travelling on the road to yesterday, hoping it will clear a path for tomorrow. My black, four-door jeep hums quietly on the blacktop as I drive along I-95. Eventually I reach exit six, which leads me to Airport Road and then Winnapaug. Finally, I see a sign that reads Watch Hill. I take a deep breath, close my eyes momentarily, and drive into town.

The minute I reach the city limits, a tumult of memories comes flooding back. The little blue summer cottage, Hill Cove Marina, Watch Hill Boatyard—it's all still there as if nothing has changed. As if four years of college and a life cycle of suffering and growing hasn't taken place. I could take time to look up old friends, see what everyone is up to these days, see who is still left in the area, find out who still visits. But I'm not here to visit with anyone, so I don't stop and search anyone out. I don't stop and say hi.

I'm here to hold a ceremony—a burial at sea.

Driving down to the ocean, I park my car in a little side drive. On foot, I begin slowly winding down the sandy path that leads to a secluded alcove with a never-ending view of the sea. Situating myself on a warm blanket of pale-colored powder, I allow a thousand episodes of precious memories to flood through my mind. Closing my eyes briefly, I experience the soft caress of a breeze floating across my cheekbones and eyelashes before opening them again. Sitting, inhaling the salty air, watching waves crash and tumble, letting particles of sand sift through my fingers, I stop and listen.

In the distance I hear the musical sound of the wind whistling through the dune grass. Then, as I listen more intently, trying to examine the noise over the thud of my loudly beating heart, I realize what I am hearing is not the wind at all, but the sweet sound of chords strumming out an intimately familiar tune.

Without hesitation I run to that sound.

Acknowledgements

~~~First of all, I'd like to thank God for blessing me with this desire and passion for writing.

~~~Also, I'd like to thank all the people who came along beside me and shared in the excitement of writing my first book. My husband, Steve, who patiently listened while I read excerpt after excerpt to him, never once making fun of my crazy ideas. My parents and my teachers who told me I had the gift of writing. My family and friends who have given their continual support. The AMU crew - who's enthusiasm is relentless - what a great place to work! My mom - Nancy Root, my daughter - Haley Flach, Maggie Frank, Christy McDonough, and Sara Quisenberry for reading the first draft and offering their opinions. Dr. Roach and Bill P. for taking the time to show me the ropes of publishing. Michelle White Photograpy for the bibliography picture. Ajoyin Publishing for giving me this opportunity. And to the many people who have approached me and said - When will your book be out, I can't wait to read it!

~~~Thank you~~~

CPSIA information can be obtained at www.ICGtesting.com
Printed in the USA
BVOW04s2056101013

333447BV00005B/17/P